# PHYSICIAN'S
# MUSE

# PHYSICIAN'S
# MUSE

RICHARD ROACH

# PHYSICIAN'S MUSE

iUniverse books may be ordered through booksellers or by contacting:

iUniverse
1663 Liberty Drive
Bloomington, IN 47403
www.iuniverse.com
1-800-Authors (1-800-288-4677)

ISBN: 978-1-5320-5415-0 (sc)
ISBN: 978-1-5320-5416-7 (e)

Library of Congress Control Number: 2018911128

Print information available on the last page.

iUniverse rev. date: 09/17/2018

To all those who encouraged me to become a physician

We started getting sick because we stopped listening to the creator.
—Ojibwa saying

# INFATUATION

I HATED SCHOOL. THE ASSIGNMENTS were so unfair. If I knew how to do a problem, why did I have to do ten that were all the same? And homework was a waste of time. If the teachers couldn't teach us during the best hours of our day, why did they have to punish us with homework to make up for their inadequacies? The worst part was that my mother was a teacher. But school was where the girls were, and since I was fascinated with them, I tolerated the torture of school.

The problem was—the more I got to know the girls at school, the more I disliked them. They were always looking at themselves in a mirror, making adjustments to their hair, filing their nails, and straightening their collars, and none of it made any difference. After ten minutes of combing and primping in the bathroom, they came out looking exactly the same as they had when they'd gone in. I knew because I paid attention.

I overheard a girl complain one day, "All boys ever talk about is themselves," so I made sure I never talked about myself when I was with girls, but they only wanted to talk about the clothes they would never wear, the latest rock band they would never see, and how pretty some other girl looked in her new outfit. It nauseated me.

October was always the worst month of my life. That was when we had parent-teacher conferences. The only good part was that my mother had conferences too, so she couldn't meet with my teachers. Dad went to our conferences to meet with our teachers, and he always came home with the same story: "Your teachers say that you're not functioning at capacity, Barak. You are able to do the work, but you're not motivated. School is important, you know."

My response was always the same: "It's too boring, Dad. I know all that stuff. Why do I have to go over it again and again? And I hate homework." I always yelled the last part for emphasis.

"You have great potential, Barak. You just need to apply yourself."

We had the exact same conversation every year. But Dad was great. When Mother came home, he knew just how to phrase the teacher's comments so I didn't get into too much trouble. My brother, Jason, on the other hand, loved school and always received glowing comments from the teachers. I was pretty sure I was as smart as he was, even if he was older and got better grades.

I would never forget the year I started tenth grade. On Thursday and Friday of conference week, there was no school. Jason and I had our parent-teacher conferences on Thursday, which meant we had Friday completely free. We always had a great time with Dad, and that year, he took both Thursday and Friday off from his work as an insurance agent. He suggested Thursday night before Mother came home, "Let's go for a hike in the city park along the Lester River tomorrow." Jason and I cheered.

The wind was blowing as a cold front came through, but doing things with Dad was always great fun. The Lester River ran through a deep, rocky chasm, so it was protected from the wind. Of course, I had to hear the "You just have to apply yourself" speech before we could go. Jason didn't get a speech; Dad just told him that all his teachers thought he was doing an excellent job in school. With Dad's speech over, we jumped into the car, and Dad took Jason and me hiking along the river all the way to the waterfall, which was almost a mile from the road. Despite the chill in the air, Dad let us wade in the pool below the waterfall. The water was still warm from the hot summer. Dad had packed a picnic lunch. We sat on rocks and ate corned beef sandwiches. Dad even peeled our oranges for us. It was great. I didn't want to leave, but we had to.

When we walked in the door, the telephone rang. Dad answered it and talked to one of Mom's friends, Heidi. I liked that name, but we were instructed that if we ever met her, we were to call her Dr. Barton. She was a physician on the Ojibwa Indian reservation north of town. I remembered hearing stories about her from my parents. Mom had gone on a canoe trip with Dr. Barton when she wasn't a doctor yet; Aunt Lisa, our rich aunt; and a French Caribbean woman, Mireille Renard, to whom Mom wrote letters. Mireille lived in Paris. Her last name meant "Fox"—I looked it up in the French dictionary at school. Someday I wanted to meet that foxy lady. When Mom got letters from her, I tore the French stamps off and hid them in my room. I even copied her address in case I ever went to Paris.

Mom, Dr. Barton, Aunt Lisa, and Mireille were good friends in college. The stories Dad told us of the canoe trip were pretty wild. He told us one night when he tucked us in bed that Mom had almost drowned and Aunt Lisa had saved her life. Mom would only say that it had been a "rough experience" and wouldn't tell us any more. Even though she hadn't seen Dr. Barton in years, they wrote to each other, and Mom called her lots of times to ask advice when Jason or I got sick.

When Dad got off the telephone, he was jumping up and down. "Dr. Barton invited us to come to her house tomorrow. You can go canoeing and fishing. They have an archery range set up too."

"Who are 'they,' Dad?" I asked questions like that because I was always curious. Adults left out important stuff.

"Dr. Barton has two daughters, Autumn and Lily. Autumn is the same age as you, Jason, and Lily is the same age as you, Barak. They aren't her real children—she adopted them."

I didn't know what to think. I loved paddling canoes. We had gone canoeing with Dad—even Mom went sometimes—and we loved fishing, so that sounded fun. I'd been interested in archery ever since hearing stories about Robin Hood, but girls? If they were like the ones at school, I wasn't sure I wanted to spend a whole day with them. "Are they Indians, Dad?" I asked.

"Yes, Barak. The correct term is *Anishinabe* or *Ojibwa*—First Nation people."

*Maybe that makes them different,* I thought.

Jason and I became more excited as Dad described what we would get to do. He said their house was deep in the woods, on a lake where no one else lived, and it was a log cabin. It sounded like a pioneer fairy tale.

Mom came home, tired from meeting all the parents of her new students. Her hair was all jumbled, and she walked like an old woman as she came in the door. She collapsed onto the couch without even taking off her coat. Jason and I were jumping around. Everyone was talking at once, but Dad was cool.

"Can we go, Mom? It'll be real fun," Jason said.

I said, "She said we could shoot arrows."

Jason added, "You always want us to improve our canoeing skills; we can paddle all over the lake." Jason always knew the right things to say to get Mother to agree to our plans.

"She doesn't have any boys our age—just girls," I said, but I wasn't sure why I said it. It just came out.

Dad calmed us down and made Jason and me stand still in front of the fireplace so he could tell the story. "I told them you would probably be willing to go. What do you think?"

Mom unbuttoned her coat and sighed before she answered. That was not encouraging. "May I humbly ask what you are talking about? Start at the beginning." She always talked like that—in proper, logical sentences. Teachers did that to make you feel bad.

"You tell her, Dad, and I will be very quiet," I said. Jason was fidgeting, waiting for Dad to begin.

Dad looked at us. "All right, guys, I'm the spokesman. Agreed?"

"Agreed," we answered in unison, and then Jason put his hand over my mouth. I brushed it away.

Dad helped Mom off with her coat and gave her a peck on the cheek. She pushed off his hug. Jason ran and grabbed her coat to hang it up in the closet.

"Your friend Heidi called just as we came home from our hike, and she invited us to come to her house on the Ojibwa reservation Saturday." Dad paused. I thought he was watching Mom's response. Then he added, "To spend the day."

"Oh, I don't know, honey," said Mom. She always called him *honey*. It made me sick.

But I listened as he explained to Mom about the opportunity to go canoeing and shoot arrows with Heidi's daughters. He added, "I hear they're quite skilled."

"It is *essential* that we go," I said, stumbling over my new vocabulary word. Jason threatened to slap my face. I made a dash for the other side of the fireplace.

"I have had two days of parent-teacher conferences," Mom said. "I was planning on collapsing in bed tonight and not getting up tomorrow. Maybe we can go another weekend. How would that be?"

Jason turned away as tears formed in his eyes. I pretended not to notice that he was crying and collapsed on the floor. I thought a more dramatic response might help.

"I sort of promised them," Dad said with a stammer that I thought had a good effect.

The house was silent. Mom kept looking around. "All right, if you promised," she said. She had a mean look on her face as she glared at Dad. We weren't supposed to notice what Dad referred to as "adult nonverbal communication."

Jason and I erupted in cheers. I started dancing around the dining room table.

Jason yelled, "Thanks, Mom!"

Then she messed it up. "If you boys have all your homework finished for Monday and show me tomorrow morning that every assignment is done, we'll go."

I groaned in despair. During parent-teacher conferences, the teachers loaded on the homework since they couldn't torture us for two days. I always did homework on Sunday night or turned it in incomplete if I could get away with it. "Why do you have to be such a school teacher all the time? Can't you be a regular mom sometimes?" I yelled. Jason pushed me onto the couch. I jumped up. Jason had pushed me up next to to Mom. Would our roughhousing make her mad?

"Barak, do your homework and you win. You get to go. Don't fight me all the time," Mom said as she pointed her finger at me. I hated that. I always suspected she could put an evil spell on me with her finger.

Dad gave me a hug to calm me and whispered in my ear, "Don't worry, Barak. I'll help you. You'll get it done."

I wiggled out of Dad's hug and grabbed Jason, and we ran up the stairs to our rooms before she thought of any more requirements. We had to start on homework right away.

# MEETING DR. BARTON'S DAUGHTERS

On Saturday morning, after some secret help, I presented my homework to Mom. She said I was qualified to go to Dr. Barton's house. Jason had helped me with my English paper, but Mom didn't read it carefully, or she would have recognized words I didn't know. Jason promised to explain the words to me Sunday night in case my teacher asked me what they meant when I returned to the school penitentiary on Monday.

It was a long drive. I wanted to ask Dad how long it was going to take us, but I controlled myself. There was nothing to do but look out the window. Along Highway 53 from Duluth to Orr, Minnesota, there wasn't much to look at other than pine trees. Getting my homework done had been such a chore that I didn't even tease Jason, because I didn't want to jeopardize our adventure. Besides, Mom fell asleep in the front seat. I leaned forward and whispered to Dad as he was driving. "Neither Jason nor I want to disturb Mom." I had just learned the use of *neither* and *nor* in English class and wanted to use them. Besides, I was afraid that if Mom woke up, she would point her finger at Dad and make us turn the car around to go back home. *If we just get there,* I thought, *we'll be all right.*

When we turned off the highway at Orr, I thought we were almost there, but we weren't. We traveled down narrow paved roads that turned into dirt roads through the woods. I thought Dad was lost, but he said he was following the directions Dr. Barton had given him. We came to a fork in the road. The road to the right disappeared down into a swamp. I could even see water over the road as I leaned over the front seat. We went left. After a couple of hills, we went down into a valley that spread out into a clearing.

Around the next corner was a house. We hadn't seen a house or a mailbox in almost an hour, so I was hoping it was Dr. Barton's. It was early afternoon when we arrived. I had eaten one of the sandwiches Dad had packed to eat in the car, so I wasn't hungry. When Dad said it was Dr. Barton's house, I let out a cheer. Mom jumped awake. I apologized under threat of some severe punishment. I wanted to explain that Mom needed to wake up because we had arrived, but I withheld my argument.

The house had a huge porch all around the front. The pine trees shading the front entrance were so large that Jason and I, if holding hands, wouldn't have reached halfway around the trunks. I thought it was neat that green and orange pine needles covered the yard. There was no grass to mow, unlike at our house.

Besides the pine-tree smell, the air smelled like things that were growing or rotting, and I could even smell a little smoke. The weather had turned warm—so warm I wanted to take off my shirt, but I didn't. Dr. Barton came out to greet us. She did not look like a doctor to me. She was dressed in black slacks and a black-and-red flannel shirt. She had long black hair pulled into a ponytail that reached to her waist. I instantly liked Dr. Barton. She seemed like an amazing adult.

Dr. Barton gave Mom a big hug, and she even hugged Dad. Then she turned to shake hands with Jason and me. She asked our names and even wanted to know what we liked to do, what classes we enjoyed in school, and who our friends were. I had never met an adult who asked those things of a teenager. None of my mother's other friends who came to our house talked to me like Dr. Barton.

As we walked inside, the house smelled spicy, like a gingerbread house. There was a rich, meaty smell as well. I looked around. It was a real log cabin. I had read about log cabins in my history books, but I'd never expected to see one or know someone who lived in one. It even had a wood stove for cooking and a fireplace. There was a stack of split wood in the corner.

Dr. Barton said, "I'm baking bear and moose for dinner. Hope you like it. Welcome to my humble home."

I had never eaten bear or moose, but the smell of bear and moose baking gave me instant hunger. I was excited about supper, and it wasn't going to be ready for a long time. Something else smelled good too, but I didn't recognize it.

Then we met Dr. Barton's daughters, who came up the stairs from the basement. They were fun to look at. They bowed when they were introduced to us, just like in an old movie. Autumn, the older, had long, straight black hair. She was taller than Jason and thin like a model in a catalog. She was dressed in jeans and a sweatshirt with an eagle on it. I could tell Jason was pretty excited.

"My real name is Waatebagaa—Bright Leaves," Autumn said, "but you can call me Autumn."

I said, "Waatebagaa," to try to get the sound right. She told me I said her name nicely, but I still decided to call her Autumn.

Then we were introduced to Lily. She was shorter than her sister but a little taller than I was. She had the shiniest black hair I had ever seen. It was cropped in the back, but on each side of her face, she wore long braids that fell all the way down her shoulders. They had beads woven into them. She wore short cutoff jeans. I noticed her great legs. No girl at school had such nice legs. I could see her wonderful muscles. She wore a tank top that our principal never would have allowed in school, with a short-sleeved flannel shirt over it. It wasn't buttoned, so I could see her belly button in the middle of her great stomach muscles. She was curvy, and her breasts were just big enough to make her look real cute. I had never seen such a beautiful girl. At least there were none like her in our school.

"My Anishinabe name is Waabigwan-atewaniin—Growing Flower."

I tried but couldn't say Waabigwan-atewaniin the right way—but I sure wanted to learn.

She laughed at my attempt and took my hand. "You can call me Lily, Barak. It's easier."

I didn't even feel embarrassed to have her hand in mine. I looked at her fingers. They were strong but delicate. Her fingernails were clean but not long, pointed, and painted like those of the girls at school, who spent all of homeroom playing with their emery boards. As my gaze followed up her arm, I noticed her biceps. She looked stronger than me, and she smelled earthy like a pine tree. She wasn't wearing any stinky perfume that made me sneeze like the girl who sat in front of me in homeroom class.

My heart was pounding. I liked these girls. They were the first girls I had ever liked in my life. I liked Lily the best, though.

"I made coffee and cardamom rolls," Dr. Barton said, interrupting my thoughts.

I realized that was the smell I didn't recognize: cardamom. We sat around the kitchen table as she served us. The cardamom rolls tasted good, but I noticed that Autumn and Lily went for the coffee first. Mom had never let us drink coffee before, so I dove for it and put lots of cream and sugar in mine. I didn't know if I would like coffee, but if Lily was drinking it, I would too.

After she finished her coffee and ate her roll, Autumn said, "Let's go down to the lake and shoot arrows. It's so nice and warm today; let's do stuff outside."

I jumped out of my chair—anything to get away from parents. Dr. Barton offered me another cardamom roll. They were good. I looked at Mom, and she wasn't paying attention, so I grabbed one and followed the girls.

Jason and I ran behind the girls down the stairs. I was surprised that a log cabin could have a basement. The girls pointed out their rooms on opposite sides as we ran out the back door. Following a trail of stones, we arrived at a dock next to a boathouse that overlooked the lake. It was a large lake, elongated like a shoe, but there were no cabins or houses anywhere.

Mystified, I asked, "No one else lives here?"

"Just us," said Autumn.

"We have the whole lake to ourselves," said Lily. "So we go skinny-dipping a lot."

I wasn't sure what skinny-dipping was, but I didn't say anything. It sounded wild, like something I should learn to do.

"So do you know how to shoot arrows?" Autumn asked.

Jason and I had shot a few arrows at Boy Scout camp, so he said, "Sure, we can do that."

I remembered that Dad had said they were pretty good at archery, so I was sure Jason should not have said that.

"Follow me," said Autumn.

They had compound bows in the boathouse—nothing like the simple bows we'd used at Boy Scout camp. There was a rack of arrows, some of which had sharp, shiny hunting tips. "What are these for?" I asked, feeling the razor tips. I almost cut my finger.

"Deer hunting," said Lily. She grabbed one that had multicolored fletching. "This is the arrow I shot my deer with last year." She let me touch the soft fletching.

"But we use these other arrows for target practice," said Autumn, clutching a group of arrows hanging in a quiver to the side. She handed me one to check out. The arrows at Boy Scout camp were chintzy in comparison.

Lily led us to the back of the boathouse, where there was an archery range. We stood by the boathouse, aiming at targets set on bales of hay at the edge of the forest. The girls let us go first. Jason managed to hit the target. I tried to aim carefully, but every arrow landed in the hay just below the target. We collected the arrows. Then it was the girls' turn.

Autumn hit the bull's-eye on her first shot. She used the arrows with the yellow fletching. The rest of her arrows were in the ring around the bull's-eye. Jason was impressed and told her how good she was. I could tell by the way he was talking to her that he liked her a lot.

My eyes were on Lily. Every chance I could, I stared at her. When she turned toward me, I looked away so she wouldn't notice. She took off her flannel shirt. Her tank top didn't cover much, and I realized she was not wearing a bra. I had never seen any of the girls at school without a bra. I thought there was a rule about it. As she drew up an arrow, I was fascinated by the movement of her arm muscles and the way her breasts—

"Bull's-eye!" Autumn yelled as Lily's arrow knocked hers out of the target. "Just a minute, Lily."

Lily lowered her bow as Autumn ran to the target and took out all her yellow-fletched arrows, leaving the one red-fletched arrow in the bull's-eye.

"Take that one out too!" Lily yelled. Autumn took out the last arrow.

When Autumn returned, Lily shot again. All her arrows landed in the bull's-eye; some seemed to be almost in the same hole.

"Can you teach me to shoot like that?" I asked.

She gave me the bow, and I notched an arrow. She helped me hold it properly. Her scent made me light-headed. It was wild and rustic. I couldn't tell if it was some weird perfume or if she just smelled like the woods, or maybe she'd rubbed pine needles on her neck.

She pushed my arm up. "Aim higher," she said.

I aimed for the top of the target and pulled the arrow back as far as I could. She helped me pull it back a little farther and braced my arm. Her face was next to mine as she sighted down the arrow. "Shoot," she commanded.

I let it go and closed my eyes, hoping for the best. I hit the target in the third circle from the bull's-eye. "My all-time best!" I yelled.

Jason tried again too. Autumn was patient with him, and he got his arrow in the ring outside the bull's-eye. We were proud of ourselves. They helped us with a few more rounds, and we improved, becoming more consistent. When I hit the outside of the bull's-eye ring, I was sure it was an accident, but we all cheered anyway.

"Are you ready to canoe?" Lily asked us as Autumn put away the arrows and bow.

"We love to paddle," said Jason. "We've even been on a trip to Canada."

He shouldn't have said that either. There were two aluminum canoes overturned on the shore. We split up: Jason went with Autumn, and I went with Lily. After the first few strokes, it was obvious they were better than we were. We paddled across the lake, boys in the bow and girls in the stern. Lily said, "That is the Anishinabe way." We headed into the narrow part of the shoe-shaped lake, where a river flowed into a narrow bay.

"I'm hungry," said Lily.

"You're always hungry," said Autumn.

There was fishing gear lying in our canoe. She told me to stop paddling. After a few casts, Lily had two walleyes. "Ready for a snack?" she asked, holding up the two fish.

"Sure," I said, but I was not looking at the fish; I was looking at the most amazing abdominal muscles I had ever seen on a girl.

We paddled to shore and pulled the canoes onto the beach. Autumn lit a fire with a flint. I was fascinated—no matches or newspaper. I had read about starting a fire with flint in the Boy Scout magazine, but I had never seen it done. In the meantime, Lily whipped out her knife and gutted one of the fish. She wove some willow sticks around it and then roasted it over the fire until the skin and scales were black. After setting it on a rock, she peeled off the skin and gave each of us a portion. The smell of the roasted fish made me hungry. In no time, I had eaten the meat off the bones with my fingers, popping it into my mouth. Jason washed his hands in the stream that fed into the lake. Autumn and Lily didn't wash their hands; they just rubbed them with some leaves, so that was what I did. Lily wrapped the other walleye in leaves—to keep it fresh, she said.

"What kind of animals do you have around here?" Jason asked.

Autumn told about the habits of some of the creatures while Lily sat munching on the rest of the fish, which I'd thought we were done with. She was eating the meat off the head and even popped the fish's eyes into her mouth. I thought it was gross, but she said the eyeballs were especially tasty. When she was done, she asked, "Do you like squirrel?"

"I've never eaten squirrel."

Autumn said, "Lily, you're going to ruin their appetite for Mom's dinner."

"Oh, I'll still be hungry," I said.

Lily got up. My eyes were fixed on her. I enjoyed watching her body move. "Come with me, Barak."

"You've got to eat it if you snare it!" Autumn yelled at her as Lily and I followed a trail into the woods. Jason stayed by the fire, talking to Autumn.

"Don't worry! I will!" she called back.

We crept along. She motioned for me to be quiet as she rubbed her hands in something slimy on the ground and then set up a snare. She edged me back behind a bush, and we crouched together. I could feel the warmth of her body next to mine. She put her hand on my shoulder and pushed me down to the ground. I could feel her firm breast on my shoulder but tried to concentrate on the snare. Our breathing became synchronized.

In a flash, a squirrel was in the snare. She jumped up, slit its throat with her knife, and then flayed off the skin. A meaty corpse was all that was left of the poor thing. "Autumn and I have been tanning our own hides. Mom taught us how to do it the Anishinabe way. We have quite a collection. You should see the squirrel-hide vest I made. I can teach you if you want."

"Wow" was all I could say.

We walked back to the fire with our trophy. Jason and Autumn were still talking. I told him about the snare. We sat on logs and talked about all kinds of things. Lily explained the habits of beaver and otters. Autumn told about the bear she had hunted with her mother and the deer she'd shot the previous fall. They knew more about animals and plants than our biology teacher did, and the way they told us was more interesting.

When the sun was low in the sky, just above the horizon, we were still on the opposite side of the lake from Dr. Barton's house. "Should we head back?" asked Jason. I didn't care.

"I suppose, or Mom will get upset, and we'll have to split wood as a punishment," said Lily.

I fantasized about watching Lily split wood. *She must have been punished a lot*, I thought, looking at her arm muscles.

As we headed toward the canoes, Lily said, "Let's race back—boys against the girls."

I thought it was a bad idea because I wanted to paddle back with Lily, but Jason agreed. We got into one canoe. Jason took the stern. I was determined to paddle as fast as I could. The girls, in the other canoe, were out in the lake before we got situated. They waited for us to get our canoe side by side with theirs.

Lily was in the stern, and Autumn was in the bow. "Ready. Set. Go!" Lily yelled.

I hit the water and pulled as fast as I could. Jason had a little trouble accommodating my stroke and had to get the canoe straight before he started to paddle. The girls were already several canoe lengths ahead of us.

I paddled harder. I saw a huge wake streaming beside our canoe. Jason had us straight, and we were going faster than we had ever paddled before. But we were no match for the girls. They were almost a hundred yards ahead, and I was exhausted. They stopped and turned their canoe sideways. I stopped paddling, and Jason and I looked up to see what they were going to do.

"I'm sure you can do better than that," said Autumn.

"Maybe they need an incentive," Lily said. Both girls stood up in their canoe. Our parents had never allowed us to stand in a canoe. "We just want to encourage you," said Lily as both girls pulled up their tops.

I had never seen a girl topless before, even in a magazine. My mouth hung open as I remembered how Lily's breast had felt on my back when we'd crouched in the bushes. Now she was standing in the canoe, and I could see her breasts and her belly rippling with muscles. I hadn't known girls could be like that. "Come on, Jason! Let's paddle!" I screamed.

I paddled so hard I thought my arms would rip out of my shoulder sockets, but my eyes were on Lily.

"Faster," she said as she dropped her shirt and laughed at us.

Suddenly, Jason and I were in water over our heads. I swam to the surface to get air. *What happened?* When I surfaced, I searched for the girls. We were in the middle of the lake. Our canoe was full of water. They were dressed as they paddled over to rescue us.

What followed was quite educational. They pulled our water-filled canoe over the middle of theirs, flipped it, and then put it back in the water. They held it next to theirs so we could climb back in. As we coughed and sputtered while treading water like we'd learned at Boy Scout camp, Lily climbed into our canoe. I climbed into the bow, and Jason climbed into Autumn's canoe to paddle home. I thought they were laughing at us, but I wasn't sure; besides, we were laughing too hard to tell.

"You hit the muskeg," said Autumn.

"What's muskeg?" I asked.

Lily explained that it was a floating mass of vegetation that came out from the mouth of the river. "It's like a green, slimy, floating carpet."

"It was like we hit a wall," I said.

"Is that what flipped the canoe?" asked Jason.

"Yep, and then you were both in the water," said Lily, laughing.

As we paddled home, Autumn explained how muskeg formed and floated. I was listening so hard that it seemed we'd been at the dock only moments before. I looked up. It was almost dark. *Oh, what will Mom say?*

Back at the dock, we turned the canoes over and laid them on the beach. I was dripping like a wet washcloth. As the stars came out, the magical light of the Milky Way lit the path to the house. We rushed inside through the basement door.

I heard Dr. Barton call, "Wash up before you come upstairs for supper."

"Yes, Mother," Autumn and Lily said.

Lily ran up the stairs with the other walleye she had caught and the squirrel she had snared, which was now reduced to meat and bones. Meanwhile, Autumn pushed us into the laundry room and gave us pink sweatpants and pink T-shirts to put on. "Quick," she said as she shut the door. We changed in a flash. It was a good thing because I was still pulling up the sweatpants over my soaked underwear when she barged back in.

"Put your clothes in the washer." She grabbed soap and fabric softener to put into the washing machine. We added our sopping-wet clothes.

As we ran up the stairs in our pink outfits, Dr. Barton said, "I hope you were good hostesses to Barak and Jason."

"Don't worry, Mother. We kept them entertained," responded Autumn. She hugged her mother and then added, "We made sure they had a good time."

# DINNER AT HEIDI'S

WHEN JASON AND I ARRIVED at the dinner table, our parents stared at us. We looked ridiculous in pink, especially with flowery T-shirts and girls' sweatpants. Autumn noticed Mom's horrified look and explained, "Oh, they had a little accident in the canoe. Their clothes are in the washer, and I'll put them in the dryer after dinner. But we made sure they had on their life jackets. Don't worry."

I looked at Jason and whispered, "I don't remember any life jackets. Do you?"

"Quiet," he whispered. Then, in his most polite voice, he asked, "Where should we sit, Dr. Barton?" She pointed to the chairs at the end of the table. Lily and Autumn took the seats opposite us.

Heidi explained that she'd shot the bear during the last bow season and that the moose had been a gift from a patient who had no money. "So he paid me with moose meat." She went on to describe how she'd wrapped the two roasts together because bear meat tended to be greasy, and moose meat could be dry. "The two bake well together."

The table was set with a large platter of meat and a large baking dish with wild rice casserole. She asked us to hold hands and said, "Let's pray and thank God for his rich gifts and thank the animals who surrendered their lives so we could have this feast."

As soon as she was done praying, we dug into our food. The flavor was wild and intense. After a few bites, Jason asked Dr. Barton for the recipe for the wild rice casserole and said, "Please teach my mother how to make this. I love it."

I asked for second and third helpings, unsure if I would ever get to eat bear and moose meat ever again.

All during dinner, I tried not to stare, but I kept my eyes on Lily. She was so graceful, even the way she held her fork. She was different from the girls at school, who scoffed at the food, took a few little bites, and then said they didn't like it, or it wasn't cooked right or whatever. I imagined Lily eating to fuel her tank for her next adventure. I sure wanted to see what that was going to be.

Mom asked about our day. I told her about shooting arrows and hitting the target. Jason told more of the story. "We went canoeing on the lake," he said. Then he added, "Because we could only lose so many times at archery."

"But did you learn something?" asked Dad.

"You can only learn so much by losing every round, Dad," I said.

"We should have let them win once," Lily said to Autumn.

"That wouldn't have been honest, Lily," Autumn answered.

"It might have been more gracious, though," said Dr. Barton.

"Anyway, we decided to go canoeing across the lake," said Jason. "I love to canoe. And your daughters, Dr. Barton, are expert canoers."

"We cooked fish on the beach on the other side of the lake," I added. "Autumn started a fire without even using matches."

Jason interrupted. "And Lily caught two walleyes, and we cooked one of them without even a pan."

"Then we all ate with our fingers," I said. "It was a great snack."

"It was nice of you to bring home some meat, Lily," said Dr. Barton.

I started telling the squirrel story. "You should have seen how Lily snared that squirrel, Mom." I explained about gutting and skinning it, but Mom interrupted.

"We are guests here. I'm not sure that is proper dinner conversation."

"Oh, sure it is, Mom. It's all about food," I said.

Mother hushed me with a disgruntled frown. "Barak, that's enough about gutting."

I looked at Jason. It was perfect. She wouldn't ask any more questions about our day now. He thanked me later, but we both tried to look disappointed.

After dinner, we had a great time. Autumn and Lily were interested in everything about camping and the habits of animals. We went to their rooms, first to Autumn's. It was pleasantly decorated and organized. She had pictures of moose, deer, and horses on the wall. Her room smelled sweet like flowers. She had dried wild roses in a vase on her dresser.

Then we went to Lily's room. The whole room smelled wild, like pine trees mixed with the smell of the hides she had tanned, which hung around the room. On her dresser was her skull collection. She had everything from wolf to weasel skulls. She had wired some of them so the jaws worked. She even had owl and chickadee skulls. She was explaining to us how chickadees survived the winter, when Mom called from the top of the stairs, "We really have a long drive home! We'd better get going."

We found out that Dad had caught a fish while we were canoeing. He always had his fishing license with him, even though he didn't get to go fishing much. Dr. Barton had cleaned the fish he'd caught, and she took it out of the freezer, adding the fish Lily had caught as she wrapped them up in wax paper. "Are you sure you want to give me Lily's fish?" he asked.

"We eat plenty of fish. I'll just catch some more," Lily said. "Do you want the squirrel too? They're real tasty."

"We'll pass on the squirrel," Mom said, but I wanted to try it. I was sure it would taste great.

Autumn ran down to the basement and got our clothes out of the dryer. We went into the bathroom to change while Mom and Dad said goodbye to everyone. It always took them a while. I closed the door and whispered to Jason, "Those girls are beautiful." Then I squealed like a mouse. "Have you ever seen a girl like that before, Jason?"

"Never. But we can't tell Mom about this. You've got to promise."

I held up two fingers. "I promise. Scout's honor."

After goodbye hugs—and I can't even explain how thrilling it was to hug Lily—Jason and I climbed into the back seat of the car. Dad sat on the passenger side, and Mom was driving. So much for her falling asleep on the way home and not asking questions. Jason and I sat still. I thought that if I was good, Mom wouldn't ask about how we'd gotten wet. I was wrong.

"So how did you boys tip over the canoe?" Mom asked as she turned onto the freeway. Dad was sound asleep, snoring once in a while, so he couldn't help us.

"They're a couple of Amazons, Mother," Jason said. He had read about Amazons in a comic book Mom had taken away from him. He had brought it home, and after Dad had tucked us in bed, Jason had called me over to his bed. He'd turned on the flashlight under the blankets, and we'd looked at the comic together. I thought it was about Tarzan, but I only remembered the women warriors. Mom had found it the next day, and it was gone forever.

"They're the coolest girls ever," I said. "The wimpy girls at school do not even come close."

"They are very accurate with a bow," said Jason. He described again how Lily's arrow had knocked out Autumn's arrow.

I thought it was just his way of distracting Mother. "I sure wouldn't want to be on the wrong side of Lily," I said. "She snared that squirrel and killed it so fast. I could hardly see what she was doing." I took a deep breath. "Lily showed me how to set snares and hide in the bushes," I said. I was trying to get to the gutting part to stop the conversation again, but it didn't work.

"So I still want to know how your clothes got all wet. You flipped the canoe, didn't you? Was it in the middle of the lake, or were you along the shore?"

I was worried that Mom was too curious. "Oh, that," I said. I looked at Jason. I was desperate, but I started to giggle. I couldn't help myself.

"I'm waiting for an answer, boys."

"You tell her, Jason," I whispered.

"They challenged us to a race in the canoes, Mother. We paddled as fast as we could, and they just laughed at us. I think they could have gone even faster, but we couldn't keep up with them. We tried to paddle faster." He held a finger to his lips and looked at me. "We ran into muskeg. You know what muskeg is, don't you, Mom?"

"I am familiar with muskeg," she said. Her tone hadn't softened.

"The muskeg must have floated out from the mouth of the river. We didn't see it, so when we hit it, we flipped over," I said.

"We had our life jackets on," Jason lied. "It was shallow, and we got covered in mud when we flipped." It was another lie. "The girls rescued us. It was really no problem." That was mostly true.

He skipped the part I was worried about. Mom didn't ask any more questions. I mouthed a silent "Way to go, Jason." I didn't tease him all the way home.

# 4

# MATURING MY ATTITUDE

"YOU ARE INFATUATED WITH LILY," Dad said to me a couple of weeks later. We were having a session, as Dad called them, upstairs in my bedroom. I was sitting on my bed; Dad was sitting on my desk chair. We were knee to knee.

Sometimes sessions were fun because I found out things I didn't know about our family—about Mom and Dad when they first met and stuff like that. Jason and I always had sessions in our room, but this time, Jason was sent downstairs so he couldn't hear what Dad and I talked about. Sometimes I was sent outside when Dad had a session with Jason. Once, I snuck upstairs and listened at the door to hear Jason's session. Mom caught me, and I had to do supper dishes every night for a week. Sometimes sessions were bad, like the time Dad found out I'd put a frog in Jason's underwear drawer.

We had a sex session once, when Dad explained how babies were made, how girls got pregnant, and why boys' penises did strange things. I had that session before I discovered how interesting girls were. It all had seemed so gross then. But now I had seen Lily almost naked. I didn't exactly tell Dad that, but maybe he figured it out since I was talking about her all the time. I guessed I'd mentioned her too many times, because Dad said we had to have a session about her.

"There will be other young women you will like when you meet them," Dad said. "You might even meet and marry a nice young lady someday. I know you really like Lily, but you are too young to think about that now."

I was amazed that Dad knew what I was thinking about. "But she is so beautiful, Dad, and I have never seen another"—I cringed at the word—"girl like her. There are none in the whole high school like her. She can shoot arrows, catch fish, and snare squirrels, and none of the other girls at school can do that." He didn't seem to know what to say, so I added, "Were you infatuated with Mom before you married her?" *What a great question*, I thought.

"Yes, Barak, I was, but I was old enough to marry her then. You need a few years under your belt before you are old enough to think about marriage."

I wondered if he meant I wasn't old enough to do the thing we'd talked about in our sex session. "All right, Dad, I will try to remember what you told me. I will try not to think about Lily too much." *Until I get older*, I thought. That ended our session, but my feelings of infatuation kept me awake all that night.

In high school, there were a lot more girls than there'd been in junior high, and for some reason, I was more interested in them. I tried hard to talk to them so I could get over my infatuation with Lily, but they would giggle, primp their hair, and walk away. No one fascinated me like Lily.

One Saturday, Dr. Barton came to town to go shopping for supplies. There were not many stores on the reservation; in the town of Orr; or even in Virginia, Minnesota, down the highway, so sometimes she would come to Duluth, where we lived. Autumn and Lily came with her, and they stopped at our house for coffee. Mom put a frozen pecan coffee cake in the oven. I was embarrassed for her. Compared to Dr. Barton's cardamom rolls, it wasn't much, but I was sure it was the best she could do.

Lily ran in the door and hugged me. I could tell she wasn't wearing a bra, just a T-shirt. Her figure was awesome. Her shorts left no leg muscle to my imagination. She had grown taller, but so had I. Now we were about the same height. Some girls who were cute when they were younger didn't become beautiful later, but Lily was more beautiful than I remembered. "I shot my first moose, Barak. What do you think about that?" she said.

"Wow, that's great."

"I brought a roast and a few steaks to share with you."

"Barak, can Autumn ride your bike?" Jason said, interrupting us. "We want to go for a ride."

"Sure, have fun." I turned to Lily. "So tell me the story." We left the adults talking and went outside to sit on the porch swing. She sat so close to me that we were touching. I saw a dragonfly land on the railing. It had fluorescent green wings. I pointed it out to Lily. She cooed.

Dad came out to the porch. "Would you like something to drink?"

"I'm fine," said Lily.

"Me too, Dad," I said, and he left. I thought he was checking up on us. "So tell me about the moose hunt."

"I saw the moose cross the field toward the lake." She leaned close to me. I could smell the scent of pine in her hair. "It was early in the morning. The sun had just crested the trees, so I snuck through the cedar swamp and then headed toward the lake. Sure enough, he was running parallel to the shore. I hid behind some bushes and shot between the branches when he stopped. The moose only had a small rack, but the meat is great—real tender. You'll love it. Your mom knows how to cook it, doesn't she? You cook it just like venison, if she remembers what my mother told her."

"If she gives my mom the recipe, she can follow it." I put my arm around her shoulders. "I bet your mom was happy about the moose meat."

"You know that she's not my real mother, don't you?"

"Dad said you were adopted, right?"

"Yes, I'm adopted." She laughed and slapped my knee. "I came from a box on her desk at the clinic."

In my sessions with Dad, I'd never heard of a baby coming in a box. I didn't know whether to be serious or laugh. I sat there dumbly, looking into her hazel-brown eyes. They had irregularities of dark brown spots and other spots that seemed fluorescent.

"Autumn's adopted too. She knows who her mom is. They go to the prison once a month to visit her. Her mother killed her father—that's why she's in prison. I don't know my mom or dad. Heidi tried to find my mom, but no one seems to know who she is. But Heidi is real good to me. I am very blessed. Besides, she knows all the Anishinabe ways and taught them to us."

I wasn't sure what *blessed* meant, but I hugged her. I didn't know if it was any comfort, but I felt like doing it. I couldn't understand what it would be like not to know who your parents were. I got in trouble with mine all the time, but at least I knew who they were, and they loved me and hadn't killed each other.

She pulled away. "Hey, you want to be my brother? I've always wanted one. I could adopt you as my brother."

I cringed. "Do I have to go through a ceremony and cut myself or something?"

"That's just in the movies, silly. No, we'll just shake hands, and I will adopt you as my brother." She paused and narrowed her eyes as she stared into mine. "But it has to be forever. Once you agree, you can't ever go back. Never."

For some reason, I felt scared. It sounded serious. *Should I ask Mom and Dad first?* I didn't know. I held out my hand. "Forever?"

"Both hands," she said. "You can't do this halfway. Forever, and you can't ever go back on your promise. This is the Anishinabe way."

*Should I think about this?* What was I doing? Did this obligate me to some ritual, or did I have to go out in the woods and starve or fast or something? I held out both hands. She clasped them so hard it hurt.

"I accept you as my adopted brother. Do you accept me?" she said.

My words came out slowly. "I agree to be your adopted brother."

"Forever? Swear by God?"

"Forever, so help me God," I said, and she let go of my hands. There were abrasions from her fingernails digging into my skin.

She gave me a hug. "So what should we do? You want to go for a walk?"

An amazing thing happened after that day—not the brother thing, as I still had no idea what that meant, but my attitude toward girls changed. None of the girls at school made me nervous anymore. Compared to Lily, they just did not measure up. Since I wasn't trying to impress any of them anymore, they flocked around me. I didn't know then, but later, I found out that there was a prize for the first girl who could talk me into a date. I could have dated anyone I wanted. They even asked me to take them out when no one was listening. At lunch, there was always a girl asking if she could sit with me.

"How do you do it, Barak?" asked my best friend, Joshua. He tried to get girls to accept a date, but he tried too hard. He started sitting with me every day at lunch just because he knew some girl would sit at my table.

"I'm afraid I disappoint them, Josh," I told him. "I never ask any of them out." The magic lasted all through high school. No one won the prize.

# OFF TO FRANCE

JASON AND I WERE BOTH in high school when our parents received an invitation from Mom's friend from college, Mireille, to come to Paris. Mom and Dad were so excited about their trip that they ignored us. We got to do things I knew they would have objected to, but they were distracted.

"Can I ride my bike to town and buy and ice cream cone?" I asked.

Dad was looking at a map of France. "Sure, Barak, just be home for supper. Here's five dollars." I took off before he changed his mind. He had never let me bike to town before. I should have asked for an advance on my allowance, but I didn't think of it at the time.

At first, I was hoping we would get to go with them to France, but that didn't happen. I decided not to be too disappointed, but my head was buzzing with what we would do while they were gone.

Dad sat Jason and me down on the couch. "I know you are two very responsible teens, but your mother and I are going to France, and that means there will be an ocean between us. You need an adult frame of reference should something come up."

"And who will that be?" I asked.

"Lisa and Troy are willing—"

Jason jumped up. "We'll get to do lots of cool stuff."

"Are they your relatives or Mom's?" I asked because I was always curious.

"Actually, neither," said Dad.

He looked around to make sure Mom couldn't hear, and he got serious as he explained. It turned out that Aunt Lisa was a friend of Mom's who'd been on the canoe trip when Mom almost drowned. In fact, Aunt Lisa had pulled her out of the water and saved her life. Dr. Barton hadn't been a doctor yet but had helped resuscitate Mom. Now they were going to Paris because the other girl who'd gone on the canoe trip, Mireille Renard, lived there and had invited my parents to visit, offering free room and board.

I became curious about that canoe trip and asked more questions. Jason and I sat as still as lichens on a log as Dad told us more of the story. They'd been in storms, seen moose, and gone down rapids. They'd camped in a tent for two weeks, paddling every day. Dad paused at one part, and I knew there was more, but he wasn't telling. We had gone on a weeklong camping trip one time. It had rained every day, but Mom knew how to get the camp fire going even in the rain. I didn't think many schoolteachers knew how to do that, so it seemed she'd learned a lot on that canoe trip.

Jason and I joined Aunt Lisa and Uncle Troy at the airport to see Mom and Dad off. Jason started dropping tears, so I pretended to be sad too. It made Mom all gushy. Dad put his arm around her as they headed through security.

After they left for France, we had a great time. Aunt Lisa and Uncle Troy owned a camping store. They had all kinds of neat stuff, from tents and canoes to cooking kits and backpacks. Behind a locked glass case, they had a whole assortment of camping knives. In the winter, they rented cross-country skis and sold the best parkas in town. I knew that Mom bought all our winter coats there. I noticed that she didn't pay the price on the tag either.

Jason and I helped at the store, carrying and stacking boxes. We stocked shelves, and Jason even talked to the customers. I thought the most fun was when we set up a display tent in the middle of the store. I held the tent stakes that were in the package, wondering what I should do with them.

"There's no wind in here, Barak. The tent doesn't need stakes." Uncle Troy laughed. He gave me fifty dollars for helping him set up the tent despite my confusion.

The first Saturday after Mom and Dad left, Uncle Troy and Aunt Lisa left the manager in charge of the store and took us rappelling down a cliff. It was exciting to look down the cliff and see how far I could fall, but with all the safety gear, I knew that wouldn't happen. Jason was scared and got tangled up in his lines, but no one got hurt.

It was a hot, sunny day, so afterward, we went to Aunt Lisa and Uncle Troy's house and swam in their pool. They said we could go skinny-dipping. I knew what that meant now, and I wanted to do it, but Jason was too embarrassed, so we jumped into the pool in our underwear. Uncle Troy was a great diver. He showed us how he did a somersault dive. Jason was too scared to try, but I tried and mostly did a belly flop. I had a pretty sore stomach, but I didn't let on. Uncle Troy laughed and taught us how to do some simple diving tricks. I almost did a swan dive but ended in another belly flop. My stomach was all red and sore for a whole day.

Later, when we went back to check our house, Jason told me to get the swimming suits. I was hoping to go skinny-dipping now that I knew what it was, so I purposely forgot. That night, Uncle Troy and I went skinny-dipping. Jason went in his underwear after he gave me a hard time about forgetting his suit. I didn't care. I jumped off the diving board and swam the length of the pool with nothing on. It felt great.

Aunt Lisa said she would stay with us at our house if we wanted, if we felt more comfortable there, but their house was special, almost like a museum. Dad told us they were very wealthy. So we stayed at their house the whole time Mom and Dad were gone. They had lots of extra rooms for guests, a library, a greenhouse, and a huge kitchen. We could have each had our own room, but Jason wanted to stay with me in the bunk-bed room. I thought he didn't trust me.

Their house was surrounded by a state forest, so they had no neighbors. In the back of their house was a swamp. Uncle Troy called it a wetlands area, but it was really a swamp. He explained that it had taken him an entire summer to put a hiking trail around it. "I sank in the mud up to my knees at times," he said. In the mucky part, he'd placed rocks out of the mud. Jason and I got up before breakfast and hiked around the swamp every morning. There was always something new to see. One morning, Jason got a cramp in his leg as we squatted on the edge of the water, waiting to see the frogs. If you just walked by, you didn't see the frogs. You had to sit on the edge of the pond and wait, and then the frogs showed themselves. One morning, we even saw a salamander.

The ducks found the swamp too. Jason and I discovered several nests. The eggs hatched while we were there, and Uncle Troy gave us each binoculars to watch the ducklings' development so we wouldn't get too close and scare them. Jason got bored, but I kept watching.

Aunt Lisa's dad, who was even richer than Aunt Lisa and Uncle Troy, had built them their own tennis court, so we played doubles. There was a net on top of the enclosure, so we didn't lose any balls in the woods. Sometimes Jason hit the ball straight up. Uncle Troy said that if the ball hit the net, it was out of bounds. I was on Aunt Lisa's team. It was a close match, but we won because Jason got excited and hit the ball straight up into the net.

We had two weeks full of adventures, fishing, hiking, and even a one-day canoe trip. Jason got homesick one night, but Uncle Troy talked to him, and he was better in the morning. By the time I thought about missing Mom and Dad, it was time to go to the airport to pick them up.

They were happy to see us. Dad told neat stories about all the things they'd seen in France. Mom had special presents for each of us. Dad said they'd even stayed in a castle one night in the Loire Valley, wherever that was. He said the bed was so huge he couldn't find Mom. I didn't think that was true. I'd snuck into their bedroom at night. They were always curled up together with no clothes on. I thought Dad was still infatuated.

# DAD'S FUNERAL

DAD GOT SICK WHEN HE came home from France. He complained that his muscles ached, and he had fevers at night. He told me that he would have gotten sick anyway and that it had nothing to do with going to France. I know that now, but it was hard to believe then. I had no idea what a lymphoma was or what chemotherapy was all about. He was weak when he came home from the hospital, but he did things with us anyway. When he threw me the ball, it had no zing to it. Before he was sick, it would sting my hand when I caught it.

We had great times together and did lots of stuff after that. I thought he was cured, so I was shocked when he went to the hospital the second time and never came home. Aunt Lisa took us to see him a couple of times, but I didn't like to stay because he looked so bad, and he had all kinds of tubes and wires connected to him. One time, I asked about them.

"What's this wire for?"

"To check my heart."

"Why is this fluid yellow? Is it like urine going in you?" I asked.

Jason hid his face in his hands. He always did that when I talked about gross stuff.

Dad laughed. "No, Barak, it has strong medicine in it that is going into my bloodstream."

"Is that your urine coming out of that tube?" I said.

Mom always made us use the correct words, not words like *piss*, which people said in school.

"Yes, Barak. There is a tube going into my bladder."

"Does it go through your penis?"

"Yes, Barak."

"Doesn't that hurt? I wouldn't want a hose in my penis."

"That's enough questions, Barak," said Mother. She had an angry look. "Kiss Dad goodbye, and Aunt Lisa will bring you boys home."

Aunt Lisa told me on the way home that she didn't understand much about medicine but had been real sick once and had had a catheter in her bladder. Of course, she was a woman and didn't have a penis, but I didn't want to know any more about that.

That was the last I got to talk to Dad. He died a couple of days later. Aunt Lisa brought Mom home from the hospital, and I could tell right away that something was wrong. Mom got real crabby after that, yelling at Jason and me for everything.

At the funeral, I looked at Dad in the casket. I wanted to say, "That's enough being dead. It's time to get up. How can we handle Mom without you?" But I didn't say that. I just stared at him. I cried a little, but I didn't think that would help anything. I must have whispered, "I wish I could have helped you fight that lymphoma," because a hand as gentle as a butterfly wing touched my shoulder.

"Maybe you should be a doctor when you grow up, so you can help people with cancer like your father."

I turned. Lily was standing behind me. She was elegant. Her hair was combed out except for a single strand braided with a silver chain. She wore a trim black dress that sparkled. She hugged me. I was afraid I got the shoulder of her dress wet with my tears, but she didn't care. "You'd be a good doctor," she said. "A sister knows these things about her brother."

"But I hate school. You have to go to school forever to be a doctor."

She took me aside and brought me to a table filled with soda and little sandwiches. We grabbed a couple and sat in a corner to talk. We talked about all the bad things that had happened with Dad dying and how upset Mom was about the whole thing. I was thankful Dr. Barton had brought Lily and Autumn to the funeral. I looked across the room to see Jason hugging Autumn. I tried to ignore them because I was having a meaningful conversation with Lily. I complained about school and how I hated it. She listened and nodded. "But medical school is a lot more fun than high school," she whispered in my ear.

*How does she know?* I wondered that night as I lay in bed with the vision of Dad lying dead in the casket. I thought about being a doctor. I had two more years of high school, and I was done. I never wanted to go to any school ever again. I fell asleep with Lily's voice nagging me to become a doctor.

# MOTHER'S GRIEF

IT WAS THE SATURDAY AFTER the funeral. I was holding my hands over my ears.

"Barak, pick up your room! Why do you have to make things so difficult for me?" Mom had been yelling for almost an hour. She'd critiqued Jason first, but she had more to say to me.

"I miss Dad. It's not the same without him," I said.

She grabbed my shirt. "I hope your wife dies someday. Then you'll feel guilty for the way you've treated me. You're living like a pig. Get this room cleaned up."

I yelled back, "If I want to live like a pig, it's my life! Leave me alone!" I didn't expect a positive response. I got grounded for a week and slapped across the face. I hadn't known Mom had such a strong swing. I should have ducked, but I didn't see it coming. She had never hit me before.

"As long as you're living under my roof, you will live as I tell you to," she said. Her volume didn't quite make it to the neighbors' houses. I thought about pitching a tent in the backyard so I wouldn't be under her roof, but I figured she would claim the tent was hers too. Maybe I could borrow a tent from Uncle Troy's store.

I hung my head and tried a different approach. "I'm so sorry, Mom. I'll pick up my room so your life can be better." I probably shouldn't have added the last part. It didn't go over well. Collapsing onto my bed and sobbing worked pretty well after she slapped me again, because she screamed and left the room. I got a cold washcloth to put on my swollen cheek and came back to ask Jason, "So what should we do today?"

"I don't think Mom will let us do anything unless we clean our room," he said.

I sat on my bed. "I sure miss Dad. She's turned into the wrath of God without him." I kicked at my clothes lying on the floor. "Some Saturday this is going to be."

"Come on, Barak. Help me, and then maybe we can do something. And don't stuff all your things in the closet like you did last time. That's the first place she'll look," he said with his hands on his hips just like Mother. "Or under the bed."

"Why can't the wicked witch just wave her wand and clean our room herself?"

"Barak, don't say that about Mom."

"Why? Are you going to tell on me?" I picked up my shirts and hung them in the closet. I kicked all my dirty underwear into a nice pile in the middle of the floor. Jason ran and got a laundry basket from downstairs, and I put the pile in it. It didn't take long, but I still felt that Mom forcing me to clean my room was an invasion of my privacy.

When we were done, we went downstairs. Mom was reading the paper at the kitchen table. Jason asked her if we could go for a bike ride. I stood back by the door, waiting for the response.

"You can go, Jason, but Barak needs to mow the wicked witch's lawn first."

*Whoa, I lost. New approach.* "If I mow it very carefully, may I go for a bike ride, most honorable mother?"

She stared at me. "Only if it is perfect."

Perfection was not my thing. This was going to be a problem. "Yes, most honorable mother, I will mow the lawn to perfection. Each blade of grass will be at a perfect height."

"Cut the crap, Barak. Get out of here, and get to work."

I curtsied. She slammed down her paper. I ran out the door.

When Mom went back to work, it gave us some peace. Jason and I still had times when we sat and cried because we missed Dad, but we had each other, and we would cry and then go for a bike ride. When Mom came home from school, we tried to disappear.

One night two months later, we came home from school, and Jason suggested we make dinner for Mom. We dropped off our books on the dining room table, and Jason pushed me into the kitchen.

I said, "What should we make? I don't know how to cook very well. Dad always made supper."

Jason said, "Don't worry. I can make some macaroni and cheese, and there are hot dogs in the refrigerator. You can heat those up, can't you?"

"Should I start a fire in the backyard and roast them on a stick?"

Jason rolled his eyes at me. "Barak, just get a pan, fill it with water, put the hot dogs in it, and heat them up. Don't be such a troublemaker all the time."

I didn't think I was a troublemaker all the time, but I let the matter drop.

We started in plenty of time to finish before Mom came home. Jason read the directions on the box, and then he made me read them to him again as he followed the recipe. We waited patiently for the water to boil, added the pasta, and then found the strainer Dad always had used to drain the pasta. I had a little trouble measuring the milk, as some of it escaped onto the stove, and Jason said I bumped his arm when he was adding the cheese sauce, but when we looked in the pot, it definitely looked like macaroni and cheese.

"We did it," I said.

"Now I'll set the table. You heat up the hot dogs. Mom will only eat one, but I want two."

I put five hot dogs in the pan and added enough water to cover them. I put a chair right by the stove so I could watch them till they started to boil. Jason said when they were boiling, they were done.

It seemed as if it took a long time to boil, but when I saw the first bubbles coming from the bottom, I turned off the stove. I lifted the pan to drain the water. Just then, Mom came home. I jumped and spilled some of the water, and one of the hot dogs landed on the burner. I tried to grab it, but I burned my finger and screamed.

Mom burst through the kitchen door. Jason was right behind her.

"Jason and I made supper for you, Mom." I pulled my poor finger out of my mouth and continued. "Did you have a good day at school?" That was what Dad always had said when Mom came home.

"It looks to me like you made a mess. Look at that stove. Burned milk and cheese powder all over, and take that hot dog off the burner!" she yelled.

I grabbed a dirty fork off the counter and stabbed the burning hot dog.

"I'm not eating that crap. Now, clean up this kitchen. I'm not hungry." She went down the hall and locked herself in her bedroom.

Jason and I ate in silence. I could taste the salt of my tears going down the back of my throat. We each ate two hot dogs. I ate the one that had escaped. Mom's hot dog sat on the serving plate till it got cold. Our macaroni and cheese tasted like paste. Most of it ended up in the garbage. Jason took out the garbage can right after we were done eating so she wouldn't see it, while I scrubbed the burned milk off the stove.

We still didn't say much as we sat at our desks, doing our homework. I wasn't in the mood to tease Jason. He was probably disappointed, but I couldn't help it. We heard Mom go to the bathroom, and the telephone rang once, but Mom answered it from her bedroom. Other than that, it was silent in the house.

"Ready for bed?" Jason asked at about ten o'clock.

My homework had been finished for about a half hour. I had just been staring at the bibliography in my civics book. "Yes," I said.

We went to the bathroom, brushed our teeth, stripped to our underwear, and crawled into bed. Jason turned out the lights.

"Jason, are you asleep yet?"

"No."

"I can't take much more of this." I covered my face with my pillow as I sobbed.

It had been two months since Dad's funeral. I still hated school, but now I hated coming home too. Jason and I tried to hide in our room. Even when I had no homework, I sat at my desk and pretended to do homework. I didn't think Mom ever knew I was pretending, but it wasn't enough for her. It seemed no matter how I behaved, it was wrong.

On a Friday afternoon in the spring, when Jason and I got home from school, there were two cars in the driveway. I recognized the jeep as Aunt Lisa's, but the other was a red sports car with all kinds of chrome. I had never seen such a fancy car. We were surprised when Uncle Troy jumped out of it to greet us. He gave us hugs. I had decided that when I turned sixteen, I wasn't going to have hugs anymore, but it sure felt good. Aunt Lisa hugged us too. She sure had nice muscles for someone Mom's age.

"You guys want to go for a ride in my new car?" asked Uncle Troy.

"Is it all right with Mom?" asked Jason. I didn't care.

"Lisa is going to wait here for your mother and tell her."

"I'm not sure we have a mother anymore," I said. "I think a wicked alien has invaded her body."

"Barak, don't say stuff like that," Jason said.

"Why shouldn't I say stuff like that? Aunt Lisa won't tell on me. Will you, Aunt Lisa?"

"Your thoughts are safe with me, Barak."

I'd always thought Aunt Lisa liked me best. Uncle Troy had told us once that she got in lots of trouble when she was a kid, so she had compassion for me. *Compassion* was one of my vocabulary words that week, so I knew what it meant.

Uncle Troy invited us again to ride in his sports car. "Jason, you sit in front on the way, and Barak can sit in the front on the way home."

"Where are we going?" I asked.

"For a long ride," he said as he started the car. It purred like a mountain lion licking its lips.

"Why isn't Aunt Lisa coming? She's taking Mother out for dinner?" asked Jason.

"Yes, she is worried that your mother isn't eating very well. She's gotten so skinny." He pulled out into the street and sped around the corner.

We went out onto the freeway, and Uncle Troy shifted through all the gears. The ride was smooth. Even in the back seat, I felt as if I were in a spaceship. The leather seats gave the car a wonderful smell, and as I looked over the front seat, I saw all kinds of gadgets on the control panel.

We got off at an exit I didn't recognize. "What's this town?" I asked.

"Eagle Lake. We are going to a little pizza place I know."

It was the strangest restaurant I'd ever seen. The tables were out on a dock, and buckets filled with fishing rods sat beside each table. Uncle Troy sat down and cast a lure out into the water. "Take a look at the menu, boys, and order whatever you want."

The waiter came to our table and spread newspaper over it. Then he took our orders. I ran my finger down through the possibilities on the menu. "On my pizza, I'd like pepperoni and sausage and ham and peppers and lots and lots of cheese," I told Uncle Troy.

"You heard the man," said Uncle Troy to the waiter. "And that sounds good to me. Make mine the same."

"We're each having our own pizza?" I was astonished.

"Yes, sir." He turned to Jason. "What do you want?" Jason wanted plain cheese. His pizzas were always boring. When we had pizza at home, Jason would take everything off his piece except the cheese. Jason was weird.

Uncle Troy reeled in and cast the line farther out into the lake. We fixed our eyes on the bobber. I had never gone fishing while eating pizza before. It was fun, even though we caught nothing. I wasn't sure what we would have done with the fish if we had caught one. I sure didn't want the restaurant to put it on my pizza.

We talked about everything—school, missing Dad, and the pukey suppers we had eaten lately. Jason said they weren't pukey, and that wasn't even a word. Uncle Troy asked about Mom, but we just said, "Oh, she's all right." I could tell he knew that was a lie. I wanted to tell the truth, but I figured I was in trouble for the alien comment already. Jason would probably tell on me—Mother would make him—and I would be grounded for a week.

My pizza was great. When I picked up the first piece, there was a long string of melted cheese that I rolled around my finger and then popped into my mouth. I was stuffed by the time it was all eaten.

Just as we were ready to leave, an eagle flew over. "So is that why they call it Eagle Lake?" I asked.

"I think it was named a long time ago, but a friend of mine who's a game warden here said there are eight eagle nests on this lake. They patrol them so that fishermen don't go too close and disturb the birds."

I turned around. "Look, Uncle Troy—the eagle is near our bobber."

We watched the eagle dive and come up with a fish in its talons. It was exciting, but I felt sorry for the poor fish. If the fish had bit on our hook, we would have let it go.

I sat in the front seat on the way home, but it wasn't as much fun as it should have been because I figured Mom would be home, and I would be in trouble for something. But the car was sure fast. Uncle Troy drove close to the speed limit, but if a cop had chased us, I was sure he would not have been able to catch us.

When we walked in the door, Mom and Aunt Lisa weren't back yet from their dinner, so we went out into the backyard and threw the football till dark. We heard Mom and Aunt Lisa pull into the driveway. They were talking as they came up the sidewalk, and they stopped on the porch. My muscles tightened. Uncle Troy, Jason, and I ran in the back door.

I thought, *If she kicks me out of the house, maybe I could live with Uncle Troy. But she would still know where to find me.* Jason and I sat like statues in front of the fireplace as Mom and Aunt Lisa walked into the living room. It was so quiet that I wanted to scream, but instead, I stood up and kicked the footstool. I didn't know why I did it. I just had to. I thought it was a reflex. I was in so much trouble already that it didn't matter.

Mom shocked me. She knelt on the floor. She was crying. "Can you forgive me, Barak?" She reached toward Jason. "Can you forgive me, Jason? I've been so selfish. Please forgive me."

Jason rushed to her and gave her a hug. "You're forgiven, Mother. I love you," he said.

I wasn't sure. Was this an act? I was confused. She was asking to be forgiven. It took my mind forever, but in the end, I decided to give her a chance. She hadn't killed anyone like Autumn's mother had, and I thought maybe I loved her. "Yeah, I suppose I can forgive you too, Mom," I said. "You know I love you." If anything would get her, that would.

Her hug felt real. She apparently wasn't angry at me for calling her an alien. Happiness hit me, but it could have been the pizza. "We're a family again!" Jason yelled.

Nothing bad happened after that. Uncle Troy and Aunt Lisa talked. I sat and watched Mom's face. I wasn't listening well, but I watched like a cat ready to jump if this was a trap.

## New Mother

Saturday morning, Jason and I slept late. No one banged on our door to wake us up. Was Mom sleeping in too? When we finally got up, we were hungry, so we decided to go look in the refrigerator to see what we could find to eat. I was tired of cold cereal, but I had tried to fry an egg the previous Saturday and had to spend an hour cleaning Mom's special pan.

As soon as I opened our bedroom door, I could smell maple syrup and pancakes. If my nose didn't deceive me, I smelled bacon too. What was happening? We slipped down the stairs like spies searching for the answer. Someone had the table set with a glass of orange juice for each of us and hot syrup. Mom startled us as she came out of the kitchen to put bacon on our plates. "I can only make four pancakes at a time," she said. "Are you boys ready for two each?"

We sat down and poured hot syrup all over our pancakes. I spilled a little on the table, but Mom didn't yell at me. *What is wrong with her?*

"These are great, Mom," Jason said as he wolfed down half of his pancakes. "I could smell them all the way upstairs."

She brought out a second batch, gave each of us one more, and put the other two on her plate. While we ate, she told us about when she, Aunt Lisa, Dr. Barton, and their friend Mireille had gone on the canoe trip. "That's when I first learned to make really good pancakes," she said. "But they usually ended up with pine needles in them." I was afraid to laugh, but Jason did. Then she told us more stories about the canoe trip and some stories about when she'd first met Dad.

"Now, boys, I need your help."

My back muscles tightened. *Uh-oh, here it comes. She was just buttering us up to work all day doing stupid jobs. Jason will probably get all the easy jobs. I'll get all the hard ones.*

"I think it is time for Barak to have his own room, so would you boys help me clean Dad's office? We'll put Barak's bed in there. Then everyone will have his own room."

I couldn't believe it. She was going to let me have my own room. I was going to be in Dad's office. Was she trying to get us to work, or was this real? Puzzled, I asked, "So Dad's office will be my room?"

"Yes, and I've made another decision. Your rooms will be your own responsibility from now on. I promise." She held her right hand up. "I will not go in them, and I will not tell you how you have to keep them." She smiled. "If they're messy, I will just shut the door." She turned and looked at me. "My only request is that you boys keep your stuff in your own rooms so the rest of the house stays neat."

"I can have my own room, and you won't go in it?" I asked. This was unbelievable. What had Aunt Lisa done to her? *She must have hit her with a magic wand or something.*

"Yes." She paused. It looked as if she were biting the tip of her tongue. "Your rooms will be private. I won't be allowed in your room without your permission." She looked at both of us. "You still haven't told me if I can enlist your help today."

"I'll help." I almost fell off my chair when getting up.

"Me too," said Jason.

I looked at him. He seemed awfully happy to get rid of me and get me out of his room. Of course, he was going to miss my teasing him every night—I was sure of that—but one had to pay a price for privacy.

We got tired and sweaty from moving furniture. Dad's big chair fit in Mom's bedroom. Jason helped me take apart my bed and put it back together again in Dad's office, which was now my room. Mom put clean sheets on the bed. She didn't even ask me to help.

We stacked Dad's books on the floor and carried the bookcase downstairs to the living room. Mom sat on the floor and sorted through Dad's books. She put some in a box to give to his business partner because she didn't understand them. Others she carried to her bedroom. I thought they were novels or history books.

The last thing in Dad's office to deal with was his desk. "Do you want this desk for your own, Barak?" Mom asked. "Then the other desk could be Jason's."

I couldn't believe she was asking us stuff instead of just telling us what to do. "I'd love to have Dad's desk."

"All right, Jason, here's a box. Get everything of Barak's out of the desk in your room, and that desk will be yours. Barak and I will sort through Dad's papers."

Jason scurried off. He seemed excited to get rid of my stuff in the desk we had shared. She set another box between us, took out a fistful of papers, and started looking at them.

I saw three green envelopes that had embossed writing on them. They were addressed to Jason Shelton, Barak Shelton, and "Amandeline, my love." Dad had called Mom that, but we weren't allowed to. Once, I'd tried and had my mouth washed out with soap. "Hey, Jason!" I yelled. "Come quick! Look what I found."

Jason came running. I handed Mom her envelope and Jason his. I tore mine open. A letter and some kind of document were inside. Their envelopes had the same thing. Mom started crying when she read her letter. I read my letter.

Dearest Barak,

I love you very much. You are very special. You have a deep sensitivity. That is why you know how to tease so well. I know you don't like school, but I want you to try going to the university anyway. I am sure you will find it totally different from high school. I pray that the gifts God has given you will be used in a way that helps other people. No matter—when you turn eighteen, you may use the money for anything you want. I trust you.

Dad

PS Be gentle with your mother. She doesn't understand teasing.

"Dad says here that I have sensitivity, Mom." The document fell out, and I picked it up. "What's this mean? It says I'm a beneficiary."

She was still crying and couldn't talk. After she blew her nose and took a deep breath, the words tumbled out. "It's a life insurance policy. There's one for each of us."

"Does this mean we're rich or something?"

She blew her nose again. "Your dad must have bought them when he first started with the company. I didn't even know he had these policies. They must have been deducted from his payroll check. I can't believe it."

Since Mom was having trouble talking, I turned to Jason. "What are you going to do with your money?"

"Go to the university."

"Yeah, Dad wants me to go too. But the letter says I can spend it on anything I want once I get out of high school."

Mom was able to talk again. "These policies are to be invested till you start college. You will have even more money by then."

I sat down in my wooden chair, which had one rung broken. "I wish Dad was here so I could thank him for taking good care of us."

"Tell him in your prayers, Barak. I'm sure God will tell him."

"I thought you didn't believe in God. You said that if there was a God, he wouldn't have been so mean to let Dad die."

"I'm sorry I said that, Barak. I have a lot to learn. Can you forgive my foolishness?"

Forgiving Mom was getting to be a full-time job. "Yes," I groaned, and I gave her a hug. "Dad said in my letter that I wasn't supposed to tease you because you don't understand teasing, so I won't give you a hard time." I looked at her. She was thin and seemed weak and fragile when I hugged her. Uncle Troy was right; she hadn't been eating well. "I'm sorry I tease you so much. Are you going to forgive me too?"

"Yes." She put an arm around Jason and one around me, and then she sat and sobbed. I was getting sweaty while standing there with her arm around me. After she calmed down, she turned to us. "We've done enough cleaning for one day. You each have your own room now. Do you want to go out for a gooey pizza?"

"We have to each have our own, Mom, because Jason only likes cheese on his, and I like lots of meat."

She laughed. "All right, three individual pizzas. I like anchovies on mine."

Jason and I said, "Yuck," at the same time.

# GRADUATION

Two years later, the spring of the year I graduated from high school was a climax for me. I'd never thought I would make it. Since Lily was the same age, she was graduating too. Jason and I borrowed Mom's car and drove up to Orr, Minnesota, to attend Lily's graduation. There were only twenty-four in her class, so it didn't take long. At the end of the ceremony, everyone took off his or her graduation gown. Most of the girls were dressed in frilly clothes. Lily only had on a T-shirt and shorts. She whispered in my ear that she was mad because Dr. Barton had made her wear a bra.

Several of her classmates had been invited to Dr. Barton's for a party, so we carpooled over to Dr. Barton's house. It was a bright, sunny day, so the party was outdoors among the pine trees. Four Anishinabe drummers dressed in black floral Anishinabe regalia sang as they beat a large, ornate drum. The music was syncopated compared to the music I was familiar with, and the singing was exotic. Lily explained that it was a celebration song. She and her friends who were Anishinabe danced a traditional dance to the beat of the drum. Feathers and embroidered flowers decorated the costumes of Lily's Anishinabe friends. Those of us without First Nation blood and costumes were invited to join the dances. Autumn danced with amazing agility in a sparkly blue dress that seemed to catch Jason's eye.

While I listened, I thought of how different this party was from the one the year before, when Autumn and Jason had graduated. They'd had a simple celebration together at a restaurant. Just family had been invited. Mom and Dr. Barton had split the cost. It had been fun but quiet. Autumn and Jason had made a quiet announcement that they were attending the University of Minnesota, Duluth. As it turned out, she and Jason even had some classes together. It all had been so sedate.

The drum beat brought me back to the present. Lily's friends raised a big commotion. I turned to see what it was about. Dr. Barton and some of the graduates' parents had set a picnic table with wild rice and bear meat. At the end of the table, where I expected to see a cake, was a platter of candy made from wild rice and maple syrup. It tasted great. I wondered what Mom would serve next week at my graduation party. I was certain that it would be inferior to this feast.

As I wiped bear grease off my mouth, Lily took me behind the house, down to the boat dock to talk. "So, my brother who hates school so bad, are you going to the University of Minnesota, Duluth, in the fall?"

I explained that my dad had left me a life insurance policy to pay for my university education. "Are you going?"

"I got a scholarship from the tribe just like Autumn, so we will both be going to University of Minnesota, Duluth. Any idea what you're going to do?"

My focus had been to get through high school without too many detentions. I hadn't really thought about where I would go to college. I felt forced into the decision. In fact, I had dreamed of using my money to buy a sports car. "Oh, I think I'll go to UMD too," I said in reflex.

"Great," she said, and she gave me a hug. It made me tingle all over. I decided then that if Lily was going to UMD, so would I.

The next week, at my graduation party, Mom had catered little meatballs and a cake from the mall bakery. It was pretty pathetic. Nevertheless, I enjoyed my party because Autumn and Lily drove down from Nett Lake to celebrate with us. They both had driver's licenses, and they drove an old pickup truck in which Lily had replaced the transmission. "The truck has purred like a cat," Autumn said, "since Lily fixed the timing."

Lily was delighted when I showed her my application to UMD and told her, "I'm mailing it in tomorrow."

"You know," she said, "Autumn is renting an apartment off campus for the two of us. We each have our own bedroom because otherwise, we would not get along very well. You can come visit any time." She wrote the address on a piece of paper and made me stick it in my wallet. It would be an easy walk from campus. I was thrilled that I would be able to visit her any time I wanted. There would no longer be a hundred miles of Highway 53 between us.

Once I started at UMD, I realized that Dad had been right about university education. It wasn't like high school at all. In most of my classes, there was a midterm and a final; that was it. Even in my calculus class, I didn't have to turn in daily assignments. "The homework assignments are for your own edification," our professor said. He asked at the beginning of each class if there were any problems we wanted him to review, and if there weren't, he went on to the next concepts. I loved math at UMD as much as I had hated it in high school.

My problem was that I didn't know what to major in. I enjoyed science, but I didn't want to be a science teacher like my mother. I supposed that was rebellion, but I didn't know what I wanted to do. I struggled with freshman physics, but my first chemistry class was so interesting that I told Lily, "It's like studying God's fingerprints." She loved that. The beauty of the chemical structures fascinated me. I even dreamed about them at night. So I majored in chemistry, but I enjoyed biology too, especially when we dissected animals and studied their anatomic structures. Sometimes Lily snuck into my biology lab and helped me with the dissections. I was impressed at how much comparative anatomy she already knew.

Autumn and Jason were still friends, but their relationship seemed to be cooling. Majoring in sociology, she had a 4.0 GPA, and Jason did too but in economics. They had some classes in common, but he realized he wasn't quite as smart as Autumn, even when he studied more than she did.

Lily decided to be a lawyer about the middle of her freshman year. She made the decision after looking at bulletins for law school and realizing there were suggestions but no required classes, so she could take any class she wanted. She did not like being told what to do. Autumn told her one time when I was over at their apartment, "You're so argumentative you'll be a great lawyer." They had been fighting over something most of the evening. I never understood what because when they fought, they spoke in Anishinabe.

"I am not argumentative," she said, but at the first opportunity to apply to law school, she applied just to see if they would accept her. I secretly hoped she would be rejected and have to apply again when she graduated, so we would be at the university for four whole years together. Besides, I was jealous that Jason, Autumn, and Lily were so focused on their careers.

One beautiful spring day when temperatures were in the seventies, I was studying for my English literature final exam out on the deck in front of UMD's cafeteria. The birds' singing and the smell of the grass that had been mowed that day distracted me. I decided to see if Lily wanted to do something. Her apartment was just a few blocks off campus. Besides, I had been over my notes enough times. Tomorrow was the exam. I needed to do something different.

Lily still treated me as if she were my sister. Maybe it was because she'd been serious about adopting me as a brother. I'd thought it was just a silly thing that high school kids did, but Lily seemed serious about the relationship. In fact, she made me feel like family, not a potential boyfriend, when I was with her. I was disappointed. I supposed I was still infatuated with her. The positive part of our relationship was that we could talk about anything. That was good, but I wanted the relationship to evolve into something more intimate.

I walked over to Autumn and Lily's second-floor apartment. The birds were flitting about in the gentle breeze. The spring air smelled good. Their apartment was small but had a sliding glass door that led out onto a miniature deck. As I approached the house, I saw that the sliding door was open, but I didn't see anyone. I figured they must have been airing out the apartment on such a pleasant day.

"Anyone home?" I yelled from the front yard.

I heard Lily's voice. "I'm out on the deck, studying. Come on up; the door's not locked."

I climbed the stairs and found the door unlocked, so I walked in. The apartment had a fifty-gallon fish tank along one wall. Autumn took care of several tropical fish; Lily couldn't be bothered. She said she would have been more interested if it had been a walleye in the tank, but then she would have eaten it. I thought that was one of the things they argued about.

As I entered, I observed clothes strewn about, and dirty dishes filled the sink. The smell of grease from burned food was wafting through the open door out into the spring breeze. To announce my arrival, I yelled, "Where are you?" I saw no one. I had a good idea that Autumn probably wasn't home, because she would have been cleaning up the mess.

"Out here."

I walked out to the deck. Lily was lying on a towel, reading a book and sunbathing. At first, I thought she was naked, but then I saw her thong.

Her bra was crumpled on the towel in front of her. Up on her elbows, she was engrossed in her book. "I'm studying for my philosophy exam. Are you all set for your exams?"

She motioned for me to sit in a chair in front of her. I hesitated because from that vantage, I caught the full effect of her dangling breasts. There was a cherry tomato plant in a rolling planter, so I scooted it with my foot to block the view. It was less distracting that way, but I caught myself staring at her muscular back, which distracted me anyway.

"You want some tea?"

"Sure."

She got up with her book in one hand and her bra in the other, still reading as she went into the kitchen. "Herbal or regular?"

"Either is fine. Should I wait here?"

"Yeah, I'll join you in a minute."

When she returned, she had added a faded T-shirt to her ensemble. She set a cup of tea on the plastic table between us and sat down. "So what have you been studying?"

"English literature. We have to write three essays on the poems we've studied. The exam is tomorrow from eight to ten o'clock."

"Have you decided to be a physician yet?"

"I've never said that I wanted to be a physician."

"That is definitely what you should be. You're sensitive to people's feelings, and you're good in biology and chemistry. Where else could you put those skills to maximum use?"

"I don't know. It seems like a lot of school. And I hate school. Well, UMD hasn't been so bad. Much better than I expected, I guess."

"Barak, the process of becoming a physician will be fun for you. I remember what you said at your dad's funeral, and I happen to know that you are fascinated by the human body." She lifted up her T-shirt. "Right?"

I was certainly fascinated by her body, but I didn't think that translated into becoming a physician. "Do you think my grades are good enough?"

"What's your GPA?"

"I had trouble with physical chemistry, but I still have a 3.72. That class was way over my head. I'm lucky I got a B-. I think Dr. Butler gave me credit on the final for explaining why I didn't understand the problems." I sipped my tea. I felt hot despite the breeze blowing across the deck and wafting the steam away. "Oh, by the way, I got that job."

"Working as an orderly?"

"It's called a certified nursing assistant, or CNA. But yes, I start my training next Monday, when exam week is over. I should have steady hours all summer, but I don't know where I'll be assigned yet."

"That's great. Don't work too hard; you don't need the money."

"I'm supposed to use my life insurance money for school, and I have to account for what I spend it on. It is part of Dad's will, so it would be nice to have some money that I could just spend." I smiled. "For example, I could take you out for dinner sometime."

"My scholarship from the tribe is all I need; plus, Heidi is always sending me spending money." She sipped her tea and then twisted the cherry tomato plant from where I had moved it back into the sunlight. It was already full of flowers. "Just before classes start in the fall, could you get some time off to go on a canoe trip?"

"Sure, when I switch from full-time to part-time at the hospital, I could take some time off. What did you have in mind?"

"There's an area in the lake region of Ontario that has one magnificent waterfall after another. It's difficult to get there—lots of portages—so there shouldn't be a lot of people up there. Besides, I love waterfalls."

"Will Autumn and Jason want to come?" I downed the last of my tea.

"That would be great—a lot safer too—but it doesn't matter. If they don't want to come, you and I should go alone."

My mind raced. What would a week alone in the wilderness with Lily be like? Would we be able to catch fish for our meals? Would she know enough edible plants so we wouldn't have to pack much food? Other possibilities presented dramatic images to my brain, but I stifled the thoughts. "Sounds good to me."

She picked up my empty cup and headed for the kitchen. "I've got to get dressed. Autumn and I are going out for supper. Do you want to join us? She'll be home soon. She always studies at the library. She says I'm distracting." She set the cups in the sink and whipped off her T-shirt and thong. "I need a shower." She headed for the bathroom.

I had to quell my emotions at seeing how casual she was about modesty, so I went to the kitchen and started washing the pots and putting the dishes in the empty dishwasher. I found a frying pan that had something burned on the bottom, and I scoured it clean. In washing the dishes, something I avoided at home, I used my pent-up energy from seeing her traipsing around naked. Besides, I knew that Autumn liked things neat, and it was part of Lily's chores to clean up the kitchen.

# DINNER DATE

LILY SCOOTED OUT OF THE bathroom with a towel wrapped around her waist and went into her bedroom. She came out wearing a silver necklace woven into her braids; long, dangling turquoise earrings; a black T-shirt that did not obscure her rippling abdominal muscles; and a black skirt covered with bright red flowers and birds. She was wearing a bra. She sat on the couch, picked up her philosophy book, and curled her feet underneath her.

I was just putting the last pan away in the cupboard, when Autumn walked in. She was dressed in a floral blouse with a blue skirt. "I see you have your boy slave doing your work, Lily. Why can't you take responsibility for doing your own chores?"

Before I could protest that I was not a boy slave, Lily jumped up from the couch. "I didn't ask him to do the dishes. He just did it on his own."

Autumn flung her books onto the coffee table and put her hands on her hips. "Why do you have to be such a lazy slob? Look—clothes all over."

I vaulted the couch and yelled, "Stop the catfight! Your mother wouldn't approve."

"At least my mother isn't in prison for murdering my father," said Lily.

"At least I know who my mother is!" screamed Autumn. The rest of the conversation was converted to Anishinabe.

"Stop!" I yelled. I let out a high-pitched whistle. Both girls stared at me. If this didn't come out right, I would be carrion. "I meant Dr. Barton."

"Heidi?" they said.

Autumn added, "We knew what you meant. That's not the problem." They reverted to Anishinabe. By the way they were yelling short phrases, it sounded as if they were calling each other obscene names.

"Stop." I put a hand on top of each girl's head and pushed them to a seated position on the couch. I turned to Autumn. "Let's start over. What's this all about? It can't be because I did a few dishes without being asked." I decided to address the boy-slave issue later.

Autumn's face flushed. "She's wearing my favorite skirt without even asking." Lily jumped up and took off the skirt. "Here. Have your skirt."

She was wearing the cutest see-through red underwear, but I tried not to notice. "Were you going to wear that skirt tonight?" I asked Autumn, trying to negotiate a peace settlement. We were all standing again. I realized I was interposed between two leopards.

"Don't take her side. She is always wearing my clothes without asking," said Autumn.

Both girls' brown eyes were intent on each other. I turned to Autumn. "May I suggest that reflects your good taste? She approves of the clothes you have chosen." I thought that sounded like a mediating approach. I held my arms outstretched with one hand on each girl's chest.

"Don't take her side," said Lily. "I've asked before."

I blurted out, "May I suggest that you're both"—I turned to look each girl in the eyes—"wrong?" I lost consciousness as I received two sharp blows to the gut and collapsed.

When I regained consciousness, both girls were kneeling beside me. Autumn's perfume and Lily's sweet breath roused me. "I didn't mean to hit you so hard. I'm sorry," said Autumn. "I meant to hit Lily."

"Stop before I die of your love for each other."

"I'm sorry too," said Lily.

Both girls were so close I could have kissed them. If I had been in different circumstances, it would have registered in my reincarnating brain how beautiful they were. "Are you both dressed and ready to go out for dinner?"

"I need a skirt," Lily said as she stood and paraded in her red underwear. The sheer fabric left nothing to the imagination. "May I wear one of your very tasteful skirts, Autumn, my adopted sister whom I love and admire?"

"Yes, you may, and thank you for asking, Lily, my loving adopted sister with whom I chose to share an apartment."

"You are looking very nice this evening, Autumn," Lily said as she put the skirt she had been wearing back on and slipped on her sandals.

"Thank you, Lily. May I accompany you the way I am dressed, or should I wear something of yours?"

"Hold it. Don't answer that, Lily." I scrambled up off the floor. "You're both dressed just fine. Let's go eat. I'm hungry."

Autumn headed for the door. "Even with your sore stomach?" she said.

"I deserved it," I said as I put one arm around each girl and headed for the door. "I should have chosen a different adjective."

When we got outside, Lily threw me her car keys. "You drive. We want to go to Harvey's Steak House, and we want a chauffeur." They both climbed into the back seat.

As I drove, they maintained an animated conversation in Anishinabe. It took twenty minutes to reach the restaurant. By the time I parked the car, both were silent. I assumed things had resolved.

The conversation was amiable as we waited for our steaks. We talked about exams, local politics, and international affairs. Autumn trimmed the fat off her steak and chewed a bite of the meat. "Good flavor," she said. "Real tender. So how is your brother's new girlfriend?"

"What do you mean?" I set down my knife. My fork was dangling a piece of steak.

"We broke up. He's dating a girl from the economics department. Her name is Beth."

Her tone sounded neutral. I sensed no bitterness in her voice. "Yes, I've met Beth once. She and Jason were studying in the library. I thought she was just a friend he studied with. But I didn't know you two broke up. When did this happen?" I cleared my throat and proceeded with caution, as my stomach was still sore.

"We broke up a couple weeks ago. But I like Beth. They seem right for each other," said Autumn as she sliced off another piece of steak.

That seemed positive. "Do you know her well?"

"She was in my sociology class. We've studied together. I think that's how Jason met her. She'll make him a fine wife. I guess I was too radical or independent for him."

I put down my fork. "Whoa, you really mean that?" I hadn't realized my brother was that serious about any girlfriend. Autumn already had them married.

"Yes, Beth is sweet. He needs someone traditional like Beth."

"He does have a strong sense of propriety. But what happened?" *That was stupid*, I thought, but I didn't know what else to say. I felt like a rabbit nibbling on two lionesses' kill.

"I just couldn't fit into his mold. But he's a gentle person. I enjoyed the time we spent together. She is better for him, and I wish them the best."

I let out a deep sigh as Lily changed the subject to disagree with some obscure philosopher. I had no knowledge base to add to the conversation. I chewed my steak and listened as the two of them ripped apart the proponents' premises. The girls insisted on paying for their own dinner when the waitress left the check. I appreciated the mundane experience of dividing the numbers by three. We had each ordered the same thing.

Lily drove, Autumn sat beside her, and I was assigned to the back seat as we left the restaurant. They dropped me off at my house. I got out of the car and thanked them both, "Great evening. I feel ready for my exams. Will you two get along without killing each other?"

"We'll be fine," Autumn said. "I love Lily. I just can't stand her sometimes."

"Thanks for mediating," said Lily. "Sorry you got hurt. You know, your belly is pretty soft. Maybe you should be doing more abdominal exercises."

"I'll see to that right away," I said as Lily hit the gas pedal and peeled out of the driveway.

# CERTIFIED NURSE ASSISTANT

DESPITE HAVING MONEY FOR SCHOOL supplied by the life insurance policy, I needed some spending money, which job as a certified nurse assistant provided. It also gave me the clinical exposure to decide whether medical school was what I wanted. I had to start applying for medical school at the end of my sophomore year or decide I wanted to be a research chemist. Lily was pushing me to apply to medical school.

The classes to become a CNA fascinated me. There was only one other man in the class. Herb was a retired factory worker who had gotten bored in retirement and wanted to do something productive. He was a corpulent fellow who always wore khaki clothes and had a great sense of humor. We ate lunch together every day. He told comical stories about his grandchildren, and I learned that he loved to fish, but other than that, I had trouble relating to him or anyone else in the class.

Except for two middle-aged women in the class, the rest were young women who'd just graduated from high school. They were pretty to look at, with their lovely hair and stylish clothes, but their puerile conversation at break turned me sour. When we were required to wear our uniforms, they all looked ordinary. The first week was mostly lectures about caring for people, showing proper respect, and fire and electrical safety. The second week focused on practical matters, such as giving a bed bath, taking blood pressures, and catheterization.

Mrs. Claussen called us to attention. "Class, today we are going to learn male and female catheterization. We have plastic models to practice with this morning. This afternoon, you will be assigned to work with nursing assistants on the floor. Hopefully you will get an opportunity to assist in the procedure. You will not be allowed to do catheterizations on your own till you have been observed and certified."

There were four plastic models: two male and two female. We gathered around our stations as the instructing nurse at each station explained the types of catheters and the sterile procedure involved. It didn't seem too complicated, but I had trouble holding the lubricated catheter with the disposable forceps in the kits.

"You've broken the sterile field, Mr. Shelton," the instructor said as she stopped me. She put the catheter back into the plastic receptacle. "Try again."

The sterile gloves inhibited my dexterity as I picked up the catheter with my right hand and spread the plastic labia with my left. This time, I introduced the catheter into the female urethra without dropping it.

I found the exercise instructive. I did notice some of the high school graduate girls giggling over the plastic penis of the male catheterization model, but they all became serious when the instructor made them focus on the imperatives of proper procedure.

Herb and I had a nice lunch that day. He was going fishing on the weekend, as it would be our last weekend free for a couple of weeks. He told me about the lake where he fished. This was much more interesting than the latest antics of his grandchildren. "They have some big walleyes in that lake. That's why I bought the cabin there years ago," Herb said.

"Are you usually successful?"

"I go out at six o'clock in the morning. By nine o'clock, I have enough fish for breakfast. The rest of the day, I have my wife's to-do list to keep me busy." He laughed. "It comes with marriage." He returned to discussing fishing. "You just have to know the habits of the fish to catch them—when they eat, where they rest. And don't forget that fish are lazy; they like their food brought to them."

"What does that mean?"

"When the wind is steady, the fish congregate where the food is blown. When there is a current, the fish go where the current drops the food." Herb looked at his wristwatch. "Break is up; back to work."

We all passed our exams, which involved making beds, transferring patients properly, demonstrating the mechanics of giving a bed bath, and inserting Foley catheters. The written exam involved an understanding of when a patient needed urgent care, when to call the nurse, how to recognize electrical equipment that needed servicing, and how to respond to a fire. The next day, we were given our grades and assigned to our departments. Herb was assigned to his preference, the psychiatric ward.

I was assigned to the emergency department. I hoped the clinical exposure would help me decide whether medical school was what I wanted.

That Monday, I reported to my new assignment. Dorothy Ross was the charge nurse in the emergency department. She had been an army nurse with combat experience before she retired and joined the civilian world, but her military demeanor hadn't changed. "Barak, I need you in room twelve. Clean that guy up before the doctor sees him," she said.

Giving bed baths was one of the first things we had learned, but I was not prepared for Mr. Jacobson in room 12. He was agitated, disoriented, and in leather restraints, screaming, "Get those bugs off me!" I couldn't tell if the smell was feces, vomit, or both. A pan of soapy water and a washcloth introduced me to reality.

I introduced myself, as if it made a difference, but we were supposed to do that. I started taking off Mr. Jacobson's clothes. His shirt was rank with vomit. It was torn, so I used the bandage scissors to cut it off rather than releasing the leather restraints. "I'm getting the bugs off you," I said. His pants were full of feces and shredded below the knees, so I cut them off as well. I covered him with a sheet for modesty, as we were taught in class, but he kept kicking it off. Four basins of water later—and complete nausea on my part—Mr. Jacobson was presentable for the physician. He looked nice with a clean gown covered with a clean white sheet. The bugs in his mind were still bothering him.

Nurse Ross poked her head in the door. "Put those soiled clothes in a plastic bag, and come into sixteen. I need your help with a catheterization. Be quick about it."

I bagged the clothes, threw my double gloves into the contaminated-waste bag, and ran to room 16. We had just finished our training and exam. Wasn't I supposed to be supervised more? I felt as if I had been thrown into the fire.

I heard the woman groaning in room 16 before I entered. Pulling aside the drape, I was confronted with a woman who weighted at least four hundred pounds. She was grunting as the physician listened to her belly. Her gown almost covered her voluminous breasts.

"Pull her leg to the side, Barak. Get this catheter in." She handed me the opened kit. "She is in labor and trying to deliver, but her bladder is obstructing the birth canal."

Nurse Ross braced and pulled the woman's leg to the side. The woman groaned. Any erotic thoughts about my first female catheterization dissipated. Nurse Ross spread the labia and shouted, "Get that catheter in!" I found the urethra with my right hand and grabbed the catheter with my left, slipping it into place. The plastic forceps lay unused in the tray. The Foley bag filled with crystal-yellow urine almost immediately. The massive woman sighed.

"Thanks, Barak." Nurse Ross's demeanor calmed. "The ambulance informed us that someone is coming into the trauma room in about five minutes. Be there. They'll need help."

I backed out of the room, still overwhelmed by what I had just seen. The woman still had her knees bent, and I saw the baby's head crowning out of her vagina. Nurse Ross covered her with a sheet as a transport person appeared to bring her to the obstetric ward down the hall. I got out of the way just in time.

The trauma room victim presented covered in mud. The ambulance attendant, a muscular but comely woman, described the scene. "He was drunk and drove off the bridge and landed right in the muck below. What an extraction that was!"

I put on gloves and a gown, stripped the patient, and started washing mud and blood from his wounds amid the foul smell of stale, vomited beer. The physician listened to his lungs and prepared to intubate the man. "He's not breathing very well," the physician said. He motioned to the nurse, who grabbed an emergency tray, and the physician intubated the patient, sucking vomit out of his lungs.

With the patient cleaned up and intubated, the emergency physician said, "Put in a catheter." He focused on the patient's lacerations, flushing them with massive amounts of saline, which flowed all over the floor. I put in the catheter using sterile gloves with no time to manipulate the plastic forceps. After I finished, the nurse grabbed the used Foley kit and handed me a mop to clean up the mud and blood that had pooled on the floor. The physician never looked up from his focus on resuscitating the patient.

Later, I catheterized a male college student. I was glad I didn't recognize him from any of my classes. He was hallucinating and kept yelling, "Red!" which didn't make any sense. The nurse grabbed a sample of urine as soon as it started flowing out of the Foley catheter.

The eight hours of my first shift flew by. I never got to indulge in the required coffee breaks or lunch break. When the afternoon CNA arrived, I felt smelly, dirty, hungry, and exhausted. Dorothy Ross, RN, said a quick "Thanks for your help today, Barak" as I left.

*Did she even know this was my first day? That I was supposed to be supervised? Was I supervised?*

I went to Lily's apartment after work. She was bringing in the mail as I drove up. "How's the life of an orderly?" she said.

"A little shell-shocking, I'm afraid. Can I persuade you to make me a cup of tea—decaf? And I'm real hungry. You got any leftovers in the fridge that I could eat?"

"Sure, what's the problem?" she said as she served me a large glass of Gatorade while she heated water for tea. A plate full of reheated wild rice casserole appeared. I took a long drink. It was so refreshing that I thought I must have been dehydrated. Then I dove into the casserole, gobbling down everything on my plate, to which she added a second helping.

Once I started talking, I couldn't quit. I told her about the emergency department and the patients I had seen. "I guess I got certified to put in male and female urethral catheters. The nurse who allegedly supervised me said I did a great job. I'm not even sure she was watching. It was the circumstances that bothered me. I'm not sure I'm cut out to be a physician."

Lily went to the kitchen as the tea kettle whistled. She returned with two steaming cups. "Careful—it's hot." She handed me a cup. "All right, continue."

"I did a male catheterization first on a drunk who drove off a bridge. What a mess. Then I catheterized a young man, a university student who presented high on drugs. The urine drug screen showed cocaine, marijuana, and amphetamines. He was totally confused. He didn't even know his name or where he was."

"That happens. And the female patient?"

"The first one was an emergency job. This very obese woman was in labor." I described the scene of the head ready to crown and the sudden necessity to get the catheter in place. "There I was, trying to get the catheter in with amniotic fluid pouring out her vagina."

I took a deep breath, sipped my tea, and sighed. "Later in my shift, a very attractive teenage girl overdosed on Tylenol because her boyfriend broke up with her." Tears dripped down my face. Lily gave me a tissue. "There she was, this beautiful young woman, dying of liver failure. She should have been at the mall, trying out new purses, instead of lying on the gurney with her chest exposed to do an EKG and a new CNA—me, Barak—with his head in her groin, putting a plastic tube into her"—I swallowed—"urethra."

Lily sipped her tea. "Could you give her any comfort?"

"She was comatose, and without a liver transplant, she'll probably die. She waited too long. The physician was in communication with University Hospital in Minneapolis to transport her for an emergency transplant. The helicopter was waiting on the roof. I was the motor for the gurney with the whole physician-nurse air flight team putting her into the helicopter."

She got up from her chair, massaged my neck, and tilted my head back. Her scent calmed me. "You've just had an overdose of reality." Her voice was as soft as a breeze through aspens. "The kind of physician I would want is one whose heart breaks for his patients and who is still able to function. Did you get the catheter in the poor girl?"

"I did." My eyes blurred with tears. Lily brought me the whole box of tissues. "You still think I can make it through medical school?"

"Now I know you will be a great physician." She invited me to sit on the couch and sat beside me, leaning my head on her shoulder. Her touch was balm to my soul. Her strong hands massaged my muscles, releasing the heart-wrenching experiences of the day.

When I felt relaxed, she jumped up from the sofa. "I got a very curious-looking letter today. You want to see what it is? I waited to open it till you came."

I took a deep swallow of the last of my tea, grabbed another tissue, blew my nose, and then answered with an attempt at enthusiasm, "Sure."

"It's from the University of Minnesota Law School. It will probably tell me to finish my bachelor studies." She opened the letter with a hunting knife and handed me the letter without looking at it. "Here. You read it, and tell me what it says."

I read the letter and then, in silence, read it again. Setting it down on her lap, I said, "It says you've been accepted to law school."

There was a click in the door latch. Autumn came in and set down her keys. As she took off her coat, she eyed the two of us on the couch with a pile of crumpled tissues sitting on the coffee table.

Lily handed Autumn her letter. In a soft, unnatural voice, she said, "Please read this letter at your convenience, most precious sister." She looked at me and resumed her normal voice. "We've been practicing being politer to each other so you don't get hurt."

"Lily, you've been accepted to law school." Autumn's eyebrows rose. "You haven't even finished your bachelor's degree. How did you do that?" She faked a smile. "I mean, congratulations, dearest sister whom I love and adore." They hugged, and Autumn spun Lily around the room. They collapsed onto the couch beside me.

"Barak, you want to celebrate with me Friday night?" Lily said.

"Do we have to wait till Friday?"

"Yes, because we might be out all night, and if we went out tonight, you wouldn't be able to get to work in the morning. Besides, isn't this your last weekend off for a while?"

Lily was euphoric for the rest of the week. I continued working in the emergency department, where I was exposed to more reality, as Lily said. When I arrived at the girls' apartment Friday night, exhausted and hungry, things were as I expected. Autumn was nicely dressed, paying attention to her fish, while Lily was still running around in a towel that almost covered her.

"Where are we going?" I asked as Autumn let me in.

"She wants to go to a seafood place. Any ideas?"

"Jason has taken a certain person whose name I won't mention to Blackwood's," I said. "He said it was really good."

"Did Beth like it?"

I blushed. "Yes."

"Beth has good taste in restaurants, so if she liked it, then that's where we should go." She knocked on Lily's door. "How does Blackwood's sound?"

Lily opened her door. She had on panties and was holding a lacy bra in each hand, one black and one red. "Dearest sister—"

"Yes, you can wear one of my dresses. Go ahead."

I almost choked. "And the black bra," I said.

She shot across the hall to Autumn's room.

As Jason had said, the food was good. The service wasn't fast, but we were in no hurry. We toasted Lily, who was excited and had plenty to talk about. Autumn and I split the tab, but Lily insisted on leaving a big tip.

When we got back to the apartment, Lily asked if we wanted to go to a bar. "Not me," said Autumn. "I'm not a night person."

Lily and I went by ourselves. After my initiation to the emergency department, I was in no mood for alcohol, so I ordered a Coke. Lily showed her ID, ordered some drink I had never heard of, and then ordered a double.

"Let's dance," she said after downing the second cocktail. We danced to the live music, but by the end of the third song, I was getting tired, and Lily seemed clumsy.

"Give me a shot of your best whiskey," she said.

"I think that's enough, Lily."

"How many times have you been accepted to law school?"

"That's not the point."

"It's my point." She drank the whiskey and started flirting with the older man sitting next to her. "Give me another, bartender."

"I think that's enough, Lily."

"There's never enough to celebrate." Her words were getting slurred. "Then just give me a cold beer. My brother here thinks I've had enough."

The older gentleman's eyes brightened as he asked me, "You're not her boyfriend?"

I stared at him. "Tonight I am." He looked away.

The beer arrived, and she chugged it down. I paid the bartender and told her, "Let's dance some more."

"I'm too tired to dance."

"Come on, Lily." I grabbed her around the waist and danced her out to the car. She fell asleep in the seat. I didn't want to drive her home. I knew Autumn would be livid if she saw her drunk. Jason was visiting Beth's parents that weekend, and Mom was at a teachers' convention, so I decided to bring her to Mom's house.

I made a left turn, and suddenly, Lily opened the car door and said, "I'm sick."

I ground the brakes to a stop as the car behind me changed lanes and honked. Lily hung her head out the open door, still restrained by her seat belt, and puked on the pavement. I eased into the parking lane and let her finish.

She was just hanging there breathing as I put the car in park, turned the key, and went around to her side. "Are you feeling better?"

"Just order me one more beer, and I'll be fine."

"No more tonight." I propped her up in the seat and tightened her seat belt.

"I just need one more drink, Barak. What kind of friend are you?"

"The best," I said as I started the car and drove home.

In the driveway, I turned off the ignition and sat there. It was silent except for Lily snoring.

She aroused enough to help me get her into the house and up the stairs into my room. I laid her on the floor, covered her with a sheet, and undressed her as we had been taught in CNA class. "Always preserve the patient's modesty," we were told. I rolled her up in my sleeping bag and took her soiled clothes to the laundry room to wash the vomit out of Autumn's dress and the black bra. I followed the instructions on the tag, finding the settings on Mom's washing machine. "Some celebration," I told the machine as I sat down to wait.

It was three o'clock in the morning before the clothes were clean and dry. I wasn't sure if I should redress her or just go to bed. I decided that if she was still asleep, I wouldn't wake her. I folded the clothes and headed up the stairs. I heard a commotion and ran to the second floor. She was in the bathroom, vomiting. Then I heard her crying. "I dirtied my panties," she said. "I haven't done that since I was five." She opened the bathroom door and stood in the doorway, naked, holding out her soiled underwear. Tears mixed with mascara streaked her face. "Oh, Barak, would you wash my panties for me? I already washed my dirty ass."

I took the panties with two fingers, trying not to contaminate myself. I averted my eyes and shut the door. I laid the bra and dress on my bed and went back down to the laundry room to rinse and wash her panties. "Oh, Lily," I whispered to myself, "you're not invincible." I slept on the couch.

In the morning, I went up to my room and knocked on the door. "Are you awake?"

"Yes. I just have a terrible headache. Come in." She was sitting cross-legged in my sleeping bag on the floor, still naked, holding her head.

I offered her the clean panties. She didn't take them, so I set them on her knee. "I washed these for you." I walked into the bathroom. "You want a couple Tylenol?" Then I remembered that Tylenol and alcohol competed for the same enzymes in the liver. "How about ibuprofen?"

"I don't care."

I gave her the tablets with a drink of water.

"Thanks." She swallowed them down with the whole glass of water. She looked up at me with her raven eyes. "Where did you sleep?"

"On the couch in the living room."

"So you didn't take advantage of me?"

"Other than seeing you naked, no."

"So there's none of your sperm swimming around in my vagina?" She started putting on her panties.

"No." I picked up the still-folded bra and dress on the end of the bed and gave them to her. "Come to the kitchen when you're dressed. I'll make some coffee and anything else you'd like."

"I need a shower. I'm filthy."

"Take a shower. I'll start breakfast."

Twenty minutes later, we were sipping coffee and eating toast with strawberry jam.

"I'm so embarrassed, Barak. I made such a fool of myself." She stirred cream into her coffee. "I don't care if you saw me naked. You're going to be a physician. You need to be desensitized to people's bodies. Besides, I have nothing to hide from you. You've seen me naked before." She swallowed her last bite of toast. "But I feel horrible about being out of control." She wrinkled her nose. "And covered in shit. Sorry about the language. I think I cleaned up the bathroom pretty well."

"I don't think you can handle alcohol," I said. "I tried to stop you, and you just ordered another drink. You wouldn't quit."

"I don't even remember that part."

"Do you remember opening the car door while I was driving and vomiting on the street? It was a good thing your seat belt was tight, or you would have fallen out of the car."

"No, I don't remember any of that." She paused and appeared to be deep in thought. "Heidi warned me that I might be at risk to become an alcoholic. She's never had a drink in her life. Did you know that? Her father was an alcoholic and died from exposure because he was too drunk to crawl out of a mud puddle. She told me that maybe the reason I was found in a box on her desk was because my parents might have been alcoholics. She said that I might have a genetic predisposition. You know how Heidi talks."

"I don't think you should drink alcohol anymore. I don't think you can handle even one drink." My voice choked up, and tears formed in my eyes. "I love you, Lily, and to see you like that was"—I closed my eyes for a second and recalled the young woman I had put a catheter into—"ugly."

She rested her chin on her folded hands. "If I make that decision, it means I can't drink for the rest of my life. I'm not sure I'm ready for that."

"Do you want to go see if your vomit is still on the curb? Would that help you decide?" It was a mean thing to say, but a week in the emergency department had made me callous enough that I didn't care whether she thought it was mean or not.

She closed her eyes, laid her head down, and folded her hands on top of her head. "That was sarcastic, but I deserved it. Now I have to decide." I could hear her mumbling to herself. I thought it was an Anishinabe chant.

I was silent as I picked up the dishes and put them in the dishwasher.

It took a while, but when she bolted up out of her chair and wiped her eyes, she said, "I never want to go through this again. I'll never drink again. I have a disease. I can't handle alcohol. It's that simple." She finished the last of her coffee. "Let's go tell Autumn."

Later that morning, the three of us sat on the couch in their apartment as Lily explained what she remembered to her sister. I filled in where her memory was vacant, detailed with discretion. Autumn handled the affair as a professionally trained social worker. She was even edifying as she set parameters for Lily's resolution. Lily decided never to drink alcohol again. She promised us.

That summer, I saw too many patients in the emergency department who couldn't keep that promise. Nevertheless, she stayed sober all summer.

# ATIKOKAN TO ELY

It was a bright summer day in mid-August when Lily and I stood on the sandy beach in front of the Atikokan, Ontario, forest rangers' station on Nym Lake. Jason and Beth had dropped us off, unloaded our gear, and driven back to Duluth. The plan was for them to pick us up the last weekend of the month in Ely, Minnesota. Our gear was packed into a lightweight seventeen-foot aluminum Grumman canoe, and we were ready to shove off into Quetico Provincial Park. She took the stern, and I took the bow.

It was just the two of us. By the end of the summer, we had not found anyone to go with us. At least Jason and Beth were willing to drop us off and pick us up, but they had jobs and obligations. Besides, Beth hated camping, so they were unwilling to go with us. Autumn had an internship required for her master's in social work, so there we were, alone.

Lily was leaving for main campus to start law school when we got back, so it was our last chance to be together. I needed one more year to finish my chemistry degree, and then, well, Lily insisted that I apply for medical school. She was sure I'd be accepted. I wasn't, nor was I convinced I wanted to be a physician. My orderly job in the emergency department had left me somewhat of an emotional wreck. I needed this vacation. I was going back part-time to work weekends when I returned to UMD in the fall.

We'd discussed just the two of us going alone at length. Hesitant, I'd been willing to cancel the whole thing. It just didn't seem safe with only one canoe. "Do you still want to go?" I'd asked her one evening while we were sitting on her deck, watching the stars tumble overhead.

"Sure, why not? I trust you."

It was more that I didn't trust myself. Seeing Lily, dressed or undressed, still excited me. I guessed my infatuation continued. If we were alone in the woods, miles from nowhere, what would she do? What would I do? Could I maintain my composure? "I really want to go, and it may be the last time we'll have a free summer to do something like this together," I'd said as I sipped my tea. "I'm just not sure it is proper."

Lily had stared at me. "No sex." She'd grasped my hands. "Do you agree?" She'd grabbed my face with both hands and scowled. "You're my adopted brother. In Anishinabe culture, that would be obscene, like incest."

Her expression had made my ears tingle. "Yes," I'd said. Her frankness had calmed my anxiety. It had relieved the tension around my concerns about her intentions. I'd assumed it had come from Heidi in order to get her permission. I was still unsure about my resolve. "Besides," I'd explained more to myself than to her, "we're just friends."

"Siblings," she'd said.

Mom didn't know how casual Lily was about nudity, but I doubted it would have made much difference. Autumn had explained to my mother one evening when the girls were invited over for pizza that we had spent hours in their apartment alone together. Then she'd added for emphasis, "If they haven't had sex by now, they can probably be trusted."

Everyone had laughed except me. I'd turned crimson. I wasn't sure I wanted Mom to know how much time we had spent alone together, but I'd let the matter drop. After more discussion, everyone had agreed we could be trusted. So there we were with our canoe loaded, looking out over Nym Lake.

Aunt Lisa canoed that area and knew the waterfalls Lily wanted to see, and she'd helped us with a proposed route. She'd offered a few suggestions about the portages and campsites. Lily loved waterfalls and had queried Aunt Lisa on all the details. Uncle Troy had contacted his previous employer, Ernie, and arranged for a canoe; Duluth packs; and canoe pickup.

Lily had packed light, but I'd insisted on my survival kit of compass, hatchet, knife, first-aid kit, bug spray, and sunblock. She'd said she would be responsible for the food. The pack felt too light as I loaded it into the canoe, even with Uncle Troy's tent strapped to the top. We'd packed our clothes together in another Duluth pack. It was light enough that I could carry the clothes pack with the canoe on my shoulders. Lily emphasized that she did not want to cross the many proposed portages on our route more than once.

We stood on the shore, listening to the waves lapping against the canoe as we scanned the sky. The sun was shining, and the temperature was pleasant. I took a deep breath and focused on the filmy clouds drifting across the western horizon. The ranger had said the weather would be pleasant all week, but maybe into the second week, there would be a chance of rainstorms since a system in the Pacific Ocean was heading for Seattle. "It hasn't rained in several weeks here, so be careful with fire," he'd warned.

A delicate breeze smelled of cedar and pine. At the edges of the imported sand in front of the ranger station, wild roses grew. By then, the flowers were gone, but the ripened hips were bright red. Lily popped several ripe rose hips into her mouth, spitting out the seeds. "Good source of vitamin C," she whispered. I wondered why we needed vitamin C with all our food, but I didn't ask. I ate one that she offered me.

The lake was huge, with a few cabins on the north shore because of road access. There were no roads or cabins at the southern end of the lake, according to the map, because it was part of Quetico Provincial Park. Crossing the first portage, we would be in wilderness until we arrived at our pickup in a couple of weeks. Lily said she could paddle the distance in a week but wanted some layover time to contemplate the waterfalls.

Both of us were runners. Lily ran five miles three times a week. I ran a three-mile course around the university almost every day. I usually had enough energy to swim a few laps in the UMD pool after my runs. Lily swam a mile on her off days; plus, she was enrolled in aerobic classes. Paddling with someone who was so physically fit and an experienced canoeist meant we could paddle efficiently. By the end of Nym Lake, I sensed the thrust of Lily's paddle and responded in kind. There was no doubt she was the better canoeist, which was why she'd taken the stern. She said it was Anishinabe for the woman to stern the canoe. I didn't argue.

At the south end of Nym Lake, we arrived at our first portage. As we approached, another group was busy unloading their gear onto the sandy beach. Stuff was all over. I thought we should wait, but Lily turned the canoe to the left. "There's another portage over here," she said. Within minutes, we were at a rocky landing. Five feet from shore, she jumped out of the canoe, pulled out the food pack, and put it on my shoulders. While still in water to midthigh, she put the clothes pack on her back and flipped the canoe onto her shoulders. "Let's go."

As we walked up a steep hill, I asked, "If you've never been here before, how did you know about this other portage?"

"Simple topography, my dear Watson. Most of these portages are from before you Europeans came here. The trails between lakes are measured by the length of a canoe; seventeen feet equal a rod."

Twenty-six rods of portaging later, we were in Batchewaung Lake. I looked to my right and saw the first canoe of the group we had seen at the other portage, crossing down to the water. I speculated that it would be a while before they had all their canoes and gear carried over the portage.

We paddled down a narrow strait on the west side and came to the next portage. We stopped for lunch on an island in Pickerel Narrows, which was little more than a cluster of craggy rocks. We drank lemonade made from water she dipped out of the lake without filtering it. I was concerned. "Shouldn't we filter the water? There's giardia in these lakes."

"Do you see any beavers or bears on this tiny rock of an island?"

"No."

"Well then, no giardia."

I drank the lemonade, picturing days of diarrhea in my mind. We ate rye crisp, candy bars, and a handful of nuts. One scruffy jack pine grew in a crack of a rock. There was no shade. "We haven't seen any other groups since that portage into Batchewaung," I said as we stretched out on the rocks to soak up some sun and digest our lunch.

"I don't expect to see anyone where we're going," Lily said. "The next portages are hard enough to weed out most tourists, and the portage into Bisk Lake is short but not the favorite route. Fishermen like to fish near the waterfalls, so we will probably have company there." She stood and stretched. "Isn't this beautiful?"

"I thought we were going into Dore Lake." I gazed up at the filmy clouds passing overhead.

"Everyone goes that way. We are avoiding the other campers." She laughed, pulled off her shirt, removed her bra, and stuffed them both into the clothing pack. I took off my shirt, and we both stretched out on the bare rock. The sun had warmed the granite to a pleasant temperature.

Her tawny caramel-colored midriff fascinated me. She was sure to tease my hormones the whole trip. She always claimed she was desensitizing me to be a good physician. "I hope I can handle my desensitization," I murmured. She didn't seem to hear me.

After a nice rest in the sun, we put our shirts back on, and instead of paddling south at Emerald Island, we paddled east into a collection of islands. Somehow, she found the sixty-eight-rod portage into Bisk Lake. So far, she hadn't consulted the map.

*Does she have the topography memorized or what?*

We discovered a hoard of blueberries along the portage, so after we set our gear at the landing, we ran back and feasted. We collected a plastic bag of blueberries for our morning pancakes and finally convinced ourselves we had enough. With swollen bellies, we crossed Bisk Lake and then went down a rapid chute to the next portage. We crossed Beg Lake and went down a stretch of fast water to Fern Lake. A muddy landing full of mosquitoes lying in wait for human blood invited us to a stretch of river with a few more portages and some large pools, and finally, we went into Olifaunt Lake.

I was exhausted. We had paddled at least two hours beyond my quitting limit. The sun was an hour from the horizon before we found a place to camp. I was sure the other way would have been much easier, but Lily was in her glory while shooting the rapids, angling the canoe through narrow channels, and seeing the string of small lakes. I set up the tent while Lily set out the cook kit and organized supper. With our sleeping bags laid out and our personal bags at the foot of the tent, I wandered over to see what was for supper. I was famished.

She had a small fire with a few vegetables cooking in a pot. She had mixed some instant pudding for dessert and then set both pots aside on a warm rock. "I didn't know we were going vegetarian," I said as I squatted beside the fire.

"We're not."

"Then where's the meat?" I shouldn't have said that with such malice in my voice.

She raised her charcoal eyebrows at me. "In the lake, silly." She turned and headed for the canoe. My stomach flip-flopped. We hadn't fished all day, and now it was almost dark, and she was planning on fish for supper. "You coming?" she yelled.

I stumbled down to the lake. Disappointment, fatigue, and hunger quelled my enthusiasm.

"Take the stern, and paddle out between those two islands," she said.

More paddling was not what I wanted to do. My hands were tired of holding the paddle, and my shoulders throbbed, but I complied. Within three casts, she had a nice walleye. "You want one too?" she asked with a cocky smile.

I looked at the size of the fish. *Is she going to eat the whole thing?* In panic and frustrated fatigue, I asked in a quiet, shrill voice, "May I share yours, please?"

"Sure, you asked nicely, and I'm generous."

"Then let's eat." I turned the canoe and headed back to camp.

The fire had gone out. I grabbed some sticks to start it again. "What are you doing?" she asked.

"Getting the fire going to cook the fish."

"Leave it."

I backed away as she gutted the fish and laid it—skin, head, and all—on the coals to cook. With two twigs used like elongated chopsticks, she flipped it over when the downside was black. When it was thoroughly black, she lifted it off the coals. She set it on a rock and peeled off the skin. The flesh was tasty and moist. Never had walleye and vegetables tasted so good. She was sucking on the head as I searched for the pudding.

By the time she let me lick the last of the pudding out of the pot, it was dark. I was ready to crawl into the tent and sleep for a long time. I wondered, *Will every day be like this?* She had promised that when we got to the waterfalls, we would take a layover day. I was already thinking about a day without paddling, and it was our first day out. I headed to the tent like a stallion seeking the barn.

"You aren't going to bed all dirty and sweaty, are you?"

I turned. She stood naked on a rock overhang. "Let's go for a swim," she said. She did a surface dive into the lake.

I stripped off my clothes at the tent, too tired to care whether she saw me or not. I picked my way between the rocks. The water felt cold on my feet. I hesitated on each slimy rock as I eased out into deeper water. At knee level, my foot slipped, so I did a quick dive. I gasped for breath as the cold gripped my chest, yet somehow, I felt euphoric. The water massaged my sore muscles, the cold eased the throbbing in my shoulders, and my fatigue melted away. Energy returned as I swam out to her. We splashed around like two freshwater otters as the stars sifted out of the darkening sky. The Milky Way shone so brightly we had no trouble seeing our way back to camp even twenty yards out in the lake.

When I started to chill, I headed in to shore. "Wow, that was great," I said as I stumbled up the slippery rocks, "but now I'm shivering." My jaw was shaking as I sprinted to the tent for our towels. I gave Lily her towel as she stepped out of the water onto the rock. *Why does she have no trouble slipping? Why isn't she shivering?*

"Lie down," she commanded.

I put my towel down on smooth, warm granite and lay on top of it. She rubbed my back with her strong arms to the point of pain. "Now, that's what I need," she said as she got up and lay on her towel beside me. "Rub my back."

I rubbed her back, as she had done for me. I guarded my gaze and focused on massaging her muscles. It amazed me how well developed her back muscles were. The moon, just cresting the horizon, scintillated across her skin. "Harder," she said. "You're not putting much force into it." I dug my fingers into her till my hands cramped.

"Thanks. I needed that," she said when she finally sat up. We huddled on a log and listened to the loons sing while watching them dance in the moonlight. They were but twenty feet from our shoreline. "You'll get better with practice," she said. She put her arm over my shoulders. "Wasn't this a fascinating day?"

I said nothing. I was processing the experience of giving a naked girl a backrub on the Canadian Shield while at least a day's paddle from the nearest road. I was sitting beside her, naked myself, listening to a pair of loons cavorting in front of us, and we weren't going to have sex—part of my desensitization, I guessed.

Awed by the beauty but attacked by hordes of mosquitos, I dragged myself to the tent. I was careful to zip up the mosquito netting as I crawled into my sleeping bag. I watched her through the tent door, humming the chorus to the loons' calls. They responded to her calls. The music was breathtaking. Why weren't the mosquitos bothering her? She was calm and still as I watched her silhouette against the Milky Way.

My leg muscle cramped, and I stretched it out, holding my breath until the spasm relaxed. I zipped up my sleeping bag, rolled over to face the wall of the tent, and prayed I would keep breathing until morning.

# NEW LAKES

IN THE MORNING, LILY WHISTLED to awaken me just as the sun peaked over the forested eastern shore. I retrieved the map from the pack while she was sprinkling blueberries into our pancake batter. "We certainly went the long way around," I said as my finger followed a much shorter route with fewer portages.

"Just to see all those pretty lakes," she said. "And we never saw any people."

"Yes," I said. *I prepared myself mentally for a lot of unnecessary paddling and portages "just to see them."*

She served me my pancakes. I sighed. "These are delicious. Wow," I said.

She grabbed the map from me and stowed it in the pack. "We won't need this today because we are going to Chatterton Falls."

"Are we going to lay over there?"

"Too many people," she said, licking syrup off her lips. "But we can have lunch there and maybe catch a few fish below the falls and then find a campsite on an island in Russell Lake—easy day."

The morning sun was warm and bright when we packed up camp. After putting a couple of buckets of water on our fire, I was sure it was out. I had no idea what time it was because Lily had stuffed my wristwatch into the bottom of the pack with an indignant "You won't need that." I was sure it was earlier than when I usually got up. Across the bay was a seventy-five-rod portage to wake me up, and then we'd head south to Russell Lake.

By the time we arrived at Chatterton Falls several hours later, I was whipped. We had to paddle up a fast-flowing stream to get into Russell Lake. My shoulders were still sore from the previous day, but then I saw the falls and knew why she had wanted to come there. They were magnificent. Resting on the rocks and listening to the roar of the falls calmed my spirit. This was a place of peace.

My mind raced through all I had been through, from my father dying to my mother's crabby months and her turnaround. Lily meant so much to me. I thought of finishing high school, attending UMD, and getting a job as an orderly in the emergency department. All had been hard things, but they had brought me to that moment. I was tired, sore, and hungry but invigorated with the girl of my dreams.

"Do you want lunch? Follow me." She held up a paper bag marked "Lunch" in front of me. "See all the logs? This is a memorial to white man's greed. There are over five hundred logs jammed in this falls." She jumped from log to log and finally sat down on one in the middle of the cascade. "Come on, scaredy-cat."

"Isn't this dangerous? The logs are slippery, and they could shift and—"

"They've been jammed here since 1942, when Mathieu Lumber Company tried to send too many logs down the falls at once. Really stupid, eh! So I don't think they'll shift under your measly weight."

I carefully balanced on one of the logs near the shore and, stepping from log to log, finally arrived at the one she was sitting on. I looked between the logs at a roaring torrent of water below us.

"Sit down. It's great feeling the vibration of Mother Earth through the logs."

I sat down, shifting my weight, unsure if in the next moment, we would be tumbling with the logs down the falls. She handed me a rye crisp with peanut butter and jelly on it.

"Wonderful, isn't it?"

The spray tickled my dangling legs. The roar beneath us was like Wagnerian music, and the smell of the water and lichens growing on the logs since—what had she said?—1942 was ethereal. I'd never imagined doing something like that. The vibration massaged my aching muscles. I imagined staying right there all day. "Are we staying here tonight? It's so beautiful."

"There are too many people coming to see the falls. There is a campsite on an island in Russell Lake. Let's check that out."

As I nibbled at my rye crisp, she squirted more peanut butter onto it. While I was munching my rye crisp, she took out the knife sheathed on her belt and cut off a piece of beef jerky. "Here. You need protein for the paddling. You're slowing down."

*I am?*

I hated to leave the falls, but I was delighted she was willing to camp early. I thought it was only an hour or so after noon, judging by the position of the sun. The campsite was small, but there were only two of us, so it was perfect. I stretched out on the rock face after we had set up camp. I was just closing my eyes, when she said, "Camp's ready. Let's go."

"Where?" I said as I stumbled to the canoe.

"Let's go down those rapids we had to paddle up and go check out the Lookout Tower in Sturgeon Narrows."

Without our gear in the canoe, we shot down the white water. Haystacks of water shot up on both sides. I felt out of control, yet with Lily in the stern, we avoided the rocks and swished through the Vs like experts. When we reached the calm water at the bottom of the chute, I turned to see that she was laughing. I was thinking we would have to paddle up it again, but maybe she would take the roundabout route or portage. I didn't know. On the western shore was the Lookout Tower she had described from the map. There was a well-traveled path up to it, and after climbing it, we had a wonderful panoramic view. I stood breathless.

"Isn't this beautiful?" she said.

"Magnificent."

"Yeah, that too." She headed down the tower, and I followed in her wake. "Let's get going. We can have a relaxing dinner tonight. There are lots of pike in Sturgeon Narrows. Is that all right, or should we try for walleye in Russell Lake?"

She fished from the stern. When she was willing to stop, I made a few casts and caught a nice thirty-inch pike. "Nice job, Barak," she said. With our fish, we retraced our route back to the rapids. I was anxious as to how we would paddle up the chute. She tied a rope on each end of the canoe. With one rope in each hand, she maneuvered the canoe upstream. I walked along the shore in amazement. "Lining the canoe is a lot easier than paddling," she said. My sore shoulders were thankful she knew how to do that.

Back at our campsite, I was glad we had already set up camp. "May I see the map?"

"Why?"

"Just to see where we should head to next."

She sat down next to me. "Barak, you are too goal-oriented. Think of this trip as a chance to wander around in Mother Earth's backyard."

She did not retrieve the map, and I wasn't sure where it was now. The forest was her home, and she seemed to need no navigational aid to explore the rooms.

"Come. I'll show you how to prepare a pike so there are no Y bones in the meat."

Her cuts were swift. She was sure of herself. She pulled lard out of the pack, and in no time, we had sizzling filet of pike on the griddle. I was instructed to make the macaroni and cheese. It was a perfect complement to our fish. I felt ravenous. I found not a single Y bone in my meat.

"What's the next waterfall we come to?" I said, licking my lips.

She pulled out the map from a secret pocket in the back of the pack. I interpreted her gaze as disgust. "See? Here's Chatterton Falls. We want to see Split Rock Falls next." She pointed her finger along the shore of the next lake. "And here's the Snake Falls."

I took a deep breath. It looked easy. There was only one portage between the three falls.

"But," she continued, "I'm afraid there will be a lot of fishermen and other groups there, so—"

I was afraid of her *so*.

"Let's take this chain of little lakes from Sturgeon Lake and come around to the falls from the south. We'll see lots of terrain that most people never see."

I was stunned by her proposed route. There were at least six portages through a chain of lakes connected by small streams. There hadn't been rain in two weeks, and the water would be shallow. Why would we want to do that, when there was a perfectly easy way to arrive at the falls we had come to see? "There should be a campsite right here," I said, pointing on the map to a campsite on a jutting peninsula that would be free of mosquitoes. "And it is right near Snake Falls."

"Yeah, that looks good. Hey, what we could do is set up camp there and then canoe through that chain of lakes and end up back at our camp, all ready for us. Let's do that. Good suggestion, Barak."

That was not what I'd intended. It added two more portages, which would be eight total, but without gear, it would be easier. This girl was insatiable.

"All right, time for a swim," she said.

The next morning, when the sun sparkled across my eyelids and my full bladder woke me up, she already had oatmeal ready. She had sprinkled it with more blueberries. Where she found them I will never know.

We portaged across Chatterton Falls and set up camp on an island in Chatterton Lake. Another group was leaving as we approached, so we waited offshore and set up as soon as they shipped off in their canoes. I was ready to take a nap and forget the whole idea of seeing all the little lakes she was curious about, but that was not to be.

After portaging back across Chatterton Falls, we canoed back down the chute to Sturgeon Lake and then off to the east into Hebron Bay. Then there were Fred Lake, Cutty Creek, and Nan Lake, and we followed a stream into Camel, Eag, and Cub Lakes. All along the way, we ran into portages, even some that were not on the map. I had to admit we were efficient without as much gear, and we took turns carrying the canoe. At last, we were in Keats Lake and got to see Split Rock Falls in the brilliant setting sunlight. By the time we had made a full circle and portaged into Chatterton Lake to find our camp on the island, it was dark.

"Did you enjoy seeing all those little lakes?" Lily asked.

"I think so. What's for supper? I am famished." I held up my hand. "But I am not complaining. Our lunch of freshwater clams was a special treat. How did you know they would be there?"

"Why wouldn't they be there?" she said.

I dug into the stew she had made with beef jerky and freeze-dried vegetables. Hunger made a wonderful spice. "When were you here last?"

"I've never been here before," she said, savoring her stew. "That's why I wanted to canoe here—to see it."

"I'm confused. How can you navigate so well if you've never been here before?"

"Oh, I just know the lay of the land, I guess. I admit that I did study the map before we left. If you think about the geography of this area, it just makes sense."

She obviously had mysterious skills. I was clearly outranked.

The next morning, we ate oatmeal again. It tasted good. I wondered if it would be a layover day, but of course, I was wrong. We packed up camp and headed back to Split Rock Falls. We sat near the falls just to hear the roar. It seemed different in the daylight.

The water shot over a rock shelf, forming a sheer wall of water about four yards long, and then crashed onto the rocks below, swirling in a whirlpool at the base. There was a campsite situated on a peninsula jutting out into the eddy current at the base of the falls "My people would never camp here in the old days," she said.

"Why is that?"

"The roar conceals the sound of approaching enemies."

"But we don't have any enemies to worry about," I said.

She smiled. "Don't you want to explore the falls?"

I hesitated. "Sure, but are we camping here?"

"Of course not. There may not be enemies here, but there are too many people."

After exploring, we canoed over to Snake Falls. There was no portage around the falls, but the portage into Shelly Lake was farther to the north. We had to paddle against strong current just to get to the portage, which was rocky and rough. Shelly Lake didn't meet my understanding of a lake. It had a swift current and long bays stretching north to south. We finally made it into Kawnipi Lake and found a campsite. It was a beauty, much nicer than any we had stayed at so far. We also saw no other campers, which suited Lily.

It had been a hot day with little breeze in the small lakes. It seemed as if I had been fighting current all day, so when we made camp, it didn't take long to decide to go for a swim. I was amazed at how athletic Lily was, even though I already knew it. She slipped through the water like a porpoise, hardly making a wake. "Let's stay here for a day. Is that all right with you?" she said.

"Yes, fine."

I thought the promised layover day would never come.

# LAYOVER DAY

I WAS READY TO SPEND the whole day swimming at our site and fishing from the shore. My muscles were sore, and we were about at the halfway point. "I am so thankful to have a rest day. This is our rest day, right?" I said.

"I suppose. You would enjoy a layover day, wouldn't you?"

"Yes, I sure need it."

"There is a poorly marked falls straight north up that bay." She pointed at a bay opening from our campsite. "And I would like you to see the pictographs on this lake with me. You do that today—it will be easy paddling—and tomorrow we will take a rest."

"Sounds great to me."

She pulled out the map and showed me where the pictographs should be and the bay she wanted to paddle up. After breakfast, we jumped into the canoe and paddled over to the rock face west of Rose Island. Then we went down into Keel Lake. The three thunderbirds in red paint on the sheer cliff awed me.

"Nobody quite knows why these were painted," Lily said. "There are hundreds of sites with different paintings of canoes and animals. On Lac la Croix, there are handprints. Most anthropologists feel that they mark completion of a vision quest."

"Would you ever go on a vision quest?"

"I did."

"What?"

"Four days. No food or water. I was put on an island in the middle of some lake. I never quite knew where I was. My mentor never told me. He just dropped me off and picked me up four days later."

"That is unbelievable. Did you have a vision?"

"Yes." She paused, touching the granite face of the paintings. "I'll tell you a little something about it tomorrow night if you help me this afternoon."

I wasn't sure why she couldn't tell me then, but I had given up trying to understand her mysterious ways.

Next, we paddled straight north into the bay she'd mentioned. It became narrower as we paddled. Just as it seemed to dead-end, she turned the canoe to the right, and there were a small stream and a waterfall with a pool at its base.

"Ready for a swim?" she said. "There's no one around."

We beached the canoe and walked up a ways to the pool and cascade. She stripped and jumped into the water. I slipped my shorts, underwear, and T-shirt off; folded them; and put a rock on top. I scrambled after her up the rocks to the falls. My Keens gave me better traction as I climbed the rocks. They were slippery with lichens yet sharp on the edges. *How can she do this barefoot?* When we came close to the falls, I halted to admire them, but she swam across the pool and climbed up onto rocks in front of the falls. She motioned for me to follow. The water was colder in the pool, obviously spring fed, and I shivered. The sound of the falls was deafening as I approached. When I reached her, she motioned for me to go through the falls. I didn't understand at first, but I followed. We edged our way behind the wall of water. There was no cave, but there was sufficient space between the rock face and the cascade to slip behind the wall of water. She tilted her head forward into the water. The sheer force straightened her hair, blurring her face like a modern-art painting. She turned, held the rock, and pushed her butt into the water.

"This is great. What a douche," she said.

I imitated what she had done, impressed with the force of the water.

She clung to the rock and arched backward so her face was in the water, holding her pose with only one foot on the ledge. It gave me the shivers. With one slip, she would crash onto the rocks below. I turned and backed into the rocks, content to let my foot feel the sheer of the water.

It wasn't that I didn't notice how beautiful she was with the water cascading down her body, and it wasn't that I was used to her being naked; it was my terror that she would fall and die that kept me from staring at her. *This is natural, and we are in nature*, I told myself, or something as ridiculous.

When we were done with our shower, as she described it, we headed to the whirlpool below the falls. We jumped into the pool. I was impressed with its depth. I couldn't feel the bottom anywhere. Current swirled us around like a carrousel.

"It's deep enough to dive here," she said, "from that rock." She pointed to a ledge above us.

"Jump feetfirst to be sure," I said. "We're three days' paddle from the nearest road, and I don't think I could portage your lovely body out of here." The *lovely* part just slipped out. She gave me an obnoxious look.

She climbed the rock shelf above the pool. "All right, here goes for safety's sake."

I got a full-frontal anatomic lesson as she leaped spread-eagle almost on top of me.

"That was great," she said as she surfaced. "It's at least twenty feet deep. I didn't even touch bottom."

I climbed the rock to try it, but I hesitated and dove feetfirst. She dove headfirst and laughed as she surfaced. I was in a panic. *What if she breaks her neck? Or if I break mine?* Several more dives left us both tired but elated. Neither of us had broken anything.

After swimming to exhaustion, we dressed and headed back to our campsite. Partway there, she was scanning the bay. "If I understand the topography of this lake, we should fish over there."

Of course she understood the lake's topography. It only took three casts for each of us to catch a fish. She threw both back.

"I thought we were having fish for supper."

"We are, but let's have some fun first. We'll keep the last ones."

I wondered how we would know which one was the last one, but I didn't ask. We paddled around the bay, catching fish as we went. Twenty- to twenty-six-inch walleyes weren't unusual. As the sun was starting to hide behind the tree line, she asked, "Do you want to catch supper, or should I?"

"You caught supper last night." I tried to put a trifle of complaint into my voice. Actually, she had caught supper almost every night except for my northern pike, but it sounded better that way.

"See those weeds over there?" She was in the bow, but she set down her fishing pole and turned around, sterning the canoe from her bow position. "Cast over there. I think I would prefer bass instead of walleye tonight."

I was good at casting. I could never have figured out where the fish were, but I could cast like a professional. I'd taken fishing as one of my physical education classes when I was a freshman at UMD. I'd gotten an A because I could cast the lure into the hula hoop the instructor placed on the gymnasium floor with every cast. I cast right where Lily had pointed. As I started to reel in my line, I felt a jerk. The fish jumped out of the water, splashed down on its side, and dove. The line screamed out of my reel. Lily was in hysterics. I wasn't sure if she was laughing at me or the fish.

I played the fish for a while, and when it seemed to fatigue, I reeled it closer to the canoe. We had drifted almost into the shore. "Bring it right beside the canoe," she said. In a flash, she grabbed the fish by the eyes and flipped it into the canoe. "Good job. Bass for supper. You hungry?"

"Starved."

With our fish caught, we headed back toward our campsite. Just before we got to our island, she shifted direction toward the mainland shore. "Come with me," she said, grabbing the ax from the bottom of the canoe. I followed her back into the woods to a clearing. "See all these little twigs? A fire here in the past allowed all these poplar twigs to grow. I want to gather some of them to bring back to our camp."

Of course, she didn't explain why we needed poplar twigs, and I had become comfortable not asking. She probably wouldn't have given me a straight answer anyway. She cut, and I was soon loaded down with sapling twigs. "Bring those to the canoe, and come back."

On my return, she loaded me up again and filled her arms with the rest that she had chopped down.

Back at our island camp, she started a fire and cooked the bass we had caught. We set it on the rock and pulled back the skin. It was delicious. I had never enjoyed eating fish so much. The ambience of the pine trees, the smell of the fire, and a soft breeze enriched the experience.

After we finished our feast, she pulled the saplings out of the canoe, stuck them in the ground, and tied the tops together to make a dome-shaped structure. I did what she told me, tying them together with cedar bark strips she gave me. When completed, I asked, "So what is this?"

"A sweat lodge." She stood back to admire her work. "Now for the proper stones. Come with me." We walked along the shore of our island, looking for large, round stones that were small enough to carry back to camp. When we had four, she set them in our campfire. "Your job tomorrow on your layover day will be to keep a nice fire going on top of these four rocks. Can you do that?"

"Sure, what are you going to do?"

She didn't answer me. I probably shouldn't have asked. She grabbed the canoe paddle and said, "See you tomorrow. Make sure you keep the fire going." She climbed into the canoe and shoved off.

"Are you going fishing again?" I was confused. Didn't she want me to paddle?

A few yards offshore, she turned to me. "I'm fasting. Take care of that fire. I'll be back tomorrow night. Enjoy your layover day. There is macaroni and cheese in the pack for your supper if you don't want to fast. Just follow the directions on the package."

With that, I stood dumbly. I watched her paddle off to the north, and then she was gone. *No canoe. Alone on an island. What should I do?*

Later, lost in thought, I discovered that my macaroni and cheese was burning. I grabbed it off the fire and set it on the log beside me. I nibbled each mouthful, unsure what had just happened. I gazed into the fire, my eyes wandering over the four rocks. "Keep the fire going," she'd said.

With minimal breeze, the mosquitoes came out in clouds. I added some sticks to the fire and danced in the smoke to ward them off. It was dark. There was no moon, but the Milky Way was magnificent. I stripped except for my Keens and dove into the water from the shore in front of the campsite. I wasn't as interested in swimming as I was in getting away from the bugs.

*I think I love Lily, but she sure is strange. She is attractive and has so many skills other women just don't have. But what is she doing now? Where did she go? Why doesn't she tell me what she is doing? What if she doesn't return? Then I'm stuck here—that's what. And then I'm dead.* A roar of the wind blowing through the jack pine invited me back to camp. There were no mosquitoes now, but the fire blazed as in a blast furnace. I built a rock shelter around it, making sure the fire was centered over the four rocks. When it smoldered to hot coals and I thought it would be safe for the night, I crawled into the tent.

I looked at her side of the tent. She hadn't even taken her sleeping bag. I stared into the darkness, realizing I missed the nightly ritual of watching my Anishinabe sister crawl into her sack. I couldn't get used to the notion of being an adopted brother, though. I questioned my emotional response to her. Was I in love, was I infatuated, or were we just friends? I fell asleep trying to envision what she was doing.

The next day was boring. I tried to make pancakes and burned them. I guessed the fire was too hot. But I was faithful in keeping the fire going. A breeze kept it burning and kept mosquitoes out of the camp. I swam; dried off; stretched out on the warm Canadian Shield, on a rock that was out of the wind; and roamed around the island. I found some wintergreen and brewed a bit of tea.

At lunchtime—at least I thought it was lunchtime, as the sun was right overhead—I dug out the rye crisp and found a couple of candy bars labeled with my name on them. I ate them while sitting on a rock, contemplating the waves rippling on the shore. I couldn't find my wristwatch in the pack, so I reasoned what time it must have been by watching the angle of the sun. I tried to set up a sundial but wasn't sure how to interpret the shadows.

That was when I noticed something black in the water. As it got closer, I realized it was a bear swimming toward the island. *What should I do?* I didn't know anything about bears. "No! You don't belong here!" I yelled. I grabbed a pot and a serving spoon and began banging on the pot. The bear didn't stop; it came onshore and smelled the air. "Go! Go away!" I yelled.

There was no response to my screaming. The bear just ambled toward our food pack. I knew it was after food, so I got between our precious food pack and the bear, screaming and banging on the pot. The bear turned left. I went left. The bear snorted and went right. I went right, banging as loudly as I could. Then I dropped the pot. *What should I do? Will the bear attack me?* Yelling, I grabbed the pot off the ground and started banging as I stepped forward. The bear backed up, snorted, and went back into the water. I watched it swim back to the mainland.

I collapsed in a lump, hyperventilating and relieved. I probably would have just sat there for the rest of my life, but the fire needed more sticks. I got up and fed the fire, as instructed. *What would Lily have done? Where is she? When will she return?*

The sun was just peaking behind the horizon, when I heard the rhythmic sound of her paddle in the water. I ran to the shore. I couldn't see her. Around the point of the island, her canoe slipped into the shadows. Without a word, she beached the canoe and approached me. "Did you keep the fire going all day?"

"Yes, and—"

"Did the bear scare you?"

"How did you—"

She laughed so hard she had to hold her belly. Where had she been? How did she know about the bear?

"I sent the bear to make your day more exciting. I thought you might be bored without her invading your camp. She wouldn't have hurt you. I asked her not to."

"Where were you that you could see the bear? What do you mean you sent her and asked her not to hurt me?"

She just shook her head and laughed some more as she checked the fire. She turned to me. "Listen carefully. Do not speak, and do not interrupt anything I do or say." With two poles she had stowed in the canoe, she picked up the hot rocks one at a time, chanting in Anishinabe, and placed them into the dome we had made the previous afternoon. She faced each of the cardinal directions so there was one stone for the north, one for the south, one for the east, and one for the west. When the stones were placed in proper position, she covered the dome first with pine boughs and then with our tarp. With a piece of leather, she covered the opening.

She seemed serious. She spoke. "I will sit opposite the door. You will sit directly opposite me by the door. This ritual is for my purification. If you get uncomfortable, you can slip out the door. Do not interrupt me, no matter what happens. I will explain later." She smiled. "And then I will make you supper." She started to take off her clothes. "Do you understand?"

"Yes." I didn't, but I promised not to disturb her. I stripped to my underwear. She entered the sweat lodge nude, carrying a bucket of water. I slipped off my underwear. *Why not?* I went in behind her.

The heat inside was sweltering. The smell of the spruce boughs permeated the air. Lily hummed, poured water onto the rocks, and then started to sing in Anishinabe. I didn't understand anything, but I loved the rhythm and the tones. I could tell when she started a new song with a different beat. She put more water on the rocks, and the heat intensified. Several times, I thought about leaving, but I stayed. It seemed magical. As I focused on her singing, I was distracted from the discomfort of the heat. Something bumped into my shoulder, nudging me with a bowl of tea. It tasted bitter, but I drank it. It left a rancid taste in my mouth. I thought about leaving to vomit, but the feeling passed.

Her chant now seemed to be asking questions. I thought I heard a drum beat. I was sure she was thanking someone, judging by the gestures she was making. Then it was quiet. A painful silence permeated the lodge like fog.

I saw a large blackbird flying around the inside of the lodge. It was graceful, seldom flapping its wings. *Am I hallucinating? Seeing a vision?* The blackbird held something bright in its beak. Around and around it flew, and as it flew, it became smaller and smaller and then dropped onto the four hot rocks. It disappeared in a flash of light.

I wiped at my brow. Lily was singing again. Sweat was stinging my eyes. I heard a voice, but it didn't sound like Lily. It was more like a bird asking, "What is her name? What is her name? Tell me her name."

I responded, "Waabigwan-atewaniin."

Lily's singing stopped.

In the dark glow from the four stones, I looked at her. Had she fainted? Had I interrupted? How long had we been there? I was paralyzed with fear and started crying. I saw my father's face in the glow and felt the intense pain of his death. Then I fainted.

When I came to, I was spread-eagle on the ground outside the sweat lodge, beside the campfire. In the firelight, I saw that Lily was dressed in a T-shirt and shorts, hunched over the fire, cooking some kind of meat. The smell made me hungry. I felt hungrier than I ever had in my entire life and as weak as if I had just run a race. "What happened? What time is it? Was that real? Did I make a mistake? I didn't mean to interrupt."

"The time is irrelevant." She left her cooking and helped me sit up. "What is important is that the Great Spirit accepted you. Explain to me what you remember, and I will interpret it for you."

I started to explain.

"Wow, amazing. Let's eat first before you tell me any more. I know you're hungry."

I wanted to ask how she knew I was hungry, but there was so much I didn't understand that I let it pass. She served a wild-tasting meat cooked in onion gravy over something that resembled potatoes. "Do I have permission to ask what this is?"

"You asked nicely, so yes, you may."

There was silence. I waited. I felt as if I were going to burst with curiosity. "Well, what is this wonderful dish that I have the privilege of eating?"

"It's a duck that gave up its life so you could be nourished. Don't worry; I asked its permission first."

I wasn't worried about asking the poor duck's permission.

"The sauce is made from a wild onion and some other spices that Mother Earth suggested to flavor our food, and I served it over some cattail roots that chose to give up their lives for you to celebrate your experience in the sweat lodge." She put a heaping spoonful in her mouth. "The Grandfather Stones wanted to thank you for your care in keeping the fire going all day. You were accepted as the fire keeper. It is a great honor."

I shook my head and finished explaining what I'd seen and felt. "I saw a large blackbird flying in the sweat lodge. Was that real?"

"That was my manitou, Raven." She paused.

*Why did she stop?* Was she unwilling to tell me more? Or wasn't I allowed to know more? This was weird and magical. Raven was her manitou? What had I gotten into?

"Raven told me about the abundance I will experience in my life, but then there will be much pain, and eventually, I will starve and die."

"What? It told you the future? Is that why it dropped into the Grandfather Stones?"

She gasped. "Did you see that?"

"Yes, and then I saw my father. I felt so bad, just like I felt at the funeral. Was I hallucinating? What was in that tea you gave me?"

"I never gave you any tea, but yes, you saw the future. It is often ambiguous. You will also experience much pain, but then you will rejoice in your sadness. I can't tell you any more than that. You will have to meditate on what you experienced."

"You did give me tea to drink. It was bitter, but I drank it."

She gave me a hug. "No, I never gave you tea. That was your acceptance by my manitou for being my fire keeper." She sat beside me, and for a long time, we both stared into the darkness.

I hugged her back. "So what did you experience? You promised to tell me."

"I am not allowed to tell you the whole thing, but since you are my adopted brother and now a fire keeper and since the Grandfather Stones accepted you, I will tell you some of it." She stared into my eyes. "You white skins are prone to be inpatient and ask questions instead of listening, so since this is sacred, don't interrupt me."

There was a long pause. I thought maybe she had changed her mind about telling me anything, but with her introduction in mind, I dared not speak. The loons called in the distance. I wondered what time it was. It had been total darkness since I'd regained consciousness. I knew better than to ask. She hadn't answered me the first time I'd asked.

"The day after my first menstruation, I asked Heidi if I could go on a vision quest. She grilled me, trying to convince me I didn't want to do it. Autumn didn't, so why should I? I knew she was determined to test my commitment. When she saw that I couldn't be dissuaded, she gave me a big hug and said she was proud of me and would find me a sponsor. The preparation was grueling, but eventually, I was tested and determined that I was properly prepared."

There was another long pause. I saw her lick her lips, close her eyes, and sigh. "For four days without food and with minimal water on an island in the middle of who knows what lake, I wandered, swatted mosquitoes, and even got dry heaves because I was so hungry. I was standing in a huge, open place in the middle of the island. It was a massive rock covered with thick lichens. It was sometime in the middle of the night, but the moon was so bright that I could see like daylight. A large raven, larger than I had ever seen before, landed in front of me. 'I will give you great wisdom,' said Raven, 'but you will have to suffer many things. You will never wed and never have children. This gift is for your people, not for your posterity.' That is my vision. There's much more, but I am not allowed to tell you. Even my brother cannot know everything about my vision."

I covered my mouth with my hand to avoid gasping. I couldn't believe what she was telling me. She'd gone without food and water for four days? I couldn't accept that her vision would mean she could never have children. What was that all about?

She said, "So that is why you saw the big blackbird flying around the sweat lodge. I am shocked that you saw her fall into the Grandfather Stones, but I cannot tell you about that now."

There was silence. The loons sang several choruses, and the Milky Way floated across the sky.

# ON TO THE MAGIC LAKE

I AWOKE IN MY SLEEPING bag with no memory of how I'd gotten there. Lily was sleeping on her side in her sleeping bag. *Was I dreaming? Did that really happen last night?*

I must have mumbled my questions out loud. Lily turned and said, "Yes."

We got up without much communication, ate oatmeal, and packed our equipment. When the canoe was stowed with our gear, I turned to see her taking down the sweat lodge. Within a few minutes, it was as if it never had existed. She left no trace. She even carried the saplings that had formed the frame out into the woods. She came back on a different trail, looked at me, and said, "I'm ready. Let's go."

We backtracked some and then proceeded south into Heronshaw Lake and down a stream into Cairn Lake. It was a geographic curiosity, as the east bank was a massive cliff easily fifty feet high, and the west was a gradual incline. One day there must have been a great geologic fault shift in Earth's crust. I wondered if there had been any people around to experience the earthquake that must have resulted. It was a hot day, so I lathered up with sunscreen and paddled shirtless. Her Anishinabe skin didn't seem to need any sunscreen, but we kept long sleeves and long pants handy for the portages because of the mosquitoes. We saw no one.

"I want to camp on that island in Kahshahpiwi Lake," she said. "It's only a few more portages."

"Sounds good to me," I answered from the bow, looking back over my shoulder and catching the rhythm of her torso with each paddle stroke, her abdominal muscles rippling with each pull on her paddle. I couldn't help but be amazed at her physical gracefulness. The hardest part to understand was that she didn't seem the least self-conscious. "You know that I have no idea where Kahshahpiwi Lake is or to what island you're referring."

"I showed it to you on the map," she said. I didn't remember.

We canoed down the narrow channel with portages every fifty yards or so. It was shallow and rocky, so I had to get out of the canoe in places to guide us along, but it was worth the struggle. The jagged rocks, patches of cedar, and red-winged blackbirds flitting from one cattail to the next revealed a changing spectacle with every paddle stroke. After the last river portage, Keef Lake opened to a beautiful vista. The water was calm, but because of the sheer cliff on the east side, it was obvious the lake was deep. The western shore was a gentle, sloping shore. A dense forest of cedar changed to birch and jack pine all the way to the horizon.

"Kahshahpiwi is only one more short portage away. That will be our home. You know, the Midewiwin Society met there."

"The what society?"

"The Midewiwin Society. Historically and even today, the Midewiwin Society is for healing. Often, the members were involved in psychological healing but physical as well. Heidi is a Midewiwin, second level. You didn't know that?"

"She's a medicine woman?"

"Yes, the tribe wouldn't pay for her medical school training until she became a member of the Midewiwin Society. She went through a gruesome vision quest, much worse than mine. She had an elderly mentor who wanted her to be strong in the ancient ways."

I developed a new appreciation and respect for Dr. Barton. I couldn't imagine what she must have gone through. Lily's description of her own vision quest was troublesome enough, and she had said Dr. Barton's was worse. "Is that why you decided to go on a vision quest? Are you a Midewiwin?"

There was silence. I knew I shouldn't have asked.

Kahshahpiwi was a beautiful lake. The narrow channel seemed to stretch to the horizon. Our island, in the northern third of the lake, was almost connected to the western shore. It was a great site, with a gradual incline that reflected the western bank. Other people had camped there, as the plants were beaten down around the rocks. There was a nice flat area for the tent right under a large white pine, a campfire area that had a fair amount of wood stacked beside it, and a small gravel beach. "This is great," I said.

She had disappeared. When she returned, she said, "It looks all right."

"What do you mean *all right*? It's the best camp we've had all ..." I hesitated. How long had we been out? I thought over our experiences—the waterfalls, the fishing, and, of course, the sweat lodge experience. It must have been ten or twelve days.

"I scouted the perimeter. There's no bear scat, but it sure has housed a lot of company," she said as she walked back to the canoe. "Well, let's make this our home."

"I've lost count. How many days until our pickup in Ely?"

She just laughed at me. "Are you going to help set up the tent? There is that nice flat place under that great white pine."

After so many days of moving camp, we were efficient. We set up the tent together. Since it was still early afternoon, we didn't need supper for several hours. I was prepared for a nice nap on the rocks.

"Time for a swim," she said as she stripped and jumped into the water.

I followed, having lost my inhibitions several days back. The water was colder than any lake we had experienced, and I thought my heart would stop as I fought for the surface. I gasped. "This is cold."

She was facing the eastern cliff. "Yeah, it makes my nipples hurt. It must be spring fed." She clutched her breasts as I swam up beside her. "See how sheer it is?" she said.

"How could I miss it?"

"That goes straight down. This water is cold, which means we should be able to catch lake trout here." She started swimming for shore. "Come on. Let's go fishing."

Without drying off, we dressed and paddled toward the steep cliff. She was in the stern. In the bow, she had stowed our minimal tackle in a small plastic pouch. "Put a couple of sinkers about a foot from your lure," she said.

I put down my paddle, picked up my fishing rod, and added the sinkers, as instructed. "Is this lure all right?"

"That'll do. It really doesn't matter that much."

We were almost to the cliff. I could have touched it with my paddle.

"Now cast as far as you can."

"Which way?"

She chuckled at my lack of understanding. "That doesn't matter. Either direction parallel to the rock wall."

I cast as far as I could. She stopped paddling and waited, having set the canoe parallel to the cliff. "Let out more line."

I wanted to say, "You're kidding," but I didn't. I was learning not to question her. There was only a bit more line on the spool, when she told me to stop.

"Hold your rod with your knees, and paddle like crazy," she said.

We made quite a wake as we paddled as fast as we could. Suddenly, the little bit of line I'd left on the spool screamed out against the tension. "Grab your rod!" she yelled, and she stopped paddling.

The fight was terrific. I would reel in, and when I thought I was getting somewhere, the line would peel off the reel again. Once, I made the tragic mistake of holding the line between my fingers to check the tension, and the line ripped through my fingers and burned, leaving nice blisters on my thumb and index finger. It didn't help my pain that Lily was beside herself laughing at the whole affair.

It was the hardest fight I'd ever had with a fish. As I pulled it closer to the surface, it jumped out of the water and then dove under the canoe. Lily turned the canoe to keep the line from snagging, but she was laughing so hard I was amazed she didn't tip the canoe over in the process. My arms were exhausted when I finally brought the fish to the surface. It appeared as tired as I was. She scooped it out of the water in a single flash of motion. On the bottom of the canoe lay a three-pound lake trout.

"These fish like cold water," she explained. "So when I saw the configuration of the lake and felt the water when we dove in, I knew there were lake trout here. Nice job, Barak Shelton."

"Thank you, Lily Barton, for the fine compliment. But did you have to laugh at me the whole time?"

"How do you know I wasn't laughing at the fish?" She covered her face and laughed into her hands. "You really were funny. You should have seen yourself."

Dinner that night was the most delicious fish I'd ever tasted, with delicate, firm meat sizzled to perfection in its skin. Lily sucked on the head.

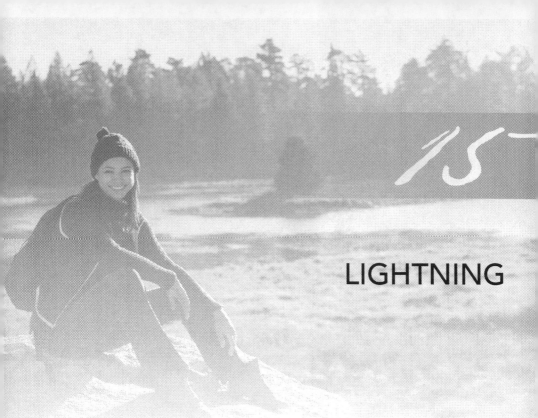

# LIGHTNING

Late that evening, we packed everything away and pulled the canoe up onto the rocks. We sat on top of a large boulder overlooking the lake. The smell of a satisfying supper still in the air and the scent of the white pine needles scattered over the sun-warmed rocks gave me a sense of contentment. There were no mosquitoes. I put my arm around her as she snuggled up next to me. "This has sure been a great trip," I said. The air was still, and the lake was like glass. The sun was about an hour from setting as the shadows of the western hillside slid across the lake.

"Let's go for another swim," she said.

"It's too cold."

"Ah, it'll be good for us." She jumped up, shed her clothes, and then folded them and put them on top of the rock beside the gravel beach. "Autumn told me to pick up after myself," she said with a laugh. She edged into the water and turned back to shore to put on her Keens. "Better keep your sandals on so you don't hurt your feet. There are lots of sharp rocks here."

I was stunned by her naked form. Hesitant about getting in the cold spring-fed water again, I followed, laying my clothes beside hers and tightening my toe-protective Keens, as instructed.

Standing naked beside her, I tried to control my desire to grab her and hold her body next to mine.

She turned to me. "Because it's cold, let's swim as far out in the lake as we can. Whoever swims the farthest without stopping wins. Ready. Set. Go."

On command, I jumped into the water. My eyes opened to a green kaleidoscope of color. I swam as hard as I could. The icy cold made my legs cramp. When I could not do another stroke, I stopped and looked up. She was about twenty feet beyond me. I expected her to be laughing at me, rejoicing in her victory, but instead, she was treading water while facing the western horizon. Her face looked strained.

"What's wrong?"

"Look." She pointed at the crimson setting sun. "See those clouds?"

Beyond the sinking sun, the clouds were greenish black, lined in a row along the horizon. Black streaks descended in an ominous curtain. Lightning was illuminating the boiling front. "Good thing we swam out here. From our camp, we wouldn't have been able to see those clouds till it was too late. Come on. We've got work to do." She swam back.

I was still breathless from swimming out into the lake, but I followed, taking a few rest breaks to tread water along the way. Every time I stopped, the water chilled me. My jaw was chattering by the time I reached the shore. Sure enough, without my Keens, I likely would have been unable to get up over the sharp rocks.

The clouds moved fast, and I anticipated a downpour. Lily scooped up our clothes and put them in the tent to stay dry. I gathered our cooking supplies and stuffed them into the food pack just as the wind howled like a sonic boom. Everything was blowing; leaves, pine needles, and dust swirled around me. I shielded my face as dirt blew into my eyes. I dropped the food pack. Disoriented, I couldn't tell where I'd dropped it. More importantly, where was Lily?

An explosion of lightning split the white pine beside our tent in two. I felt the tingling in my feet and up through my body as the electrical bolt descended through the tree and across the campsite. I ran to get out of the way as the falling tree landed next to me. Then I saw Lily running from the blaze as everything—the tent, the tree, and all our belongings—exploded into flames. The wind hurled flaming embers from the trunk that had collapsed onto our tent. I ran to grab her as she stumbled. A flaming branch flew through the air and hit her square in the head. I grabbed her and screamed, "Oh God, no! I need her!"

As I held on to her, we were flung through the wind, smashing into the rocks along the shore. She was limp. I dragged her into the crevice of the large rock shelf that faced the water and away from the inferno that was our camp. I huddled over her. "Lily, wake up!" I yelled till I was hoarse. "Lily." It was futile; there was no response. I checked her pulse, which was bounding; I laid my ear to her chest and listened to her lungs, which were clear. She was breathing as if she were asleep. I put my hand to her breast and felt her heart pounding against her chest wall.

The green sky turned black as the forest burst into flames up the sloping western hillside, filling the sky with inky smoke. I laid Lily on the gravel under the massive boulder next to the shore. I crawled to the edge to see what was left of our camp. A massive blaze under the torched tree engulfed our tent, packs, and belongings. The blazing limb that had hit Lily lay on top of the food pack where I had dropped it. It was on fire. There would be nothing left of our food. The smoke thickened like soup and clouded my vision. I could barely see in the swirling gray mass.

Then the sky revolted with multiple explosions as lightning struck all around the hillside to the west. Despite the cloud of smoke, I could see the trees burst into torches. The air was heavy. I had to hold my face next to the ground to breathe. I crawled back to where Lily was, under the protection of the boulder. I prayed the water would protect us. The waves were violent in the wind; the spray pelted my skin like needles. I screamed but could not hear myself above the roar. I squirmed beside her, protecting her unconscious body from further insult. Her singed hair smelled acrid as I cradled her head in my hands. Electricity shot through the rocks again. Thunder blasted my ears. The residual ringing made me deaf. I felt a wet towel splashed up by the waves and grabbed it. I draped it over our heads to filter the air. With my hand on her ribs, I monitored her breathing and heartbeat.

A shock wave of heat forced me to curl tighter next to Lily under the rock shelf. My exposed back burned as I cringed in front of her. I glanced over the protection of our boulder shelter just in time to see the canoe catapulted off the rocks and up into the fury of the wind. A screaming backdraft blew it into the surf and out of sight, lost in the maelstrom.

How long the lightning and thunder lasted, I had no idea. Time didn't matter when one was surrounded by crashing blasts. When it stopped, I peeked out across our campsite. *It must still be the middle of the night. Have I been unconscious as well as Lily?* Despite the fog of smoke, I could see in the firelight that all the trees up the hillside were smoldering embers. There was still a bright blaze on the crest of the hill.

"What should I do? Oh God, what should I do?" I couldn't hear my voice despite yelling with all my strength over the roar of the inferno on the hilltop. Sparks flew like fireworks out of control. The roar of the fire was punctuated by blasts of pine trees, rich with sap, exploding. I hugged the granite boulder protecting us, but I could still feel the intense heat blowing against my back. In a time frame I couldn't comprehend, the roar subsided as the fire raced away from us to the west. I didn't know what to expect, and I didn't dare look, but my exposed back was soon pelted with hail, an overture to a subsequent deluge of rain.

*That will put the fire out*, I thought as I lost consciousness.

# STILL ALIVE

I AWOKE SHIVERING AND STIFF. Lily's respirations were rhythmical. She was still unresponsive. I felt the lump on the back of her head. There was a large, squishy hematoma. I palpated her skull and found no apparent fractures. "Oh God, she has to recover. I can't get out of here without her."

I eased out from under our rocky shelter. I had to move, but I was so stiff. The sight was unreal, and the smell was putrid. Small wind devils of ash swirled around the rocks. The rain had stopped. I didn't recognize our campsite. The entire island was burned. Every tree was black. The fallen part of the white pine still smoldered over the cinder that had been our tent. The base of the tree stood like a black obelisk. The western shore of the lake was scorched, pocked with black sticks that used to be trees. I could see an orange fringe of fire still burning on the ridge in the distance, under a canopy of smoke. I turned to look up the sheer rock cliff on the eastern shore. The trees stood untouched like jewels on a crown. Not a single tree showed signs of the fire. They were the only reference that we were still at the same place. The wind must have blown the fire up the western shore and spared the eastern.

I didn't know what to do. I wandered around camp more to move my limbs than with any purpose. I was afraid to look at the tent—or what had been our tent. Besides, there were still flames from the tree licking the remnants of our gear. *Should I put the fire out? With what? What is left? Everything was destroyed.* That was when I realized I was naked. I had on only my Keens, which Lily had wanted me to wear when we went swimming. I wanted to get dressed. I shivered even though I wasn't that cold. I remembered Lily running up the rocks to put our clothes in the tent so they wouldn't get wet. Was there anything left?

I heard her moan and ran to her side. "Is it snowing?" she mumbled.

Was she delirious? I felt her belly. There was no tenderness, and she didn't seem hypothermic. I felt her pulse. It was strong and regular. I rolled her from her side onto her back. "Lily, it's me—Barak. It's not snowing. That is ash falling down. You were hit on the head by a flying branch in the fire."

Her voice was weak. She was speaking Anishinabe.

"I can't understand you, Lily. Speak English."

"Fire. East." She swallowed. "Rain. South." She put her hand on her head and moaned. "Wind. West." She turned her head and opened her eyes. "Only thing left to happen is snow from the north."

I sat beside her and checked the abrasion across her forehead. It was superficial, but her right eye was badly swollen. There weren't any signs of significant blood loss. "We had hail. Does that count?"

"Oh, good. Then it won't snow." She grabbed her head with both hands. "I have a terrible headache like when I had that hangover. You didn't get me drunk, did you? I'll never forgive you if you did." She paused as if waiting for a response. I didn't know what to say. She seemed delirious.

She laughed and put her hands on her belly. "That was a joke, Barak. Don't look so serious." She boosted herself up onto her elbows. "What happened? I remember putting things in the tent, and then I remember feeling hot and cold." She shivered. "Help me up, Barak. I'm so stiff." I helped her up. She seemed clumsy at first, but as she stretched her arms and legs, she improved. She felt her head. "I've got quite an egg on my head. We should eat it for breakfast."

I knew she was making another joke, but I couldn't laugh. "Am I being too serious? Look at our stuff," I said, and I pointed to what used to be a tent. "Everything's gone. Packs, tent, cook kit, food pack—all of it burned to cinders. And I saw the canoe fly away in the wind. We're going to die out here. We have nothing!" I yelled and cursed till I was hoarse.

"Not everything," she said. "But we need a fire to keep warm." She walked up the rock ledge, a little shaky at first, and grabbed a piece of the pine that was smoldering. She blew on it till it burst into flame. "Get some of the branches off that white pine. Some of them are still smoking, so be careful; they might be hot."

I followed her command, and soon we were warming by the fire. "There's plenty of firewood around here, so let's keep this going for starters," she said. As we warmed up, we started investigating. "Did you see which way the canoe went?"

"I think it blew that way before everything burst into flames, and the sky filled with smoke." I pointed to the east.

She climbed on top of the rock shelf that had protected us and searched the distance. The sun was peeking over the horizon through the dark mantle of smoke and clouds. "I see something in the shadows over there. I think that's our canoe."

I looked where she was pointing, but I saw nothing.

"Let's check out what's left of our gear." She scurried down off the boulder and grabbed a stick to poke through the embers of our tent.

We had to move several burned tree limbs. They were still smoldering and too hot to handle, so she levered them away with her stick. She pulled at the tar ball that used to be our tent. We sorted through the debris. It surprised me that the floor of the tent was intact. It had a few burned spots, but it must have been insulated by our sleeping bags till the rain squelched the fire. Our clothes were cinders. Our sleeping bags were layers of black coagulate the intense heat had made of the synthetic fiber. Lily found the hatchet, and I found my hunting knife and compass under the sleeping bag. The compass was melted. It was worthless. The handle of the knife was burned, but the blade was still useable, as it did not seem to have lost its temper.

Lily encouraged me as I cried over the remnants of my compass. "We don't need that anyway. I can tell directions without it."

I sorted through what used to be our food pack. A burning limb had fallen on it, holding it in place in the wind. The aluminum cook pot was distorted from the heat. I bent it back into shape and held it up to the morning sun to see if there were any holes. I saw none and assumed it would still hold water. The dehydrated food must have blown away in the fierce wind generated by the fire, as I found no remnants. The plastic bags with our lunches were sizzled brown globs. For some unknown reason, the oatmeal was preserved but scorched.

Lily watched as I sorted through the mess. "Try cooking up some of that oatmeal. I'm hungry."

I thought about the carcinogens in burned plastic as I cupped as much of the scorched oatmeal into the pot as possible. Then I went down to the lake. The surface was covered with ash. I stood immobilized.

She must have sensed my consternation because she splashed away the surface debris. Cupping her hand, she scooped some of the deeper water into the pot. "Is that enough?"

I started sobbing and couldn't stop. I blurted out, "We need one cup of water for each package." I knew it was an absurd thing to say, but it just came out. I shook with grief.

She hugged my convulsing form. "We can handle this, Barak," she said. "Hang in there, brother I have chosen. Neither of us died."

"You had a concussion."

"Sure, and I have a bad headache and a swollen eye, but we're alive, Barak. We're alive. Rejoice." She let go and did a little dance in front of me. "Look. We're just like Adam and Eve, naked without shame."

I wasn't sure I was without shame. At that moment, with her dancing in front of me, I thought she was the most beautiful woman in the whole world, and I felt as if we were the last humans on earth. I blurted through my tears, "But what are we going to do?"

She grabbed a wet leaf from under the water and helped me blow my nose. "Take one step at a time. You cook up that oatmeal, and I'll scrounge around a little more."

I put the oatmeal into the water and set it on the fire. It seemed odd to stoke the fire. The fire would give us breakfast, but it had taken everything away from us. When the oatmeal was cooked, despite the floating black things in it, I called out, "Breakfast is ready."

"Look. I found our spoons. They're a little warped." She bent them back into shape and gave me one. We sat on the charred logs that had been our fireside benches, facing each other with the pot in between us, and spooned oatmeal out of the pot. It tasted smoky and disgusting, but watching Lily eat distracted me from the nasty taste.

"I'll let you lick the pot, and then go wash it," she said.

I stood and turned to bring the pot down to the lake. She started laughing. I turned, annoyed. "What's so funny?"

"Your butt is all black from sitting on that burned log." She got up and turned so I had a good view of her charcoal butt, and then she leaned over to peek at me between her legs. "That should give you something to laugh about."

"Right," I said, and I turned away. Lily's blackened buttocks, exposed genitalia, and delicate breasts hanging beside her face as she looked at me between her muscular hamstring muscles were just too much. I moved like a zombie to the water's edge to clean the pot.

When I returned, she had everything that was usable sorted out on the rock beside our campfire. "We are very blessed, Barak," she said, contemplating the assortment. "Knife. Hatchet. The tent floor can still be used as a tarp. A little more oatmeal till we find better food, a pot, spoons, and my flint for making fires—everything we need to survive." She looked over her shoulder. "I just hope the canoe is intact."

"No clothes," I muttered.

"The towel that you covered our faces with—we have that."

I was angry with her optimism. I held the rag up and said, "Sure, you can sew a little outfit for each of us."

She hugged me and put my head on her shoulder, rubbing my back. "The Great Spirit will provide."

Her naked caress against my bare chest was no encouragement under the circumstances. I pictured our naked bodies bloated and dead, laid out for the forest service to discover in a couple of weeks. That was what God would provide.

She whispered in my ear, "I heard you praying for me during the night. God answered your prayer. I survived." She released me and did a couple of jumping jacks. "Here I am, in all my glory."

"Be realistic!" I yelled. "We are several days' paddle from the nearest road. We have nothing except"—I pointed to the collection on the rock—"that junk, and I'm supposed to do jumping jacks?" I did a couple out of sarcasm.

"Your penis looks funny when you do that." She stopped jumping and started laughing.

"Well, your breasts are pretty comical, bouncing around when you do that." I was embarrassed the moment I said it. "I'm sorry. I shouldn't have—"

"That's the spirit of the Barak I know and love." She turned and looked across the lake. "First job: we need that canoe, or I'll have to make one." She scanned the eastern shore. "See that glint in the morning sun? I think that's our canoe."

I remembered how cold the water was as I searched the far shore of the lake for the glint she'd described. It did look like our canoe. "That's a heck of a long swim," I said.

"Can you swim with the knife?"

"I suppose."

"I'll strip off a piece of the tent floor and tie it to your wrist. We can't lose it. I'll take the flint. We'll swim over there and check on the canoe. If we get too cold, I can build a fire to warm us up once we're there." She searched my less-than-enthusiastic expression. "Look, Barak, we've eaten, and we've been warmed by the fire. We'll never be in better condition to swim across the lake than we are right now. Waiting could be fatal."

Still dejected, I gave an unenthusiastic response. "All right, I'm ready." I didn't like the sound of *fatal*.

"Swim at about eighty percent of your maximum. You should be able to sustain that. We stay together and use each other to rest and warm up along the way. We could tow a log behind us to rest, but it would increase the work of swimming. Are you ready?"

"Wait a minute. What if the canoe is all busted?"

She took my hand and led me to the water's edge. "Then I will fix it or call on my manitou to tell me how to make a canoe." She pulled me into the water. The water was so cold it grabbed my heart when I jumped in. The ash on the surface tasted bitter like soap, but I swam for my life, too afraid to be left behind. I caught up with her. After a few minutes, she asked, "Is this too fast? Can you sustain this rate?"

"I think so."

I swam to exhaustion, yet the glint of aluminum on the opposite shore seemed no closer. Lily sensed I was struggling and paused. We trod water face-to-face. She pulled me toward her, warming me with her body and rubbing my back. "You know, women have more endurance. I suppose it's because of our extra body fat."

Her breasts felt warm against my chest, and I felt her nipples soften. "Very nicely distributed," I said.

"You're ready to swim again," she said, pushing me away and laughing.

When we got to the opposite shore, drowning seemed a pleasant option. I couldn't force myself to one more stroke. Lily bounded up the shore to examine the canoe, turning it over to inspect the interior until she was satisfied with its integrity. "One of the fishing poles is still tied inside!" she yelled with glee. I collapsed, shivering in the moss on the shore.

"I need some help here, Barak. The wind wedged it between some roots. I can't pull it out by myself. Give me your knife."

I untied it from my wrist. With a few quick slits, she snapped off several limbs, and we pulled together. The canoe came free. We walked it into the water. It had several dents and was leaking from popped rivets. "We should be able to fix that," she said with a practiced eye. She returned to the shore and cut some twigs from a cedar tree. She poked them into the rivet holes. "Ready to paddle back to camp?"

"We don't have any paddles." I started to cry, overwhelmed by the circumstances.

Apparently undaunted, she told me what to do. "We'll use our hands. Lie down on the bow, and use both hands. I'll take the stern." We got into the canoe. It was still leaking despite the rivet holes she had plugged, but with just our weight, we were able to scoot along fairly fast before it filled with significant water. The sun poked through the smoky canopy and warmed my back as I lay on the bow, straining to use my hands as paddles. We started to cross the lake. It seemed to me as if we would never make it, but it was warmer than swimming back to our camp. Noise suddenly shattered the stillness. It sounded like an airplane, but smoke in the western sky obscured whatever it was. We were almost back to our island, when a streak of sunlight highlighted something wedged in the weeds along the western shore. "Look over there, Lily. Are those our paddles or just sticks floating in the water?"

Without saying anything, she turned the canoe. Stuck in the reeds along the shore, we found our paddles.

"How did the canoe blow over to the eastern shore and the paddles land on the western shore?" I said.

"The wind does odd things in a fire."

I fished out the paddles from among the reeds and cattails and handed one to Lily. "This is great. What luck," I said. I was feeling more positive that we wouldn't die in the wilderness.

"That's the spirit, Barak. Yeah, this saves us a lot of time."

"What do you mean?"

"I could have carved new paddles, but now I don't have to."

I spent the afternoon pounding out the dents in the canoe with a smooth rock. Lily was busy doing something. I wasn't sure what she was up to, but whatever it was, it smelled bad. I didn't pay much attention, as I was focused on my job. My psyche was doing strange things. There I was, in the middle of nowhere with the most beautiful woman my mind could conjure, running around naked, and I was focused on dents in a canoe. *My brain is damaged*, I thought as I pushed the canoe into the water to check for leaks. It glided straighter, but the rivet holes leaked like a watering can.

"It's leaking all over," I said. "We'll never be able to bail fast enough to use it."

"Pay attention to where the leaks are, and bring it up onshore."

I dragged it up onto the rocks. I was careless and discouraged; my muscles were sore from pounding with rocks. "Turn it over," she said.

I turned it over, and we inspected for cracks where I had pounded out the aluminum. I was worried about the sun burning my naked Caucasian body. I looked at Lily. She seemed darker. Her caramel skin was almost like dark chocolate now, and her areolas were like chocolate mint paddies. I shook my head. What was my problem? I was comparing her body to candy. I scooted into the shade of a big rock. "I think I have sunstroke. I need to rest."

She carried a flat rock covered with a gob of black gunk. "Forget it. I need your help. Crawl under the canoe, and see where the light is coming through." She handed me some white pine needles. They were orange, scorched by the heat but not burned. "From under the canoe, you can see the sunlight coming through. Stick pine needles out through the holes, and I'll patch them as you find them. I cooked some pine pitch." She smiled. "The fire burned so fast even the trees sweat. I collected enough pitch to patch the holes. This is a little gift from the Great Spirit."

Not sure I understood the process, I obeyed and crawled under the canoe. A planetarium of holes lit up across the bottom of the canoe. With the handful of pine needles, I directed her to where the pitch needed to be spread. She plugged the larger holes with some kind of stuffing.

"What's that?"

"Moss to fill the holes and hold the hot pitch."

When it was all dark under the canoe, I crawled out. "It looks good. No light show."

"Great. I was hoping I wouldn't have to make another batch." She set down her rock with the black pitch and stood behind me to rub my back. "Do you feel more rested now?"

"Yes, but now I'm hungry. Are you going to catch us a fish?"

"The fish won't bite after that storm—no use even trying—but I'll see what's in the pantry."

I thought she was joking. I forced a smile. She swam across the narrows between our island and the western shore and then ran into the woods. I was amazed how agile she was despite her head injury.

I didn't follow but sat on a log to check my feet. The Keens had helped a lot. Slipping my feet out of my sandals, I examined the soles. They were tender but getting tougher. The hairs on my legs were singed. *Too close to the fire.* I recalled the burned glop my boots had become and was thankful I had worn the sandals when we were swimming. "The portages are going to be tough on you boys," I told my feet. I inspected my body. I had scratches and abrasions in places that usually never saw the sun. My face was flushed from the intensity of the fire before I'd found shelter under the rock, and my butt felt sunburned despite being blackened from the soot smeared on my backside from sitting on the burned log. "God, I wish I had some clothes." I looked up at the sky. It was still churning with smoke, but the overcast was higher. "A nice steak dinner would be good too, God, since I'm asking for stuff."

"Your prayers have been answered," Lily said as she ran into camp.

I didn't even look up. "Right," I said with as much sarcasm as I could muster. I stood and turned to her. My shoulders drooped as a reflex.

"You have no faith in God, and you don't believe me. What an ass you are, Barak Shelton."

"Come on, Lily. Be realistic. Our clothes are burned. We have one stupid wet towel and nothing to eat. My butt is sunburned, and my poor exposed genitalia are sore and swollen. How am I supposed to feel?" I figured I might as well blurt it out; she could see everything anyway.

She walked up to me and slugged me in the gut. I doubled over in pain. "Everything is provided if you listen carefully. Grab the hatchet and knife, and get in the canoe."

I hesitated.

"Quickly," she commanded. Her face looked stern.

We paddled south along the burned shoreline. It was desolate. The rocks were black, and some were even split from the intense heat. The trees that had been so lush the day before looked like used matchsticks. She beached the canoe where the burn stopped and lush undergrowth resumed. The transition was dramatic. *How did that happen? The fire scorches one area, and five feet away, it's like there never was a fire.*

I mumbled and complained about something. She held her hand up for silence. She was listening for something. I heard nothing. She said nothing, but I understood by her hand signals that she meant for me to follow at a distance. Slowly and cautiously, avoiding branches, she moved in stealthy silence.

Despite my Keens, my tender feet required deliberate placement along the twisted undergrowth. Besides, I didn't want my bare thighs scratched by malevolent branches. I was focused on the ground, so when we came upon a massive fallen tree about four feet in diameter covered by a blanket of moss, I jerked to a halt. She directed me to squat. I understood by her hand motions that she wanted the knife. She traded me for the hatchet.

She was listening—to what, I didn't know. Then she slipped off her Keens, burst up on the log, ran barefoot along its length, and jumped off where the dead branches impeded her progress, out of my sight. I had no idea what she was doing. I just stood confused, slumped against the log for support, and waited. From the dense underbrush, I heard singing in Anishinabe. Then she yelled, "All right, you can come now! Bring my Keens and the hatchet."

I walked along the log, not sure of my footing, as the moss was slippery, and I had trouble keeping my balance. How had she run its length barefoot? When I reached the other end, where she had jumped off, I stood horrified. Lily was covered in blood. It was smeared across her face, and clots dripped off her breasts and belly.

"Are you hurt?" I asked.

She shook with laughter.

I slid cautiously off the log. The moss felt slimy against my bare skin. Once on stable footing, I scrambled to her side. She wiped her bloody hands down her flanks, making macabre patterns on her skin. Then I focused on where the blood came from. A large doe lay dead at her feet.

"I slit her throat after I thanked her for giving up her life for us. You didn't want me to let her suffer, did you? Her leg was broken, probably in the panic of escaping the fire." She grabbed me and smeared bloody stripes across my chest. "Steak dinner tonight, O ye of little faith."

"Is this some kind of ritual?" I asked, trying to wipe the blood off and smearing it on my hands.

"Nope. I'm just trying to get your attention."

"You got it. Now, how did you know this deer was here? How did you run down this log and slit its throat? I'm confused. How did you do what I just saw you do?"

"I heard the poor thing crying while I was gathering firewood. I assumed she must have gotten trapped somehow while trying to escape the fire." She held up the right front leg with a dangling hoof. "When I heard you complaining about not having any meat to eat and no clothes to wear, I just had to laugh. We can make doeskin clothes and have some nice, tender venison steaks for dinner tonight."

She laid the deer on its side and slit the hide down the thorax and belly. She disarticulated the first joints of the legs, sliced under the skin, and pulled the lower hide off like four sleeves. "Use the hatchet to cut the head off. We need it."

I set about my grizzly task, hacking at the neck, as she disemboweled the creature, removed the hide, and examined the entrails. "Too bad. The liver is no good. I love liver." She held it up so I could see the white nodules peppered across it and then threw it in the brush. "The wolves will be well fed tonight. In fact, I'm surprised they didn't find her first. They must have run west ahead of the fire. This poor doe ran south. She almost made it."

"These mosquitoes are terrible." I stopped hacking at the doe's neck to swat and swing at the clouds swarming around me.

"Three reasons," she said.

I paused to look at her. There were no mosquitoes bothering her. "Yes, what are they?"

"First, you're working too hard, sweating, and not pacing yourself. Second, you're all upset, so you're breathing too fast. Mosquitoes are attracted to carbon dioxide." She went back to work, slicing off the meat.

I swatted the swarm around my head. "And third might be?"

"You haven't asked nicely if I have any insect repellent."

I got down on one knee in a puddle of clotted blood and folded my hands. This was ridiculous. Our insect repellent had been burned up in the fire. "O wise, beneficent Anishinabe maiden, do you have any insect repellant, please?"

"Yes, I do, most humble, unbelieving Barak, my brother whom I love and adore." She ripped a plant up by the roots, cut it in two, and squeezed out some white juice. She rubbed it across my face and neck and then turned me around and rubbed it down my back and across my butt. It felt cool and soothing.

"Thank you." There was instant relief from the bugs. Without the swarm of mosquitoes around me, I could calm down, breathe slower, and focus on hacking the doe's head off.

"You're welcome. If the mosquitoes start bothering your penis, let me know," she said as she spread out the hide on the ground. "I can rub some repellent on it too."

"Lily."

She held her tongue between her teeth and giggled. "All right, I'll stop teasing you, but I want you to be thankful for what nature provides." She cut off two chunks of meat from the spine and held them up. "Does filet mignon fulfill your request for supper?"

The smell of blood, meat, and hides reminded me of a butcher shop only more intense. Her bloody smile beamed with satisfaction. "That sounds"—I gagged and swallowed—"delicious." I had trouble equating *delicious* in context with the present gore, but I refused to be ungrateful. I couldn't imagine what she would do to me.

"You and God need to have a talk tonight. You have a lot of confessing to do for all your complaints today. Too bad there's no priest around. You'll have to confess to me." She slit large hunks of thigh meat off the bones and threw them onto the hide she had spread out. I noticed that we were attracting flies, but she seemed as oblivious to them as to the mosquitoes.

I finally severed the head and held up my trophy. "Good work," she said. "Now help me haul out this meat before too many flies discover what we've done."

*So she did notice.*

Leaving the skeletal carcass in place for the wolves, we each took a corner of the hide and hauled it through the woods to the shore. The canoe was beached a few yards north of where we came out. I waded into the water and pulled the canoe over so as not to dislodge the pitch-filled rivet holes. We lifted our load into the canoe.

"Back to camp?" I asked as I took the stern.

"Right." She smiled like a child retuning from shopping at the toy store.

She chatted as we paddled. "I know we planned three days to the landing from here, but I don't want to leave till we're ready. Besides, I think we can do it in two or maybe one day, paddling all night. I'm sure the firefighters are busy, and our pickup will understand if we're late." She held up her paddle and pointed with it to the west. A rim of fire and smoke still crested the horizon. "Besides, we've got work to do." She didn't explain what work we had to do, but I was getting used to the Anishinabe perspective of need-to-know.

I gazed at the deer's head I had chopped off. "I'm hungry, but I am not eating this head," I said, kicking it in the bottom of the canoe.

"It's a delicacy, but I won't let you eat it," she said. "It's too valuable."

"Can we wash off when we get to camp? I feel like I've been in a massacre. This blood you smeared all over me is starting to itch, and I don't like the smell." I looked down as I paddled and saw clots of blood congealed on my skin. There were even dark globs clotted in my pubic hair. It was grotesque.

# FRESH MEAT

BACK AT CAMP, WE SECURED the canoe. I rubbed my stomach, and the horror of the blood and guts was dissipated by the hunger that would soon be satisfied. *Food is coming,* I told my empty belly. I salivated at the thought of a juicy steak.

I plunged into the lake to loosen up the dried blood smeared across my torso. Gobs of blood stuck to my skin. Lily whistled at me as she pulled up some horsetail plants growing along the shore and showed me how to scrub with them. When we finished our bath, I felt clean again.

She called me ashore. She pulled the hide out, leaving the meat in the bottom of the canoe. She laid out the hide over a log, gave me the hatchet, and instructed me to sit. "Hold the blade by the sides, horizontal to the hide, and scrape off every bit of flesh." She demonstrated how to scrape off the fat and membranes stuck to the hide. I practiced, and she adjusted my angle. "Good. And when you have to urinate, let me know."

*Now what?* I wondered. *I have to inform her when my bladder is full?* This was getting far too personal for comfort. I felt rebellious. I wanted to run into the woods and piss just to spite her. *But oh well.*

I started scraping the hide, as instructed. The hatchet blade made a pretty good scraper, and I found contentment in my work. When I thought I had done a decent job, I asked her to inspect my work. "See these membrane things?" She twisted bits of tissue between her fingers. "They need to be scraped off. Keep at it."

I went over the whole hide again. *This is so tedious. Have I been at this for hours?* Without my watch, which had been in the bottom of the pack, now melted in the fire, I had no concept of time. Weary from the repetitive motion and with wrists sore from the work, I got up. "I've got to go potty, Mommy." I stood up and directed my penis into the burned shreds of bushes.

"Stop!" she yelled. Her scream stopped my stream. She grabbed the smaller of the cooking pots and held it in front of my penis. "All right, now you can go."

This nudity stuff was getting way too familiar. Sure, it was delightful to see this lithe young maiden running around the forest naked—I admitted to the sensual pleasure of that—but did she have to watch me piss too? I bounced my shy penis to get the urine stream flowing again. I closed my eyes, as I couldn't bear her scrutiny. When I finished, I was an embarrassed wreck. She touched the pot to the tip of my penis, intent on catching the last hanging drop. After setting the pot on the ground, she squatted over it and added her urine. "Do I have to see this?" I complained, covering my eyes. "Should we watch each other take a crap too?"

"Human feces has been used for tanning hides, but with all the ashes from the forest fire, I think I can do the job with just urine and boiled ash."

It dawned on me. *All right, I'm slow at this survival stuff. She is using our urine to cure the hide.*

She scrutinized my scraping progress. "Not quite finished."

I couldn't imagine scraping the whole thing again. I was going to have nightmares that night about scraping hides. Resentment built up inside me.

"But I have another job for you," she said.

I felt instant relief. I had paid no attention to what she was doing while I scraped, but when I looked at the campfire, I saw that she had built a frame of sticks and laid out thin slices of meat over it. "I need you to keep a smoky fire going. Use this rotted wood. Remember, no flames and lots of smoke," she said.

"I'm hungry."

"We'll eat after sunset. We need the sun to help us jerk this meat and work our hide."

I didn't want to wait for the sun to set, but I did my job, making a smoky fire. When I had to urinate, I did it in the container now that I knew the reason for collecting our urine. I watched her do the same. A switch in wind directed the smoke into my eyes. I backed away from the smoke and glanced at Lily working the hide. Her muscles rippled with strength, and she moved in rhythm with her scraping motion. She caught me staring at her.

"You like what you see?"

"Yes." I hesitated to answer, but honesty seemed best. "You are quite attractive, you know." I didn't want to be slugged again, which I figured would probably be the punishment for deception.

She stood up, held out her arms, and rotated slowly. "There's the whole thing. Do you need to see my orifices too?" She tilted her pelvis and spread her legs. I cringed. "My body is just the house I live in, Barak. It's not me. For cripes' sake, you've seen me naked for a week now. Get over it, and get back to work."

She returned to her work on the hide. "It reminds me of a wolverine—dangerous and unpredictable," she said.

"What does?"

"Your penis."

I felt embarrassed but rejected too.

She wasn't even looking at me, but I covered my erection and turned back to my smoky fire, returning my focus to the strips of meat I was smoking, not eating. I sneezed.

By sunset, she had made a tub by digging out a round depression and then securing with a border of rocks what once had been our tent floor. She placed the hide in the hollow and then poured the urine we had collected all day over it, mixed with ashes. The venison was almost dry, so I was surprised when she went down to the lake and produced two slabs of meat tucked away in the other cooking pot. She had kept the pot in the cold water with a rock over the cover to hold it down. She added dry wood to my smoky fire, and it burst into flames. Now that it was dark, I could see only her silhouette against the red-hot coals as she roasted the tenderloins on two sticks.

When the meat was golden brown and sizzling, she handed me one of the sticks.

"So where are the vegetables?" I asked.

She jumped up, grabbed my meat, and pushed me to the ground. "Ouch!" I yelled as I landed on a sharp rock. "What was that for?" I grabbed at the sharp pain on my butt. In the firelight, I saw blood on my hand. "I'm bleeding."

"Stand up, and turn around," she said as she turned my backside toward the fire. "Yep, you have a nasty cut. It's bleeding a lot." She took a small rock out of the fire with a stick and seared the cut. I screamed. "There. The bleeding stopped. I'll put some salve on it in the morning." She spun me around to face her. Her eyes burned with fury. "You've been complaining all day. What's wrong with you, Barak Shelton? God has given you a doe hide for clothes; we found the canoe, which we patched, and even the paddles; and you're having a fireside dinner of filet mignon with a beautiful naked girl. What's to complain about? No vegetables?"

The loons started singing across the lake. She turned her ear to listen and then looked back at me. "I know guys who would kill for this experience. How much do you have to have before 'Thank you' comes out of your rancid little mouth?"

I held my hand over my laceration, hoping it would stop bleeding. I answered in slow, deliberate phrases. "I'm sorry. I am very thankful. I was making a joke." It did not dissipate her anger much.

"Are you thankful? I want to hear the list. Tell me what you're thankful for." Her grip on my arms was painful.

I enumerated everything I could think of, starting with the canoe and patching material and finishing with filet mignon. Her hazel eyes softened as I added, "I am very thankful for you. I would have died without your expertise."

"God provided for us, so don't be thankful to me."

"I meant that I am thankful for food and a deer hide and a canoe with paddles." I repeated the list. "And a towel, a knife, flint, and you, most beautiful naked girl."

"Now, that sounds a lot better, doesn't it?" She picked my steak up off the rock she had set it on and blew away the dirt. "Here's your steak back. No more complaining." She went to the shore and grabbed a leaf off a submerged water plant. "Here. Sit on this. It'll stop the bleeding."

The steak was tender and delicious, and I said so many times. The loons sang their enchanting melodies, which changed Lily's mood. She sat next to me, our flanks touching. "It's going to get cold tonight," she said. "We'll need each other for warmth. The hide isn't done soaking."

I reached my arm around her back and hugged her. "You mean we have to sleep together?"

Her smile was lit up by the smoldering fire. "But—"

"I know. No sex." We laughed. It eased the tension.

I hauled the canoe up and tilted it open toward the fire. She scanned the situation and said, "I want to be able to check on the meat during the night. You probably wouldn't wake up if it was disturbed, so you crawl under the canoe first, and I'll sleep in front of you."

I crawled into position. I was shivering in the chilling breeze, but what choice did I have? She knelt in front of me and laid our rescued towel over my back. "That should help some, or do you need it over your little wolverine to keep him out of trouble?" She palmed her breasts in my face. She didn't wait for an answer but snuggled her back up against my front. "Will that keep you warm?"

In the distance, we heard the howl of wolves—first one, and then there was a chorus of others answering. "They found the guts and bones we left for them. Can you hear how happy they are?" she whispered.

"I'm not sure I can interpret their happiness," I said, "but I'm glad they found all that glop." We listened to the chorus crescendo, and then it stopped. I adjusted my shoulders to get comfortable. "I'm glad we made the wolves happy. I hope they don't think we are part of their meal."

She sat up and howled a couple of short yips and then a long, mournful howl. A lone wolf answered her. "The wolves are thankful. I was just telling them that they were welcome to my kill," she said.

*What is with this woman that she can even talk to animals?* My nose was up against her back. Her scent was like earth covered with pine trees. I quivered. After what we had been through that day, I didn't even question that she could communicate with the wolf pack. I laid my hand over her belly. Her muscles tightened as my fingers slipped into her pubic hair. I didn't mean to. She adjusted my hand's position. Her hand on mine felt rough from working the hide.

# NEW CLOTHES

THE SUN IN MY EYES awakened me. She was already busy. She had the hide tied around a sapling, and with a branch as a tourniquet, she was squeezing out the solution of urine and alkali water.

"Are you making oatmeal?" I mumbled.

"No. We're saving it. Get up. I need your help."

"More urine? I have to go."

"No. I'm done with that part."

I crawled out from under the canoe. The sky was clear, but there was a large mushroom of smoke on the western horizon. I saw no rim of orange flames, as I had the previous day. I urinated on what had once been a bush, chuckling at my natural response to turn my back to her.

"Have some jerky for breakfast. It's pretty good. It's dry enough that the flies won't bother it anymore." She pointed to the large rock at the water's edge. "I laid it out there."

I took a bite. I was going to say something about it being chewy and not spiced like at the supermarket, but my throbbing butt laceration convinced me not to say anything that might sound like a complaint. "It's very good, and I am very thankful."

She looked up from the hide and smiled. "Use the blunt end of the hatchet to break the skull. I need the brains. And see that pot of boiling fat? It's boiled long enough. Set it in the lake to cool. I need the rendered fat off the top."

I set to work on cracking the skull. It was much harder than I expected, but it finally cracked. I removed the bone chips and shook the contents into the small cooking pot now emptied of urine. The brain came out like clotted toothpaste. It even had streaks of red across the white goop. I presented my trophy.

"Whip it till it looks like a strawberry daiquiri. We'll smear it over the hide, and then we need our smoky fire again." Our eyes met. "Can you do that?"

"Consider it done." I went about my jobs as assigned. I held some twigs together to make a whip, and in no time, I had a strawberry-daiquiri solution. She had stretched the hide on a hoop made from a small green tree. She must have paddled to the area outside the burn, as every small tree around camp was gone. She smeared the brain mixture on the hide, working it into the surface. By then, I had a nice, smoky fire. She laid the hide on the frame near the smoky fire. I admired her work.

"Let's go for a swim. We can't do anything with the hide for a while," she said.

I joined her at the water's edge. "Just a minute," she said. She stopped me and knelt down to inspect my laceration. "When was your last tetanus shot?"

"Last year."

She smeared a bit of deer tallow over the laceration. "That should protect it." She stood and hung her head. "I apologize. I shouldn't have gotten so angry. It's going to heal with a nasty scar. It really should have had stitches. Will you forgive me?"

I lifted her eyes to mine. "Am I forgiven?" We hugged. That was the moment when I realized we would survive.

"Yes, my brother who has learned to be grateful, you are forgiven." She bowed her head. "And thanks for forgiving me."

"I'm going to wear clothes when we get home, so who but you will ever know that I have a scar on my butt? Besides, it will remind me to be thankful." We embraced again. Euphoria came over me as her warm breasts softened against my chest, and her abdominal muscles tightened against my belly. "Wolverine alert," I said.

She stepped back, laughed, and slapped my penis. "Behave yourself, Gwiingwa'aage." She grabbed my hand. "Come on. Little wolverine wants to go swimming."

Ever after, Gwiingwa'aage—Wolverine—would be her pet name for me. We jumped into the water and played like a couple of otters. I didn't think wolverines were interested in swimming, but otters were.

That evening, she spread the rendered fat over the hide and showed me how to stretch and soften it. Sometimes she used her teeth until the hide was malleable and velvety. That night, as we listened to the loons sing their mournful songs, we cuddled up under a soft blanket of doe hide. It smelled like leather, but in my mind, I pictured urine, ashes, and deer brains, even though I didn't quite remember what deer brains smelled like. But the smell of the acrid smoke was distinctive. As I curled up next to Lily, her scent put me to sleep.

"We have to leave tomorrow," she whispered so as not to interrupt the loons.

"We're two days behind. Do you know the way? I didn't find the map. It probably burned in the fire or blew away."

"Basically," she said. The water was lapping on the shore, when the loons paused in their chorus. Frogs croaked in the distance, resuming their songs for the first time since the fire. She twisted under the hide and faced me. I felt the soft caress of her nakedness. Her voice was so gentle I barely heard it. "I love you, Gwiingwa'aage, but—"

I reached over her and pinched her bottom. She jumped. "I love your butt too, Lily." She laughed at my pun and fell silent. It was funny, but I regretted interrupting what she was going to say next. She never finished her sentence; she just rolled over and fell asleep.

In the morning, she cut the hide in half and made a vest for herself from the top and one for me out of the lower part. She cut the neck hide in two and made a loincloth for each of us. "That should keep your wolverine calm." I wasn't sure whether her loincloth or mine was supposed to accomplish that feat.

With scraps she had woven together, she made belts. Mine had a loop to hold my knife. With rawhide ties, she pulled her vest together. She braided thin leftover pieces into her hair. "Those are a nice touch," I said.

"They are in case we need ties for something later."

We packed our venison jerky with our other prize possessions: two pots, a hatchet, flint, and the last serving of dried, scorched oatmeal sewed into a birch bark container, all rolled up in the tarp that used to be a tent floor. She set the bundle on two pieces of wood so it wouldn't get wet in the bottom of the canoe if the canoe leaked.

"Ready to go?" she asked with a smile of satisfaction. We stood in our finery, paddles in hand.

"I'm as ready as I'm ever going to be," I said, parading around in my new suit. Then I scrutinized her from head to toe. After seeing her naked every day since the beginning of the trip, why did she look more erotic dressed in her loincloth and a laced vest that just hid her nipples? Was it that the vest pushed her breasts together, forcing them to bulge over the top? Yet it was short enough that it accented her muscled midriff. Seeing her dressed made me anticipate our evening swim, when I could watch her undress. *How absurd*, I thought. *What will I see that I haven't seen before? And why do her clothes make me more aroused? What's wrong with my brain?*

"Let's go," I said, and I crawled into the bow.

We were fast on the portages. On the first one, I carried the canoe, and she carried the rolled tarp. On the next portage, we switched. The tarp was awkward to carry, so on the next portage, I paid more attention to how she carried it.

The lakes to the south were free of burn. The wind had blown the fire west. We must have been on the eastern fringe. It was pleasant to be in lush greenery again instead of our stark, burned campsite. Several portages and lakes later, the sun was straight overhead. We were in Shade Lake, just a few portages from North Bay of Basswood Lake. There would be no portages for a long time once we reached Basswood, so we stopped for a snack of venison jerky. "This really is good—quenches my hunger," I said.

"I'm glad you are so thankful. That's a good attitude you're developing."

"I'm glad you appreciate my developing maturity."

"I'm sorry I was so rough on you, but we needed to get things done. I like you, Barak—a lot. That is why I chose you to be my brother."

I swallowed a mouthful of well-chewed jerky.

We entered a small stream. We were going against the current, but the water was so shallow that it wasn't difficult. We were cautious with our patched canoe. When we came to a portage, we stopped before coming to the shore, so the bottom of the canoe never touched any rocks. Only gobs of moss-soaked pitch were keeping our craft from leaking. Aluminum canoes floated even when they leaked because of the foam in the bow and aft, but half-filled with water, they sure were a lot harder to paddle. In the shallow stream, we slid across the bottom several times. I cringed and inspected all the patched holes, but there were no leaks.

Red-winged blackbirds announced our progress as the stream snaked through a wide floodplain. Wild rice was growing all around us. Lily encouraged me to try some of the grains, although it was a few weeks until they would be ripe enough to harvest. The taste was nutty, but the unripe rice hinted of green tea.

Poling with our paddles through mud, we discovered the reason for the relative lack of water: a large beaver dam loomed ahead. I got out of the canoe at the dam's base, and hand over hand, we lifted the canoe up and put it in the deeper water on the other side. The water was mucky and smelled slimy.

I gazed ahead. "It's going to be a lot easier paddling in the deeper water," I said, emphasizing my positive attitude.

I turned back to see if Lily was ready. She had removed her vest and was taking off her loincloth. The look on my face communicated confusion. "What are you doing?"

"Didn't you want vegetables for supper? God has provided," she said. "Again. Get in the canoe, and paddle over to those arrow-shaped plants near the cattails." She placed her folded doeskin clothes neatly on top of the tarp.

I held the stern in place as she slipped into the water and swam along holding the bow. I paddled where she directed and nosed the canoe into the water plants. My water sprite pushed herself deep in the water till only her face showed. Holding the canoe with one hand, she manipulated something with her feet. Tubers started popping to the surface, which she captured and threw into the canoe. "We can cook these tonight. They taste like mashed potatoes."

"Really?"

Her floating face smiled. "Really."

When she'd collected enough arrow-plant tubers, she grabbed some leafy green plants growing on the surface before hoisting herself into the bow. Standing in the canoe with perfect balance, she scooped the gobs of muck off her legs, flipping them back into the water. Then she sat in the bow and grabbed the paddle. "Let's go. We're having a grand supper tonight." Her voice trilled with anticipation.

Seeing her naked again, I said something stupid. I couldn't help myself. "Aren't you going to get dressed?"

She didn't even turn. "Not till the next lake. I can't rinse off in this mucky water. I'll get my nice new clothes all dirty." She pulled a powerful stroke to set our direction. "Keep the canoe in the middle of the stream." She was letting me stern the canoe—women's work.

That night for supper, she soaked some of our jerky in water while cooking the arrow root. It didn't smell like mashed potatoes, but it looked like it. When it was done, she added some tallow from our reserves and some of the leafy greens and fried the soaked jerky. She left some of the arrowroot drying on the rock, mashed it with a clean rock, and added it to the sauce. It thickened to bubbling gravy. With the hatchet, she slit a piece of cedar into two flat boards. She served my plate. "Mashed arrowroot and venison with gravy on a shingle. You can't get that at the finest restaurants."

The flavor was wild. The taste exploded in my mouth. "This is great." I started eating too fast, but I realized there were no seconds, so I slowed down, savoring and chewing each mouthful. I scooted next to her and held her face, cleaning the gravy off her chin with my finger and putting it on her tongue. "I am very thankful."

She licked my finger. "I'm glad."

After a refreshing swim in the moonlight, we crawled under the canoe to listen to the loons and fall sleep. We used our tent floor to cover up, rolling our vests for pillows. I was so comfortable that I knew I would have no trouble sleeping. Besides, we had paddled enough to make my shoulders sore.

I kept my loincloth on, but Lily didn't. "I can't sleep with anything constricting me," she said. "I've always slept nude, even as a little girl. It exasperated Heidi. She was forever buying me pajamas that I never wore." My hand found its proper place near her umbilicus.

Breakfast the next morning was jerky washed down with wintergreen tea. She found the leaves along the portage trail next to our camp. After a morning swim, we dressed. Lily said, "Inspect the canoe for leaks. There is a lot of sap on these trees, and we can fix them if there are any."

I hauled the canoe into the water and inspected each of the now-black nubbins on the bottom of the canoe. "No leaks!" I yelled.

"Great. Let's get going then."

Paddling from sunrise till sunset compensated for our two lost days. Her navigation was flawless. How she found the portages and kept her sense of direction across multiple small lakes leading into the large bays of Basswood Lake mystified me. But this was her backyard.

Once we hit Basswood Lake, we felt the strength of the wind. White-capped waves slapped us from the northwest. Our vests staved off the chill. It would have been gruesome to paddle totally exposed. Still, I chilled, but we quickened our pace to stay warm. Not only had my paddling skills improved, but my endurance had as well.

When we arrived at camp just before sunset, she ran off into the woods. I was uncertain why. Did she need privacy to defecate or what? I soon found out when she returned carrying some red things, wild onions, and several varieties of mushrooms. Supper that night was again rehydrated venison steaks with mashed cattail roots and greens but with the flavorful addition of sautéed mushrooms and wild onions flavoring the gravy. Satiated, she offered tea.

"What kind of tea is this?" I said as I sipped the flavorful brew.

"I found some wild roses along the shore and harvested the rose hips. What do you think?"

"It's great. Refreshing."

"Glad you like my culinary delights." Then she became serious. "We should make it to the landing tomorrow. Close to our pickup time if we leave before sunrise."

"Paddle in the dark? Is that safe?"

"With me it is." She smiled. The light of the dying fire cast an orange glow over her face and torso. She had already undressed.

I choked on my tea and swallowed to regain my composure. "I can't tell you what this trip has meant to me. I've never really been in the wilderness, and you have taught me so much. I've learned to be thankful." I had never spent so much time with a naked woman before, but I didn't add that.

She got up from the log she was sitting on and sat next to me, putting her arm around my shoulders. "Does your laceration still hurt?"

"Yes, but I'm healing just fine."

"This trip has meant a lot to me too. After what we've been through, I feel like I could trust you in any situation. I've always been distrustful of men. I didn't like the way guys treated me in high school. They were always fawning over me and didn't really want to know me, the real person."

"I would have died without you, Lily. I respect you and admire your survival skills. I confess that I struggle with you being attractive. But after what we have been through, the physical you is not what makes me respect you."

She hugged me close. "I struggle with that too."

*Did she mean my physique or hers?* I wondered. I didn't want to know, and I didn't ask.

Lily woke me well before sunrise. We went for an awakening swim. It was dark except for the planetarium light above us. Although the moon had set, the stars were bright. I had never seen the Milky Way in such brilliance. Looking out across the lake, my eyes followed the contour of the trees.

She pointed my attention. "See that dip in the trees? That's where the channel is to Jackfish Bay. We are going to swing southeast down to Pipestone Falls. From there, it isn't far to our landing."

We had a breakfast of cold rose hip tea she had brewed the night before and venison jerky because she didn't want to take time to start a fire. In a flash, the canoe was packed, and we were paddling down the lake in the glow of the stars. There was no wind. I took the bow, as I had no idea where to head in the dark. We didn't talk much as we paddled. I had no idea what time it was, but Lily seemed to know. We paddled hard and soon found ourselves paddling down the channel. Without a map, in inky darkness, she paddled right to the portage. I had no experience following a portage trail in the dark and feared I would trip. I wished my flashlight had made it through the fire. However, as my pupils dilated, starlight lit up the trail enough for me to navigate the roots and rocks. We traveled in silence. Lily seemed hypersensitive to the environment, so I didn't want to disturb her concentration.

After sunrise, we switched positions, and I was in the stern as we headed across a large bay and followed the channel of some large lakes. After turning a corner through a narrows, I recognized the bay ahead of us from previous trips out of Ely with my father. I headed for the small island in the distance because I knew the landing we had chosen when we planned the trip was just around the corner to the west. With a few minutes of paddling past the island on the other side, we would be back in civilization. My heart quickened.

"Dock over there," she said, pointing to a gravel beach on the island.

"Do you have to urinate?" I asked, using my proper medical terminology. I felt comfortable now with blunt descriptions of bodily functions.

"Might as well, but I need to do something before we hit the landing."

I urinated in a bush, turning my back toward her to give her privacy. It seemed absurd. When I finished, I turned to find that she wasn't there. I called.

"Over here," she said.

"What are you doing in the bushes?"

She had her vest off and was making holes in our salvaged towel with a stick. "There's another group coming across the lake behind us. Didn't you see them?"

"No, but I haven't been looking behind us." It was probably the last time in a long time I would have the opportunity to see her topless, so I decided to savor the moment.

She saw me gawking and covered her nipples. "You are so male, Barak! Quit staring, Gwiingwa'aage."

I swallowed my drool and shook my head as she went back to working on the towel. "Sorry. It's just that—"

"You're insatiable," she said. "That lecherous look was totally inappropriate." She resumed her work.

"But I'm thankful …" I didn't finish my sentence but put on a serious look, pausing to try to understand what she was doing. "What are you doing?"

"I'm making a bra. There might be other people at the landing. This vest doesn't cover me well." She grimaced at me. "As you happen to know." She tied the long ends of the towel around her trunk and twisted them to the back. She took a leather thong from her hair, tied it to the left triangle, looped it over her neck, and tied the other triangle. "Voilà—a bra. All right, Gwiingwa'aage, let's go," she said, tying her vest so it was snug.

As we paddled around the island and approached the landing, there was quite a commotion. An ambulance was flashing its red-and-blue lights, and a crowd was gathered. "What do you think this is all about?" I said. "I don't have my watch, but I don't think we are that late, are we?"

"Now aren't you glad I made that bra, or wouldn't you care?"

"I'm glad, and I care." I suddenly saw our families. "Hey, I think that's Autumn talking to my mother." I waved and shouted. "There's Jason and Beth. This is exciting to have a greeting party. But what are they all doing here?"

"And there's Heidi. I wonder what's up." She waved. "Hey, Mom."

As we hit the shore, a cheer went up. The EMTs swarmed around us. "Are you all right? Were you affected by the fire?" one of them asked.

"We're fine." I squeezed my way to Jason and Beth as Lily raced toward Heidi and Autumn. "What's this all about, Jason? Are we late for our pickup? I lost my wristwatch."

Jason, Beth, and my mother hugged me with tears streaming down their faces. I turned to see Lily engulfed by Autumn and Heidi.

"No, Barak, you're not late; you're right on time." Jason burst into tears. "But we heard about the storm and the lightning causing massive fires. The rescue squads were searching for you. Helicopters and firefighters were rescuing other campers but hadn't seen you. After that hundred-mile-an-hour wind and seventeen separate fires started by lightning strikes, we feared you were trapped or maybe killed. A hundred and fifty thousand acres of Quetico and BWCA have been reported burned to the ground. Some of the fires still aren't controlled, and we knew you were canoeing right through the middle of it. Four people have already been found dead. Lots of people were rescued with major injuries and broken legs and arms. One man is in a coma with a head injury from a tree falling on his head."

"I was so afraid," Mom said, clenching my arm. Tears dribbled down her cheeks. "I thought I'd lost you."

I hugged her. "But we're alive," I said. "We're all right."

She cried on my shoulder. "I lost your father; I didn't want to lose you."

Jason pinched my flank. "Looks like you ate well."

I smiled. "Steak every day for the last three days. Filet mignon venison-style."

"Come on. You're kidding."

"No, that's the absolute truth. Ask Lily. You know that she never lies." I waved. "Lily, come over here. My brother doesn't believe that we ate steak every night."

Lily, Heidi, and Autumn clustered around us as the crowd reformed around an arriving canoe. The ambulance was flashing its lights; the EMTs hovered over the canoe as it hit the landing. The EMTs prepared to remove two campers from the bottom of the canoe. They were covered in blood and looked pretty bad. A young woman had sticks tied to her legs. The boy looked as if he had bad burns on his face and hands.

Heidi hugged me. "Lily told me that you saved her life during the lightning storm."

I looked around. Every eye of our two families riveted on the two of us. News reporters rushed to our sides and pushed their microphones into my face. "Lightning hit a white pine and split it in two. It burst into flames and fell on our tent. A branch of the falling tree hit Lily in the head, knocking her into the rocks. She was unconscious." Lily rubbed the now yellow-green bruise on her face. "All I did was drag her to shelter under a massive rock facing the water. It protected us from the blaze and wind that engulfed our island. It was so hot, and the smoke was so dense it was hard to breathe. I put a wet towel over our faces to filter out the intense smoke so we could breathe. The next morning, she regained consciousness. She had a few bruises and a concussion, but she recovered. Then Lily saved my life. I would have died out there without her survival skills."

The reporters looked delighted with my interview. A photographer asked to take pictures of us, thanked us, and ran to where the EMTs were pulling the victims out of the canoe. Their skill and equipment soon had the two in the ambulance and speeding off to the hospital in Ely.

Ernie, the outfitter, appeared, standing over the canoe and inspecting the damage. I took his arrival as an opportunity to get out of the fray of family. "That canoe is pretty banged up," he said. "But don't worry. I'm just glad you're safe; we have insurance for acts of God."

*Is that what this was?* I wondered.

As we looked over the dents in the canoe and the patched holes, I noticed the crowd and the news reporters gathering around Lily. In my peripheral vision, I saw her sister bring her some clothes from the car to cover her for the cameras. I continued to explain the condition of the canoe to Ernie. "The wind whipped it like a pickup stick all the way across the lake. I straightened out the major dents, and Lily patched the holes with pitch." I smiled at Ernie. "It doesn't leak." I picked up the rolled tent floor. It still held enough jerky for a few more days and the rest of our survival gear.

"Still, I can't rent it out. Do you want it?" asked Ernie.

"Lily!" I yelled. "Do you want the canoe?" She shook her head. "I guess not, Ernie. Maybe you could use it as a trophy for your outfitting business. You could say, 'Our canoes can withstand forest fires,' or 'Sheer-wind tested.' Something like that might be good advertising."

Ernie smiled. "Good suggestion."

Autumn pulled me aside and whispered amid the din. "Nice outfits," she said as she ran her hand down the back of my doeskin vest and padded what my loincloth didn't cover of my buttocks. "It would take Lily at least two days to make these after she killed a deer. What did you two wear while she was making them?"

"I noticed that you got something for her from the car that was less revealing."

"Yes, I did, but you haven't answered my question."

"Nothing," I said, and I looked deep into her brown eyes. I paused and then turned to yell, "Hey, everyone! We need some hot showers and some gooey dessert. Lily only fed me meat and vegetables." She ran up and jabbed me in the rib. I gasped and whispered, "And I was very thankful." I gave her a hug, slipping my hand under the sweatshirt in which Autumn had dressed her. My fingers found their way under her doeskin vest to caress her bare back. "Are you ready for dessert?"

"Sounds good as long as you're thankful, Gwiingwa'aage."

# BACK TO THE UNIVERSITY

SITTING IN THE CAFETERIA AT UMD, I watched snow flutter down outside. Icicle stalactites formed curtains over the large picture window. I missed Lily. I had helped her pack her stuff to transfer to University of Minnesota Law School and helped her move into her apartment 250 miles away. I missed not being able to help her unpack everything, but classes started, and I had to leave her among her boxes. I had no choice. I called a couple of times. She sounded cheerful but busy. She asked about what I was studying and what my professors were like, but we hadn't seen each other in months.

I was tired. In the middle of the night, I screamed awake with images of the lightening and fire. I saw the burning branch striking Lily in the head and her unconscious body falling to the ground. I was drenched in sweat, and my heart was racing. After a cold shower, I returned to bed. Recalling the songs of the loons and the howling of the thankful wolves calmed me enough to fall back to sleep.

Eating mashed potatoes and Salisbury steak made me think back to eating arrowroot and cattail tubers. One bite of Salisbury steak reminded me of the exotic flavor of the venison fillet steaks grilled on a stick. I daydreamed about Lily preparing the hides, cutting the meat to make jerky, and digging arrowroot tubers with her feet while she clung to the side of the canoe.

"May I sit with you, Barak?"

I turned and recognized the silky, waist-length black hair before I saw her face. "Sure, Autumn. Sit down." I stood and held the chair for her. She set her books on the table and sat down with her yogurt and an apple.

"Thanks. Aren't you the gentleman today? How are your classes this semester?"

"Pretty easy. I finished all the requirements for my chemistry major and have all the prerequisites for medical school, so I'm taking fun classes, like geography. How about you?"

"Master's-level classes are much easier than I expected. And I'm having a great time as a teaching assistant." She ate a spoonful of yogurt and took a bite of her apple.

"Have you heard from Lily?" we asked each other simultaneously, and we both answered, "Not for a couple of weeks." Then we laughed together.

"We're getting along better as sisters now that I don't have to guard my wardrobe." She smiled. I realized what beautiful features Autumn had as she brushed her long hair back behind her ear and took another bite of her apple.

"I've struggled," I said in a whisper. "She always provoked me to study, so I've been less disciplined since she left."

"She was such a slob in the apartment I can't imagine how she made you more disciplined."

"She chastised me if I hadn't spent time studying, no matter how sloppy you thought she was."

"I suppose." She spooned the last of her yogurt into her mouth and munched on her apple. "So how are your professors this semester?"

As we talked about classes, I noticed how long and delicate her fingers were, yet her hands looked strong. She wore little makeup that I could tell, as her Anishinabe complexion needed little enhancement, and her lips needed no accent. As she changed positions, her lanky frame shimmered in her satin blouse. The silver jewelry on her wrists tinkled when she moved her hands. She smelled like roses. I recalled the smell of her room the day Jason and I had visited many years ago.

She set down her spoon and put her hand on mine. Her touch was like silk. "You avoided my question at the landing."

"What question?" But I knew which question I hadn't answered, and I was still afraid to tell her that we had spent the time naked together.

Her dark brown eyes met mine. "Let me ask you again then. What did you wear for two days while Lily was tanning the doe hide?"

I swallowed hard. The Salisbury steak seemed stuck in midchest. "I did answer you. Maybe you didn't hear me. I said, 'Nothing.' Our clothes were burned up in the fire. We were skinny-dipping when the lightning struck. Our clothes were in the tent. Lightning hit an old oak tree near the tent. It split the tree in half, and the blazing timber landed on our tent. It exploded. We lost everything. All we had was the scorched bottom of the tent. I think that was because of the deluge of rain that followed."

"And you slept together under the canoe?"

"For warmth. It got cold at night."

"And you never had sex?"

"Never." I swallowed. "I think Heidi must have made her promise no sex when she agreed to let us go together."

"I was there, Barak. Heidi never said anything like that. If Lily said that, she made it up."

"Lily never said that; I presumed it." Now I was confused. "I do love her, you know."

"Do you really?" She put her elbows on the table. "Why should I believe you?'

I thought about how I should answer. Anything I said could and would be used against me. I stared at her. "To start with, she is very beautiful." I didn't want that to be the criterion, so I added, "She's intelligent, athletic, and skillful." Unsure how she was taking my answers, I added, "And she saved my life."

"That's all vanity, Barak. Would you still love her if all that was taken away? Everything you said only benefits you. I would say that you like her because she runs around naked half the time, and that flatters your fragile male ego. Do you love her more than that?"

I puzzled over her question as I stared into her expressionless face. *What should I say?* Lily was fun and exciting, but maybe that was vanity too. I decided to plead ignorance. "What do you mean, Autumn? I took her home when she got drunk that time. That did not flatter my ego."

She braced her fists on the table, looking at me like a voracious wolf. "What sacrifice would you make for her? That's the kind of love she needs. Granted, you took her home when she got drunk, but prove to me that you love her for her benefit." She stood, gathered her books, and walked away.

Did Autumn like me, or was she just trying to protect the sister she was always fighting with? I couldn't tell. She seemed suspicious of my affection toward Lily.

Lily promised to come back to town for Christmas vacation on her way north to Nett Lake. We agreed to meet at an Italian restaurant for dessert. Autumn, Jason, Beth, and I were seated at a round table in the corner, waiting for her. Jason and Beth were celebrating their engagement.

"When is the big wedding day?" asked Autumn.

"We want to get married April fifteenth," Beth said as she took a sip of her champagne. "Jason will be ready to take his certified public accountant exam, and he already has some nice job offers."

"That's great." Autumn took Beth's hand and admired her diamond. "I certainly wish you the best. If I know Jason, he will make a kind and gentle husband."

Beth lowered her eyes. "I really feel blessed." She turned and gave Jason a kiss.

"So what are your colors going to be?"

I was not the least interested in wedding plans, so I turned to Jason while the women continued. I was drinking beer. "Are those CPA classes difficult?"

"Pretty easy compared to undergraduate classes but a lot of detail." He was holding Beth's hand to his cheek.

"Where are you going for your honeymoon? Made any plans yet?"

"I've thought about Jamaica."

We talked about resorts and beaches, flights to various destinations, and exotic cuisine. It kept me distracted from worrying about Lily. She was a half hour late.

When she walked into the restaurant, all eyes turned, the restaurant hushed, and I stood. She gave me a warm hug after she walked to our table. She looked vibrant. She had her hair cut short in the back, with dangling braids beside her face, just like when I first had seen her. Silver strands and thin green satin ribbons were woven into the braids that bounced on her chest as she walked. Her tight forest-green sweater did not even come close to meeting her short leather skirt. A thin silver chain belt accented her midriff.

"Is that what you wear to law school?" asked Autumn.

"Usually I wear less." She paused, smiled at her sister, and then finished her sentence. "Formal clothing." I watched her abdominal muscles ripple as she took a chair between Jason and me.

"Still exercising?" I asked.

"Run three to five miles a day and work out at the gym three days a week. It helps me study."

"You still have time to study?" asked Autumn.

"I read all this stuff, and then when I'm exercising, I play it over in my mind. Then I'm ready for the tests."

The waitress came to take our dessert orders and asked Lily what she wanted.

"Diet Coke and chocolate cheesecake," she answered, raising her eyebrows at me. When the waitress left, she whispered in my ear, "Had a lot of desserts lately, Gwiingwa'aage?"

No one else seemed to catch what she said, but I caught the sarcasm. Besides, the table conversation focused on the upcoming wedding plans. The others ignored us.

"Several fine desserts, and I've been thankful for each one," I said. "You heard that I was accepted to University of Minnesota School of Medicine?" Though I was only speaking to Lily, suddenly, the whole table erupted in congratulations. Lily made me stand up and gave me a hug.

After heartfelt hugs from Autumn and my brother and a sweet handshake from Beth, Lily announced to the whole restaurant, "My best friend, Barak Shelton, has been accepted to University of Minnesota Medical School!" The restaurant erupted in applause. Lily took me to the center of the dining area to dance. The maître d' turned up the background music, and we danced. She was hard to keep up with and led the entire dance.

Breathless, I resumed my place at the table, embarrassed by the scene we had made. Lily squeezed my thigh under the table. I was going to return the squeeze, but her skirt was so short, and I was having enough problems with her outfit and what had just transpired. I didn't need more limbic stimulation.

"What's law school like?" Autumn asked after we were all situated and calm. Lily provided an animated description of her professors and some of her classmates. She soon had the whole table laughing. Beth seemed stunned by some of Lily's vocabulary, but she couldn't help giggling over her antics.

Lily asked about Beth and Jason's wedding. They recited the details of dresses and church decorations. I contributed little to the conversation, and Autumn didn't seem to have much to say either. We finished our desserts.

After Lily spooned the last of her cheesecake into her mouth, Autumn stood and excused the two of them. "Lily and I need to head north to the reservation for the holidays. Heidi is expecting us tonight, and we still have a long drive. It was great seeing all of you." She turned to say something to Lily. I strained to hear their whispered conversation, but they were too far away.

All of my feelings surfaced for this magical woman. Lily was amazing and unconventional. She was the only woman I had ever felt that strongly about. Seeing her made my spirit feel refreshed.

# MEDICAL SCHOOL

AT LILY'S INSISTENCE, I HAD applied to medical school, still uncertain if I would be accepted. In the back of my mind, I thought I would have appreciated being rejected to prove to her that I'd had enough of school. But I was accepted at the University of Minnesota, Minneapolis. I moved to the cities and started classes the following September. I felt ambivalent. Medical school was tough. All my dread of school returned in a flash. I moved into the medical fraternity house. I wasn't a joiner, but everyone else in the frat house was a medical student, and the rent was cheaper than any apartment I could find.

Now that I was in the cities as well, I considered moving in with Lily. She probably would have let me, considering my brother status, but her apartment was on the wrong side of campus, and besides, I figured two weeks naked together was as much as I could handle. I didn't want or need the distraction. However, we did spend a lot of time together. She resumed her role, challenging me to study.

I was excited the day I received my new oto-ophthalmoscope. It arrived by parcel post on Friday, and I wanted to use it as soon as possible. We had been learning how to take a history from a patient, and the next phase was to learn to perform a physical exam. Monday morning would be our initiation to head and neck examination.

I called Lily. "Are you busy this evening, studying for a test or anything?"

"I have a test on Monday, but I just need to review my notes Sunday night. I'm free tonight. Why?"

"I just got my new toy for examining eyes and ears, and I wanted to practice on you."

"Then come over. I was just going to watch a movie."

On the way, I reviewed the head and neck exam in my head: *Check the pupils to see if they react to light, check eye movements, check hearing, and look at the tympanic membranes.* Our professor had told us to learn a pattern so that we did the exam the same way each time. I thought through my routine as I drove.

I tapped on her door. "Come in," I heard between deep breaths. She was doing chin-ups on a bar wedged in her bedroom doorway. She was wearing sweatpants and an oversize T-shirt. She was tall enough that she had to keep her knees bent. I could do chin-ups, but she was a lot faster and smoother than I was. I hoped she didn't ask me to do a set.

"Hi, Barak. Be done in a minute. Forty-eight. Forty-nine. Fifty." She straightened her legs and landed like a cat in the doorway. She gave me a hug. "Where's your new toy?" Her sweat smelled like pinesap.

I opened the shiny black case and showed her my oto-ophthalmoscope. I put in the batteries and attached the otoscope. "Can I look in your ears?"

"I hope they're clean." She sat on the kitchen chair. The hair behind her ears curled with perspiration.

I started with her right ear. I had to adjust my head so things were in focus. At first, I saw a red blur. I moved my head back and forth and still saw nothing. I turned the scope to the left.

"Ouch. Straighten your approach."

*How does she know what I'm doing wrong?* I wondered. But she was right. My hands were sweaty as I straightened the scope, and there was her tympanic membrane, as crystalline and beautiful as I had seen in the textbook. "I can see it, and it's normal," I crowed. "And there's no wax."

"Good. I'm glad I have no excess cerumen. Now look in the other one. I have two ears, you know."

*Where did she learn that?* I was always amazed at her vocabulary. Looking in her left ear was awkward. I was so right-handed. As I switched hands, I fumbled with the scope and stepped back to take a breath.

"Don't hold your breath when you're doing the exam. Just breathe normally."

*Who does she think she is, telling me how to do this?* I took a deep breath and forced myself to breathe in a rhythm. My hand was less shaky, and though it felt awkward, she was correct; I now could see into her ear canal. "Your left tympanic membrane is normal too."

"Great. There's no blood dripping out? No trauma?"

I relaxed my arms. I was getting a cramp in my shoulder. "You sound like a lawyer. Of course there's no blood."

"I'm not a lawyer yet; I haven't taken the bar exam."

I ignored her, pulling off the otoscope. It became a bright flashlight. "Open your mouth, and say, 'Ah.'" She did. "You have beautiful tonsils."

"No one has ever mentioned my tonsils being beautiful." She giggled.

I set down the scope and felt her neck for lymph nodes. I ran her thyroid between my fingers. "Your lymph nodes are nice, and your thyroid is as smooth as silk." I was really getting into the exam. "I need to look in your eyes."

I had talked to some of the second-year students at school, and they'd told me that using the ophthalmoscope was tricky. You had to look through the tiny hole, adjust the lenses to see the cornea, and then zoom back to see the retina. I put the ophthalmoscope head in place and turned the light onto my hand. It worked. I leaned over to look through the hole. I couldn't find her eye as the light wandered over her face.

I stood up and took a breath. "Open your eye real wide," I said, as if that would help. She sat motionless as I tried again. I felt like a bombardier trying to find the target.

She moved her head away. "You're holding your breath, Barak. You'll run out of oxygen before you find my eye."

"Could you sit on the table? When we examine patients, they are up on an exam table, which is a little higher. That might be easier." I said it with authority, as if I really knew the solution.

She pushed aside the place mats and sat on the dining table. I took a deep breath, exaggerating my breathing so she wouldn't criticize me. I searched for her eye. As soon as I found her pupil, I started turning the lenses. For just a flash, I saw the blood vessels in her retina. "I saw them!" I shouted.

"Are mine normal?"

"I have no idea, but I saw them."

"Before you start dancing, try my left eye."

I knew that would be difficult. I had to hold the scope in my left hand and then use my left eye to look through it. Everything was black. I had closed both eyes. I held my right eye closed with my right index finger and stared with my left eye through the tiny hole. I was on a mission to find her eye.

"Breathe," she commanded.

I started breathing slowly as I edged closer to her face. Her breath wafted into my nose. It smelled of wintergreen. I found her sclera and knew the pupil was nearby. Slowly edging up, I caught a whiff of her perfume. I turned and sneezed, knocking my head into my scope.

She jumped off the table. "Did you bring your running shorts? Let's go for a run. You can try again when we get back." She stripped off her sweatpants and T-shirt. She had on jogging shorts and a sports bra underneath.

"My stuff is in the car."

"Change, and let's go."

I ran down to the car, brought my gear back, and changed. We ran out the door together. A block away from her apartment was a trail that wound around a series of city lakes. There was a paved trail for bicyclers and a dirt trail for runners. I could beat her in a short sprint but not in an endurance race, so she let me set the pace. The lakes were choppy, but the wind felt good on our skin. The scent of flowering trees and shrubs spurred us on. We passed most of the runners on the path, but a thin, emaciated person with a faded marathon shirt shot past us. About three miles into our run, we slipped past the back side of a canoe rental and returned on the other side of the lake. "I just couldn't sit still any longer," she said. "Too much pent-up energy. I needed this run."

I was panting too hard to say much. "Yeah, me too," I managed.

A block away from the apartment, I was ready to cool down to a walk. She noticed my slackened pace. "Race you to the shower!"

I tried to sprint, but my legs felt like rubber. She beat me to the door and then sprinted up the stairs. I gave up and climbed the stairs in pain, trying to catch my breath. The apartment door was unlocked. I could hear the water running as I came inside. She'd shed her sports bra, shorts, and panties outside the bathroom door. I collapsed onto a kitchen chair with my elbows on my knees.

She exploded out of the bathroom door with a towel wrapped around her waist. "Your turn," she said, and she dashed into her bedroom. "Extra towels in the cabinet."

"Gosh, she's beautiful," I said to myself as I picked my aching body off the chair. My bare legs stuck to the wood. My pants pinched as I stood. I was desperate for a shower.

As I learned more history-taking and physical exam skills, Lily let me practice on her. It relaxed me when I went to the hospital to examine patients. I was desensitized to Lily's torso, so when I practiced a heart and lung exam, I felt calm and professional. An abdominal exam was difficult because she was so muscular, but I was sure I felt the edge of her liver. It seemed firm. I was sure our professor had said the liver was supposed to feel soft. I couldn't find her spleen, and her deep organs were obscured by her muscles. An extremity exam was easy, as her muscles were well defined, and her joints were so flexible I could practice all the exam tests without hurting her.

She seemed cavalier about the whole thing and sometimes read a book she needed to study while I was examining some distant part of her anatomy, such as checking lower-extremity reflexes. She would tease, "You done yet? If not, I need another book." One time, as I was going through the knee exam, she said, "If you don't hurry, I will be diseased before you finish, and you'll have to start all over." We always finished with a big bowl of popcorn before I drove back to the frat house. They were lax about curfew, but I had decided I would never stay overnight in her apartment.

The last part of our training before we were allowed to do complete history and physical exams on admissions at the hospital was a breast and genital exam. We divided into two groups and practiced on plastic models in the simulation laboratory. On the day we were to practice on people, my half of the class was to do a male exam the first day and then switch to a female exam the next day. We had male models from the art school, but it was no problem. I examined myself for practice the night before. One of the women in my class told me she was squeamish, but we performed the exams with faculty present to monitor our professionalism. She gave me the victory sign as she walked out of the exam room. She told me later she had maintained her composure with the male model.

The night before the female examination, I reviewed the details and called Lily.

"Sure, come on over. I'll make popcorn," she said.

When I arrived, she was sitting on the couch in a flannel shirt and shorts, watching the National Geographic Channel—something about lemurs in Madagascar. I sat on the couch, and she passed me the popcorn. My hands were sweaty, and the popcorn felt greasy. I ate a few kernels, but they didn't seem to sit well. When the program was over, she turned off the television, grabbed my hand, and took me to her bedroom. "All right, what do we do first?"

"I'm supposed to inspect your breasts for dimpling or skin changes."

She whipped off her shirt. "Do you see any?"

I inspected her breasts, forcing myself to be clinical in my observation. "They look completely normal."

"Good. What's next?"

"I'll have you lie down and palpate for lumps."

She got comfortable on her back and raised her arms over her head.

"I'm supposed to use the flat parts of my fingers, not the tips," I said. "When was your last menses? I am supposed to ask that first. Breasts feel different just prior to menstruation."

"My last menses was ten days ago."

"All right." I had no idea how breasts felt different, but I was glad Lily was not about to menstruate. As I put my fingers on her breasts, I realized that despite the canoe trip, listening to her heart, and all we had been through together, I had never touched her breasts. My hands were dripping with perspiration. "I am supposed to go in a circular motion like this." I started with upper breast and followed the pattern outlined in our textbook. "I'm supposed to finish palpating over the areola and the nipple, and then I check each axilla," I said as I followed my spoken instructions. Her axillae were moist.

She looked up. "Is the wolverine supposed to come out of the forest, Gwiingwa'aage?"

I looked at my pants and was embarrassed.

She covered up. "I don't think that's particularly professional, Barak. Go take a shower, and you can try again another time."

I was so embarrassed that I left for the bathroom.

When I came out of the shower, dressed and feeling more composed, she was dressed, sitting on the sofa. She handed me some hot chocolate. We sat on opposite ends of the sofa and watched the news. When the news was over, I got up to leave. I was still sweating. I swallowed. "I'm so sorry."

"Don't be embarrassed, Barak. That reaction was natural. Isn't that my job as your sister to desensitize you so that doesn't happen when you examine patients? That is my role, you know. I'm your"—she smiled—"physician's muse."

Tears dripped off my cheeks. "I was supposed to learn to do a pelvic exam too." I held up the disposable plastic speculum I'd brought.

She led me to the door. "Later, Barak. I've got to get up early tomorrow. I've got a long day planned."

As I walked to my vehicle, I was glad she had refused, although she hadn't really refused. Maybe my foible had made her embarrassed too, but I doubted that. Still, I felt the experience of palpating her breasts would make me more confident and professional in the morning when we were supposed to examine female models. I hoped none would be as attractive as Lily.

Professor Lewis was consistently serious as he explained the process of eliciting history and examining patients. His teaching provoked the confidence we needed to obtain a complete history and perform a comprehensive examination. The next week, we would be assigned patients on the medical ward at the hospital. This was our last chance to master our skills. He reviewed the breast exam and asked for questions. No one raised a hand.

"Now, the pelvic exam is vital to a woman's health. Routine Papanicolaou smears have saved more women's lives than any other examination. It is important that you learn to do this properly. We have paid female models for you to practice the exam. They have had many pelvic exams, so do not feel intimidated. Feel free to ask them questions about your technique, such as if the speculum insertion is uncomfortable or not. They have been instructed to tell you. When you have completed the exam, the physician attending will ask the woman for feedback about your performance. Listen carefully to what she says."

He looked at his clipboard and held it up. "You will be graded on your performance according to the printed criterion. Review your sheets before you begin. Are there any questions?" He looked around the room. No one raised a hand. "You must pass this examination before you will be allowed to examine patients in the hospital or clinic."

The student behind me whispered, "They're probably prostitutes."

Professor Lewis might have heard him, because he added, "You will be graded on your professionalism." Then he said, "All right, you will take turns, so we have stations set up with plastic models. Practice the breast exam and pelvic exam on the plastic models until it's your turn to examine the women who have agreed to teach you this important exam."

I was glad I wasn't first, but I was nervous being last. I had practiced on the jelly breast models and the plastic half woman enough to be bored. Yet my stomach knotted up when my name was called. *I'm supposed to introduce myself and shake the model's hand first,* I reminded myself.

I walked into the exam room and grabbed the doorframe to keep from fainting. There was Lily, sitting on the exam table in a hospital gown. I was trembling as I extended my hand to her. "I am medical student, Barak Shelton." The preceptor, standing to my left, noted my introduction on his clipboard.

"It's nice to meet you, soon-to-be-doctor Shelton. I'm Lily Barton."

Next, I was supposed to explain the procedure. I hesitated, trying to recall what I had memorized. Thinking through the phrases and automatic speech helped slow my heart rate as I recited the explanation, but my hands were sweating, and I felt the sweat dripping down my back.

Approaching her did not improve my confidence. "I need to do …" *What next? Oh, I need to examine her breasts.* I stumbled in forming my words. "A breast exam." I untied her gown and explained the breast inspection. Lily had a tiny red spot on her right breast that I had seen innumerable times. I focused on it to stabilize myself.

"Is this mole anything to worry about, Doctor?" she asked.

"No, I believe it is benign. It's called a Campbell de Morgan spot." I remembered that from the dermatology lecture and hoped I sounded authoritative. "Let me have you lie down. The next step is to palpate your breasts." I explained the procedure and noticed that the attending made another check mark on his clipboard. I was thankful for the practice the night before. The texture of her breasts at least felt familiar as I asked about her last menses. I put her exam gown back over her shoulders and tied it behind her neck. "Now I am going to perform a pelvic exam. Have you had one before?" It was part of the protocol to ask, but it seemed foolish in the present situation. She had probably had a dozen that day alone.

"Yes, I have, Dr. Shelton. I am familiar with the procedure."

I explained the procedure anyway and noted that the attending put another check mark on the clipboard.

"Slide down as I put your feet in the stirrups." I put on my exam gloves. "Till you feel my hand on your bottom." I bit my lip. She slid into position. "That's right. You're perfect." *She probably already knew that.*

"Now you will feel me touching you." I raised the sheet. I saw perspiration between her thighs and labia. *Maybe she's nervous too,* I thought to console myself, but I wasn't convinced. I divided her labia and put my fingers into her vagina, attempting to relax her pelvic muscles. I felt her cervix touch my finger. "Is that uncomfortable?" I was supposed to ask that. Another check mark went on the faculty's clipboard.

"No. It feels fine."

"Now I'm going to insert the speculum. There will be a clicking sound. It's just the speculum clicking into position." I put some lubricant on the speculum, but I wouldn't have needed to, as there was plenty from my classmates' exams. The speculum slid into place, and I opened it. Her cervix popped into view.

"Can you see the cervix?" the attending asked.

"Yes."

"Let me check the position." He leaned over, noted the proper position of the speculum and the position of the cervix, and put another check on his clipboard. "Now, under normal circumstances, you would use the cervical brush to remove cells for the Papanicolaou smear. Can you describe the procedure to me? We won't actually do it now."

He handed me the brush, and I explained the process of obtaining the specimen.

"Excellent. You may remove the speculum and do the bimanual exam." He focused on his clipboard, checking several boxes.

I went back to Lily's vagina. She had snuck a stickum on her inner thigh. It read, "O'Duffy's 7:00 p.m., Gwiingwa'aage." I clicked the catch. "I'm removing the speculum now, and I am going to perform a bimanual exam. One hand will be on your belly, and the other will be in your vagina. I will be feeling your uterus," I said as I palpated her uterus between by examining hands, "and each ovary. This may be slightly uncomfortable." I felt Lily's ovaries slide between my fingers. "Everything is normal. You may slide yourself up and sit up."

She slid up the table and sat up. Her gown flopped into her lap. She turned to the attending. "He did a good job—made me feel comfortable and explained things well. But he should have tied my gown back up so I wasn't exposed when I sat up." The attending set down his clipboard, lifted Lily's gown, and tied it behind her neck.

"Correct." He made a note.

After her evaluation, I was supposed to acknowledge her willingness to be examined. "Thank you, Ms. Lily Barton, for allowing me to do this exam. It has been very important for my education."

"You're very welcome, Barak Shelton. You will make a fine physician."

"Ms. Barton, this was the last student," the attending said. "You may get dressed now. We appreciate your patience with our medical students. You may pick up your check at the secretary's desk."

The faculty physician and I walked out together. My heart rate slowed as I thanked him for his feedback. I really didn't care, but it calmed me to tell him.

# O'DUFFY'S BAR

SEETHING WITH ANGER, I DROVE to the bar. O'Duffy's Bar was notorious among students for brawls. Why were we meeting there? Why were we meeting at any bar? *If she returns to drinking, this is going to be ugly. She knows better. She knows she can't handle alcohol. She's in law school. What if she got a DUI? It could tarnish her career. She might be denied taking her bar exam.*

I thought over the afternoon. *She seemed calm, more than I. Did the exam bother her? It bothered me. She planned that stickum-on-her-thigh trick. It wasn't an afterthought. And I remember tying her gown. I know I did.*

I parked my car in the enormous lot and rushed into the bar. It smelled of stale beer and peanut shells. There were already some rowdy students yelling at each other, with the bartender warning them to quiet down. Back in a dark corner, I saw Lily. She was dressed in jeans and a University of Minnesota sweatshirt. Three martini glasses sat empty in front of her. I picked up my pace.

"Lily, you know—"

"Is this your brother?" the bartender asked, bringing a fourth glass. "He doesn't look like you."

"We have different parents. I'm adopted."

"Oh. What can I serve you, sir?"

"Diet Coke would be fine, with a squeeze of lemon. Thanks," I said.

As he left to get my order, my face flushed with anger. I gave Lily a chastising look. "What do you think you're doing?"

"Taste it," she said, "before you say anything you might regret."

I took a sip from her glass. "This tastes like 7Up," I muttered.

She laughed so hard her belly shook. "It is 7Up. That look on your face is priceless. It was well worth four martini glasses of 7Up."

"All these glasses were just 7Up?"

"They were. I promised you I wouldn't drink." She grabbed my hand. "Don't you trust me?"

The bartender brought my drink. "Anything else?"

"Two orders of spicy wings, please," I said.

"Coming right up." He turned to get our order.

"You're buying me wings? How special. I'm the one who got paid." She waved the check over my face. "You had to pay me out of your tuition." She grabbed my cheeks in her hands and drew our faces together. "So tell me," she whispered. "What do my vagina and cervix look like? And were you surprised to see it pop into place? Some of the other students struggled with that."

"Yes, your vagina looked nice," I said. I covered my face. "I can't believe I said that." I shook my finger at her. "Lily, I will never forget what you did to me today. I nearly fainted."

"I know. You looked as white as a ghost. It was so funny I had trouble keeping a straight face."

"You had trouble?" I said, my teeth grinding. I took a deep breath. "And that gown trick. I know I tied it when I finished your breast exam."

"You did." She laughed as the wings arrived.

"I'll get graded down for that, you know."

"Not much." She put a wing in her mouth and stripped off the meat. "These are great."

"Professor Lewis said that the models have worked for him before. That you are experienced." I choked on the word as I tasted one of the wings.

"It's my little contribution to medical education, Barak. Did you think you had my breasts and vagina all to yourself?" She sucked the meat off another wing and tapped the clean bone on my nose. "There is another benefit, you know."

I nibbled some of the meat off my wing, careful to chew before swallowing. I didn't ask; I didn't want to know.

"I get a free Pap smear every year. The first student each year does take a specimen. I'm cancer-free and no gonorrhea, herpes, or chlamydia. Isn't that great?"

"Maybe I don't want to know, but how long have you been doing this?"

"I'm proud to say that I have educated every physical exam class in the last couple years, since I started law school."

"So that's how you knew whether I was using the ophthalmoscope properly and how to breathe so I could listen to your heart and lungs?"

"That's why. Aren't these wings good?"

The bartender appeared. "Can I bring you a 7Up in a regular glass now? And how are the wings?"

"Sure, bring me one more 7Up. The wings are great."

I wasn't finished with my first wing, and my drink was still half-full, so he just brought a 7Up in a regular glass for Lily.

"You still haven't answered me," she said.

"What was the question? I must have forgotten."

"You said my vagina looked nice. What about my cervix? Lots of medical students have gotten to see it, but I've never seen it."

I described her cervix in anatomic terms.

"Like a smiling face, eh? And you said that my vagina looked nice."

I turned red. "Yes, your vagina is all pink and silky. Can we change the subject?"

"All right, but I've been planning this for over a year, ever since you got accepted to medical school. Think of it as my little gift to you." She squeezed my chin. "I was serious, Barak—you will make a fine physician."

The didactic part of medical school seemed routine after that. There were no more Lily surprises. She graduated from law school top in her class, much to the chagrin of some of her classmates who had labeled her as a goof-off.

She studied much less than most. She aggravated her friends when she explained, "I read it once; I got it."

When she graduated as valedictorian, she invited Heidi, Autumn, and the whole Shelton family to her graduation party. She rented the upper floor of a local restaurant and packed the room. Jason and Beth were impressed by the political leaders, including the mayor and several state legislators, who accepted invitations. I overheard Beth when she whispered to Jason, "She looks like a normal person in a black suit with some makeup and modest jewelry. I never expected to see her with her hair in a bun."

She introduced me to several of the dignitaries as "My special friend Barak Shelton. He is soon to be a physician." I brimmed with pride. She was going to introduce me as Dr. Shelton, but I refused. I had one more year of medical school to complete.

Lily passed her bar exams with little effort and joined Cohen, Shapiro, and Associates, specializing in corporate law. When their firm was asked to negotiate with the county the reburial of Native Americans found when they widened Highway 53 to a four-lane freeway, everyone in the firm recognized Lily as the best choice to represent tribal interests. J. T. Cohen offered his help, but she handled the case with skill. That case gave her notoriety in the tribe as well as the county and state government. She soon became involved in several other government corporation negotiations. She became the firm's expert in government disputes and corporate law. Other companies recognized her expertise, and she was instantly busy as well as productive. The Anishinabe community respected her because she continued to negotiate contracts for her tribe gratis. Government lawyers feared her, and Native Americans respected her expertise.

# THE PROPOSAL

DURING MY CLINICAL YEARS OF medical school, I applied for the Rural Physician Associate Program. It provided an opportunity for Minnesota students to work with a rural physician for six months in lieu of basic rotations, such as family medicine. When I was accepted into the program, I found that Dr. Barton was an approved preceptor, so I asked her to be my preceptor. She readily agreed. We got along well, and she was an excellent instructor. I stayed at her house during the rotation and, at her suggestion, occupied Lily's bedroom.

One weekend many months later, Lily said she was coming home for a visit. I took my stuff out of her bedroom and moved into Autumn's room. It was more formal and immaculate, even though she hadn't been home in months. It smelled sweet and delicate from rose and lavender perfume but a little too girlie for me. Lily's room smelled of leather, pine, cedar, and birch. I much preferred her room.

I was excited about the weekend. I helped Dr. Barton make some special pastries that we knew Lily liked, and we roasted bear and venison, served with a wild rice casserole for dinner. We worked together to make her favorite dessert: pumpkin pie. Of all the women I had met, including some attractive, highly intelligent medical students, I loved Lily best. I really wanted to marry her despite how she seemed to shun my advances. There was no one like Lily. I thought her trip home would be a perfect opportunity to propose. I had considered that she might refuse, but I felt it was worth the risk. No one else had made such an impact on my life. I had bought an engagement ring, and I planned to get her alone when Dr. Barton was busy and propose marriage. I planned to pop the question on Sunday night just before she left for the city.

We had fun canoeing and hiking around the lake, and we even caught a few fish. Lily had exciting stories about the court cases she was involved in, as well as funny stories about people mistaking her for a secretary. The weekend was going as planned. I was nervous with anticipation. After dinner on Sunday, I suggested we walk down to the dock. The air was still and fragrant. As the sun set on the horizon, the loons started singing. The bats swarmed into the sky, and the mosquitoes went into hiding.

In the twilight, we sat on the dock, dangling our feet in the water. I stumbled a couple of times while getting ready to ask her and changed the subject. I felt the ring box in my pocket, and my hand was sweaty. "What would you think about getting married someday?" I stammered.

She jumped up and pushed me off the dock. I grabbed the box with the ring in it as I hit the water. I spun around, gasping with aspirated lake water in my lungs.

"Barak, that's ridiculous. I can't marry you. You know better than that. You heard my manitou. You're my adopted brother. That would be incest. Do you think I would walk around in my apartment half-naked and share my innermost thoughts with you if I thought you were some romantic Don Juan?" She looked angry and disgusted. "We have a special relationship granted by the Grandfathers who accepted you as a fire keeper. I can tell you anything. We were like yin and yang on the canoe trip, not ashamed to reveal anything about ourselves to each other. We can tease each other. I love you more than anyone in the whole world. I trust you. You've proven yourself. We've slept together, and you had the integrity not to take advantage of me. I was drunk in your room—something I'm very ashamed of, by the way—and you preserved my dignity even to my prim, proper sister. Don't ruin our relationship." She stormed up the dock, turned on the path to the house, and screamed, "What's the idea? You need to stick your penis up my vagina to satisfy your Gwiingwa'aage? Are you trying to possess me like a thing, destroy my vision, and get me pregnant so I abandon a baby like my parents abandoned me? Forget it. That's disgusting."

My hand cramped as I held the ring box and waded to shore. By the time I got to the house, she had said goodbye to Heidi and left. I slept in Autumn's room that night. Actually, I didn't sleep at all.

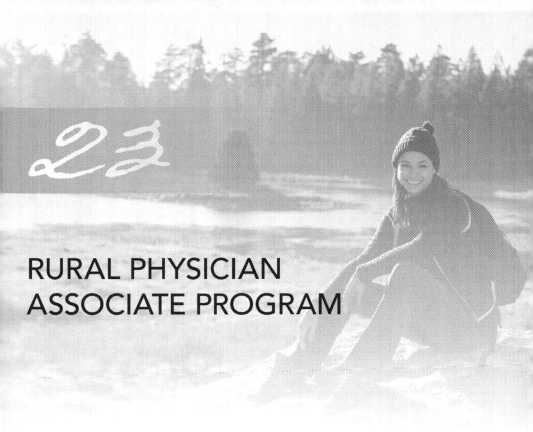

# RURAL PHYSICIAN ASSOCIATE PROGRAM

THE NEXT MORNING, AS I lay in Autumn's bed, my emotions were reeling from Lily's reaction. *She's the one who made me go to UMD. She's the one who made me go through all these medical school requirements. She's the one who made me apply to University of Minnesota Medical School. And now she's rejected me.* I wanted to quit medical school, run away, and never see her or a patient ever again.

There was a knock on Autumn's door. "Barak, I got a call from the nursing home. There's a new admission. I have an office full of people at the clinic. I need you to go do a history and physical on the admission. Then give me a call?"

"Yes, Dr. Barton, right away." I showered and got dressed. As I climbed the stairs, I found that she had hot cinnamon rolls set out for me.

"Just give me a call when you're done," she said as she ran out the door.

I decided to take my time and do an exceptional job. It would take my mind off Lily. The new patient was a Native American woman who was confused, weak, disoriented, and incontinent. She had been transferred from Memorial Hospital in Virginia, Minnesota, after an acute illness because she couldn't care for herself. I did a careful exam and focused on any neurologic deficits. I tried to obtain a history from her, but she couldn't give me much, so when I finished the exam, I reviewed the transfer records of her acute hospitalization in scrupulous detail. When I felt as if I could present her in formal medical school fashion, I telephoned Dr. Barton's office.

"I finished the history and physical you asked me to do."

"Good," said Dr. Barton. "What did you find? The nurse told me the patient was an elderly Native American woman."

"That's partly correct. She is Anishinabe, but she's not even fifty years old, although she looks much older. Her name is Natalie Cross. Her blood pressure, temperature, and pulse are stable. She is confused and disoriented to where she is but knows her name. Her eyes are yellow; she is quite jaundiced, with rather nice hair. She has lots of spider angiomas all over her chest—no breast nodules. Her heart and lungs sound normal. Her belly is swollen with ascites, and her liver edge is as hard as a rock. There is some edema in her ankles. The pelvic exam shows an inflamed cervix, and she has large rectal hemorrhoids. I'm certain she has cirrhosis of the liver. The records document that she's an alcoholic, but I think she is too cirrhotic for just alcohol."

"You think she had hepatitis in combination with alcohol abuse?"

"That's what I think. May I order a hepatitis profile? The referring physician thought she was just an alcoholic, treated her for aspiration pneumonia, and transferred her here, so none of that's been done."

"Sounds like you have put some good thought into the case. Go ahead and order whatever you think she needs, and I'll cosign it when I finish with clinic. I still have a few patients to see."

"Dr. Barton?"

"Yes, Barak?"

"There is one more thing."

"What is it?"

"When she was more lucid than she is now, she told the doctor …" I paused. "I read this in her transfer records. She had a baby and, I quote, 'left it in a box at the doctor's office.' I think she may be Lily's mother." I choked, hardly able to get the last words out of my mouth.

"Are you sure, Barak? I have searched all over the reservation to try to find Lily's mother. Check the records carefully, and I'll review them when I get there."

"The time fits with Lily's birthday, although I know that was plus or minus a day or so from when she appeared on your desk."

"Barak, try to get more records from her previous physicians, and I'll get there as quickly as possible."

The hour I waited for Dr. Barton was the longest hour of my life. I got more records faxed to the nursing home from a hospital where she had been five years prior, checked dates, and confirmed the latest physician's report with a history taken when she was completely oriented. The same history was recorded.

Dr. Barton was silent as she reviewed the reams of faxed documents. She put her glasses down and let out a deep sigh. "I think you're right, Barak. But let's treat her with lactulose and see if she becomes more lucid. That often decreases the hepatic encephalopathy, and even in end-stage liver disease, the patient's orientation improves."

I paid special attention to Natalie's laboratory results. I checked her orientation every morning before I joined Dr. Barton at the clinic. Four days later, her mind was much clearer, so I called Dr. Barton. "She knows who she is and where she is. She's completely oriented this morning." I swallowed. "She repeated the story of having a child when she was a teenager."

"Things are slow here at the clinic, so I'll be right over."

When she arrived, she introduced herself. "Mrs. Cross? Natalie Cross? I'm Dr. Heidi Barton." She paused to see if there was any spontaneous recognition.

"It's nice to finally meet you, Dr. Barton. This handsome young fellow has been doing a good job taking care of me. He is quite attentive."

"I am glad to hear that. I saw you a couple days ago, but you were a little confused. How are you feeling now?"

"Much better, Doctor. What's wrong with me?"

"You have very severe liver disease—chronic hepatitis."

"Oh." She paused to scrutinize Dr. Barton's face. "You're Anishinabe. Do you speak the gentle people's tongue?"

"I am, and I do."

Natalie switched languages, and periodically, Dr. Barton translated for me. She finally looked at me and said in English, "Here goes." She switched back to Anishinabe, and I could tell it was an intense conversation. Mrs. Cross started to cry, and Dr. Barton put her arm around her. She turned to me. "She remembers the whole incident. She even knows details I have never told anyone. She's Lily's mother. She would like to see Lily before she dies."

"I sure would," Natalie said. "I'm sure she is a fine girl, but I couldn't take care of her. You understand, don't you, Dr. Barton?"

"I understand, Natalie."

I sat down on the chair beside the bed. I felt faint. This was Lily's missing mother. "Natalie?" I said.

"Yes, Doctor?"

I had given up trying to convince her I was still a medical student. "I'll call your daughter tonight, and we'll arrange a meeting."

"Thank you, Doctor. I never dreamed I would see her again. She was such a cute little thing; I wanted her to live—to have a chance to really live. Not like me." She started sobbing quietly.

Dr. Barton and I walked out of the room. "Barak?"

"Yes, Dr. Barton?"

"Your job is to watch her electrolytes and give her lactulose so she stays lucid until Lily can come." She stopped and sighed. "If she wants to come." She opened the chart to the order page, signed my previous orders, and handed it to me. "It will be a challenge; she'll get diarrhea from the medicine, and the nurses won't like it, but you must do it."

"Yes, Dr. Barton." I started writing new orders for the lab tests to monitor and the medication Dr. Barton dictated.

"Barak, I meant to tell you this sooner: when we are not in the hospital or clinic, you may call me Heidi."

"Yes, Dr. Heidi Barton, I will."

We walked out to the parking lot. Our cars were parked next to each other. Heidi smiled. "Let's go home. I'm tired, and I put bear ribs in the Crock-Pot for supper. They should be done by now."

"Sounds good, Heidi."

"It will be, Barak."

That night, Heidi had an emotional telephone call with Lily. Most was in Anishinabe, but she switched to English as she told her what Natalie had said to me and that Natalie wanted to see Lily before she died. "Can you handle that, Lily? You don't have to come see her if it will be too difficult."

Heidi handed me the telephone. "Lily wants to talk to you."

I hesitated. "Yes, Lily?"

"So you found my mother. What a brother. You're my best friend. You know that?"

"I love you, Lily."

"I know you do. I love you too, but please don't put any of that romantic crap on me ever again, all right?"

"I'm sorry."

"You ought to be. Now, are you willing to be with me when I come see my real mother?"

"I'm here for you."

"Thanks. Then I'll come. Tell my mother, Heidi—no, both my mothers—that I'll drive up to the reservation on Friday night after work."

"I'll be here. She'll be here too."

"You sleuth, Barak." There was a pause, and I heard a sniffle over the telephone. "I owe you big-time. See you Friday. This is a little emotional for me, so don't be embarrassed if I cry."

"I won't. I might cry too."

"You baby. I'll see you Friday. Oh, did you get your money back on the ring?"

How did she know I had bought a ring? I let out a deep sigh. "Yes, most of it."

"Good. You shouldn't have done that, but I apologize for being so harsh. I'll see you Friday."

"Thanks for the apology," I said, but she had already hung up. I handed the phone back to Heidi. "She's coming Friday."

"Your job is to keep Natalie cogent till Friday. Don't let her slip into a coma. Watch her labs."

"Like a hawk." *For the raven*, I thought.

Natalie became delirious at times during that week, but I checked her laboratory tests, and when something was abnormal, I checked with Heidi as to how to correct it. Friday evening, Natalie was lucid and excited, if not a little apprehensive, to meet Lily. She was incontinent of stool and urine, so fifteen minutes before Lily came, I asked the nursing assistant to help me clean her up. She was surprised I was willing to help.

"None of the other medical students ever helped," she said as we rolled Natalie onto her side and wiped the stool off her bottom.

"I was a CNA before I went to medical school. I'm certified to help you."

The nursing assistant smiled as we worked together. When we were done, I chose a frilly white blouse to put on her that Heidi had donated for the event and pulled the sheets up to her waist. I raised the head of the bed as much as she could tolerate with her distended belly full of ascites.

"Very nice, Dr. Shelton," said the charge nurse.

"I'm not a doctor yet."

"Whatever. You will be soon."

I was standing at her bedside in my white coat with my stethoscope around my neck, when Lily entered. I could tell she was distraught but didn't want it to show. She squeezed my arm so hard I thought her fingernails would draw blood.

"Mother?"

"Yes, dear?"

"I'm Waabigwan-atewaniin."

"You're my daughter?"

"Yes, Mother." Lily swallowed hard at the word. Tears dripped down her cheeks. I grabbed for the bedside tissues.

"You're a beauty. Let me hold your hand."

Lily extended her hand. Frail, emaciated fingers reached out and clasped Lily's hand. "I'm Natalie. Before you say another thing, I have to ask you something."

"Yes, Mother?" Lily wiped her cheeks.

The frail woman winced with discomfort, patting her distended belly. "It's just like being pregnant." She tried to push herself up in bed.

Lily gave me a questioning look.

"It's fluid from her liver failure." I let go of Lily and helped Natalie get comfortable.

"Waabigwan-atewaniin, my dear, can you forgive me? I couldn't take care of you. I was doing drugs and drunk all the time. And the guy who got me pregnant beat me and left me in a dumpster behind a cheap motel. That would have been no life for you."

"Mother, I forgive you. You did make a good decision in giving me to Dr. Barton. She has taken good care of me."

"You give her a hug for your old mother because you came out beautiful. She is taking good care of me too. She sent this handsome young doctor to watch over me."

"Thank you, Mother. Yes, I'll give her a hug. This is Barak. He's a medical student working with Dr. Barton."

"I would say he has mostly been working with me. Now that we've gotten that over with, sit down here, and tell me what you have been doing."

Lily sat down on the edge of the bed but grabbed my hand for support. "I'm a lawyer, Mother. I work for the tribe sometimes." She changed languages and started talking in Anishinabe. Natalie clapped her hands, obviously delighted. They talked for a long time. Periodically, Lily would switch to English because she did not know a word or phrase in Anishinabe. I just stood there, oblivious to the conversation.

Natalie put both hands on Lily's cheeks. "You turned out just fine. I'm awful tired now, but thank you for coming. Your Anishinabe is pretty good. Dr. Barton taught you well." She reached for the electric controls and lowered the head of her bed. "You go now. I'm too tired to talk anymore." She closed her eyes. "Besides, the Great Spirit has answered all my prayers."

Lily collapsed in my arms as I helped her up off the bed and walked her out of the room and down the hall. The sanitized air betrayed the dying patients in the rooms we passed. The fluorescent lights were dimmed, as it was past midnight. The charge nurse waved as we passed the bustle of activity at the nurses' station. I pushed the security lever to let us out the door into the night air. Lily relaxed as she took a deep breath of cedar and pine.

She let go of my hand, and I examined the deep gouges in my skin. "Oh, Barak, I'm so sorry. I didn't realize." She rubbed my hand. "It looks like a lynx clawed you. Now you'll have more scars that I've caused."

"I'll heal. Let's head home. Heidi has a wild rice casserole and a moose roast ready for us."

A week later, Natalie Cross died. I accompanied Lily, Autumn, and Heidi to the funeral at the small chapel on the reservation. A few nurses from the nursing home and some friends of Heidi's came, but the pews were mostly empty. Lily sat beside me, gripping my hand, her perspiration stinging my healing skin.

"I wish I could have gotten to know her better," Lily said at the grave site as they lowered the casket.

Heidi put her arm around her shoulders. "But she was just suffering."

She cried on Heidi's shoulder. Then she turned and hugged me. "Thanks for being a great physician for me, Barak."

Later, I drove her to Autumn's apartment in Duluth. Autumn and I hugged her and let her cry, be angry, yell, and cry some more, but neither of us said much. After Lily ran and locked herself in the bedroom, Autumn turned to me on the couch. "Now I know you love her."

Many things changed after that day. I finished my requirements for medical school and started residency. Autumn got a job as a social worker in Minneapolis. Jason passed his exams and moved to St. Paul to work as a CPA for a multimillion-dollar business. I matched with the internal medicine residency program at Hennepin County Hospital. It was my first choice since it was clinically oriented, not research oriented, and Hennepin County Hospital had impressive faculty. The best part was that I didn't have to leave Minneapolis, where I had finished my half dozen rotations required for graduation from medical school after completing the Rural Physician Associate Program with Dr. Barton. We kids, as my mother called us, were all moving to the Twin Cities.

# RESIDENCY

"ARE YOU STILL DATING THAT shark? You're going to get bit," Alex, my senior resident, said. I had been an intern for just a few months. This was my first academic medicine rotation. Alex was my supervising resident. He had met Lily at the resident Christmas party.

"Are you sleeping with the enemy?" Kate, the other first-year resident on academic medicine, teased.

I laughed it off. "You guys are just jealous."

"Well, she is one sharp-looking woman. I have to admit that, and I enjoyed talking to her," Alex said. "But it's tacky bringing a lawyer to our residency parties."

"She is a corporate lawyer, not a malpractice lawyer," I said.

"Same ocean of fish," Alex said. "Now, let's get these patients seen. Barak, you have eight patients. You had a new admission last night: an alcoholic with pancreatitis in room 823."

Internal medicine residency was intense, but I loved it. I had graduated from medical school in the bottom of the top third of my class. Lily said I could have done better if I had applied myself, but that was easy for her to say. I still hated hearing the speech, even if it was coming from Lily. But she arranged a surprise graduation party and paid for everything. That was embarrassing because I still had money from Father's life insurance investment fund. I could have used that. Despite the embarrassment, when

Autumn, Jason, and Beth arrived at the party with Mom and Heidi, I was thrilled.

Now, in the middle of my first year of residency, I was learning a lot. Alex Faustino was a sharp senior, despite some of our disagreements about his social and political views. He knew more about my patients after a cursory exam than I knew after an hour-long history and physical, but he sure made us work hard.

Residency was so unlike medical school I had to pinch myself. In medical school, there was time to sit and talk about cases, and we had a few lectures, even during the clinical rotations. Now I was the responsible physician, and it was frightening at times.

Alex looked through his patient list. "Check that chest x-ray on Mrs. Turner. You should have cultures back on Mr. Richards; I'm sure he's septic. Get your notes written with all of today's lab reports so Dr. Brandon knows you've reviewed everything. Know your patients, team. Dr. Brandon doesn't hold your hand; she wants you to know your patients. Now, get going. Faculty rounds are at ten thirty." With that, Kate and I were off to see our patients.

"How are you breathing today, Mrs. Turner?" I asked as I listened to her lungs. Between breaths, she rattled on about her ex-husband. I heard good breath sounds on both sides, but when I looked at the chest x-ray, it looked worse. She had no fever, and her cell count was improved.

"He was just a total idiot, that husband of mine. I should never have married him, but my dad thought he was the best man for me. If Dad wasn't dead already, I'd kick him in the butt."

"I'm sorry about your husband, but your lungs sound pretty good today. You've improved a lot."

"No credit to my idiot husband. He smoked most of my cigarettes."

The nurse interrupted. "You need to see the man in 823 now, Dr. Shelton." It amazed me how much disdain a nurse could put into "Dr. Shelton," but I was just a first-year resident. I needed to show some humility. "His blood pressure is dropping, and he has a temperature of 39.5 centigrade."

I hadn't even seen my new admission yet. The night call team had admitted him and said he was "just an alcoholic with pancreatitis—nothing unusual." When I entered the room, he was flat in bed, breathing in short, panting respirations. I looked at the chart. "Mr. Sprow, I'm Dr. Shelton." He didn't respond, so I yelled, "Richard Sprow, can you hear me?" Still, there was no response. I listened to his lungs. He was gasping for air, and his heart was too fast for me to tell if he even had a murmur. I pulled down his hospital gown. His belly was distended like a balloon. I listened and heard high-pitched tinkling sounds like water dripping in a well. I turned to the nurse. "Please page Dr. Faustino stat."

She ran out the door. In a moment, he answered his page.

"Alex?" I said. "Richard Sprow, the patient with pancreatitis, is very unstable. His blood pressure is dropping, he has a fever, his respirations are agonal, and his belly is blown up like a balloon. I ordered labs and an x-ray, but I think he belongs in the intensive care unit." I paused to listen for his response. The nurse budged my arm with a scrap of paper. "His blood gases are back. He's very acidotic." I read him the results.

"I'll be right there."

Then things got hectic. Mr. Sprow was evaluated by the critical care team and, within twenty minutes, transferred to surgery and whisked off to the operating room. The high-pitched tinkles were a sign of an obstructed bowel. Peritoneal signs suggested he had perforated. "Look at these labs, Barak," Dr. Brandon said. "The amylase is elevated but not the lipase. The night team misinterpreted the elevated amylase because Mr. Sprow was an alcoholic, but pancreatitis causes both lipase and amylase to go up. Besides, this amylase elevation is way beyond what one would expect for simple alcoholic pancreatitis."

Down the hall, we looked at Mrs. Turner's worsening x-ray. I was admonished that there was a lag between radiology and clinical improvement. Mrs. Turner was getting better. In fact, why had I not done the paper work to discharge her? Dr. Brandon wanted to know. I was grilled on the lab reports of my other patients, which I hadn't had time to review because I'd been occupied with Mr. Sprow. When I sat down for a cup of coffee at the end of the day, it seemed like a sedative.

I telephoned Lily when I got home. "Residency is exhausting. I don't know if I can take this. My senior resident is demanding, and my attending wants me to know everything about my patients. I get there an hour early, and I still can't seem to know everything I'm supposed to know. I'm just so tired."

"Call Heidi," she said. Her tone was unsympathetic. "I am sure between patients, she will have time to feel sorry for you."

"Thanks for the compassion," I said.

"That was your problem on the canoe trip: lack of thankfulness. When are you going to learn that lesson? Now start over. Tell me what you are thankful for today, or I will hang up."

I started over. "I'm thankful for what I'm learning. I am thankful that I can make a difference in people's lives."

"That's better. How do you feel now?"

"Better."

"Why is it so hard for you to be thankful? You're very privileged, Barak Shelton, to be able to have such an intimate relationship with people when they're sick and vulnerable. Do you know that for every student who got accepted to your medical school, there were seventeen who did not?"

I changed my tone, and we talked. She listened for a while longer and then said, "I've got to go. The National Geographic Channel has a special on Madagascar. You can come over and watch it with me if you want. I'll make popcorn."

"Thanks, Lily, but I think I'll go to bed. I have to go to work tomorrow at five thirty and find more things to be thankful for."

"Say it again without the sarcasm."

I monitored the tone of my voice and repeated the phrase.

"Hang in there, Barak. You're a fine physician."

"You have more confidence in me than I have. Love you. Bye."

She had already hung up.

Each day was a little easier, especially if I stopped to correct my attitude. When Lily came over for supper, she allowed no complaining. If I started, she would stand, put on her coat, and go to the door to leave. That always stopped me. I never did persist long enough in my complaints to see if she would leave. I was too intimidated.

I did enjoy my patients—well, most of them. They had such interesting tales to tell. Alfred Johnson was missing all the toes on his left foot and three toes on his right. I admitted him for pneumonia and asked how he'd lost his toes.

"I was foolish in my younger days. My friend Hank and I were prospecting for gold in Colorado. We found some too. Not enough to fill your pocket, but just enough to buy a case of whiskey. Hank and I headed back up to the mountains to try to find some more. While we were up there in the mountains, we drank our whiskey and got so drunk we didn't notice that the weather was changing. We almost froze to death. Hank and I spent two weeks in the hospital. He lost parts of his ears, and the end of his nose fell off." Alfred laughed. "It was too long to begin with."

"That must have been very painful."

"I escaped the hospital before he did. I left my toes there, but Hank left his feet." He coughed up some green sputum. "They're probably burned up in the incinerator by now, mixed with the smog over Denver."

His white count was elevated, and his chest x-ray looked terrible, but with antibiotics and breathing treatments, he survived. Every day he had a new story about some misadventure in his life that had ended in disaster, so I wasn't surprised when the discharge planner told me he was homeless. I wanted to take him home with me and have him tell me stories every night, but the social worker helped him apply for county assistance and got him a small apartment to live in. His only request was to be within walking distance of the public library. I wondered if some of his stories were fiction, but his missing toes were real.

I loved the stories of the veterans. One older woman was a nurse who'd landed in Germany a couple of days after D-day. She'd gotten a Purple Heart for wounds sustained when a mortar hit the hospital where she was working. She had shrapnel in her legs and chronic phlebitis from the wounds, but her friend had been killed, one of only four women buried in the US Normandy cemetery.

Of course, Lily was right. It was a great privilege to be a physician, and as I became more efficient, I was able to understand that. There were still things that got me down. One night, when I was on the trauma service, I was called to the emergency department for three admissions. The emergency resident, Phil Henderson, was trying to resuscitate a young man in a tuxedo. It was shocking to see so much blood all over the fine, pressed formal clothes. He had several nurses assisting.

"Anything I can do to help?" I asked.

"Go to trauma room two, and check on the bride," Phil said.

"What happened?"

"Drunk driver. He's in trauma room three but seems to be all right."

I ran into room 2. There was only a smattering of blood on her wedding dress, but she wasn't moving, and I got no response when I checked her eyes. The pupils were dilated and fixed. I applied sternal pressure to her chest enveloped in the delicate lace of her wedding gown. Her arms came up, and her feet strained downward. I stroked her feet. The toes went up. "Decorticate posturing, just like I learned in neurology," I said out loud to myself. That was when I noticed something coming out of her nose. I inspected more closely. It was brain tissue mixed with spinal fluid. Her ethmoid plate must have fractured in the crash. Her brains were coming out her nose. I took a quick look at the monitor. Heart rhythm was sinus bradycardia; blood pressure was high but would soon crash. She was brain dead, and I knew she wouldn't make it through the night.

I reported my findings to Phil. "All right," he said, "I'm almost ready to call it quits on the groom too. I'll call neurosurgery for her, but why don't you check over the perpetrator in room three and see if he sustained any injuries?"

I checked the man in room 3. "Mr. Axton, I have to check you over. You've been in a car accident."

He was thrashing around, but his left leg was handcuffed to the bed. I looked out the door and saw a police officer writing his report. "Leave me alone!" Mr. Axton screamed. "Get your shit ass out of here. I need some sleep."

He was moving all extremities well. "Mr. Axton, I'm the doctor. You're in the hospital. You were in a serious car accident. I have to check you."

"No, you don't. I don't care if you're the queen of Sheba. Now, get the fuck out of here. I need some sleep."

I didn't know what to do. I felt like killing him, but that was not my calling. I turned out the lights. He was asleep in no time. In the dim light through the curtain, I examined him without waking him. I listened to his heart, which was normal. I listened to his lungs. There were a few rhonchi and lots of wheezes. He had clearly aspirated. He groaned when I palpated his belly, but there were normal bowel sounds and no rebound tenderness. There was no need for surgery.

I walked out to fill out his chart. "Need any help, Doc?" the police officer asked.

"Thanks, but no. I examined the important things. I think I'll let him sleep and check him more carefully later." I perused the chart. The routine labs were back. They were all normal except for his blood-alcohol level, which was four times legally drunk. I looked up. The nurses were covering the groom with a sheet. Phil had given up. I knew the bride would be dead by morning. The neurosurgeon would try, but his best skills would be futile. Mr. Axton would go through alcohol withdrawal and then refuse to admit he was an alcoholic. He'd spend a few months in jail to protect the public because he would refuse rehab. I had seen this before. I wanted to scream.

I loved cardiology and even thought of specializing. It was exciting to diagnose a myocardial infarction, rush the patient to the catheterization lab, and fix his or her blocked coronary artery. Thirty minutes later, the patient was pain-free, and the heart muscle was salvaged. The patients were appreciative.

"Thanks, Doc. That was a close one," one patient said as he shook the cardiologist's hand. "I could see the gates of heaven before you put that stent thing in me." He turned to me. "Are you going to be a cardiologist when you grow up, Dr. Shelton?"

"Maybe," I said as I discussed his discharge medications. The cardiologist waved goodbye, leaving me to do the discharge orders.

What held me back from becoming a cardiologist was the lifestyle. They were always in the hospital, managing new crises. During the rotation, I spent a lot of time in the hospital just because my attending cardiologist was there. I was exhausted at the end of my cardiology rotation, and it was only one month.

When I turned in my hour logs to our director's secretary, she took one look at them and asked me to wait as she took them to the director. "Dr. Shelton," he said, calling me into his office. "This is unacceptable."

"But I was learning a lot."

"You want to jeopardize our whole internal medicine residency program because you learned a lot?" He sat back in his chair. His expression was strained. "If the American Board of Internal Medicine sees this as a trend, they will put our program on probation. I can't have that. Now, you know the rules. I will call the cardiology group, but you know they will tell me they didn't keep you in the hospital. It's your responsibility to go home on time. No more violations, Dr. Shelton. Is that clear?"

"Yes, sir, I will watch my duty hours, sir."

"You're a fine physician, Barak, but it is important to keep your sanity too. I don't want to see you doing this to yourself. You look exhausted."

"I am. Thank you." I walked out. I started nephrology the next day. There would be lots of consults, according to my fellow residents, but when the nephrologist left for the dialysis center, I would be free to read in the library or head for home. It would be a saner rotation.

The rotation I enjoyed the most was infectious disease. It was busy and had lots of consults, but every organ system in the body could be involved with an infection. My physical exam skills improved by the day, and doing spinal taps became routine. When I told Lily about all the different infections I had seen, she brightened up and poked me in the ribs. "Did you see anyone with malaria yet?"

"That's a tropical disease, Lily."

"I know. They have four different kinds of malaria in Madagascar, according to the Pasteur Institute. They don't have *Plasmodium knowlesi*— that's only found in Southeast Asia. I was just wondering if you had seen any cases yet. There are many students from tropical countries at the University of Minnesota. Keep looking. I'm sure you'll find a case. Then come tell me all about it."

I hated it when she knew more about a medical problem than I did. I knew it was because of her skills at research and remembering everything she read or saw, but I still resented it. "Yes, Lily, I will be on the lookout for malaria," I said, but I was thinking, *What's the chance?*

A week later, I was consulted for a student from the university with a high fever. The emergency department physician noted a temperature of 104 but could not discern a cause, so the student was admitted, and infectious disease was consulted. He went into kidney failure, so our nephrology service was consulted as well. He was from Ghana and had recently spent a month back home before returning for his junior year at the university. He'd gotten sick the day after he returned to classes. The emergency resident suspected malaria and ordered a smear, but the laboratory reported the smear as negative for parasites.

Dr. Douglas, the attending on infectious disease, met me in the hall outside the patient's room. I had just finished my consult evaluation for nephrology. I documented in the chart the recommended fluid replacement and careful attention to electrolytes.

"So," Dr. Douglas said, "what do you think is going on?"

"He is a twenty-four-year-old African man, a student here at the University of Minnesota. He has been febrile for four days and presented with a headache. On exam, he has a few wheezes in his lungs; his heart rate is fast; and abdominal, rectal, and neurological exams are normal. Presently, he is in mild renal dysfunction."

"Did the admitting doctors do blood and urine cultures?" asked Dr. Douglas.

"Yes," I said, "and a CT of his brain, abdomen, and chest and even a spinal tap. Everything is normal in his labs except protein in his urine and an elevation of his blood urea nitrogen and creatinine. His renal dysfunction is mild."

Dr. Douglas folded his hands in his lap. "It's suspicious for malaria."

"The emergency department physician thought of that, but the smear was reported negative."

"Let's go see for ourselves." He invited me to join him. We went to the lab and got the smear slide from the technician. "Dr. Hartman, the new pathologist has returned from working in Kenya. Let's have him look at this," Dr. Douglas said.

Dr. Hartman was sitting at his microscope, surrounded by slides. He was focused on a surgical pathological specimen. "Dave," Dr. Douglas said, "can you look at this smear? I strongly suspect this patient has malaria."

"Sure," he said, "haven't seen a good case of malaria since I left Kenyatta Hospital in Nairobi." He put the glass slide under his scope and adjusted the lens. "You're right. It's full of parasites. Falciparum malaria and maybe some vivax as well. Does the patient have a fever? With vivax, they often get lung involvement, and both can cause kidney damage."

"Thanks, Dave. You will need to dictate an addendum. The tech reported it as negative."

"Yes, they don't see it often, so they miss it. Sorry, guys. A new report will be in the computer today."

We walked back to the patient's floor and ordered the appropriate medication. "Let that be a lesson to you, Barak. Don't trust a lab report; trust your instincts, and find a pathologist who has seen what you're looking for."

My nephrology attending was impressed with the diagnosis and instructed me to research renal dysfunction associated with malaria. He said I would have to present the case at nephrology grand rounds. That meant more work to do that I hadn't counted on, but I knew Lily would be excited.

Lily was fascinated that night. She wanted to know all about malaria. Without violating confidentiality, I explained the entire life cycle of the parasite and how the patient presented.

"Now that you've seen a case, you know how to diagnose and treat it, right, Barak?"

"I suppose I would be more likely to pick it up. But there are variations of the disease that I would need more experience to know how to treat."

"You could go to Madagascar and treat people with malaria now that you know what you're doing. That is so neat."

There was seldom a disease that Lily wasn't interested in, but she was particularly interested in tropical medicine. "The people in the tropics need good doctors, Barak. They've been neglected. Why don't you specialize in tropical medicine?"

"I never thought of it." I was thinking about mosquitoes and swarms of bugs.

"Well, it's time to think about it. You want some popcorn? There is a National Geographic special on Madagascar. You should watch it with me."

# OUTPATIENT CLINIC

ONE AFTERNOON A WEEK, WE served the Internal Medicine Outpatient Clinic. As a senior resident, I looked forward to seeing my continuity patients. I had taken care of most of them in the hospital on academic medicine and then followed their chronic problems in my clinic. I had cared for some of them for almost the whole three years of my residency. I always anticipated great conversations and expected to see them progress toward better health.

Julia Essenhausen was my favorite patient. I had admitted her for a kidney infection my first month of residency. She was seriously ill but had survived. She was ninety years old and had heart-valve disease, which made the kidney infection even more serious. She wanted her valve fixed, but the surgeon was reluctant. Eventually, he gave in but warned her of a poor prognosis. Within a week, she was ready to go home, walking the halls to see if she could find her surgeon to discharge her.

I had followed her in the clinic ever since. She always came elegantly dressed like a European countess. In fact, she claimed her grandfather was a Prussian officer. I was delighted to see her name first on my schedule.

I walked into the exam room. She was already up on the exam table with a clinic gown tied in place, waiting for me to examine her. Before I even had a chance to greet her, she said, "Now I'm getting frail, Dr. Shelton. I'm not as active as I used to be, but I still do my workout at the

YMCA every day. I can still swim five times a week, and I am faster than some of those young people."

I listened to her heart. She had the soft murmur of a bovine heart valve.

"I told that surgeon I wanted the cow valve, not the pig valve," she said.

"Quiet now, Mrs. Essenhausen. I need to listen to your lungs."

"Call me Julia, Dr. Shelton. Remember, you saved my life."

"You had a kidney infection. I just gave you antibiotics."

"I had pyelonephritis, remember? And that other doctor was going to give me some pills and send me home. I would have died. You knew I was sick and gave me those IV antibiotics. You saved my life. I've had three great-grandchildren born since then that I never would have gotten to see if it wasn't for you."

"Yes, Julia. Please don't talk; I'm trying to listen to your lungs." I focused as she took four deep breaths. "All right, you can talk now."

"I brought you some pastries made in the old Bavarian style. We Prussians stole the recipe," she said with a laugh. "I hope your nurses haven't eaten them all while you have been attending to me."

"I'm sure they saved one for me." I smiled.

"Did I ever tell you about the time we sailed in the North Sea?"

She was the last patient on my schedule; I still had enough time to listen to one of her mesmerizing stories.

One afternoon clinic, the schedule was booked, and half of the patients were new. It was Friday, and I dreaded the usual raft of unknown patients attempting to get narcotic prescriptions with the complaint "My regular doctor is out of town. I just need enough Vicodin till he comes back. The pain is killing me, Doc." The patient would then usually cross his or her arms and smile. I hated the word *Vicodin*. It sent evil thoughts through my brain. I rarely gave those patients anything, and as I offered more appropriate alternatives, they usually walked out on me. It was still stressful.

When I was finished with the last patient, my receptionist said there was an officer waiting for me in the preceptor room. I had no idea what to expect. As I walked in, Dr. Slater, my preceptor, looked distressed.

"What's this about?" I said.

"Are you Dr. Barak Shelton?" He had his hand on his holstered gun.

"Yes."

"I have a summons for you, sir." He gave me a thick white envelope and left.

I opened it.

"What is this about, Barak?" asked Dr. Slater.

I read the top lines of the document. "It says that I'm being sued for failure to diagnose a bowel perforation on Richard Sprow."

"Who is that?" my attending physician asked.

I felt flushed and ready to faint. I was being sued. What had I done? Nothing. This wasn't fair.

He placed a hand on my arm and said, "Sit down, Barak, and tell me about this case."

I let out a deep sigh and dropped into a chair beside Dr. Slater. My explanation cramped my throat. "Richard Sprow was a patient I admitted on academic medicine when I was an intern. The night team told me in morning report that he had pancreatitis. He was an alcoholic with an elevated amylase. But when I examined him, his belly was blown up and rigid. He was comatose and very acidotic. He went to surgery, and they found a bowel perforation. He died in the intensive care unit several days later. I only saw him for one hour at most before we transferred him to surgery. How can I be sued for that?"

Dr. Slater took the paper from my paralyzed hand. "You need to meet with the risk management lawyer as soon as possible, Barak."

The clinic charge nurse came into the preceptor room to get some papers signed for a portable potty chair for a stroke patient and diapers for an adult with severe cerebral palsy. "Are there any other patients?" asked Dr. Slater.

"Nope, done for today."

I wanted to add, "Done forever," but I never said anything. I walked to my car, carrying the envelope and holding my coat. It was terribly cold. I thought, *I should put my coat on.* The snow swirled around my face as I unlocked the door. I stood paralyzed in the parking lot. I got in the car, fastened my seat belt, and turned the ignition. If it hadn't started immediately, I might have sat in the lot and frozen to death. As the heater blasted in my face, I eased out of the lot and followed the route that I always drove to my apartment. I almost ran a red light but stopped halfway through the intersection. The driver behind me was gracious enough to let me back up. As I waited for the green light, I changed my mind. I put on the right turn signal and headed for Lily's. She would know what to do.

After being served with the lawsuit, I questioned everything I did. I got stymied over clinical decisions that, with previous patients, had been automatic. When I heard that Alex Faustino was named in the suit as well,

I dreaded the encounter with my former chief resident. He had been in practice for two years in Iowa, and I could only imagine how he was going to deal with coming back to Minneapolis for his deposition.

As much as I wanted to quit, I had to take care of my patients. I found that taking a history was a pleasant distraction as I anticipated the dreaded day of my deposition. Even doing the physical exam was not a problem, but when I sat down to write orders on the chart, I struggled. What if I had forgotten something? What if I hadn't interpreted the laboratory tests correctly? What if the patient deteriorated during the night? Should I check them again?

Almost every night afterward, Lily counseled me. She gave me tips about how to act in court and what malpractice was all about—correcting my misconceptions, she called it. More important was the confidence she had that I was going to be a good physician despite this experience. She said a "better physician," but I didn't believe her.

I met with the lawyer the malpractice insurance company assigned me, Attorney Goldstein. He was gentle with me. He reviewed what I should wear and how I was to answer the questions and explained legal terminology. "Just state clearly what you did and why you did it. Do not speculate about what other physicians did. Do not—" He paused. "Are you listening, Barak?"

I guessed my mind was distracted by the leather chairs, polished oak desk, and shiny framed diplomas and awards on his wall. I turned to give him eye contact. "I'm sorry, Attorney Goldstein. My mind is so jumbled over this."

"You will come through this just fine, Barak," he said as he reached across his desk and took my hand. "I've read through your documentation. You have a ninety percent chance of winning this case if you are poised and confident."

Confidence—that was what I lacked. I would be sued, and my practice would be ruined. I would go into the courtroom and make a fool of myself. I couldn't do this.

"Now, listen to me," he said, and I focused, readjusting in the chair. "Do not speculate about what other physicians did. Do not cast aspersions on the emergency department physicians. Do not say anything negative about the night crew that admitted him. Just stick to what decisions you made and why you made them."

His words clanged like a broken bell in my aching head. I repeated what he'd said to try to make it stick. "But I didn't do anything wrong." Tears came to my eyes. I held my aching head in my hands.

"We've been over this before. Lawsuits are not about doing anything wrong—that's criminal law. This is tort law. It is Richard Sprow's brother's constitutional right to sue you if he chooses. He lost a brother and is angry. This is his way of dealing with his anger. What we are going to show in court before a jury is that confident, compassionate Dr. Barak Shelton's decisions were not causal to the tort."

I tried to synthesize what he'd said. "So this is Richard Sprow's brother's money-making scheme to get a bundle of dough out of the doctors who did nothing wrong."

He looked disgusted with me. "That may be how you see it, Barak, but I do not want you to have that attitude in court, or you will say something that could lose this case for you."

We spent another hour correcting my attitude and going over the facts of the case. When I left his plush office, I rushed past his attractive secretary in her low-cut red dress, fine fingernails, and blue eyeliner; past the fake birch tree at his reception door; and out into the hall. I looked back only long enough to see "Attorney Joseph Goldstein" and some letters after his name in gold leaf on the massive oak door. Then the elevator came.

That night over wild rice casserole, Lily explained everything to me again. "This is not the end of the world or your career. Nothing bad will happen to you. Just be honest, and state the facts. Joseph Goldstein is an excellent lawyer."

"That's easy for you to say. It's not your leg that's caught in the beaver trap." I took a mouthful of food and choked. When I caught my breath again, I said, "This casserole is really good. What did you do differently?"

"I put bear meat in it instead of hamburger." She smiled. "It'll give you strength."

"Mrs. Essenhausen was admitted last night," the intern on academic medicine told me at morning report. "She is confused and disoriented, with a 102.3 fever."

"Did you culture her blood and urine?" I asked.

"We did. I started Levaquin IV on her."

"Better pick something else," I said as I thought back to her last admission. "Her last Gram-negative bacteria was resistant to Levaquin."

"That's what the attending wanted."

"That's a default. Check the sensitivities from the last admission." I was on gastroenterology and was supposed to report to outpatient for scheduled gastroscopies. "I've got to go. Just promise me you will check, please. She is my favorite clinic patient. I know her well."

"Okay, Barak. I'll check."

"And give her a dose of gentamicin while you're waiting." I ran out of the physicians' lounge toward outpatient services.

One gastric cancer, one Mallory-Weiss tear, and four duodenal ulcers later, it was time for lunch. I caught up with the intern at the noon infectious disease conference.

"You were right, Barak. Her previous infection was resistant, but the attending wants to wait for the culture result from this infection before he changes drugs."

I raised my hand. Dr. Douglas, the ID specialist who ran the conference, acknowledged me. "Dr. Douglas, I would like to present a case."

"Go ahead, Barak."

"A ninety-plus-year-old woman presents febrile and confused. Urine is full of pus. There is no other obvious source of infection, even though she has a prosthetic bovine valve. Her previous admission was for Gram-negative sepsis resistant to Levaquin. Would you use Levaquin while waiting for cultures?"

"Of course not. A single dose of gentamicin would be ideal while waiting for the culture and sensitivities because the organism is very likely to be resistant to Levaquin, and if she is febrile, a ninety-year-old is likely to be septic. She might die before the sensitivities are available. Studies show no evidence of renal failure with a single dose of gentamicin, even though it has renal toxicity, so that is an excellent choice." He paused. "Good question, Barak. That's a common problem. Any other cases?"

I leaned over to the intern and whispered, "Change it, or I will. She's my clinic patient. I told you. Tell your attending that Dr. Douglas recommended gentamicin when the case was presented at ID conference."

He got up and went to the telephone in the back of the room to give a verbal order to the nurse.

Dr. Douglas answered a few other questions and then presented a case of a febrile middle-aged woman with a pulmonary infiltrate. The medical students all agreed it was pneumonia. Some of the residents suggested fungi or sarcoidosis. One asked where the patient had been employed.

"She works in a lab that puts computers together."

There was no such factory in our city, so I became curious. "Dr. Douglas, may I ask where this factory is and if she has any travel history?"

"Very perceptive, Barak. She is here visiting her son, who is a student at the university. She just came from India."

"Then I would add pulmonary malaria from *P. vivax* to the differential."

"And what test would you order?"

"A malaria smear, but there is one pathologist here who has worked in Kenya; I would have him read the smear."

"Correct. The smear was read initially as negative, but the pathologist who reviewed the slide found the parasites." Dr. Douglas finished the conference by explaining the pathophysiology of how *P. vivax* malaria caused pulmonary edema and the appropriate treatment.

The day Mrs. Essenhausen was discharged after she finished a course of IV gentamicin for her Gram-negative sepsis resistant to Levaquin was the day before my deposition. I couldn't sleep that night. I scrunched my pillow, drank warm milk, and even got up and watched a Dracula movie on the late movie channel. It was worthless. I couldn't get the case out of my mind. I reviewed what had happened a hundred times and couldn't think of anything I could have done differently.

The program director had given me the whole day off—for "business," my duty-hour report said. But even without patient responsibilities, I was exhausted as I sat outside the hospital boardroom where our depositions were scheduled. When Alex Faustino arrived, I was afraid to look him in the eye.

"So, Barak, how's it going? You must be almost done with residency."

"Next June I'm done."

"Hey, I am really enjoying practice. I've got great partners and love my patients." He leaned over and whispered in my ear, "And I don't have any jerks like Richard Sprow in my practice." He straightened his tie and brushed his expensive pin-striped blue suit. "Where are you going into practice?"

"Not sure yet."

"Have you married that shark girlfriend yet, or has she bitten your pale ass?"

"No, I haven't married her, and she has not bitten me. We're still seeing each other." I couldn't admit to him that I had proposed, and Lily had turned me down.

We were mostly silent after that. I couldn't think of anything I wanted to ask him about his practice, and he wasn't volunteering. He sipped coffee from a Styrofoam cup. I got a cup with him, but it tasted awful, so I didn't finish it. I just sat holding it in my lap, watching the brown scum form on the top. I was too tense for regular coffee, but there was no decaf.

We waited.

When the emergency department physician came out the door, it startled me. His face was flushed, and he was followed by his attorney. I looked in the door and didn't see Attorney Goldstein. He was representing Alex and me since there was no apparent conflict in our testimonies and we weren't opposed to any of each other's decisions. But where was he? I caught a quick glance of a woman dressed in a black business suit, but I couldn't see her face. When the door closed again, my eyes focused on the weave of the carpet.

"Dr. Alexander Faustino."

I hadn't even heard the boardroom door open, but I stood when Alex did and stared at the young lawyer.

She was dressed in a formal business suit. Her hair was coiffed in a no-nonsense cut. She extended her hand. "I am Attorney Barton, and I am pleased to inform you that you have been dismissed from the case. We will not need your deposition. I am sorry for the inconvenience this has caused you. You may send a bill for your mileage to our office." She gave him a business card.

The color drained from Alex's face. He placed his hand in hers like a hound responding to "Shake." "I can go? I've been dropped from the case?"

"Correct."

"This is great news. Thank you. And thank Attorney Goldstein," he said, and I could see the sudden recognition in his eyes. "Are you—"

"Yes, I am, as you referred to me, Barak's shark girlfriend." She stared at him. He backed away from her.

"Oh, Attorney Barton, I'm so sorry. Really. I didn't mean anything by it."

Lily dropped his hand. "You're excused, Dr. Faustino. And you are very welcome for Attorney Goldstein's intervention. You will subsequently receive written notification that you have been dismissed from the Richard Sprow case. Thank you for your attendance." Lily was statuesque. Alex looked at me and looked at her again. He picked up his briefcase, turned, and shot out the door.

I gasped. I recognized the smell of her perfume, but after work, the scent was usually mixed with perspiration from her weight lifting and exercise. Its fragrance was much different in the hall facing the boardroom. I waited. As Alex left, she turned to me.

"Do you have time to take me out for lunch, Dr. Shelton? This shark is very hungry."

I was afraid to ask the question, but I needed to know: "What about my deposition?"

She laced her hand in mine, and we walked out to the parking lot. "You've been dropped. There was no case against you. Attorney Goldstein cross-examined their expert witness yesterday, and he described your involvement as 'quick and expeditious care that might have saved Richard Sprow's life.' After he said that, Goldstein moved for dismissal. The plaintiff's attorney lost his case with that single remark. Goldstein would have had the clerk read his testimony to the court if he'd tried to change his opinion." She squeezed my hand, stopped, and looked at my vacant face. "Oh, you want to know why I'm here."

"Well, yes."

"Attorney Goldstein is one of my partners in the malpractice division of our law firm. He sent me—I'm just a junior partner, you know—to inform you that you had been dropped."

"But I thought you were in corporate law?"

"Right. Isn't that clever? Goldstein sent me, a corporate lackey, over to show that the plaintiff's case was so weak that he didn't need to be here. It's a lawyer trick. He would have come to represent you if it hadn't worked." She put her arm over my shoulders. "Now, are you going to feed me, or should I take a bite out of you? Sharks aren't fussy."

Euphoria pulsated through me. "Seafood?"

"Sure."

"You sure looked intimidating." I opened the car door for her and then ran around and climbed behind the wheel.

"I'm supposed to." She took the clip out of her hair, shook her mane, and unbuttoned the top buttons of her suit. She looked like Lily again.

After the malpractice case was dismissed, I was emotionally and physically spent despite being thankful. Lily proposed a Caribbean vacation. My faculty mentor agreed that it was a good idea. We considered the options and chose St. Martin because she wanted to practice speaking French and because they had clothing-optional beaches.

She arranged the transportation and hotel and planned our itinerary. I had just enough energy to show up with my suitcase at the airport. I wasn't even sure what I had packed. I didn't remember much of the flight. I wasn't too alert, as visions of IVs, intensive care units, and patients' faces flashed through my mind during my fitful sleep on the airplane.

When we arrived at our bungalow, I relaxed to the repetitive flow of the waves on the beach and the smell of flowers, and each morning, I awoke to the cooing of doves as I ate my croissant and sipped mango juice. All the stress of preparing for the deposition, checking lab tests, and presenting patients to attending physicians melted into the humid, floral air. The first day of our vacation, I left the beach just long enough to eat and take a shower.

I was surprised how fluent Lily was in French. She had taken French as one of her university classes, and since becoming a lawyer, she had continued in advanced French in the adult education classes on Monday nights at the university. In retrospect, I realized that explained why I could never get her to answer her telephone on Monday nights. She ordered at the restaurants, checked in at our hotel, and arranged transportation in French. She even tutored me since my French was sorely neglected despite four years of French classes at UMD.

We were sitting at a bar on a clothing-optional beach. Lily was nude, sitting on her beach towel, sipping a nonalcoholic version of my tropical drink. I was more comfortable in my Speedo.

"I would really like to go to Madagascar, Barak."

"Why is that?"

"They have all kinds of strange plants and animals there. You know about the lemurs. We watched that special together on television, but they have thousands of unique orchids as well." She took a bite of her baguette while we waited for our order of broiled shrimp and pineapple. She flicked a crumb off her breast. "And the people there are so poor. They have an NGO—nongovernmental organization—called SALFA that has hospitals and clinics all over the island. I can't say the Malagasy words that it stands for, but anyway, SALFA is providing medical care for all these poor people. I've been supporting them as much as I can."

"We have plenty of poor people in the United States."

"Yes, but lots of people know about them. Except for the lemurs, people ignore Madagascar."

"So what do you propose?"

"When you finish residency, we could go there together. You could work at the hospital, and I could see the orchids and lemurs."

"That doesn't sound very realistic."

"They needed a generator, Barak, in a small rural hospital in Manambaro. They don't have municipal electricity there. A few months ago, I bought them a generator and donated the money to have it shipped there and then arranged for an electrician to install it."

Our shrimp and pineapple arrived. She dipped her shrimp in the jerk sauce and took a bite. "I love this sauce." She dipped a piece of pineapple in the same sauce. "Wow, what a treat." She nibbled another shrimp. I was glad I wasn't trying to share an order with her. I wouldn't have gotten any shrimp. "So I propose we go to Madagascar and check on my generator."

"I finish residency June thirtieth, but I need to study for my internal medicine board exam the first of October." I didn't have any interest in Madagascar, but I thought maybe it would be a nice vacation. Didn't she understand? I was an internal medicine specialist. Did they even have those in Madagascar?

She continued. "The orchids bloom in March in Madagascar. We could go then."

"I should be starting my job as a hospitalist. I already signed the contract. I doubt if I could get vacation that quickly. How about the following March, two years from now?" *That should put her off,* I thought.

She dipped her finger into the last of the sauce on her plate and stuck it in her mouth. She wiggled off her barstool and threw her towel over her shoulder. "All right. We'll plan on that."

I followed her down to the waterfront. I was fascinated with the way her buttocks and thigh muscles moved when she walked. They undulated in a silent rhythm with the smoothness of ballet. *So different from the woman in the business suit,* I thought. *Vulnerable, not intimidating.* Our rented beach umbrella was a few feet from the approaching tide of the ocean. We found our clothes still folded on the two lounge chairs.

"Are you ready for a swim, or are you content to watch my bare butt all day?"

My face flushed. "Sure, let's swim."

"You'd better take off that Speedo so you don't get it wet. Besides, your wolverine needs some sunshine, Gwiingwa'aage."

I hesitated and looked around. Nude couples were sunbathing and dashing into the waves all around us. I hesitated with my thumbs stuck into the sides of my trunks.

"You need help?" she said as she yanked my trunks down.

"No, I don't." I kicked off my Speedo and chased her into the surf.

# TIRED—TWO YEARS LATER

"I FEEL TIRED," SAID LILY.

We were sitting around the table at Heidi's, having just feasted on roast bear meat and wild rice, the traditional Barton Christmas dinner. Autumn held her drink to her mouth but didn't take a sip. I paused with a mouthful of dessert and didn't swallow.

"I know my schedule has been hectic with all the court cases, but I slept all day Saturday and still don't feel better. I even cut back on my exercise program the last month. I thought I was overdoing it. But, Heidi"—her brown eyes focused on her adopted mother—"I just can't get my energy back. Check me over, Barak." She stood and started unbuttoning her blouse while heading for the stairway down to her room.

"No, Lily, I'm too close to you. I might miss something. Please see someone else," I said.

Heidi nodded in agreement.

"All right, but I can't go on like this. Maybe I'm just anemic, although my menses have been pretty light."

Autumn visibly cringed at the nature of the table conversation.

We all went to Lily's room, where she lay on her bed. Heidi provided the stethoscope and observed my exam. Autumn stood at the door. I couldn't tell whether she was skeptical or worried. "Heart and lungs sound all right," I said as I placed my hand on her belly, expecting to find nothing.

But I felt her liver edge despite her developed abdominal musculature and asked Heidi to confirm.

"That isn't normal," Heidi said. "Barak's right. Your liver is enlarged, and the edge is firm and abnormal. You need to see a physician, Lily. Maybe you even need a hepatologist."

When we got back to the city, I set her up with one of the community internal medicine specialists I respected. She agreed much more passively than I expected. After the first visit, he encouraged her by saying, "Your liver is enlarged and tender. We'll do some blood tests, but I am sure it is just infectious mononucleosis or some other viral hepatitis. That explains your fatigue. At your age, you should bounce back quickly." He advised her to rest, and to my surprise, she did—but she didn't get better. A week later, the physician's office called and scheduled a follow-up appointment. I went with her.

Lily asked me to come with her into the examining room. As she disrobed to put on a gown, I noticed that her ribs were more prominent and her breasts less firm. "Have you been trying to lose weight?" I asked.

"You know I have never tried to lose weight in my life," she said as she put on a gown and sat on the exam table. She spread the sheet the nurse had given her over her knees.

I was sitting in the chair beside the desk when Dr. Hanson came in. He greeted us and turned to Lily. He had her lie down and briefly palpated her abdomen. "When I examined you last time, your liver seemed a bit large and firm. Your liver enzymes are elevated, so I did some other screening tests. Your hepatitis panel was positive for hepatitis B."

"Where did I get that?"

"Have you ever done any IV drugs or had a blood transfusion?"

"No."

"Have you had many sexual partners?" Dr. Hanson looked at me.

"No." Lily pointed at me. "We've never had sex. He's my adopted brother."

"Oh, I didn't know. I worked with Barak at County Hospital when he was a resident."

I said, "Lily was adopted as an infant. Her natural mother had hepatitis as well as Laennec's cirrhosis." I paused as Dr. Hanson appeared to be thinking through what I'd said. "I took care of Lily's biological mother in a nursing home until she died."

"What kind of hepatitis?" Dr. Hanson asked.

"Hepatitis B."

"If you've had no other exposure …" He peered over his glasses, giving Lily an opportunity to respond.

I knew what he was doing. Most of the patients I had at Hennepin County Hospital refused to admit to IV drug abuse until they were confronted a couple of times. "She has never done drugs," I said. "I've known her since junior high."

"And I haven't had sex partners with hepatitis," she added.

Dr. Hanson said, "Then you may have gotten it from your mother when you were born. Babies are usually asymptomatic. What's important is that we get you to a specialist to get this under control. You must have developed chronic hepatitis B, and there is reasonable treatment for that."

A week later, she went alone to the gastroenterologist office. One of the partners was a liver specialist, a hepatologist. The night after the appointment, we had supper together at her house. "The gastroenterologist pored over my chart, reviewed all the lab tests, and then examined me," she said, and she pulled up her sweatshirt and pointed at her right upper belly. "I wish people would quit poking me right here. It's getting tender from all the prodding."

"Lily, they have to examine you."

"I know, but I thought she would just want more blood. But she said that Dr. Hanson did all the correct blood tests. She wants a liver biopsy."

"I suppose that is the next step." I sounded clinical, but I couldn't think of any other way of saying it.

"She's going to poke a big needle into my liver. Is it painful?" She furrowed her brow, an expression I had never seen on Lily's face.

"Just for a moment. Then it's over. Most patients don't complain."

"Sorry. I'm thinking like a lawyer, but what are the risks and benefits?"

"The most serious risks are bleeding and infection, according to the published literature. I've done a few liver biopsies on my gastroenterology rotation without any problems." I saw her raise her eyebrows, so I added, "No, I will not do your liver biopsy." Then I added in my clinical voice, "The benefit is that you will know exactly what you are dealing with. The pathologist will be able to look at your liver under the microscope and tell what's going on." What I said was a canned speech I had given my patients many times.

"I am not getting better sitting here." She took a bite of her steak and swabbed it in ketchup. It was venison from a doe she'd shot the previous fall. "I'll call the office nurse tomorrow and schedule it for next week." She chewed her meat, and I could tell she was thinking through the possibilities. "Can you come with me to my liver biopsy? They won't let me drive myself home."

"I'm free at noon on Thursday. See if you can schedule it for that afternoon."

I picked her up at her apartment, and we drove to the hospital outpatient surgery department. She seemed apprehensive and didn't say much as she discarded her clothes and put on a hospital gown. She was silent as we waited for the gastroenterologist.

Dr. Toumala was a tall, thin blonde woman with a Finnish accent. She wore a pastel-blue coat that reflected her eyes but wore no makeup to accent her pale skin. She greeted Lily and then turned to me, apparently somewhat surprised. "Barak, how are you? I enjoyed having you on my service. That was a couple of years ago now, wasn't it?"

"Yes, I'm a hospitalist now and faculty for the academic medicine team two months of the year."

"Excellent. I am sure you are a good instructor." She turned to Lily.

I explained my relationship to Lily and why she'd asked for me to stay during the procedure.

Dr. Toumala nodded agreement and turned to Lily. "All right, I explained the procedure to you during your last visit, and you have signed permission. Do you have any questions?"

"I have no questions. Barak has explained everything to me as well."

The nurse came into the procedure room with a tray of equipment. After she prepped Lily's skin with antiseptic, Dr. Toumala injected lidocaine for local anesthesia and made a small incision. "Take a deep breath," she commanded. "Now hold it." Lily held her breath until told to relax. "That was the practice. Now I am going to have you take a deep breath again. This time, I will do the biopsy. Ready?" Lily nodded. "Deep breath. Hold it."

I watched the large bore needle slip into Lily's flesh all the way to the hub. I covered my mouth.

"There. We have a nice specimen," Dr. Toumala said.

"What does it look like?" Lily asked.

"I have to send it to the pathologist. The results will be available Thursday."

"But I want to see it." She sat up, and her gown fell into her lap.

Dr. Toumala held up Lily's gown with one hand and showed her the specimen that had been placed in formaldehyde with the other hand.

"It looks kind of pale. Shouldn't it be more dark brown?"

My mind raced to the liver Lily had tossed to the wolves after she'd cut it out of the deer on our canoe trip. She knew her comparative anatomy.

Dr. Toumala paused. She probably had few patients like Lily. "Yes, it should be. But I can't tell you what the problem is until we have a pathology report." She smiled, handed the edge of Lily's gown to her, and gave the specimen to the nurse to label before Dr. Toumala left the room.

The nurse gave Lily some last-minute instructions and then told her to get dressed but to wait in the room so she could check her blood pressure. "When everything is stable, you can go. The doctor will want to see you for the results next week."

"I've had worse mosquito bites," said Lily after the nurse left. She threw her gown onto the gurney and held up her right breast to examine the biopsy site, removing the bandage the nurse had meticulously applied.

"Are you going to work tomorrow?" I asked.

"Yes, I have to be in court all day." She stared at me. "There is nothing to worry about until next Thursday, Barak." She slipped into her skirt and then put on her bra and blouse. "That was sure slick."

I hung my head. "I won't be free next Thursday."

"That's all right. I'll get the report and bring it to you so you can explain all the medical words to me."

# DISASTER

THURSDAY WAS A BAD DAY. Being academic medicine faculty meant I had to supervise a senior resident and two first-year residents. I tried to be compassionate. I remembered my resident years, and for the most part, the faculty physicians had been gentle, coaching me. Our team had quite a few admissions during the night, and as the first-year night residents signed out their histories and what they had discovered on physical exam that morning, I got them all mixed up because I kept thinking about Lily's biopsy report. I had to read the notes on the census sheet several times to keep each patient straight in my mind, but still, the patients blurred together.

The intern explained his patient's case. I said, "He may have had a myocardial infarction—the EKG is suggestive—but he has severe renal failure and missed his dialysis Monday, so the lab tests are confusing." The intern shot a quizzical look. I recognized his lack of understanding. This was supposed to be a teaching moment, but I was too tired to explain.

After morning report, with a large cup of coffee in hand, I guided our team to see the patients. My interns knew their patients well, and the senior resident was supportive of his interns as well as cognizant of the patients' needs. I stood in the background and let them explain lab results and clinical course and review x-rays.

After I reviewed the discharge plans on two patients who were being sent to nursing homes, it was time for lunch. I had some nonspecific casserole that had too much grease in it with a large portion of cauliflower and broccoli to ease my conscience. After lunch, we reviewed the plans for our patients as a team and called the nursing floors for changes in patient medications. It was late afternoon when I went to the coffee bar to get another cup of coffee in order to drive safely home. I used the back roads so there would be fewer traffic decisions.

After walking into my apartment, I dropped my clothes onto the living room floor, wrapped a comforter around myself, and lay on the couch. The light from the picture window was too bright, but I could not motivate myself to draw the blinds. I covered my head with the blanket and fell asleep. My dreams were vivid, with bright hospital lights, flashing ambulance lights, and EKG monitors scintillating through my mind.

A banging sound seemed like the beginning of a headache. Then it stopped. I was glad. It started again. *Is this a new dream? Do I need an aspirin?* The banging started again. I flipped the blanket off my face. What was it? The room was completely dark. What time was it?

I heard more banging and then, "Barak, are you there?"

I shook my head. The blinds were still open, but there was no moon, and the stars must have been obscured by clouds. For a moment, I could not remember where I was.

I heard more banging. "Barak, I need to talk to you."

I sat up. "Who is it?"

"Lily. I need to talk to you. Open the door."

"Oh, Lily." I stumbled to the door and unlocked it. She burst through the door, turned on the lights, and grabbed me. I held my hand over my eyes till my pupils adjusted. Orientation was coming slowly. I was only wearing underwear, and the door to the hall was still wide open. I held her back to close the door. Lily smothered me. Her face was red and swollen. Tears poured down her face.

"What time is it?" I asked.

"Midnight," she said, "but I can't wait. I need to talk to you now." She wore what looked like flashy pajamas.

*What is she doing here?* I was confused. "Are we in my apartment?" I asked.

"Of course."

I switched on the lamp beside the couch as I oriented myself out of dreamland. It was so bright my eyes had to adjust again. "What's the problem?"

She cuddled her face in my chest. "I'm full of cancer."

I gasped at the word. For a moment, I was paralyzed. I choked, swallowing my drool. She twisted on the couch. "How could it be cancer?" I said.

She sat up, grabbed a tissue, and wiped her eyes. The bright light transilluminated her form through her pajamas. *How could that beautiful body have cancer?* I thought.

"The doctor explained that my blood tests showed that I had hepatitis B."

"Right. I was there," I said.

"I probably got it from my mother when I was born." I knew that and wanted to interrupt again, but she always had to explain things in a logical order. "I've probably had chronic hepatitis all my life, which put me at risk for hepatocellular carcinoma."

My mind transferred to lectures the gastroenterologist had given in our medical conferences. Some patients with chronic hepatitis B developed cirrhosis of the liver if the body didn't clear the virus. Twenty-some years later, they were at risk of liver cancer. But that happened to my patients, not Lily.

"My liver biopsy was full of cancer. She even showed me the slides. I knew you'd want to see them, so she made me copies." She pushed the photos to my face.

My blurry eyes focused on the photos. The typical mitotic cells of cancer filled the frame. Picture after picture showed the malignancy. "Are you sure this is your biopsy?" It was a stupid question, but I was incredulous. My liver began to hurt in sympathy. My hand went to my right upper belly, and I took a deep breath.

"Could you call Heidi and Autumn? I just can't talk to them right now, but they need to know."

"Lily, it's midnight."

"They won't care."

I picked up the telephone and dialed the numbers. I knew them as well as she did. First, I called Heidi, and then I talked to Autumn. My training allowed me to answer their questions, but when I hung up the telephone, I burst into tears. We collapsed onto the sofa, hugging and crying, clinging to life. "How can this be true?" I said.

"I wanted you to go with me to Madagascar. This can't be happening." Then she sat up, suddenly calm. "This explains what my manitou told me would happen."

"But I love you, Lily." I sobbed and hugged her, and somehow, we must have fallen asleep, because my alarm in my bedroom, perpetually set for six o'clock, woke me. Lily was curled up on my shoulder. I eased her to a more comfortable position, slipped off the couch, and headed for the shower. I had to get to work. There was a lump in my gut as I thought about Lily having hepatocellular carcinoma. The words were emblazoned in my head.

The steam from the hot shower soothed me. The routine was stabilizing. As I reached for my towel, the bathroom door burst open. Lily hugged me. "Thanks, Barak. I really needed to talk to you. You're so wonderful. I'll see you tonight."

"Where are you going?" I dropped my towel and fumbled in picking it up.

"I have to be in court at nine o'clock. I have to get home and change. We still have a dinner date tonight, right?"

"Right."

"Good. We'll talk some more then," she said as she ran out the door. I covered myself with the towel and ran across the living room to close the door.

A month later, she kept an appointment with an oncologist who reviewed the available chemotherapy and treatment options. We sat together on her couch as she told me what had transpired. Lily said she reviewed the statistics as if she were reviewing a court brief. "I insist on unbiased nonpharmaceutical studies to review," she'd told the oncologist.

Lily said she'd reviewed the mortality curves. I was impressed with how much medical terminology she knew. She'd told the oncologist that she saw a statistically significant benefit to chemotherapy with hepatocellular carcinoma but did not really see that benefit was clinically important. She also decided that the side effects were profound.

She'd thanked the oncologist for showing her the data and for respecting her decision.

Lily went back to work the next day. From what appeared on the news that night, she represented an impressive case in court that day.

Three months later, she was too weak to work. The day she cleaned out her desk at her office, Autumn and I decided it was a good time for her to go on vacation. I didn't think she had taken a real vacation since our trip to the Caribbean. Autumn arranged flights, and I arranged a hotel on Hilton Head. We thought maybe some sunshine would be good for her.

After checking into the hotel, we headed for the beach. The sun was warm, and there was a delicate breeze off the ocean. We found a strand of beach that wasn't too crowded and spread out our beach blanket. I couldn't help but notice when they discarded their wraps to reveal only minimal bikinis that Autumn had a model's figure. Her white bikini accented her caramel complexion. Lily still had her muscular physique, but the cancer had made her pale and emaciated.

"I sure hate having to wear this stupid bikini on the beach. I've lost weight, and it doesn't fit well. Do you think anyone will mind if it falls off?"

Autumn looked disgusted. "Don't be such a maverick, Lily. It won't hurt you to wear a little piece of cloth over your erotica."

"There is a spa near here where you can get a massage in a private garden," I said as I turned over onto my back.

"Quit encouraging her, Barak, or we'll all be in jail for aiding and abetting lewd behavior," said Autumn.

"I'm not lewd. I just don't like to wear clothes. Take that back, most perfect sister."

"All right," I said, "we're on vacation. Let's stop arguing before I get hurt." I crawled over and put a hand on Lily's belly. Her liver was hard and nodular. "I have a hot tub attached to my room, remember? They upgraded me. You can be as naked as you want when we get back to the hotel. Okay?"

"Can I join in on your nudist colony?" asked Autumn.

My ears felt hot. I hadn't seen Autumn naked except maybe that time in junior high school, but I still wasn't sure. I guessed I was desensitized to Lily. I wasn't sure about Autumn. "Sure, if you want," I said.

Lily rolled off her towel. "I have to go wash off this sand."

"Stay legal!" Autumn yelled at her as she ran into the gentle surf.

After a formal dinner, both Autumn and Lily were too tired to do much else, so we sat on the hotel veranda and watched the sun set. When it was dark and the stars came out, Lily got up. "I'm going to bed. See you both in the morning."

When she was out of earshot, Autumn turned to me. "She is not doing as well as she acts. She spent last night in the bathroom, vomiting. You can see that she has lost weight."

"Yeah." I sighed. "Her ribs are so prominent. Even when we were on the canoe trip, I never saw her ribs as prominent as they are today."

"She's dying, Barak."

I choked on my Diet Coke. "I know."

# DEATH OF MY MUSE

When Lily became too weak to care for herself, Heidi invited her home. She spent most of the day sitting on the porch, watching the birds, squirrels, and an occasional deer that wandered through the yard. One Saturday, I had a long weekend free from my hospitalist duties, so I asked Heidi if I could come up for a few days. She thought it was a good idea, so I traveled north and arrived in the late afternoon.

After unpacking my stuff into Autumn's room, I joined Lily out on the porch. "You want to go fishing?"

"Sure, from the dock. The boat makes me too nauseated." She started walking, but she almost collapsed. I saw her knees buckle, so I grabbed her and carried her down to the dock. I set her at the end so she could dangle her feet in the water. They were terribly swollen. The cancer had taken a terrible toll on someone who had been so fit and healthy. I wanted to cry just seeing how wasted she had become. I baited her hook and cast it out into the water with a bobber. She set the reel beside her. We watched the bobber diligently.

"If I get a bite, Barak, would you reel it in for me?"

"Sure. That's what friends are for."

"That's what a brother is for," she said. A gentle breeze blew the aromatic pine and cedar to our noses. "I sure enjoy sitting here fishing," she said. "Remember how much fun we had fishing on the canoe trip?

You were so funny because you thought I had forgotten to pack meat for the trip."

"I admit that you abundantly supplied my carnivorous needs."

"Those venison steaks from that doe were sure good." She looked at me. "Does your scar still hurt from where your butt was cut by the rock when I pushed you down?"

"No."

"Good. I felt bad about my temper tantrum. You were sure gracious to forgive me."

"You saved my life."

"Nope, you saved mine."

"I did not."

"You did too."

I laughed. "You know, we sound like a couple of children."

"Yeah, I guess we do. The other thing I felt bad about was—"

Heidi brought drinks, and the three of us sipped lemonade as we watched the bobber dance on the gentle waves. I reeled in as the sun sprayed gold and crimson across the cloud formations. The bait was gone.

"No wonder I didn't catch anything. The fish stole my bait."

Heidi collected the glasses. "I'm going up to make your bed, Lily. I washed all your sheets." She headed up the hill.

"I threw up all over everything last night. The bear meat I requested for supper was too rich, and I didn't eat very much." The sunset darkened to purple and then blue. We lay back on the dock and watched the stars tumble into view. Several shooting stars accented the impenetrable universe.

"I love you, Lily."

"I know you do, Barak."

Tears filled my eyes. "I wanted to marry you."

"That's the other thing I regretted. I shouldn't have pushed you off the dock." She took a deep breath. "But aren't you glad you didn't marry me? You would have contracted hepatitis B when we had sex. Your wolverine, Gwiingwa'aage, would have gotten you sick."

"I was vaccinated for hepatitis B in medical school. I wouldn't have gotten sick."

"Oh. That's good to know. But my vision quest manitou told me I would never have children or a husband, or I would lose my power. Then you wouldn't be a physician."

There was a lot I wanted to say, but I lay silently, watching the stars, supporting her head on my arm.

She sighed and said, "Marrying you would have ruined our relationship. The Grandfathers told you that."

*That is so childish, so mystical. I'm not your brother. We aren't related. I would have made a great husband. It would not have ruined our relationship,* I thought, but I said nothing. Instead, I rolled onto my side and caressed her gaunt face with my hand. "You are one very special woman. I'm glad you talked me into becoming a physician."

"I'm glad you went into internal medicine."

"Why is that?"

"I really dreaded getting pregnant so you could practice deliveries." She laughed at her joke and rolled away from me, so I stood up. "Now I'm getting cold. Are you going to leave me on this dock to freeze to death?"

I crouched beside her and cradled her in my arms. "I'll tuck you into bed with nice, warm blankets." As I carried her up the hill, I was aware of how light she was.

Heidi met us at the back door.

"I think she's asleep," I said.

Heidi turned down her bed, and I cradled her among her pillows. I covered her with the quilt Heidi had made for her years before. I gave her a gentle kiss. "See you in the morning, kid."

I stood in the doorway, looking at her as the moonlight through her window made macabre shadows across her face. I heard Heidi go upstairs.

Her eyes popped open. "Aren't you going to take off these silly clothes? You know I can't sleep with clothes on. And don't call me a kid; I'm not a goat."

As I took off her sweatshirt, her breasts flopped like empty plastic bags on her protruding ribs. What had the cancer done to her? I pulled off her pants and covered her with the blanket to her chin. She shoved it down to her waist.

"Isn't that neat? I can look at my belly and count my pulse."

Her liver was an enlarging mass, but her abdomen was so emaciated that her aorta pulsated visibly. My gut cramped at the sight.

"Open my briefcase, and give me that manila envelope, would you, Barak?"

I retrieved the envelope and brought it to her. Her arm went around my neck, and she pulled my face to hers and kissed me. Her frail lips graced mine like silk. I had prayed for a kiss since I first had seen her standing in the canoe as a young teen, but now there was too much pathos to enjoy it. "Good night, Barak. I love you like no one else. You've become a fine physician. You don't need me anymore. I have finished my tasks. Except one."

"What's that?"

"You'll know in the morning. You're so impatient, Barak."

"Good night, Lily. I wouldn't have been a doctor without you. I feel like I still need you."

"Forget Lily. Tonight, Barak, use my real name."

I stumbled through it, and she corrected my pronunciation till I got it right. "Good night, Waabigwan-atewaniin."

"That's better, you silly Gwiingwa'aage." Her smile melted to stillness.

I pulled the quilt up to her chin again and stood in the doorway, listening to her breathe.

In the morning, Heidi knocked on the door to Autumn's room, where I was sleeping. I jumped up, and she collapsed in my arms. "I checked Waabigwan-atewaniin. She's gone. She has taken the long journey."

I accompanied her to Lily's room. Lily was motionless, as cold as clay to my touch. I checked for a pulse and respirations, but there were none. As I held Heidi, I pulled the manila folder from Lily's rigor mortis grasp. In three shaky letters, she had written "Mom" on the envelope.

Heidi opened the envelope. Enclosed was a letter. "You read it, Barak." She passed it to me gushing with tears.

I adjusted my blurry vision. "She's donated her body to the medical school, University of Minnesota, Heidi. She wants me to present her case in a clinical pathologic conference to the residents." I choked at the thought and coughed before I could finish explaining to Heidi. "She has made all the arrangements for her body. We just have to call these telephone numbers at the time of her death."

I would have fainted if I hadn't been trying to keep Heidi from falling. What was I going to do? She was my inspiration. I felt like quitting and giving up becoming a physician. What about Madagascar? We'd never gotten to go. She'd never gotten to go. I looked at the letter again. Now I knew what her last task was: to teach with the remains of her body. That didn't help my anguish at all.

# THE FUNERAL

Tribal leaders, law school professors, her partners at the law firm, and many people who claimed they were her close friends attended the funeral. More than four hundred crowded the pews at Our Savior's Catholic Cathedral in Duluth. She had spoken to the priest, chosen the scripture passages, and even given him an outline for his sermon. My mother bought all the lilies the florist had available to decorate the sanctuary. She tied white ribbons to each pew. As the eleven o'clock mass started, a bright shaft of sunlight shone through the stained-glass windows onto the coffin.

It was hard for me to focus on the coffin, knowing the embalmed body was heading to the University of Minnesota Medical School. In fact, I wasn't sure her body was even in the coffin because I knew the protocol for donated cadavers. It was probably just a donated coffin for the memorial funeral.

Medical students were probably already cutting her open, dissecting her muscles, and scrutinizing her pelvic organs to study anatomy. I realized I was privileged to have known her anatomy alive. My mind recalled those intimate moments of listening to her heart, listening to her breath, and palpating her breasts for lumps. I recalled how she had volunteered to be the model for the breast and pelvic exam. How had she tolerated all those students pawing her breasts and finding her cervix with the vaginal speculum? Now the students would have her on the stainless-steel table, flayed open in the anatomy lab. I couldn't get the image out of my mind. Then I recalled what she'd told me many times: "This isn't me, Barak. This is just the house I live in." Now the house had been discarded to the anatomy lab.

The priest interrupted my thoughts. "I'm paraphrasing John 11:25. Jesus said, 'I am the resurrection and the life. She who believes in me will live, even though she dies.' Lily requested that I read that passage to you." I didn't hear the rest of the sermon. Waabigwan-atewaniin wouldn't be a dissected cadaver; she would be alive in my soul.

As Heidi gave the eulogy, Autumn slid over on the pew next to me. She grabbed my hand, squeezing it as Heidi told about the box that had appeared on her desk with the little baby in it. "I chose to love Waabigwan-atewaniin," Heidi said. "It was a struggle fighting the state to finalize the adoption since I am unmarried, but it was worth the effort. I am so thankful to God that she is—was—part of my life." Tears dripped down her cheeks. "And I know we are all thankful to God for what she has done for our tribe." The church filled with an "Amen" that shook the cathedral.

Autumn cried gentle tears on my shoulder as Heidi continued, and then she hugged me as the organ postlude intensified our anguish. She was so different from Lily. She had a strong sense of propriety and poise. Lily hadn't cared about those things, often making fun of her sister's sensitivity.

"You would have made her a good husband, Barak," Mom said, hugging me from the other side.

"I couldn't be her husband," I said, but I didn't think she heard me, and even if she had, she wouldn't have understood.

Later, during the reception, I heard Heidi say to my mother, "Barak has been such a comfort to me." We stood outside the church in the reception line. "I am so thankful for his support. I feel like you and your sons are part of my family."

"Thank you," Mom said. "You know how important you were to me on the canoe trip. I might not have been a mother without you, Lisa, and Mireille." She hugged Heidi with more emotion than I had seen in Mother since Dad died.

I put my arm around Heidi. She had mothered me through my clinical years of medical school. "You have been such a mentor to me, and your daughter taught me so much."

The guests filed past to express their condolences. Heidi had insisted we stand in the family line. "Lily considered you her adopted family."

"I need to talk to you about a sensitive matter," Attorney Cohen said as he shook my hand on the way out the door. He turned his gaze to Heidi and Autumn. "Can the three of you meet at my office next week?"

I assumed the sensitive matter was Lily's will, but I couldn't imagine she'd had anything to pass on to us. I also couldn't understand why an attorney from Minneapolis would come to a funeral in Duluth.

# THE WILL

BACK AT MY APARTMENT IN Minneapolis, I took vacation time since human resources said that Lily was not family, and her death didn't qualify in my contract for paid time off for death of a relative.

I went for long walks. I sat on my couch and cried. I ran five miles every day because I knew Lily would have wanted me to do that. I couldn't eat, but I managed to gulp down some juice to stay hydrated. It tasted sour. I was still puzzled about going to Attorney Cohen's office. Maybe "sensitive matter" was just a lawyer phrase. It was probably nothing.

I picked up Autumn at her apartment. She was dressed in black with a silver chain necklace. The wind whipped her silky black hair across her face as we crossed the parking lot to my car. Her hair was much finer than Lily's. My mind played back the scene of the gangly teenager in the canoe. Now she was tall, elegant, and stately. "What do you expect this will thing is about?" I asked.

"I have no idea," Autumn said as she put on her seat belt. "She didn't have much in her apartment. Mom and I cleaned that up when she moved home. But my sister is—was—always full of surprises. You were there when she died. What was in her room?"

"Some old deer hides, a bear hide, and a vest made from squirrel hides." I chuckled, but it hurt. It had been a long time since I had even smiled. I added, "I know she gave away all her good suits and dresses to Goodwill when she quit work."

As we walked into the office building, it smelled of plastic and glass with a hint of air freshener. We scanned the directory for Attorney Cohen. I recalled that Attorney Goldstein's office was on the third floor. I said a quick prayer that I wouldn't need his services again. Attorney Cohen's office was on the fourth floor. As we got off the elevator, a middle-aged woman met us. She had short-cropped hair and was dressed in an azure suit with a colorful scarf. "I'm Miss Tweed, Attorney Cohen's secretary. You're right on time. He's expecting you. Come this way, please." She escorted us into her office, expressed her condolences and poured us each a cup of coffee.

I whispered to Autumn, "We're sure getting the royal treatment."

Then Miss Tweed sat at her desk and pressed the intercom button. "The rest of Lily's family is here."

*The rest? Who else is here?*

Miss Tweed opened the door and escorted us into Attorney Cohen's office. It was bathed in sunlight from two adjoining picture windows. *The corner office*, I thought. Fresh flowers were on his desk. Backlit by the light through the massive windows, his desk was intimidating. I turned to look at the walls. Diplomas filled one, and taxidermy ocean fish filled the other. The scent of flowers and leather upholstery filled the air. He rose and ushered us to overstuffed chairs, interrupting his conversation about a fishing trip with Heidi. He drew his blinds so the sunlight would not be in our eyes. Heidi stood and gave us each a hug.

"Thank you for coming. Please be seated," he said, picking his reading glasses off a pile of papers and sitting in his overstuffed chair. "Let's begin." The buttons on his three-piece suit bulged as he leaned forward to take a blue folder from the reams of papers before him. "Lily Barton was a very productive young lawyer. It was one of the best decisions I have ever made as senior partner to hire her out of law school. As you know, she made one of the highest scores on the bar exam that the state of Minnesota has ever recorded."

"I had no idea," I said.

He ignored me and continued. "And I'm sure you are well aware of the work she did for the Anishinabe tribe."

We all nodded.

"What you may not know is that as our corporate law specialist, she was also very productive. No other junior lawyer has ever made such a reputation for our firm." He shuffled his papers and continued. "Her estate has a life insurance policy with each of you as beneficiaries." He handed the copies to Heidi, and she passed one to Autumn and one to me. He nodded at us. "There are no contingencies to this insurance money."

"Very generous," I said, flabbergasted by my portion.

"Oh, that's a minor part of her estate. The remainder is divided into three parts." He passed a page to Heidi. I saw her face turn ashen.

He spoke to Heidi. "She states in her will that she would prefer you use some of the money to go on vacation." He took off his glasses. "I understand you have not taken a vacation in years." He put his glasses back on. "But there are no contingencies; you may spend the money however you please." He turned to Autumn. "Your part, Miss Barton—may I call you that?" He handed her a sheaf of papers.

"Please call me Autumn."

"Your part, Miss Autumn Barton, is to allow you to work in whatever capacity of social work you choose without having to worry about income. Again, there are no contingencies."

I could see her Anishinabe complexion drain as she scanned the papers he'd handed her. For a moment, she looked Caucasian.

"I'm afraid that your part of the will does have contingencies, Dr. Shelton. Before I give you the documents related to your inheritance, let me explain."

I squirmed in my chair and felt perspiration drip down my back. *What did Lily—*

"Are you aware of Miss Lily Barton's interest in Madagascar?"

"Yes, I am."

"Where's Madagascar?" Autumn whispered.

"It's the big island off the coast of Africa," I said.

Autumn nodded. "Oh."

"Good. Because your inheritance requires that you work for a minimum of one year for an organization called Sampana—I cannot pronounce it."

"SALFA," I said.

"Yes, that's the acronym. You are required to work for SALFA for one year, and"—he took a drink of water from a glass on his desk—"this part I don't understand completely. You must bring back a picture of the hospital generator at the Manam ..." He stumbled over the word.

"Manambaro Hospital," I said.

"Yes, Doctor." He spelled the name, unable to pronounce it. "Rakotojoelinadrana, the director, must be in the picture, and he must sign it. Do you understand this stipulation?" He smiled. "Because I don't."

I was laughing and crying at the same time but regained my composure enough to answer. "Yes, I do. She donated the money for that generator and paid for its shipment. She even paid an electrician to go to Madagascar to make sure it was hooked up properly. We had plans to go see the generator together before she got sick." Tears streamed down my cheeks. I felt faint. I was falling out of my chair. Autumn grabbed me. Heidi pulled a tissue out of her purse and gave it to me. I cleared my throat, sat up straight in the chair, and asked, "Should I bring the picture back to you?"

He laughed. "I'm glad you understand this contingency. I was dreading trying to explain it to you."

Heidi shook her head and said, "That girl." Autumn gave me a hug.

"I didn't know anything about her interest in Madagascar," said Heidi.

"I knew it wouldn't be simple," said Autumn. "That's my sister—always full of surprises."

I lifted my aching head and turned to Attorney Cohen. "How should I contact SALFA?"

"SALFA has already been contacted. She did that before she died. The information for you to make travel arrangements is included in this document. You're encouraged to use the travel agent she indicated, but that's not a requirement." He handed me an envelope.

"I will have to give notice at work. I am under contract as a hospitalist at Hennepin County Hospital."

"Yes, I understand that you will need to give your present employer proper notice." He handed me a paper. "The top figure is the money you will receive to pay the expenses to travel to Madagascar, and a monthly stipend will be put into your account here in the United States while you are working there. The money should be retrievable by ATM." He laughed. "True to form, she already checked to make sure that ATMs exist in Madagascar, but they only take Visa. Do you have a Visa ATM card?"

I choked on the memory. "Yes, she made me apply for one a few months ago. She never told me why I needed it."

"Upon completing your requirements, you will receive the bottom figure on your return. A certain portion of money is invested in bonds. You may use the dividends as you choose while in Madagascar. Your account will receive the money on a monthly basis. If you do not go to Madagascar within the five-year period, you lose the money, and it is donated to SALFA. If you go to Madagascar and serve SALFA for a minimum of one year, the entire amount is yours. You may continue receiving the money on a monthly basis or even cash the bonds if you choose. Do you understand these contingencies, Dr. Shelton?"

I was trying to count the zeros on the paper. As my eyes blurred, I couldn't figure out how much money there was, but there was a lot. I looked at Heidi and Autumn. They were mute. I directed my attention to Attorney Cohen. "May I ask where all this money came from?"

"That's confidential to our firm, but suffice it to say that she was a very productive junior partner. Her abilities writing briefs and her charisma in court will be sorely missed. She would have made—" With a brisk motion of his handkerchief from his suit pocket, he wiped his eyes. "Senior partner this year." He stood. "Now, if you have no other questions about your inheritance or Lily's will, I thank you for coming."

He gave Heidi a hug. "You are blessed to have had such a fine daughter. Your eulogy overwhelmed me." He shook Autumn's hand. "Your sister had great admiration for your career choice." He put his hands on my shoulders. "I am the executor regarding your contingencies. You are welcome here anytime you have a question. Fax me a copy of your flight plan, and you will receive the first installment to your account to pay for travel expenses. She must have thought very highly of you, Dr. Shelton."

"She's the one who talked me into going to medical school, sir."

"A wise decision," he said as he ushered us out of his office. "I need to review *Welton vs. Harrison Corp.*, Miss Tweed." His face turned red, and I thought I saw tears in his eyes as he turned and closed his door.

# DESPAIR

I FELT MISERABLE. LITTLE THINGS would set me off. I opened the cupboard, and there was a bag of wild rice. What was I going to do with that? I didn't know the recipe Lily had used. The freezer still had a filet of bear meat. I sat in my chair by the table, too tired from work to change out of my hospital scrubs, and succumbed to intense loneliness.

I was angry too. Why hadn't Lily been willing to try chemo? Why had she been so stubborn? But it wouldn't have made any difference. I knew that intellectually. I knew she had made correct decisions. Then there was the will. She was still trying to manipulate me. I resented that. But if she hadn't been so manipulative, I would never have been a physician. I loved being a physician.

The telephone rang. It was Beth, my sister-in-law. "Barak, would you be willing to come for dinner Saturday night? Jason and I would love to make you something special."

Since I had the weekend off and nothing planned, I agreed. Maybe some brotherly love was what I needed. Beth promised baked salmon with spinach soufflé and apple pie for dessert. How could a bachelor refuse?

I slept in and arrived in the early afternoon. Jason and I went for a hike along the St. Croix River, north of Stillwater, Minnesota. It was good exercise, and I enjoyed the fresh air. Somehow, Jason seemed out of sorts, not his usual self. But we hiked, had a snack along the river, and laughed at inconsequential trivia. I couldn't tell what was wrong. Brothers knew these things.

When we returned to his apartment, Beth took a beautiful pie out of the oven. Jason and I lit the grill on the porch and soon had the salmon ready. We sat down to a spinach soufflé that towered above its pan. I devoured the delicious food.

When Beth served the apple pie with copious scoops of vanilla ice cream, the reason for my invitation came to the surface. "You're not really going to go to Madagascar, are you?" Beth said as she swallowed her ice cream flavored with Malagasy vanilla.

I thought the best tactic was ambiguity. "Well, I'm still thinking about it."

"You don't need the money, Barak," said Jason. "You still have the life insurance money that I heard you received from the will. I'll be glad to invest it for you. It will make a nice nest egg when you retire."

"Besides," said Beth, "it's so far away."

I was glad I'd never told them how much money was in the insurance policy or the will. That might have colored my brother's interest in investing my nest egg. "But it is an amazing opportunity to expand my expertise in tropical medicine," I said as I gobbled down my apple pie. I wanted to finish it before the conversation curdled my stomach.

"How much tropical medicine will you see in Minneapolis, Minnesota?" Jason said.

I wanted to tell him about the cases of malaria and schistosomiasis I had encountered at Hennepin County Hospital, but I countered with "Yes, I suppose you're right." Then I looked at my watch, remarked how late it was, and excused myself to go home. "I've had a rough week, and I'm tired. Thanks for the excellent meal. I'm not much of a cook myself."

Later, Jason apologized and explained that Mother had put Beth up to the invitation to try to manipulate my decision. Mother didn't want me to go to Madagascar; that was the truth. I didn't think Beth cared whether I went or not, as she was focused on her upcoming pregnancy.

When the insurance money came to my account, I felt rich. I decided to start dating. It was a disaster reminiscent of high school: "Do you like this new dress? Do I look pretty in pink? There's a rock concert next weekend. Are you going to take me?" I took several of the nurses out for nice dinners. They ordered salads while I ate my steak. We talked about patients for a while, and then the conversation fell to silence.

One Friday morning several months later, I put the bear roast in the Crock-Pot with onions and carrots. It looked like a lot of meat, but I intended on inviting anyone for dinner who was willing to come. I tried to invite the social worker on our medical floor. "I'm fixing roast bear meat."

She said, "Yuck. How disgusting." Several of the nurses turned out to be vegetarians, and those who weren't were vicious environmentalists who thought it criminal to kill bears. I was the main subject of the gossip tree all day. By that evening, I expected to eat the roast by myself. Bear-meat sandwiches from the leftovers might be tasty.

Discouraged by my attempts at social interaction and tired from admitting a host of patients, I went home without inviting anyone. When I arrived, Autumn stood at the door to my apartment building. "You are so predictable," she said. "I haven't been waiting more than five minutes."

She followed me up to my apartment despite no expressed invitation. I opened the door, and she said, "Ah, bear meat. My sister's kill? Am I invited for dinner?"

I nodded. She had always been so formal, criticizing me about my relationship with Lily. What was she doing there? Had she changed her mind about me? It was hard to break through Anishinabe communication.

She waltzed through my apartment, inspecting my counters and the things I had left out and checking for dust on my shelves. "I intended to take you out for dinner and pay for it," she said. "I'm rich, you know, but this is better." She opened the Crock-Pot and smelled the roast. "Nice job, Barak. Do you have a wine to go with it? Have you cooked the wild rice yet?"

"No, I don't have any rice, and I'm unsure of the wine to have with bear meat." I stared at her. She was dressed in a business suit with her hair in a bun. She took off her suit coat and flopped it over the couch; stretched like a lioness in her laced satin blouse; and unraveled her silky black hair, letting it fall to her waist. A blank stare and silence were my only responses. She pulled out a pan, in which she put wild rice from a package in her purse, and instructed me to watch it so it didn't burn.

"I'm not an alcoholic like my sister, so I think a nice bottle of Bordeaux would taste great with bear meat. You set the table; I'll be right back. And watch that rice." With that, she was out the door.

I set the table with cloth napkins and my best china, which had been a wedding gift to my parents, but Mother didn't want it anymore. Crystal wine glasses and fine silverware looked great on the table. I was just slicing the roast, when Autumn returned.

She took a look at the table, checked the rice, and smiled approval. "Nice." She went to my cupboard drawer and pulled out the wine opener.

*How does she know where I keep things?* I wondered.

The wine opened with a nice pop. She smiled. "You're acting more Anishinabe than I am. You've hardly said a word since I came."

"I'm stunned," I said. "I didn't think you liked me."

"Oh. I didn't. You were such an egocentric, obnoxious, lustful …" She paused. "But you've improved. You are much more authentic now." She took the platter with the sliced meat from me, forked out some carrots and onions from the Crock-Pot, served the rice, and set it all on the table. She smiled, gave me a hug, and said, "Let's eat."

Conversation opened like a flood. We talked about everything that night—Heidi's practice, her childhood memories, and growing up with Lily. She included some of the comical anecdotes of things Lily had done as a child that I hadn't heard before. "She was always in trouble." We talked about some of her clients. I added stories of my recent patients.

It was well after midnight—and the wine bottle was empty—before we ran out of things to share. "You're not on call tomorrow, are you?" she asked.

"No."

"So have you turned in your resignation at work yet to go to Madagascar?"

The next day, I gave notice at work that I was leaving the following April. I still had months to prepare, but the decision was made. The problem was that my family was still opposed to my leaving. I was dreading spending Thanksgiving home in Duluth, but I decided to go and not make excuses.

As I entered the house, havoc broke out in the kitchen. The turkey was burning on the top and still raw inside. Beth rescued the bird by resetting the oven temperature and covering the breast with foil. Dinner was tasty despite the disastrous beginning.

After dinner, Beth and Jason's expected child was the focus of conversation. Mother danced around the living room. "I'll be a grandmother soon. This is so exciting. Do you have enough baby clothes? And diapers? You need lots of diapers." I relaxed, happy not to be the point of conversation.

The peace didn't last. Madagascar and I became the focus on Saturday morning. Beth and Mother corned me in the kitchen. "Madagascar is so far away," Beth said. "You could get some bad disease and die. Why don't you just stay in Minneapolis?"

Mom said, "Isn't Hennepin County Hospital giving you enough money?" Then she added that I hadn't given her any grandchildren. "Are you going to become a celibate priest?"

*Enough*, I thought, and I made some excuse and left. I gave everyone a warm hug and walked out the door.

Christmas was better, as I signed up to be on call for the holiday. At the end of April, I discovered I was easily replaced as a hospitalist at Hennepin County. I received a letter from Mireille Renard, my mother's friend. She offered me free room and board at their home outside Paris. She made a point that I should take an immersion course in French if I were to go to Madagascar. She even had talked with her personal physician, who'd agreed to let me accompany him on rounds so I could become comfortable with medical French. I kept the secret from Mom that Mireille was encouraging me to go. She mentioned in her letter that it was a great opportunity. That was refreshing instead of her knocking sense into my head, as my mother expected of her.

I explained my plan to Attorney Cohen. He thought spending time in France to become more fluent and learn medical terms was a legitimate use of the money from Lily's will. He warned me that if I didn't then go to Madagascar, I would be responsible to refund any money spent in France back to Lily's estate. I agreed and danced out of the office, delighted that Lily was providing for all my expenses in France.

By the time I was ready to leave, the only person to see me off was Autumn. Jason and Beth had been up all night with a croupy baby, and Mother was back at work, teaching school. Their disapproval was palpable. Autumn drove me to the airport, gave me a big hug, and even had tears in her eyes. I was surprised she cared that much. "I thought you didn't like me when we were in college."

I ran to my gate.

# 32

# PARIS

THE FLIGHT WAS EIGHT HOURS over night, so I arrived in Paris at nine thirty in the morning local time. I had read that one should not even think about what time it was at the place of departure because it prolonged jet lag, so I promised myself not to think about it.

Mireille was supposed to meet me at the airport. Mother said she had been at Dad's funeral, but I didn't remember meeting her. Mom had shown me some pictures of Mireille from when they were in college together. She'd described how Mireille went to UMD on a track-and-field scholarship. She looked in Mom's pictures like a Caribbean beanpole, tall and slight, an obvious runner. Now she was a woman my mother's age, so I wasn't sure I would recognize her from college pictures. I'd sent her my picture, so I hoped she would recognize me if I didn't pick her out of the crowd. I went through immigration, went down to baggage claim, and exited through the *rien* à *déclarer* (nothing to declare) door, dragging my suitcases.

In the crowd, my eye caught an astounding woman who stood out from the rest. She was tall, stately, and distinguished, with a dark complexion. She walked like a fashion model and was dressed like one as well. I tried to distract myself to look for Mireille, when the amazing woman walked right up to me and said, "You must be Barak. I'm Mireille."

I had planned on saying something clever in French, but all that exited my mouth was a deep sigh.

"Well, come along, Barak. My husband, Claude, is waiting for us in the loading zone. Did your entire luggage arrive?"

"Yes."

"Good. Sometimes Delta loses luggage. You should have flown Air France."

I felt like a stray mutt following an adopting master. Mireille took my heaviest suitcase and pulled it along as if it were nothing. Despite her model physique, she was strong and athletic. I had trouble believing she was my mother's age.

It was a chilly morning, but when we arrived at the parking garage, Claude had the Citroën warmed up. My luggage almost fit in the back of the car, which meant I had to hold one of my suitcases on my lap. Claude spoke English with a heavy French accent. "We don't have *la* car. We rent this one. *Joli, n'est pas?*"

I just smiled and said, "*Oui.*" I learned later that I should have said, "*D'accord*" (I agree).

Mireille continued to explain. "We ordinarily take the train to Gare du Nord, but then we have to take a metro and change to another one to get to our apartment. We thought this would be easier for you with your luggage."

I was glued to the window. Everything looked strange—the tall buildings mixed with sidewalk cafés, the apartments with multiple chimneys, and a huge soccer stadium. I practiced reading the advertisements along the way, preparing my mind for French vocabulary. The traffic was heavy, so it was a slow process driving to their apartment. Claude pulled into a space with an odd meter. "I'm checking *la* car," he explained. I learned that renting a car off the street was efficient and practical. He swiped a credit card into the meter, and the car was considered returned.

Claude took my heaviest suitcase. "This one very heavy."

"Sorry. It has medical supplies in it for Madagascar—surgical stuff."

He smiled as Mireille took the other suitcase, and I took my carry-on bag. We trudged up the stairs to the fourth floor. I was gasping for breath by the third floor. Neither of them was the least bit out of breath.

Their apartment living room seemed like a Louis XIV boudoir. Chairs had cabriole legs and lion-paw feet. The Italian carved ceiling gave a bright glow to the room. The tables were covered in lace. I was afraid to sit on the chairs, which seemed to be antique museum pieces. Mireille laughed at me standing in front of a chair. "Sit down; it won't break. It is only a replica." Lace drapes graced the windows, and antique lithographs of ancient Parisian streets framed the walls. "Come. I will show you your room," she said.

My room was small but had a tiny desk and a small poster bed. It was elegant. The smell of lavender permeated the room. "Rest. Be comfortable. The bathroom is that door on the left." She pointed down the narrow hallway. "We will have *déjeuner* later."

I wasn't that hungry, as the airline had served breakfast an hour before landing, but I was intrigued by what would be served. I flopped onto the bed. It felt good after a restless night of trying to sleep while sitting upright in an airplane. I should have flown first class. Lily's trust would have allowed it, but it had seemed a waste of money.

I must have fallen asleep, because a knock on the door awoke me for lunch. It was one o'clock. I popped up to join my hosts. Baguette, four different kinds of cheese, and a small glass of wine were set at my place. I had never had alcohol for lunch before, but sipping my wine seemed like a nice new lunchtime custom.

"How is your mother, Barak? Is she eating well? She was so thin when she and your father came to visit. And at the funeral, she seemed so despondent. I was worried she wasn't eating again—that her anorexia had recurred."

I was shocked. I knew my mother was thin, but I guessed I'd been too self-focused to realize she had an eating disorder. I recalled that after Dad died, she hadn't eaten much until the day Aunt Lisa had taken her out to dinner. I said, "Were you at my dad's funeral?"

"*Oui*, of course, but you probably don't remember me. You seemed so intrigued by Heidi's adopted daughter. Lily was her name, right? I heard that she recently died. I'm so sorry. Your mother said you two were quite the pair."

"Yes, she was my best friend." I choked up. "She wrote me into her will. That's why I'm here and preparing to go to Madagascar."

"I'm sorry, Barak." Mireille put her hand on my shoulder. The smell of her perfume seemed like a comforting incense. "I heard about Lily's will from your mother." She paused as Claude stared silently. "Now, how is your mother doing?"

"She is doing well. Beth and Jason had a baby, and she is pretty excited about being a grandmother, so I think that is keeping her healthy." I sampled one of the cheeses on my plate. "Mom had problems with eating in college, didn't she?" I tried to ask the question as if I knew about her problem. As I thought back, many of my childhood experiences became clear. Mother had anorexia nervosa, an eating disorder.

Mireille laughed. "*Donc, oui.* That's why she flipped the canoe over when we went on our trip together. She wasn't eating, was hiding her food, and passed out. You know, I first met your mother while preparing for our all-women canoe trip." She pulled apart her baguette, put a piece of Roquefort cheese on it, and took a bite. "She was avoiding breakfast that morning, discarding her pancakes behind a rock, so when we got into some wind, she fainted, and the canoe flipped over. She was still unconscious when Lisa rescued her and pulled her underneath the canoe to recover. You knew that, didn't you?"

"Oh yes, Father told me some of that story."

Mireille laughed. "Lisa—how do you say in English?—bit into her and made her eat everything the rest of the trip." She ate another bite of her baguette with a slab of cheese. "We called it DOE—directly observed eating—for the rest of the trip. We teased her unmercifully." After a sip of wine, she continued. "That made all the difference. Your mother seemed much happier after that. I think almost drowning provoked her to righteous eating."

I chuckled as if I knew the story, but inside, I was shocked. As I thought back, it made sense. Mother stopped eating whenever she was stressed. I didn't want Mireille to know that I hadn't known about my mother's problem. I was curious for her to continue.

"I was worried about her at your dad's funeral. She didn't seem to be eating again."

Now I understood why Lisa had taken her out that afternoon when Jason and I had gone for pizza with Uncle Troy; she'd been biting into her, as Mireille said, treating Mom to DOE: directly observed eating. Lisa had saved Mom again. It sure had made a difference in Mom's attitude.

Mireille continued, not giving me time to comprehend what I had just learned. "By the way, as part of your emersion experience, we planned to speak only French unless, for reasons of safety, you don't understand something. Claude does not feel comfortable speaking English. Oh, and my physician said that you could accompany him on rounds at the hospital in a couple of weeks. That way, you can learn medical French terms for your experience in Madagascar. You will love Madagascar. Claude and I went there for a vacation. It is beautiful, and the lemurs are so cute."

That was the last I heard English. They switched to French in the middle of lunch. I struggled to understand, but they spoke slowly, and it was a great learning experience. Some things they wrote out since I read French better than I understood spoken French. Claude and Mireille explained that they owned a perfume factory and distribution company. Claude managed the manufacturing, and Mireille was the financial officer. During the day, they would be at work, so Mireille gave me a key for the apartment and suggested a list of places I should see. She emphasized that even if people spoke English to me because they recognized I was a tourist, I should respond in French. She explained that when people started answering me in French, then I had arrived as a temporary resident.

The first couple weeks were full of new experiences as I visited the tourist spots, such as Tour d'Eiffel, Musée Louvre, and Chateau d'Versailles, but then I went to less-well-known spots, such as Cluny, Museé de Moyen Age, and the Museé Rodin. After a couple of weeks, people did start responding in French. Claude and Mireille were pleased when they heard it. I still had a steep learning curve to understand what people said, but I was delighted with my improvement. No matter how many As I'd received in four years of college French courses, this was stressful, and I felt like an idiot multiple times a day, especially when a ten-year-old child understood something that I did not.

After two weeks, I had seen everything I wanted to see as a tourist, so Mireille gave me assignments: go to the post office, set up a bank account, and buy tickets for the three of us to go to the opera. These were much more challenging situations. I did well in getting the tickets but understood nothing of the French opera we attended. Mireille explained some of it on the metro back to their apartment, so I at least understood the plot.

One afternoon, it seemed as if nobody understood my French. I sat at a bistro and contemplated just giving up and going home. This was never going to work. I would never get rid of my American accent, as people told me. But that night, Mireille had no supper ready. She told me to go with Claude. "Where are we going?" I asked in polite French.

I received no answer, but I discovered that we were going to a soccer match—football, as they called it in French. It was a whole new set of vocabulary; plus, I met some of Claude's friends and was invited to participate in the conversation. I was stressed, but on the way home, Claude told me I'd done well for an American. I felt both honored and insulted.

When we returned to the apartment, Mireille dished me some homemade soup with a baguette and cheese as she informed me that she had made arrangements for me to accompany her physician on hospital rounds. She explained where and when to meet him. I was concerned because she said he spoke no English. I felt paralyzed and wanted to protest, but there was no room for discussion. Besides, my mind went blank for French words to disagree.

Monsieur Dr. Menars was gentle with me and spoke slowly, writing words out that I didn't understand. I was impressed with the warm rapport he developed with each patient we saw in the hospital. My anxiety slowly dissipated as we discussed medical issues. I was in my element as a physician.

I learned not to address him as Doctor because he was not my doctor, an interesting French custom. I was to address him as Monsieur Menars. He introduced me to his patients as Monsieur Sheldon. I was not his patients' doctor either.

Learning French medical terms was easier than I expected. There were only a few terms that were not Latin- or Greek-based, such as *foie* for "liver" and *rein* for "kidney," but many words were just French versions of medical terms, such as *gastronomique* for "gastric." In a matter of weeks, I felt quite comfortable making rounds and even discussing medical problems with his patients, except those who spoke a French dialect. Dialects I hadn't realized existed in France needed to be translated. At the end of the month, I thanked Monsieur Menars for his willingness to allow me to accompany him on rounds. It was a great experience.

A new anxiety hit me that night as I came home from the hospital. I had to decide whether I was going to Madagascar or not. I had a suitcase of medical supplies. What would I do with them if I didn't go? Why was I feeling so ambivalent? Until that night, I could have turned back. The next decision would be irrevocable.

Mireille had made a lamb roast with potatoes and vegetable sauté. She explained in French that the Air France office was right in town. She described the metro stop I should take and where the office was. There was no discussion about if I should go. I felt like a baby bird being ejected from the nest. I knew it was time.

She ate a mouthful of lamb and then opened a conversation in French. "Have you seen the painting of your mother at the art gallery at University of Minnesota there in Duluth?"

"What painting?"

Claude said, "Ooh la la."

Mireille slapped his knee. "The painting of your mother when she was modeling. Nude."

That was dangerous ground. "Ah, no." I swallowed hard, afraid I was going to choke. "My mother used to model nude?"

"Yes, when Lisa had a class conflict, your mother modeled for the art class. One of the graduate students painted such a great picture of her that it was premiered at the grand opening of the gallery. Now it's part of the permanent collection. We saw it when we checked out the new art museum when we attended your father's funeral."

A sip of wine seemed to help. "No. Lisa modeled nude too?"

"Yes, she was the main model for the art classes during the time we all went to UMD. Your mother only substituted when Lisa had a class conflict. You should see the painting. It is quite remarkable."

I decided that night that it was time to leave before I learned anything more about my mysterious, anorexic, nude-modeling mother. There were some things I didn't want to know. Madagascar was waiting for me.

# MADAGASCAR

THE AIR SMELLED LIKE FLOWERS, fragrant and humid, with a hint of jet fuel as we left the aircraft. A gentle breeze blew us along our way between armed guards. The airport was chaotic as more than four hundred people went through immigration one at a time. An hour later, when my bags arrived, I carried them to the customs table, shaking my head to the official porters. The officer had me open my bags. The SOA bag was full of needles, surgical equipment, and medical supplies. The officer spoke in French, but I purposely didn't understand him.

"I'm sorry?" I said in English.

He changed to perfect English. "What is this? Are you trying to sell this in Madagascar?"

"No, sir. It's for SALFA." I was worried by the tone of his voice that he was going to charge duty or confiscate everything. In that moment, a short, slight man dressed in a three-piece suit despite the eighty-plus-degree temperature appeared at my side. He looked Polynesian, like someone from a National Geographic special about Tahiti. He spoke with confidence in Malagasy. The official smiled and waved his hand at me. "Thank you for coming here. Your bags are okay."

"I'm Anderson, director of SALFA," he said in lilted English. "Welcome to Antananarivo, Madagascar, Doctor."

"Barak Shelton. I'm glad to be here."

Anderson took the heavy suitcase, and I followed with my backpack and other suitcase. "Thank you for intervening. I thought he was going to confiscate my bags."

"He might have. It would be no problem."

I followed him to his vehicle, a white Mercedes in a style I did not recognize. It looked like a cross between a Land Rover and a Jeep. The traffic away from the airport was hectic, even though it was just after midnight. Crowds of teens were walking the streets in the marketplace all along the road. We drove for miles between hotels and small shops and then on a straight road with rice paddies on each side. I could see the lights of the city on the hills ahead.

"We are so thankful to have your help for SALFA, Dr. Shelton," Anderson said. "We have many poor people in Madagascar who need help."

"SALFA has quite a few doctors, though. I read about that."

"And they are all waiting for you to teach them."

My image of just helping out was shattered.

We drove down a straight boulevard with a canal between the lanes and then curved up a steep hill. "This hill is Isharaka." He dropped me off at l'Hotel Louvre on the top of the hill. The hotel was surrounded by jewelry stores, and across the boulevard was another hotel, the Colbert. "Best pastries in Madagascar," Anderson said. The porter at l'Hotel Louvre exchanged a few words in Malagasy with Anderson, and I was suddenly treated like part of the family. He insisted on carrying both of my bags to the check-in desk. I tipped him with euros from my sojourn in Paris. He seemed delighted. When I got to my room, I stripped; enjoyed a long, hot shower; and then lay down to sleep off my ten-hour jet trip. I tossed and turned in the bed, got up, turned on the Malagasy television, turned it off, and went back to bed. I was sound asleep when the telephone rang.

It was a sweet Polynesian voice in French-accented English. "Dr. Shelton, your ride is here to bring you to the hospital."

"Thank you," I said, and I hung up the telephone. My heart raced. I had overslept. I wasn't ready. I splashed water on my face, ran a comb through my hair, put on my clean underwear from my backpack, and got dressed in slacks and a sports shirt. I grabbed my white coat and stethoscope out of my suitcase and ran down to the lobby. I smelled the fresh fruit as I ran past the free breakfast to the front desk. Anderson was standing in the same three-piece suit, waiting for me.

"I am sorry I'm late. I overslept."

"Have you had breakfast?" he asked.

"No, but I suppose—"

"Have your breakfast. Not a problem." He escorted me to the dining area and sat at the table while I ate the juiciest, sweetest pineapple, papaya, and guava that had ever entered my mouth. Hot coffee served with hot milk accompanied my fruit. I looked in the corner and saw the omelet chef standing ready to take orders and decided I would wake up on time tomorrow morning. Anderson didn't say much. He seemed relaxed and not in a hurry.

"I'm ready, Anderson. Thank you for waiting." I felt much better. I followed him to his vehicle, which was waiting right outside the hotel. A chauffeur sitting at the wheel jumped out to grab my white coat and stethoscope. Anderson opened the door as the chauffeur climbed into the back seat. I thought that was odd, but so far, everything in Madagascar seemed odd. I was directed to sit in the front passenger seat.

"Good morning," I said.

"*Salama tompoko*," he responded. I had just learned my first Malagasy words.

The drive to the hospital was more hectic than the ride from the airport. My eyes were filled with the sensation of people walking, bicycling, and herding cattle and goats, with taxis weaving in and out of the crowd. The air smelled of animal dung, Malagasy dust, and the sweat of two million people living in the capital. When we arrived at the hospital, Anderson directed me into a doorway.

More than a hundred people stood and started to sing as I entered. I was directed to sit at the front of the gathering. I looked around the room, embarrassed that all those people had been waiting because I'd overslept.

A young woman in a black dress and white coat, with a stethoscope around her neck and a wide, dimpled smile on her face, pulled up a chair next to me and introduced herself. "Dr. Julie." She then explained, "This song is praise to God. We are thankful that you are here." More songs followed. Dr. Julie would whisper a paraphrase at the beginning of each song. The crowd's enthusiasm matched the exceptional melodies.

Then an older gentleman, also in a three-piece suit, stood at the podium. Everyone sat down. He started speaking. There was a hush around the room. His Malagasy sounded smooth and musical, but it was clearly formal, judging by the reaction of the audience. They were squeezed together on benches that would have seated half as many people in the United States. Some people were standing along the wall in the back. I noticed an elderly man carrying a long stick with a wrap over his shoulders. Some of the people wore uniforms, and I noticed a group in surgical scrubs. In front of me was a group wearing white coats, who I assumed were physicians.

Dr. Julie whispered, "He is introducing you. I will translate. We are very glad to have you here to help us and teach us and ..." She paused. "And lots of other nice things." She seemed embarrassed at her translation.

The room hushed with expectation. Was the meeting over? What was going to happen next? I slipped my hands under my seat to calm myself. Dr. Julie whispered, "The hospital director will translate for your speech now." My heart raced. So he was the hospital director, and now I was going to give a speech? A look of pain crossed my face. "You have to stand when you give your speech," Dr. Julie said, helping me to my feet.

*What speech?* The crowd clapped to welcome me.

"I want to thank you for a warm welcome." I had no idea what to say. I'd panicked every time I had to give a speech in high school. *This is a nightmare. I must be still sleeping. I just need to wake up.*

"I am very grateful for the opportunity to come to Madagascar." Each choppy phrase had to be translated. It gave me a moment to think. *What should I say?* "The reason I came to Madagascar is because"—I waited for the translation—"a very special friend told me to come." *So far so good,* I thought. "She had a special place in her heart for Madagascar and passed that on to me." *Do I dare explain my relationship to Lily?* "She talked about Madagascar all the time, and we even planned on coming together. She told me—"

The hospital director interrupted. "I have to translate, please."

I was getting the hang of the translation thing. When he finished, I continued. "She told me that she loved the Malagasy people very much, but unfortunately, six months ago, she died and sent me by myself." *Now, where should I go from here?* I wondered.

The hospital director translated and turned to me. "What was your friend's name?"

"Lily. Lily Barton," I answered.

He didn't translate. A murmur ran through the crowd. "Did you say Lily Barton?" He pronounced the name with a French accent: Lee-lee Bar-toe.

I was puzzled. I wrote her name on a piece of paper and passed it to him. "Yes," I said, "Lily Barton." He started talking, and the crowd erupted, each person excitedly talking to his or her neighbor.

After the noise dimmed, he asked, "Do you have a picture?"

I pulled her high school graduation picture out of my wallet. He picked it out of my hand as if it were an icon of a saint. With both hands, he passed it around to the front row and then gave it to one of the physicians. He stood and went row by row, showing it to everyone in the crowd.

"In her picture, she looks Malagasy. Is she?"

"No, she is Anishinabe."

He translated what I had said and then followed with a long dissertation. *What is he talking about? He isn't translating anything I said.* I stood silently.

The physician who had shown the photo to everyone returned it to me. He cradled it in both hands and bowed as he returned it. "Tell us about Lily Barton. We want to know what kind of person she is."

*Is* reverberated in my head. It was if she were still alive. I explained about her personality, her adoption by Heidi, and finding her mother, and finally, I explained how she'd died. I choked as I tried to explain about her last wishes and her will. When I stopped, the crowd spontaneously started singing with more enthusiasm than I had heard even when I was welcomed.

The hospital director whispered in my ear, "You give very good speeches. You have blessed us this day by telling us about Lily Barton."

I sat down, overwhelmed by my emotions. Dr. Julie whispered, "Thank you for sharing your heart. Malagasy people never forget this."

I was exhausted and weak with perspiration. The crowd dispersed, still singing as they left the auditorium. I stood there, not knowing where to go or what to do next. I asked Dr. Julie, "Where is everyone going?"

"To work. These are all hospital employees. But some are patients you will see."

The physician who had shown Lily's picture to everyone came up to me and shook my hand with both of his. "Dr. Shelton, I am Dr. Solomon. Please. We are needing your help. Follow me."

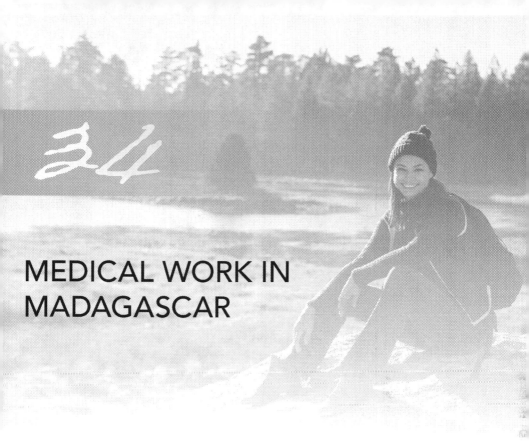

# MEDICAL WORK IN MADAGASCAR

In the men's locker room, Dr. Solomon and I changed into surgical scrubs. I tried to ask what was happening, but he did not seem to understand much English. I asked in French, but I did not understand his answer. We scrubbed at the sink and then dressed with nurse assistance in surgical gowns. I guessed I was needed in surgery and was glad I had taken a surgery elective in my first year of residency. I tried to explain that I was an internal medicine specialist and didn't do surgery. He didn't seem to understand.

We walked into the surgery suite. The anesthesiologist had a young woman asleep on the table. She was naked; the surgical nurse was scrubbing her abdomen. Judging by the form of her breasts and tight midriff, I guessed she was about eighteen. Dr. Solomon explained, "She just came in this morning before your speech. She was in shock. Abdomen was rigid. Her last menstruation—" He looked at me. "Did I pronounce that right?"

"Yes. Her last menstruation," I repeated.

"Yes. It was two or three months before." He hesitated. "I mean ago." He smiled.

The problem was coming to me as the history sank in. "You think she has a ruptured ectopic pregnancy?"

"Ectopic is ruptured, yes."

I could see his eyebrows rise and a smile creep across his face.

The nurse finished scrubbing the abdomen. The anesthesiologist increased the fluids, and we placed the surgical drapes. In what seemed like moments, Dr. Solomon was cutting her open.

As soon as we were in the abdomen, we saw blood. The dead conception poured over the incision into my hands. The nurse grabbed a basin for me to put it in, and then I turned to help Dr. Solomon tie off the left salpinx, the uterine tube that the ectopic pregnancy had burst. The bleeding stopped immediately, and I helped clean the belly of blood.

"She'll have to have a cesarean section if she gets pregnant again," I said.

"Possibly, if she is willing to come to the hospital." He was focused on his suturing.

I finished suturing the skin, something I knew how to do.

"Blood pressure is much better now," said the anesthesiologist.

My internal medicine curiosity got the best of me. "What was the pressure?"

"Four over two," he said. "Now eight over four. Much better."

I looked confused. Dr. Solomon smiled. "In English, that is eighty over forty. We drop a zero in the French system."

I took a deep breath. Eighty over forty was a sustainable blood pressure for a young girl. Dr. Solomon smiled. "God will let her live now." He turned, and I followed, taking off my gloves but unsure where to put them. The nurse took my gloves and gown from me.

We passed through the area where they put the surgical trays together. I noticed that the sterilizer had a name etched on the surface: Lily. "Dr. Solomon, why is Lily engraved on the sterilizer?"

"She donated it to us."

"Oh." I gasped. Lily's intervention had been more than just a generator. What else had she done?

We went on hospital rounds. Dr. Solomon explained each case to me. His English was good if we stuck to medical terminology. Several times, we switched to French. My French was pretty good as long as we stuck to medical terminology, so we muddled through the patients. Several had common problems with which I was familiar, such as strokes, pneumonia, and skin infections, but many had diseases I had seldom seen in residency, including malaria, schistosomiasis, and amoebic liver abscesses. It was one o'clock in the afternoon before we had seen all the inpatients assigned to him.

"I am hungry. Are you able to eat now?" he asked.

I was starving. My bowl of morning fruit had been used up hours before. Tomorrow I was definitely eating an omelet. "Yes, I am hungry now." I repeated his sentence structure.

He led me to a small dining room, where I saw Dr. Julie. She introduced me to several other physicians who were standing along the wall as we entered. A long table was set for us with large plates of tomatoes and eggs with carrot slaw. The director came and said a blessing, and we all sat down. The physicians who spoke English sat next to me and translated the questions of the others. They discovered that if they spoke slowly in French, I could understand, but sometimes I had to answer in English if I was deficient in vocabulary. Then one of the English-speaking doctors would translate. Every conversation was communal.

Large bowls of rice arrived through a side door. Three young women and one older woman carried in trays of chicken and fish with several different sauces. A bowl of steaming vegetables was placed at each end of the table. Everyone started chattering in Malagasy while Dr. Julie, Dr. Solomon, and the director whose name I could not pronounce carried on a conversation with me in English mixed with French.

While I was enjoying my experience at the hospital, I remembered the requirements of Lily's will. I turned to the director. "Where is Manambaro?"

The director asked, "Are you wanting to go there?"

"Eventually," I said. *I need to go sometime this year to fulfill the requirements Lily directed in the will*, I thought.

"It is way far south in the jungle, Dr. Shelton. Hot and humid. It rains every day there. It is right on the ocean, where the cyclones hit. You should work in the mountains. It is better." The director smiled, and his mustache twitched with his grin.

Dessert was a platter of pineapple and bananas that we passed around. The bananas were dark green with black spots but yellow and sweet when peeled. The pineapple was the sweetest yet, even better than what I'd had for breakfast.

I spent the afternoon with Dr. Julie, working in the outpatient clinic. There was no consideration for my being an internist. I saw children with ascaris and asthma, obstetric patients with preeclampsia, and elderly adults in congestive heart failure. By the time Anderson picked me up to bring me back to the hotel, it had been dark for more than an hour.

Somehow, I managed to order something to eat from the French menu at the hotel restaurant. The other choice was the Malagasy menu. I wasn't sure what it was, but it was tasty. Culinary French was quite distinct from medical French. I went to the desk to explain my need for a wake-up call. I was thankful that the receptionist, Ramona, spoke English, not just Malagasy. Then I hit the bed like a rock.

When Anderson picked me up in the morning, I was ready. I had eaten a cheese omelet, plenty of fruit, and two croissants.

"So Lily Barton sent you?" he asked.

"Yes, she was a very good friend of mine, like a sister." The word stung in my mouth.

"She has done a lot for SALFA. We are very thankful for her. Does her mother still live?"

*Which mother?* I thought. I decided to describe Heidi. "Yes, her mother, Heidi Barton, is a physician."

"You should invite her to come. We would be honored to meet the mother of Lily Barton."

"She could maybe come for a visit, but she is very busy taking care of poor people."

"Are there many poor people in the United States?" he asked.

"In certain places." I went on to describe the Anishinabe reservation. He was aghast at the tribal conditions I described.

"Just like Malagasy people," he said. "Did Lily Barton help her tribe too?"

"Yes, a lot."

When I arrived at the hospital, they were singing. I found Dr. Solomon, and we made rounds together, checking the patients we had seen the day before. The young woman on whom we had performed surgery was bright and alert. She even had normal bowel sounds. I was amazed.

One new young teen had been admitted during the night with meningitis. He had a stiff neck and high fever and was in a coma. We reviewed the choice of antibiotics. "We use chloramphenicol for these patients," he said.

I had never prescribed the drug during residency.

Lunch was good, and outpatient clinic was busy, as always. I was beat when Anderson came to get me. "The plan is for you to work with the tuberculosis patients in Antsirabe. I will bring you there on Sunday."

"Where is Antsirabe?"

"Down south along the Norwegian road."

Manambaro was in the south, so maybe I would be closer to my goal, I thought.

That night in my room, I wrote a letter to Heidi, suggesting she come sometime while I was in Madagascar. I gave the letter to Ramona, and she helped me apply three different stamps to approximate the required postage. "Are you visiting more of our island while you are here?" she asked.

"I understand that I will be working in Antsirabe. That is where SALFA wants me for now."

"Oh, it is very nice there." She smiled, took my letter, and put it in a cubicle behind her.

I saw a map of Madagascar behind her and asked, "Can you show me where Manambaro is? I don't see it on this map."

The porter ran behind the desk. "Ramona is from Antsirabe. She does not know Manambaro. I am from the south." He pointed to the southeast tip of the map. "Manambaro is here, not far from Fort Dauphin."

"It looks like a long way from here."

He smiled, revealing his decayed teeth. "Oh yes, very far."

On Sunday, while people sang and rejoiced in the Christian churches along the route, we traveled to Antsirabe. At least we were heading south, one step closer to Manambaro. I recalled Lily admonishing me on the canoe trip to enjoy the journey, not to focus only on the goal. I was fascinated by the rice paddies interspersed between the mountains. For a while, the road paralleled a wide river that accentuated the terrain with spectacular waterfalls and rapids. I looked down the cliff at the river and fantasized about Lily and I canoeing downstream, fighting through the rapids, and portaging the waterfalls.

That highland area was fertile for crops. Rice and cassava grew well because the crops were supported with plenty of rain and moderate temperatures. One valley we drove through had a huge market. I spotted carrots, tomatoes, and even strawberries. However, erosion was evident where the trees had been cut from the hillsides, and now bear-claw rips in the green landscape bared the bloodred soil underneath.

When we arrived, the churches were spilling the faithful onto the streets. Still rejoicing in their bright-colored clothes, the people were clustered in conversation, walking nowhere in particular at a casual pace. Anderson slowed for the clumps of people as he drove through town and then turned in at the gate to the hospital.

Anderson explained about Antsirabe. "*Tsira* means 'salt,' so the name means 'the Town of Salt Springs.' The *be* suffix means it is a big one." He went on to explain some of the history of the town. In the early 1900s, it had been a resort town for rich French tourists. A hotel built with a large front porch extending the entire length of the hotel had featured mineral spring baths. It had faltered and been rebuilt and now was a luxury hotel, Les Thermes. Les Thermes had a great swimming pool, and rich tourists came to enjoy it as opposed to the not-so-clean mineral springs.

We turned a corner into the hospital grounds, driving past the security guard with a hand wave. The main hospital was an impressive Scandinavian-style building. "There is a new surgery wing," Anderson said, pointing to the left of the main structure. "Dr. Jacques, the surgeon, is also the director of the hospital, and he has done an excellent job here." He drove around the hospital and up to the concrete veranda of the guesthouse in the back. "Here is your house." He stopped the vehicle and carried my heavy bag of all my possessions. I carried my backpack. My second bag with the medical supplies seemed to have disappeared. I assumed the supplies had been dispersed among the SALFA hospitals.

"I am very sorry, Dr. Shelton, but I must return to Tana. Will you be able to have dinner at one of the restaurants we passed? The Chinese one is very good."

"No problem," I said.

"The cook we hired for you will visit this afternoon. She will start cooking tomorrow morning. She has a key to the house and has worked for many of the volunteers. She knows how to make clean food, so you will not get sick. And she can be trusted with money."

He showed me the house. "Tin roof." He smiled as if it were an extravagance. There were two bedrooms, a small kitchen, and a bathroom at the end of the hall. The house was concrete with high ceilings, so it was quiet and cool. The lighting consisted of dangling lightbulbs. I expected it to smell stale, but instead, it smelled of vanilla. I asked why. "Vanilla perfume is made in Madagascar. We sprayed it in the house to welcome you." He gave another broad smile. There was a large plastic bucket in the shower. "If you keep the bucket full, then you can bathe even when the water doesn't work."

The living room was furnished with two hand-carved rosewood chairs. They looked as if they had been carved for the king of Siam. There was a bookcase with several novels, mostly in French. A low coffee table of rosewood was similarly carved.

Anderson interrupted my scan of my new living quarters. "I am most sorry, Dr. Shelton, but I must go. It is a four-hour drive back to Tana, and it is not safe to drive the roads at night."

I gave him a hug, and he departed.

I slumped in one of the Polynesian chairs. Despite their appearance, they were incredibly uncomfortable. I twisted my back while trying to get out of it. I was glad there was no one to see me fall to my knees to perform the task. Crumpled on my knees, alone in what I assumed would be my house for most of the year, I was overwhelmed with emotion. I doubted if anyone within a hundred miles—220 kilometers, I reminded myself— spoke English as his or her first language. There was no one to talk to, and I felt lonely, hungry, and tired of the twisty mountain road we had traveled for almost four hours. What was I doing there? Lily's words echoed in my brain: "That's the trouble with you, Barak. What are you thankful for?"

I rolled over onto my back. "I don't have diarrhea, Lily. I'm thankful for that." I wondered for a moment if I were becoming psychotic, talking to someone who had been dead for six months. With no one around, I yelled, "I'm thankful for this house! I'm dry, I can get food, and I'm a doctor! Are you satisfied, Lily?"

There was a gentle tap on the door. I stopped my ranting and went to the door. A petite, thin Malagasy woman stood at the door with her head bowed.

Dressed in ragged slacks and a pullover sweatshirt, she looked to be in her twenties, but when she smiled, half of her teeth were missing, and her single front incisor had a large cavity. "You being Dr. Barak?"

"Yes." I was embarrassed by my ranting. "I was praying out loud," I said.

"Is someone—Lily—here?"

"No. She is someone I am very thankful for. I was praying and thanking God for her."

"Okay. I am cook for you. Okay? Jacqueline my name."

I shook her hand. "Nice to meet you, Jacqueline. I am Dr. Barak Shelton."

"Too hard for me. I call you Dr. Barak, okay? I can say those words." She smiled, demonstrating her need for a dentist. "What you like to eat?"

I mentioned several possibilities. There was no sign of recognition.

"Write, please," she said, handing me a stub of a pencil and a scrap of paper that used to be a wrapper for sugar.

I started to write.

"You not know French words?"

I switched to French. She looked at what I wrote. There was still no recognition. "You eat *boeuf et porc et poulet?*" she asked, mixing languages.

"*Oui.* Yes," I answered, mixing the same two languages.

"Good. I make it good for you. You eat fruit?"

"*Oui.* Yes."

"I make you good *petite-dejeuner* too." She held out her hand.

I had no idea what she wanted. Did she want to shake hands on the deal? Was she asking for something? She lowered her face and said, "*D'argent.*"

*Oh, money.* I was supposed to give her money. I pulled out a fistful of ten-thousand-ariary notes and gave them to her.

She scurried into the kitchen and set them on the counter. "Too much. Only *deux* need now." She took two and left the others next to the sink. "*Au revoir.* In morning, I be here, Dr. Barak," she said, and with a bow, she ran out the door.

"I guess that means I'll be fed," I said to the empty house. For the rest of the afternoon, I settled into the bedroom, putting my stuff in drawers and checking out the books on the shelves. When I looked into the empty refrigerator out of habit, I realized I was hungry and decided to hike into town to find something to eat.

At six o'clock, it was as black as ink outside. There were no streetlights; a few lights from stores that hadn't closed yet and light from the windows of the restaurants lining the boulevard were the only guides. I had my flashlight in my pocket for security, but I preferred to find my way in the dark. The Chinese restaurant was only a few blocks away, so I chose that.

It seemed odd. The smell of ginger and soy sauce changed the street smell of Madagascar to something almost recognizable from Chinese restaurants in the United States. Faded photos of China and plastic fans decorated the palm-tree-bark walls as I entered. The waiter came immediately and seated me at a round table for two. He lit a candle on the table, and it sputtered as he laid down the menu. He spoke in French, only part of which I understood.

The menu was in Malagasy with Chinese subtitles. This was going to be a challenge. *Should I just point?* The waiter returned and asked what I wanted to drink. I answered in French. He took my menu, flipped it over, and then retreated to get my Coca-Cola. I felt a rush of relief. The other side of the menu was in French with Chinese subtitles. At least I could get the meat right. As I glanced at it, I was still confused by the culinary terms. *They need to teach menu reading in college French*, I thought.

I picked something that included two words I recognized and decided to be satisfied with what I got. I took a drink, thankful that Coca-Cola tasted the same in Madagascar as it did in the USA.

My mind went wild. This was the place I would call home for a year— well, at least until I figured out how to get to Manambaro. I wondered how many times I would come to this restaurant. Would I always come alone? What would my cook fix for me? At that moment, as I sipped my drink, waiting for some Chinese delicacy to quench my hunger, a year seemed eternal.

A large bowl of rice appeared with another dish with sauce and what I presumed was pork, since that was the word I'd recognized. Bright-colored vegetables and some kind of pasta were mixed with it. It looked festive. I had no idea whether that was what I'd ordered or not. I thanked the waiter in French with a broad grin.

The food tasted great. My mind recalled where on the menu that selection was, so I could order it again. I wondered if my cook had a day off. Chinese food might be my regular diet if she did. The flavor of ginger and the spice of tiny peppercorns made me slow my eating and order an *encore, s'il vous plait*, of Coca-Cola. I avoided biting into a peppercorn by removing them, but by candlelight, it was challenging. The meal was tasty, so when I finished, I decided to try ordering dessert. I recognized bananas flambé. I ate slowly, relishing the flavor, since I had nothing else to do.

I didn't want to leave. There were people there, and I was going back to my concrete house with a tin roof, which was silent and empty. Several armed guards along the road caught my eye, and I looked away. I walked into my house and switched on the light. It pulsated and then lit up. I looked at my watch and realized that in less than an hour, there would be no electricity. Anderson had warned me that the electricity went off at nine o'clock unless there was a surgery. My house was not on Antsirabe electricity, which was unreliable, but on the hospital generator. I decided I'd better get my bed arranged.

I crawled into bed and reread my book from my backpack, not wanting to struggle with trying to read a French novel or a medical text, the alternatives on the bookshelf. When the electricity went out, I turned on my flashlight, finished a paragraph, and then lay down to sleep. I felt comfortable as I drifted into my dreams.

Sometime in the middle of the night, the lights came back on. I hadn't thrown the switch. I got up to turn it off and crawled back into bed. *There must be an emergency surgery.*

My skin felt itchy. I couldn't fall back to sleep. Since the electricity was on, I went to the bathroom to check the itching. I had red spots all over my trunk, and looking in the mirror, I saw the same spots on my back. "What's this?" I cried, scratching. I went back to the bed and lifted the sheet. I saw nothing. On a hunch, I lifted the mattress. As my eyes focused, I saw thousands of moving black specks. I screamed, "Bedbugs!"

I went to the living room and tried to go back to sleep on the couch. I just tossed and turned, trying to scratch where I couldn't reach. I decided to take a shower.

There was no hot water, but the cold water felt good on my bedbug bites after I gasped and convinced my heart rate to slow down from the shock. The brown soap smelled antiseptic and worked well, but I shampooed with my own supply from my backpack, samples from my hotel in Antananarivo. The towels were musty, but I managed to dry off and get dressed in scrubs and a white coat. Somehow, I fell asleep on my couch until the morning light through the window woke me. I returned to my room and examined the mattress again. Thousands of bedbugs scampered away from the light. How was I going to sleep at night? What an introduction to Antsirabe.

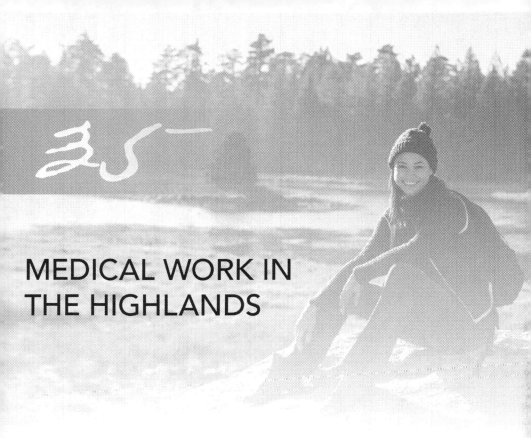

# MEDICAL WORK IN THE HIGHLANDS

DRESSED AND READY FOR WORK despite my itching back, I walked into the kitchen. Hot rice with bananas and sweetened condensed milk was laid out. A bowl of sliced fruit sat beside it with a folded cloth napkin over an empty bowl. "How did she do that?" I said. *Was she fixing this when I was in the shower? When I was running around in my towel?* I yelled, "Jacqueline?" There was no answer. I checked the door. It was locked. Mystified, I sat down to eat. The fruit was outstanding. Between mouthfuls of rice, I decided I needed to be more careful how I ran around in the morning.

I met Dr. Jacques in the courtyard in front of the hospital. He was tall and thin and in constant motion. I was thankful that he spoke excellent English. "I have been to the United States of America twice." His broad smile set me at ease. "I liked the rice at Taco Bell. Do you ever eat at Taco Bell?"

"Yes," I answered, although it had been a rare occasion. He gave me a tour of the hospital, outpatient clinic, surgery suite, and obstetrics building. There were covered walkways to each building, so I assumed it must rain quite hard at times. Last, he showed me the tuberculosis ward, which would be my primary responsibility. We were almost done with our tour, when a hospital worker ran to his side and sputtered something in Malagasy.

He smiled at me. "I would appreciate your help, Dr. Barak." I guessed that Dr. Barak would be what I would answer to for the next year. I followed. He walked fast, but he managed to issue orders to nurses along the way. We went directly to the surgery building and started scrubbing for a case. "We have a trauma case to do," Dr. Jacques explained. "A young woman was planting rice and was gored by a bull. She's six months pregnant."

We walked into the surgery suite with the young woman already anesthetized. I could see dried blood and lacerations over her protuberant belly. The scrub nurse applied butadiene as we scrubbed, gowned, and gloved. Dr. Jacques placed the sterile drapes over her as I noted the lacerations. He proceeded with the incision.

She was a mess inside. We counted seven holes in the small bowel and two in the colon. The cow's horn had gone right through the uterus, and the fetus was dead. "I'm afraid she is going to get infected postop," Dr. Jacques said. "Did you bring any antibiotics with you?"

I held the retractor as he repaired the uterus. "I brought some Augmentin IV."

"That might just save her," he said.

"I'm surprised you are trying to save the uterus." I was puzzled.

"I have to, or her husband might abandon her, or she might commit suicide." He finished sewing the peritoneum and started sewing the skin. Several drains were left in place to drain any abscesses that might develop. My head was swimming with Malagasy logic. It was so different from my training.

After surgery, I saw all the medicine patients with Dr. Narina. She was efficient and focused on the decisions that would make a difference for her patients. Meningitis, out-of-control diabetes, and pneumonia were all common. I did not expect or understand the number of children with malaria, rheumatic heart disease, and schistosomiasis.

One teenage girl with a delicate frame and pretty face was paralyzed from the waist down. When she had helped her mother plant rice, she'd gotten a heavy dose of parasite, and the schistosomiasis had lodged in the blood vessel to the spinal cord. She had no chance of recovery, although Dr. Narina said that some recent studies showed some improvement in rehabilitation potential by using steroids, but the steroids had to be given right away. The young girl's family had waited two weeks before they'd brought her to the hospital.

By noon, I had seen about thirty patients and was exhausted. I sought out Dr. Jacques, as he had invited me to his home for lunch. As I walked into the dining room with him, I was impressed with the spread his wife and their cook had prepared: fried fish with a spicy sauce served over plenty of rice. Of course, there was fruit for dessert. After a delicious meal, I thanked everyone, took Dr. Jacques aside, and told him about my bedbug bites. He spoke to his housekeeper in Malagasy and smiled at me. "Rest on the couch."

I wasn't sure that was the solution I wanted, but when I got back to my place, I rested on the couch. The electricity went off at one o'clock and wouldn't come back on until two thirty, so there was nothing to do but take a nap. I switched on the living room light, even though nothing happened, and lay down on the couch cushions. *When the generator turns back on and I can do something at the hospital, the light will come on and wake me up,* I reasoned.

I squirmed around to scratch my bites, but I was so exhausted from my restless night that I soon fell asleep.

Sure enough, when the electricity came on, the bright light woke me up. *What a great idea.* I scratched my back on the doorframe as I returned to the hospital.

In the afternoon, I reviewed my tuberculosis patients. I examined each one, reviewed the charts, and noted the medications they were on. My nurse, who translated for me, explained that the treatment was by protocol from an organization in Switzerland, and we had to follow their rules to obtain the medications for free. One of the rules was that the patient had to have acid-fast bacilli, tuberculosis organisms, seen on a smear to receive free medications. It seemed reasonable.

There were no new patients, and the ones we had were in stable condition. I reviewed each case with the x-rays the patients brought with them. In one day, I had seen more TB than in all of residency. The different manifestations on their x-ray films were fascinating.

When I finished, I checked the young woman who had had surgery. She was diaphoretic and feverish. I made sure she was getting the antibiotics I had brought and was getting the right dose. She looked as if she belonged in the intensive care unit. There was no such thing there. I checked her urine output and how fast the IV fluids were running. I listened to her heart and lungs to make sure she was not in heart failure. Her abdomen was rigid from peritoneal irritation. I hoped it would improve. All the drains were functional.

It was already dark when I went home. My plate was laid out with a spoon, knife, and fork. A fruit salad was set on top of my plate; a large bowl of steaming rice was under a plate for protection; and a simple note read, "Oven." I checked the oven. In a cast-iron skillet was a pork roast bathed in a tomato sauce. I brought it to the table. That was when I noticed the large canister labeled "Raid Yard Guard" sitting on the table.

*Ah, for the bed,* I thought.

I took the first spoonful of sauce and rice. The flavor was spicy and fragrant. Never had I eaten pork so flavorful. *But how did she do it without my seeing her? And how did she know when I would come home? How did she know what I would like?*

After supper, I sprayed the mattress. That was the end of the bedbugs, although my first night, I felt enveloped in insecticide. I wasn't sure whether Raid Yard Guard was toxic, but there were no more bedbugs, and my bites healed. By the end of the week, when I counted the bites, I felt assured there were no new ones. I was confused. Should that have worked? Maybe bedbugs in Madagascar were more sensitive to Raid.

The next day in the hospital, the woman gored by the bull met me at the door. She walked with obvious tenderness, but records showed she was afebrile. I walked her back to her bed. Drains were still leaking fluid, but it was clear fluid, not purulent. I was amazed. Two days later, she was insistent on going home. I pulled the drains and coaxed her into waiting one more day. The next day, when I made rounds, I discovered that she'd left at sunrise.

# TUBERCULOSIS

AFTER A FEW WEEKS, SEVERAL things became clear. I was learning more than I was teaching. The Malagasy physicians had enormous compassion for their patients. They used their limited resources to maximum benefit. I struggled because some of the patients who died could have been cured with the resources available at Hennepin County Hospital.

I also learned that it was nice to have a cook. I discovered that leftover food disappeared, and it probably fed my cook's family, so I modified my eating, making sure there was always plenty left. Besides, I had started to gain some weight—not judging by the scale, as there wasn't one, but judging by how tight my pants and belt were.

I realized I needed some exercise, so I started running in the morning before going to the hospital. Antsirabe was higher in elevation than Denver, so I needed a few weeks to adjust to the altitude. By the end of the second month, I was eating better and feeling less winded when I ran. On weekends, I went swimming at Les Thermes, the French spa with a great pool. It was a refreshing weekend treat.

Then I met Jora. She appeared for rounds one morning. Dr. Jacques introduced her. "Jora is a nurse from Norway. She is doing a tropical medicine rotation here. Would it be all right if she went on rounds with you in the mornings?"

Jora was a tall, thin, muscular, athletic young woman with almost white blonde hair. She smiled with the cutest dimples. Other than the lilt of a Norwegian accent, her English was flawless. "I am very pleased to meet you, Dr. Shelton. I'm Jora Torgersen."

It was the first time in two months that someone had used my last name. "I'm delighted to meet you too, Miss Torgersen."

Her lanky frame shook with laughter. "Just call me Jora."

"I usually go by Barak myself." We laughed together.

"I'm needed in surgery," said Dr. Jacques. "You two okay?"

"We'll be fine," I said. "Come along, Jora. Let's see some folks."

"I am very interested in global health, and that is why I took this rotation. I was glad to hear that you were in charge of the tuberculosis ward, as I wanted to learn to care for all aspects of TB patients."

Soon my translator nurse, Justine, joined us, and we started rounds on the hospitalized patients. There were two new admissions: a teenage brother and sister who both had huge spleens. They were in adjoining beds. "Their malaria smears are positive," Justine said. I examined them and reviewed their laboratory tests while Jora repeated the exam.

"What causes this?" Jora asked as her hand felt the edge of the young girl's massive spleen.

"This is tropical splenomegaly. It's caused by a reaction in the sinusoids of the spleen to falciparum malaria antigens."

"How do you treat it?" She put the sheet back over the patient.

"In the not-too-distant past, they did splenectomies. But the patients were susceptible to Gram-positive bacterial pneumonia. Now we treat with chloroquine for three to four months. Eventually, the spleen returns to normal, and they don't need any surgery. But it's difficult to get the patient to keep taking the medicine for such a long time." I turned to the nurse. "Justine, can you explain to them how they need to take their medicine?" While Justine admonished the two teens in Malagasy, I asked Jora, "So how long are you going to be here?"

"Six months. And then I have to write a paper about some aspect of my experience. I thought I should write about the TB patients, but these tropical diseases are interesting as well."

"What do you do for fun?" I asked. Justine was still explaining how the two patients were supposed to take their medicine and answering questions. I understood neither what she explained nor the questions they asked.

"I brought my bicycle from Norway. I am hoping to do some bicycle trips on weekends."

Justine interrupted. "They want to know if they can work in the rice paddies, or do they have to stay in bed?"

"It is all right to keep working. They should not stay in bed," I said. Justine translated, and they both smiled.

When we finished rounds at the hospital, Jora invited me for lunch. We walked south of the hospital, past Les Thermes, to a large gate in a brick-walled compound. As we walked in, the guard smiled at Jora. "I'm back," she said. The Malagasy guard smiled and waved.

"This is the Norwegian Language School," she explained. "The Norwegian pastors, teachers, seminary professors, and nurses"—she paused with a smile—"all come here to learn Malagasy. There has been a Norwegian presence in Madagascar since the 1880s. Come. I'll introduce you."

Jora and I entered a large room on the main floor of the dormitory. There was a table situated in the middle of the room, with a buzz of people standing at their places. Jora introduced me to the crowd.

Off to the side of the room was a kitchen. I could hear the bustle of preparation as we sat down after grace was said in Norwegian. I found myself between Jora and a bright-eyed, garrulous young woman, Thorey. A salad of fresh fruit was passed around. I was thrilled to converse in English with those seated around me—college students studying anthropology and seminary professors and their families. An engineer and his wife who were there "fixing things" sat across from us. The atmosphere was lively and energetic. I realized that those at my end of the table were speaking English for my benefit, because the chatter at the other end of the table was in Norwegian.

"What are you doing here in Madagascar?" I asked Thorey. She had long brown hair coiled in braids in a crown around her head. She wore a floral skirt and white T-shirt that accentuated her sinuous figure. *Are all young Norwegian girls so attractive?* I looked around the table; there were several young women, and none of them were an exception to my hypothesis. *Maybe just the Norwegian women who come to Madagascar are beautiful.*

Thorey's answer interrupted my mental wandering. "I'm working with the children at the school. I'm not a certified teacher yet, but this is giving me a great experience."

"But the children speak Malagasy, don't they?"

"They're taught in French. I've studied French since grade school, so that is no problem. But on the playground, they yell and scream in Malagasy. I'm getting pretty good at playground language." She smiled.

"Do you like the food here in Madagascar?" asked Jora as I took another bite of my fruit. "I could live off tropical fruit," she said.

The cooks presented a huge plate of rice accompanied by a bowl of beef swimming in a sauce of cooked greens. I ate enough to consider telling Jacqueline to forget supper. Then a dessert of cardamom rolls glazed with frosting followed. I wondered how I was going to stay awake long enough to see the TB patients in the afternoon.

Jora refused her cardamom roll and excused herself from the table. I assumed she was going to her room to take a nap.

Jora suddenly returned, dressed in a skintight biker's bodysuit that left nothing of her anatomy to the imagination. Her form was streamlined, interrupted only by the pleasant shape of her breasts. "I'm going for a ride. I will see you, Barak, at the TB ward at two thirty." With that, she turned; grabbed her bicycle, which was in the hallway; and disappeared.

I excused myself from my Norwegian hosts, still licking the sweet cardamom from my lips. Thorey stood to shake my hand. "It has been a pleasure to meet you. I am so glad we have a good physician here in case I get sick."

I decided not to think about examining Thorey as a patient. As I walked back to the hospital, Jora whizzed by on her bike. I still needed a nap.

*Who would have thought there would be this enclave of Norwegians here in Madagascar?* I decided the Vikings must have gotten around the world a lot farther than I'd been taught in school. Judging by my conversations at lunch, the Vikings' progeny had become quite sophisticated as well.

As I walked into my house, Jacqueline was filling the refrigerator with supper supplies. I thought, *This is my opportunity to tell her to save it for tomorrow,* but then I realized that her family might not get fed. If I didn't eat too much, they would be able to feast. I greeted her with the few Malagasy words I knew and went to my room to sleep off my Norwegian lunch.

Tuberculosis management became routine: see the patients, listen to their hearts and lungs, make sure they had adequate nutrition, tap off the fluid in their chests if needed, and make sure they were responding to the medication. However, one aspect of my role as TB doctor was not routine, and it caused me intense distress: making a new diagnosis. One case gave me nightmares the whole time I was in Madagascar.

A teenage boy was brought in from a neighboring village. He had a high fever, and his neck was stiff. His face was paralyzed on the left. I knew he had tuberculous meningitis the moment I examined him. There were few types of meningitis that caused paralysis of part of the face and were treatable. I was sure of my diagnosis: this was tuberculosis.

I did a lumbar puncture while Jora held the boy. The procedure was difficult because of his agitation, but Jora's muscular grasp of his arms and legs kept him controlled while I got spinal fluid for examination. "I'll take this specimen to the laboratory," I said when I finished.

"Will you use antibiotics while we wait for the result?" asked Jora.

"I'll give him one dose for meningococcal meningitis in case I'm wrong, but that facial paralysis is almost diagnostic of TB. Most other forms of meningitis do not cause cranial neuropathies."

Jora started an IV, and I made a few quick notes in the chart. The Malagasy nurse took my orders and ran to the pharmacy. The family hovered over the boy and seemed to understand the gravity of the situation. Jora and I went to the laboratory with the precious fluid to confirm the diagnosis.

The technician took the fluid, ran some chemistries, and then spun the fluid to examine the cells under the microscope. We stood watching the process. "Do you see any red snappers in the spinal fluid?" I asked the technician as he peered into the microscope.

"What are red snappers?" asked Jora.

I laughed at my American terminology. "It's a slang expression for acid-fast bacilli. It's what TB looks like under the microscope."

The Malagasy technician, a short, muscular man with graying hair, looked intense as he viewed the field under the microscope. "Lots of white cells, mostly lymphocytes," he said.

"That's typical of TB," I said to Jora.

"The spinal fluid sugar was very low," the technician said, still scanning the specimen.

"The lowest spinal fluid sugars ever reported are with TB meningitis," I added.

The technician looked up from the scope. "But no acid-fast bacilli."

"I can't believe it," I stammered. "They should be there. I'm sure of the diagnosis." I scanned the specimen, realizing I was not as good at scanning the specimen as the technician, but I was desperate to find them. I saw nothing.

As I looked up from the microscope, the Malagasy technician gave a sardonic grin and said, "Those TB—they do not like to live in the spinal fluid."

The patient's Malagasy nurse was standing beside me as I gave up my search. I looked at him in desperation. "Can we treat the boy without the smear being positive?"

"No, it is not allowed. The medicine must be given by protocol, and the Swiss are very particular. His family can't afford the medicine off protocol. They would have to buy it themselves at the pharmacy."

Every morning, the young fellow was worse. He moaned with headache, and the paralysis of his face was more severe. I had given him high doses of antibiotics for pneumococcus and meningococcus, common forms of meningitis, in case I was wrong, but they were ineffective. Every morning, I did another spinal tap to see if the telltale acid-fast bacilli would appear.

On the fourth morning, the lab technician found acid-fast bacilli. Justine ran to meet me in the general hospital ward with the laboratory slip. "Now we can treat him!" I yelled for joy. I returned to his bedside and initiated the protocol medications, triumphant in my persistence.

Two hours later, while I was seeing outpatients, the male TB nurse supervisor came to the clinic, walking like a wounded sheep. "The boy has died now," he said. "The family has taken him home."

My face flushed, and tears dripped down my face. Jora looked at me as I cried. "Why couldn't I find them four days ago? I knew they were there."

She put a hand on my shoulder. "Barak, you did your best. Would it have made any difference clinically?"

"I'm not sure."

"You're the kind of physician I would like to care for me. I can see that you love your patients." She hugged me, but I couldn't speak.

She handed me a tissue from her backpack of supplies she carried with her, and I wiped my face. We still had to round on the TB ward. Despite the devastation I felt, I couldn't neglect the other patients. The empty bed where the young fellow had died haunted me. I turned my back to it as we examined an elderly man's lungs in the adjoining bed. Through the translator, I told him that his lungs sounded clear. He displayed a broad grin. "I was so sick I could not even sit up when I came."

Justine translated the patient's remarks. He seemed to understand some English and agreed with satisfaction. "They don't all die," I said as I held back my tears. Justine did not translate.

# BICYCLE TRIP

Several weeks later, I met with Jora to plan a bicycle trip. I needed a break.

We met at a French restaurant about six blocks from the hospital to plan our trip. I had asked Justine to explain to Jacqueline that I did not want supper, so there would be no waste. There were plenty of leftovers, so her family would be fed. I felt like an escapee on the run as I relaxed over an exquisite dinner. "I have two problems with this bicycle trip idea, Jora. First, I do not have a bike, and second, I could never keep up with you. I've seen how fast you ride."

"I have solutions to your problems," she said. "You met Thorey, my friend at the language school who is studying to be a teacher. She brought her bike from Norway too. I already asked her if you could use it. And I promise not to go so fast that you get lost."

I gave her a quizzical look, not sure if I wanted to risk the perils of Malagasy roads on someone else's bicycle. What if I fell and damaged it? "Where would you like to go?"

"I heard that there is a volcanic lake not far from here to the south. You can see the whole crater, and the water is supposed to be hundreds of feet deep."

"Sounds intriguing. You're sure we won't get lost?"

"I learned the Malagasy name for the place, and Thorey taught me how to ask directions. It seems fairly simple. I asked the lab technician, and he said it is just straight down the road to the south. There is only one road. It is not that far. We can be back before dark."

We expanded our plans as we walked back to the Norwegian Language School. It still amazed me how dark it was in the tropics after six o'clock. We stopped in the middle of the street to gaze at the stars, some of which were not visible from the Northern Hemisphere. "There's something you can't see in Norway," I said, pointing to a constellation.

"Or in the United States," she added. Our hands touched. My fingers encircled hers and then let go. We saw some rickshaw drivers, who greeted us and asked us if we wanted a ride, but Jora told them in Malagasy that we needed the exercise.

When we arrived back at the dormitory, there was no one in the dining room. Jora ran her fingers down my arm. "You want to come to my room?"

My mind undressed the biker's bodysuit that had demonstrated her anatomy that day at lunch. I fantasized about what she must look like naked—her silky white hair, her muscular abs, and those tremendous thighs. Did she have perfect breasts like Lily's? Lily's image on the canoe trip interposed itself. Then I remembered her saying, "It's just the house I live in, Barak. Get over it."

I stepped back. "Maybe some other time, Jora. I need some rest if I am going to bike with you tomorrow."

A brisk morning rain shower evolved into a warm, bright sunrise. The rain would keep the dust down. Jora looked pleasant to my male eyes in her anatomy suit, but I hoped that what Lily had taught me would keep me focused. I felt psychologically bruised, not ready for another disappointment with a woman. The specter of Lily dying still haunted me. On the other hand, I looked like a biker's reject in my cutoff shorts and a surgical scrub top. In addition, Thorey's bike was uncomfortable, but I hated to adjust the seat to my legs. The back of the bike had a place to strap my backpack filled with sunscreen, insect repellent, and a snack lunch the Norwegian Language School cooks had put together.

We weaved through the people in town going to market. Twice, we had to stop and walk our bikes because of the crowds. Once we were outside of town, the road was clear, and we sped up—well, Jora sped up, and I gasped for breath while trying to keep up with her. The novelty of watching her back and gluteal muscles pumping in rhythm wore off like eating too much candy. I was desperate to keep up with her. When I felt like I was losing her, I yelled out, "Hey, let's stop for a drink!"

She stopped several turns up the road, pulled out two water bottles from her pack, and gave me one. "Don't drink too much, Barak; you'll get cramps."

I drank a few sips. A young boy with a stick was leading his herd of cows along the road. An older man stopped his work in the rice field to stare at us. A hawk glided through the sky above us. "Ready?" She seemed to command more than ask.

"Can you slow down a bit?" I asked as I took a gulp of water.

"There is a turnoff up ahead where the trail goes to the volcano. If we get separated, I'll wait for you there."

I gave her my water bottle, not wanting to load my pack with anything more. "All right," I said, but it seemed wrong. We climbed onto our bikes, and she took off. I slowed to a speed I could sustain. A moment later, all I could see was her dust.

*At least I haven't made any turns*, I thought. *I can find my way back to the hospital.* I was now riding uphill through a forest too rugged to farm. There was not even a farmer walking along the road to ask directions—if I knew enough Malagasy to ask, which I didn't. There was also no sign of Jora, although I stopped a couple of times and saw the print of her bicycle tire in the mud. I pressed on.

It was almost eleven o'clock when I spotted her at a lonely kiosk. She was sipping a Coca-Cola. "This is where the road goes to the volcano, Barak." She tossed me my water bottle. "Want anything before we head up? I think he still has a Fanta. They aren't cold, though."

I took a deep swallow of the tepid water. "No, I'm fine." I searched the terrain. "So where is this road to the volcano?"

"Right here." She motioned with her hand.

I came closer, as I still didn't see it. It was an overgrown footpath that disappeared into tall grass and then forest. "That?"

"Yeah."

"Should we leave the bikes here?"

"No way. They'll get stolen. We'll just ride them up to the rim." She climbed onto her bicycle and headed up through the forest. The Malagasy man at the kiosk smiled.

I walked Thorey's bike most of the way up. It was too steep, and the trail was too rugged. I had no idea how Jora made it up the trail. I perspired, soaking my clothes in the hot, humid air. I felt breathless as I climbed up the muddy trail. There was not a whisper of breeze.

Jora was resting on the rim of the volcano when I arrived. I set the bike up against a tree and turned to take in the view. An impenetrable deep azure depth of water sat like a gem inside a forested rim. It was a perfect circle, and with the bright, warm sunshine, the smell of pine permeated the cauldron. We left the bikes by a tree, scampered down to the water's edge, took off our shoes, and tested the water. The rocky core was visible to a depth of thirty or forty feet at least. There were no plants along the edge.

"Must be spring fed. It sure is cold," I said as I slipped in a toe.

"It is beautiful," Jora said, "but too cold even for a Norwegian to swim in, I'm afraid."

I hadn't even thought about swimming. I certainly did not want to get my clothes wet. The bike trip back to Antsirabe would be miserable in wet shorts. They were wet enough from sweat. We walked back up to the rim and pulled out our lunch: baguette and cheese with two bananas. We didn't say much but just stared at the sapphire lake. The air was cool, wafting off the water's surface like an air conditioner, clearing the sweat from my skin. It was quiet, and the peaceful environment soothed my soul.

Jora jumped to her feet. "Ready to go."

Taking a nap was more what I had in mind. "All right." My eye caught her tight abdominal muscles as she stretched her arms to reach the sky, and she bent backward. I ached as I scanned her figure stretching and contorting through her routine. Did I want a relationship or not? I felt ambivalent. I wanted Lily. Could anyone replace her?

"I'm ready too." She climbed onto her bike and headed down the trail. I followed, but I almost hit a tree. I swerved, the front wheel caught in the mud, and I was thrown into the grass. Neither the bike nor I was seriously injured, but I had to pull a few grass leeches off my legs. I walked the bike the rest of the way to the kiosk. The Malagasy man was still smiling. He said something I didn't understand, but his frantic pointing down the road was comprehensible.

Back on the road, I sped up, and on a straight stretch, I saw Jora in the distance. "Wait up!" I yelled, not sure if she could hear me. Down another steep hill, I saw her waiting. I sped up and was breathless when I screeched to a stop.

"There's a lake right over there." She pointed. "Let's take a quick dip." Without waiting for an answer, she headed down a footpath to a small lake. When I arrived, she was stripped naked. She was a beautiful young woman. Her breasts drooped more than my imagination had expected, but that was about all I noticed as she dove into the water.

I stripped off my shirt and approached the edge. My memory brought back visions of swimming with Lily. "Come on in!" she yelled as she frolicked in the water.

My eye caught the edge of the lake, and I paused.

"Are you coming?" She dove and surfaced. "You Americans are such prudes. Are you afraid to be naked in front of a girl?"

I squatted by the edge. "No," I said, and I fingered the silt on the edge. "There are snails here. I don't think this is safe for swimming."

Her affect changed as she stood up in the waist-deep water. I repeated, "I don't think this is safe. Snails mean schistosomiasis."

"Oh, what does that mean?" She walked out of the water.

I forced myself to look only at her face. "Do you want me to strip to prove I am not an American prude?"

She ignored my question. She took a towel out of her pack, dried, and then put her biker's outfit back on. "Let's go."

We got back on the road, and she took off. I knew the way back to town, so I wasn't concerned that I didn't catch up to her on the way back. Despite going mostly downhill, it was dark by the time I got back to the Norwegian Language School. Clouds obscured the stars and the moon. I parked Thorey's bike inside the dormitory door. There was no one around.

On the walk back to the guesthouse, my muscles felt sore. I was cautious not to twist my ankles in the potholes as I inched my way back to the guesthouse. The only light came from candles in the windows of the kiosks along the road. The electricity was off in my part of town.

I fumbled while trying to put my key in the lock, but I got it open. Inside, I headed for the fireplace mantel, where I had put my flashlight for nights when the electricity was not on. I searched for candles and matches, as I was unsure if I could replace the batteries in my flashlight at the local market. I remembered that Jacqueline had shown me where she kept the matches in a kitchen drawer. It took five matches to light the candle. The matches kept crumbling in the humid air. Once the candle was lit, I saw in red letters on the matchbox "Made in China." *Maybe they light better in China*, I thought.

I felt tired and achy. I wanted a hot shower, but without electricity, there would be no hot shower. I was thankful for the full bucket of water Jacqueline had drawn and set out in the middle of the shower. She must have anticipated the problem. I thought a bucket bath by candlelight might be romantic with the right person, but I hadn't found the right person.

In the morning, every muscle in my body hurt, but I was thankful I had no new bedbug bites. The Raid Yard Guard was working. There was still no electricity, but light through the windows directed my path as I waddled into the kitchen. There were three bananas set in a bowl on the table, but I ventured to open the refrigerator because I was intensely hungry. The supper Jacqueline had prepared for Saturday night was a pleasant surprise. Sunday was her day off, so I knew she would not suddenly appear for breakfast, and I heated up my food. I was pleased that the gas stove did not require electricity, but I used five more Chinese matches before I could get the burner lit.

Sliced roast beef over rice with a carrot salad and fruit for dessert made a wonderful Sunday morning breakfast. I pretended I was at a high-class restaurant for brunch. When I was satisfied, I remembered that I'd been invited to go to Dr. Narina's for dinner.

With a quick look at my watch, I realized I had time to go to church. I loved the singing—it was inspiring—but I walked out when the sermon started. No one seemed to mind. They knew I couldn't understand enough Malagasy to comprehend what was said. Besides, Dr. Jacques had mentioned that some of the hospital workers were impressed that I always put money in the offering, which was just before the sermon. People got up from their benches and marched past the plate to put in their offering, so it was public knowledge whether I contributed. On my way back from the offering plate in the front of the church, I just walked out instead of returning to my bench.

The music was great that morning. A choir from another town was featured, so it was like a battle of the choirs as the local choir matched the visiting choir song for song. It was almost noon before the sermon started, and I headed out. Dr. Narina expected me at two o'clock, so I had time to rest. The electricity was back on, so I stretched my sore muscles and read a book. It would be dark before I returned from Dr. Narina's. I had learned that a Malagasy dinner invitation was a long, drawn-out, formal affair.

# RURAL TUBERCULOSIS

WE WERE NIBBLING ON FRESH pineapple after a grand five-course meal, when Dr. Narina reminded me, "Tomorrow you are going with the TB van to see the patients in the country."

"Oh, I don't remember anyone telling me about that."

"Dr. Mamy is in charge of the TB program and will be here to pick you up at sunrise. Make sure you have some clothes packed. You will not be back till late Tuesday night. I will see the patients while you are gone."

"Is this how TB patients discharged from the hospital are followed?"

"Yes, after they are discharged, Dr. Mamy checks on them to make sure they are taking their *fanafody*." She smiled. "I mean medicine. The Swiss require a follow-up program to pay for the medicines. We were having difficulty before Lily Barton bought us a brand-new vehicle."

"So Lily paid for a vehicle to run the TB program?"

"Yes, and then she sent you. We are so happy about Lily Barton."

I was amazed. Lily had touched every aspect of patient care, from the sterilizer to microscopes, surgical instruments, and even a van for the TB program.

Dr. Narina interrupted my thoughts. "Yes, be ready in front of the hospital at sunrise. You have a long ways to go to the villages, so he will be very early."

"So Dr. Mamy will pick me up?"

She nodded.

I was used to things not happening on time. A half-hour or forty-minute wait after something was supposed to start was not unusual, so I was startled by a tap on my bedroom window. I jumped up, grabbed my flashlight, and pulled back the drapes. I recognized one of the nurses from the hospital, who said, "Dr. Mamy is waiting for you." I looked at my watch. It was well before sunrise.

With no time for breakfast, I jumped into scrubs; grabbed my backpack, which I had packed the night before; and ran out the door. I noticed a note on the door, explaining to Jacqueline that I wouldn't need any meals till Wednesday morning. Still wondering who'd put that on my door, I ran to catch up with the nurse walking up the hill to the hospital.

Dr. Mamy was a tall, thin fellow. He wore a double-breasted suit that was too big for him. His hair was in a crew-cut style reminiscent of an old movie. He smiled when I arrived. His left upper teeth were missing. He greeted me, shaking my hand with both of his. The white van was short by American standards; it looked more like a four-wheel-drive jeep with extended panels. The oversize tires had deep tread. "Lily" was painted in black on the door. "We are ready, yes?"

I climbed in and noticed a petite young woman sitting in the back, on top of supplies. Dr. Mamy introduced us. "She is our lab technician. She will check the sputum for us."

I asked her name and tried to greet her, but her name was difficult to pronounce. She laughed at my attempt, covered her face, and responded in quiet Malagasy. Dr. Mamy smiled and explained, "You may call her Tech if that is easier for your American tongue."

"Wouldn't that be disrespectful?"

"Not from you," said Dr. Mamy. "To mispronounce her name would be worse. What you said sounded like *large buttocks*. She prefers that you call her Tech instead." It was my turn to blush.

We drove into the darkness. I fell asleep jostling along the smooth road out of Antsirabe. It was good that I'd gotten some sleep, because we turned off the main road an hour later. The sun still had not risen. Dr. Mamy shifted into first gear as we drove up a rutted trail into the forest. Branches screeched along the sides of the vehicle as he avoided deep ruts in the road. We drove into a small village and stopped in the marketplace. The sun was peeking over the mountains on the horizon.

"We have several patients here." He held up the charts. "And then we will go—how do you Americans say it?—into the bushes."

"In the bush," I said, although I felt as if we were already there.

Tech set up the microscope, running the light off the van battery. It was ingenious how she arranged her open-air lab in the back of the van. Slipping on my white coat from my backpack, I slung my stethoscope over my neck. We set out to find the patients.

Several of the patients lived in brick houses with tin roofs. We were greeted like distant relatives. As I knelt beside straw mat beds on the floor, I heard rhonchi and wheezes. If the patient coughed up any sputum, Tech ran the specimen back to the van and tested it. She was spry and athletic and was never gone long. By the time we had another specimen, she had returned.

At about ten o'clock, we stopped at the village elder's house. It was much nicer than the other houses we had visited that morning. A printed tablecloth, stuffed chairs, and a buffet in the corner of the living room presented a homey environment. Tea was steaming from the pot on the table. As we entered, the elder's wife brought in pastries. I was famished.

I missed out on most of the conversation, which was in Malagasy, but Dr. Mamy translated a few things. The village was concerned about TB and had been careful about sending villagers who had suspicious symptoms to the hospital. A few people had coughs, and we needed to check their sputum. If it was positive, our protocol allowed us to start therapy without hospitalization.

After our break, we visited a family with two teenage daughters, one seventeen and the other fifteen, whom the village elder had asked us to check because they had been missing school. Neighbors heard them coughing. Welcomed into the house, we were offered chairs at one end of the room, and the parents called for the two girls. In demure resignation, the two sisters came and sat together on a wooden bench opposite us. Wearing only tattered shorts, they sat bare-chested with their hands folded in their laps as their mother explained the history to Dr. Mamy. He translated for me. They had been coughing for a month, bringing up gray sputum. Both had stayed home from school for the previous two weeks because they felt too tired to do their schoolwork. A month previous to their illness, their grandmother had died of a coughing disease.

I left my chair and listened to their lungs. I heard focal areas of rattling in the right upper chest of the older girl and wheezes in the left chest of the younger. I listened to their hearts and heard normal heart sounds and normal rates. In the United States, I would have immediately gotten a chest x-ray. I asked Tech to check their sputum, and she gave them each a small plastic container while I sat back down in the wooden chair provided across from them. They both gave a hearty cough and produced large purulent specimens. Neither spoke.

I felt vulnerable for the two of them and wanted to say, "You can get dressed now," but I didn't know how. They were attractive girls, and I felt embarrassed for their having to sit in front of two strange men while stripped to the waist. I hoped we would be able to treat whatever they had. Visions of the young boy who had died of TB meningitis haunted me as I stared at their naked torsos. I waited as Dr. Mamy and the girls' mother finished talking.

"I'm very suspicious that they have TB," he said. "The grandmother's illness sounds like she died of TB, and they helped take care of her during her last days."

"Did the grandmother get tested?" I said.

"No, she told her daughter, the girl's mother, that she was too old to take medicine." He grinned, showing his missing teeth. "This is a common attitude among Malagasy people."

The mother asked if we would like tea. Dr. Mamy asked me but told me we would politely refuse since we had just had tea, and he was concerned about our exposure should the girls actually have TB. Tech returned as we sat in our places. "The sputum tests are both positive," she said, walking in the door with two plastic bags.

At least they met criterion for treatment, I reasoned. Tech gave one plastic bag with prepackaged medicine to each girl while Dr. Mamy explained how they were to take their medicine. They stood and bowed, thanking Dr. Mamy. They approached me, and I stood. They extended both hands to shake my hand and bowed again. A silent nod from their mother allowed them to go to their room. They reappeared in lambas, Malagasy wraps that could be used as skirts or dresses, and sat down again on the bench, still silent.

As we left the house, we shook everyone's hand and said, "*Yeloma tompoko.*" Dr. Mamy squirted my hands with a bottle of alcohol that he kept in his briefcase as soon as we were around the corner. Nothing was said, but I was appreciative. When he finally spoke, he said, "The next village is hard to get to. We may have to walk. The elder said the road is closed."

"How will we test the specimens? Will Tech run them back to where we leave the vehicle?"

"You are understanding things Malagasy, Dr. Barak." He patted my shoulder.

We wove between the houses of the now familiar village and climbed into the vehicle. We were able to drive partway up the hillside, but soon the road degenerated into muddy ruts. He drove the van into the brush on the side of the road, and we started unpacking. "Bring your backpack; we will be staying overnight up that hill." He pointed to what looked like a mountain to me. It was going to be quite the hike. A thin older man with an impressive spear appeared, and Dr. Mamy talked with him before we shouldered our packs. Then we started up the muddy trail.

"Who was that?" I asked.

"He's our guard, so no one steals our equipment. Our technician will come with us and run down here to do the testing, but in the meantime, we need someone to make sure nothing is tampered with."

I looked back. The man was sitting next to the oversize tires with spear in hand, singing a song.

The hike was rough for me. Dr. Mamy didn't seem to exert much energy. It was soon clear that the road had not been traveled in a long time. We took a shortcut up a footpath where slippery steps were cut out of the clay. I tripped a couple of times, but Tech was there to help me. It was humbling for a woman half my size to be my source of stability, but the whole experience there in Madagascar had been humbling. This was only symbolic in comparison.

All of the houses in the village below had been made of bricks. Up there, only half were brick, and the others seemed to be pole-barn construction. "Where do they get these panels to make their houses?" I asked Dr. Mamy.

"They slice down one side of a palm tree, unwrap the bark, and lay it out flat in the sun. When it dries, it makes a panel that they attach to the upright poles."

"How ingenious," I said between gasping breaths. We entered one of the brick houses. It was clean and neat. The woman who greeted us shook our hands with both of hers and made us feel welcome. I had just sat down on a comfortable place on the couch, when Dr. Mamy stood again and said, "Off to work. We will come back here. This is where we will be staying tonight."

The first house we visited was a palm-tree-bark-panel construction. On a grass mat in the far corner was an elderly man lying on his side. Gobs of sputum dried on the floor beside him. Dr. Mamy motioned to have me listen to his lungs. Tech gave him instructions on putting his sputum into the plastic container. As I listened to his back, he coughed up a huge blood-tinged gob of green mucous into one of the containers. Tech covered it and rushed off.

"This is the grandfather of the boy who died of TB meningitis in the hospital. I'm sure he's the source," Dr. Mamy said. I heard tubular breath sounds suggesting a huge lung cavity. I backed to the far corner of the hut.

The old man's daughter, the mother of the boy who had died, explained the old man's illness to Dr. Mamy. "He's been sick a long time," she told me. I needed no other history.

I asked for a generous squirt of alcohol as we left. The next three visits were patients I'd treated and discharged several weeks before. We checked on their medicine and made sure they were improving and were compliant with their medicines. All were incredibly grateful. Their gratitude was refreshing in comparison to many of my patients in the United States. Besides, I was delighted to see how much they had improved.

It was completely dark by the time we left the last house. The stars were brilliant, as there was no town on the horizon in any direction with electric lights. The light from the moon led us back to the brick house where we were to stay. Tech disappeared. "Where did Tech go?" I asked as we were welcomed into the elder's home.

"Oh, she sleeps in the van. She feels more comfortable there."

There were handshakes all around, and I could smell a spicy aroma wafting from the kitchen. A large bottle of Coca-Cola sat on the table. All the plates were upside down. Our host invited us to sit on the sofa. Unable to understand the conversation around me, I wondered how the sofa had been brought up the muddy footpath we'd ascended to the village. The rumble of my stomach distracted my thoughts. Dinner in a Malagasy home was formal, and protocol couldn't be rushed, especially with two physicians as honored guests.

About an hour after I thought I would faint from hunger, we were served. The village elder spoke some English and about the same amount of French. I enjoyed the rice with spicy beef sauce and greens. I ate slowly, unable to contribute to the discussion. Midway through the meal, the elder asked me something. Dr. Mamy translated the elder's question: "How do you like Madagascar?"

"I am overwhelmed with joy."

Dr. Mamy translated. Our host smiled and slapped his knee with delight.

"I really appreciate being invited to your home. The food is wonderful, and I have enjoyed the Malagasy people very much. I can see that hospitality is very important to you." I took a drink of Coke as Dr. Mamy translated.

I continued. "It makes me sad to see so many sick people."

Dr. Mamy did not translate but whispered to me, "It is not time to say such things. Wait until after dessert." The conversation switched back to Malagasy.

An hour later, our host served the sweetest bananas and juiciest oranges I had ever eaten. I was still savoring the fruit, when Dr. Mamy turned to me. "Now it is time to talk about sick people."

I restated my sentence, adding, "But I am thankful that we can treat many of the sick people and see them recover."

The elder spoke, and Dr. Mamy abbreviated the translation. "He is very thankful to you that someone from the United States would be willing to come here to his village to care for the sick people."

*I wouldn't have come either if it wasn't for Lily*, I thought.

It was after midnight before we went to bed. The upstairs bedroom was nice. It was the parents' bedroom, Dr. Mamy explained. We were being honored. An embroidered lace covered the dresser, a floral Malagasy print hung near the window, and our bed had a handmade quilt. Dr. Mamy and I were sleeping in the same bed. I put on clean scrubs for pajamas. The springs were noisy as I sat on the bed. I thought it was going to collapse.

Dr. Mamy motioned for me to get off the bed, pulled out a can of Raid Yard Guard, and sprayed under the mattress. "I hate bedbugs," he whispered. The generator noise that I hadn't been aware of suddenly stopped, and then I understood why he had lit a candle. The elder had his own generator, and he had just turned it off. I climbed into bed, rolled over, and closed my eyes as scenes from the day barraged my brain. Dr. Mamy was reading by candlelight in the chair when I fell asleep.

In the morning, he was already up when I awoke. I made my side of the bed to match his and wandered downstairs to the kitchen. Everyone was sitting at the kitchen table. There was a large plate of rice with sweetened condensed milk to put on it, brown sugar, and a large bowl of fruit. The sweet smell of a tropical morning was blowing through the open door.

"Good morning, everyone," I said.

"*Salama Tompoko*" was the response.

My place was obvious, so I sat down. Tech was sitting on a stool by the wall, eating a bowl of rice. She looked well rested. Dr. Mamy greeted me. "The old man's sputum was positive. I brought the medicine to his house this morning and explained that he must take all the pills."

"Good. I'm glad we found something we could treat."

"The elder would like you to check him. He has been having pain in his stomach."

In front of everyone, he related his history. He unbuttoned his shirt so I could palpate his belly. The epigastrium was tender, a classic ulcer finding. He needed a gastroscopy, which Dr. Jacques did at the Antsirabe hospital, but Dr. Mamy suggested we treat him and do the scope if he didn't respond. The elder's wife handed me a scrap of paper torn from a child's notebook. I wrote down the medicine he needed.

He was jubilant. Dr. Mamy said, "Put the doses, how he should take them, and how many pills you want him to take."

"Why? I thought I was just telling him what medicine is available."

He chuckled. "If you sign your name to that paper, he can use it as a prescription."

"But it's just a piece of paper torn from a notebook," I said.

"At the pharmacy, they will recognize your signature as a legitimate prescription."

I finished writing out the information. "I would have written it on a whole piece of paper if I had known that." Dr. Mamy ignored me.

We finished our breakfast and then went to visit five other patients who had been discharged from the hospital. Tech took specimens from them, but their sputum looked pretty clear. She would tell us the results when we returned to Antsirabe, since we would not change treatment at that point.

At noon, we returned to the elder's house. His wife had more rice with a chicken and vegetable *loaka*, a sauce to put on it. After our fruit dessert of pineapple and mangoes, we had to go, but just before we left, the elder presented me with a gift of a kilogram of vanilla beans, at least fifty beans. They smelled great. "Why am I receiving a gift?" I asked Dr. Mamy.

"He sent a runner down the mountain to get the medicine you prescribed. After he took the first pill, his pain went away. He wants you to know he is grateful for your wisdom."

Lots of handshakes followed, and the elder and his wife even walked halfway down the hilly footpath with us. My hands and everything in my pack smelled of vanilla. I laughed to myself, thinking of wearing vanilla-scented underwear.

Our armed guard greeted us with smiles and handshakes. The van was intact, and a wad of money exchanged hands. Dr. Mamy started the engine, and we turned the van around. The long trek back to the road in first gear took all afternoon. It was as black as the morning we had left by the time he dropped me off at my house.

As I crawled into bed, I reviewed the list of patients at the hospital, confident that Dr. Narina had taken good care of them. Then I wondered how Jora and I would get along on rounds in the morning. Would she even talk to me? Maybe she would decide to work with Dr. Jacques instead. The morning would tell. I smelled the vanilla on my hands and fell asleep.

# SPINAL CORD TROUBLE

I HEARD A RATTLING IN the kitchen that woke me up. Jacqueline was making my breakfast. I had overslept. There was no hot water, so a quick bucket bath sufficed. I dressed and met her in the kitchen just as she was leaving. I thanked her for breakfast and sat down to bananas, sweetened condensed milk for my rice, and a cup of her great coffee. It bore no resemblance to the coffee at County Hospital.

At the hospital, I reviewed the patients with Dr. Narina. Most of my patients had improved. There was no sign of Jora. "Did Jora make rounds with you while I was gone?" I asked.

"She did not come to the hospital," Dr. Narina said as she put a chart in my hands. She then asked about the significance of a patient's lab result.

When we'd finished discussing the hospital patients, I asked, "Did Jora make rounds on Monday or Tuesday?"

"It was said that she had diarrhea and stayed home."

When we finished rounds, I happened to look out the hospital window. There was a rickshaw—*pousse-pousse*, as the Malagasy called them—stopping at casualty, the equivalent of the emergency room. I was surprised to see Thorey struggle to pull Jora out of the rickshaw's seat. I gave the last chart to the nurse and ran down the stairs to casualty.

Thorey met me at the door. Her cheeks swollen from crying, she explained, "Our Norwegian secretary, Rolf Bjorn, wants you to assess Jora and tell him what is wrong with her health. He will be here soon to decide what to do with her."

Two Malagasy nurses lifted Jora onto the clean sheet draped over the exam table. They removed most of her clothes and covered her with a gown and sheet. One stuck a pillow under her head and asked her if she was comfortable.

I grasped her trembling hand. "What's wrong, Jora? I heard you had diarrhea."

"That's a minor problem." Tears formed in her eyes. "I can't walk. My legs won't work. What's happening to me, Barak?"

The admonitions of medical school reverberated in my mind: *A careful history and physical will make the diagnosis ninety percent of the time.* I focused, acutely aware that no CT or MRI was available, and we had minimal laboratory facilities. "Tell me what happened." The two Malagasy nurses stood at the bedside. Dr. Narina appeared at my side and seemed concerned. Thorey stepped back to the doorway, covering her face with her hands.

"Sunday I had a little cough. I thought I was coming down with a cold." She arched her neck and called, "Thorey!" and said something in Norwegian. She held out her hand, and Thorey came to the bedside and grabbed her friend's hand.

"Dr. Narina, could you assist me?" I said. If this was a tropical disease, I wanted her expertise. "Go on." Thorey squeezed Jora's hand. Jora appeared desperate as she spoke. I started writing notes on small card the nurse put in my hands.

"Monday I felt a burning in my legs. It was nothing severe at first, but later, it was like electricity shooting down my legs. I had some diarrhea when I went to the bathroom, so I decided to stay home. I sent Thorey to tell Dr. Narina that I was sick and would not be making rounds with her." She cleared her throat. "That night, the pain down my legs was excruciating, like when you cross your legs for too long, only it was both legs. I couldn't sleep the pain was so bad. I asked Thorey to stay in my room. In the middle of the night, I needed to go to the bathroom." She turned her face to the wall and sobbed.

I gently stroked her shoulder. "Continue, Jora. This is very important."

"I had already wet myself and didn't know it. Thorey tried to help me to the bathroom, and I couldn't stand up."

I reasoned that this was a neurologic problem. "I need the rest of your history, Jora. I know you have been pretty healthy. Have you been hospitalized before?"

She looked at Thorey and emitted a weak "No."

"Do you take any medicines?"

"Just my malaria pills." She swallowed and looked at Thorey.

"He needs to know everything, Jora. This is important," Thorey said. She seemed insistent.

"And birth control pills."

I wrote it down. "Allergies?"

"None."

"Tobacco, alcohol, or recreational drugs?"

"Wine with dinner—you know that."

"Do you have any brothers or sisters? Are your parents healthy?"

"My brother is twenty-seven and healthy. My parents are too."

I swallowed. "I need to check you over carefully. I don't mean to embarrass you, but it is important. Dr. Narina will be right here with me."

"Can Thorey stay too? She's seen me naked before."

Thorey blushed.

"Not a problem." I started my exam. Her eyes were normal, her face was symmetric, and the neck exam was normal. That was good. There was no sign of meningitis. She sat up with help from Thorey. Her lungs were clear, her back was not tender, and her pale Norwegian skin had no rashes. I looked at Dr. Narina and Thorey as I exposed her chest, careful to place the sheet for modesty. I listened to her heart. It was normal. I palpated her breasts. They were softer than I expected for someone in her early twenties. I tied her gown back around her neck and pulled it up to examine her belly. I folded the sheet so it just covered her pubic hair and groin. Her liver and spleen were normal size. I had Dr. Narina verify that. I listened to her gurgling bowel sounds, probably the aftermath of diarrhea.

Below her umbilicus, I saw a series of stretch marks. Not thinking, I asked, "Have you ever been pregnant?"

She turned her face to the wall and moaned. Thorey looked at me. "She had an abortion because the guy she was living with got her pregnant and then left her, so she got rid of the baby."

I gently touched her trembling arm. "I'm so sorry, Jora." I forced myself to continue. Pulling her gown down, I exposed her groin. There were no abnormal lymph nodes. I put on exam gloves. Her vagina had no unusual discharge, but she was leaking urine, and her rectum had no sphincter tone. I covered her and checked her reflexes. Her arms were normal, but I could not get any reflexes in her legs. Her muscles were so weak that she could not even lift her legs against gravity, but she could still wiggle her toes.

I looked at Dr. Narina as I took a pin and scratched her leg. There was no response. I did it again. "Do you feel me touching your legs?"

"Tell me when you're going to do it," she said. I was already sticking the pin in her thigh.

I turned to Thorey. "Stay with her. I need to talk to Dr. Narina."

Thorey bent over and gave Jora a hug.

Dr. Narina and I stepped outside. "She has no reflexes in her legs," I said. "You saw that she is numb, and her rectum has no tone, which is why she is incontinent of urine, and she will be incontinent of stool as well. This is a transverse myelopathy. I suppose it could be Guillain-Barré, but that disease doesn't usually affect the sphincters."

Dr. Narina nodded agreement. I looked up at the sky. Wisps of clouds floated by. "Saturday, when we were bike riding, she went swimming in a pond south of here. I didn't go in because I saw lots of snails, tiny ones, washed up on the beach. Do you think this could be schistosomiasis mansoni?"

Dr. Narina nodded. "That is what I was thinking, but I thought she only went swimming at Les Thermes."

"No, she went swimming in that pond beside the road when we came back from bicycling. Is the time course right?"

"Yes, and her story of cough fits with someone who got schisto who is not immune, just like the young girls when they first help their mothers with the rice planting."[1]

Tears came to my eyes. "I've read about this since we saw that young girl when I first came. Praziquantel and steroids are the treatment, right?"

"Yes, that is how we always treat them, but it doesn't always help."

"I know. But Malagasy don't come right away. This is acute. Besides, if it is Guillain-Barré or another virus, the medicine won't hurt her."

"It might help. I agree," said Dr. Narina.

We walked back into casualty. I looked at Jora, and my heart ached. My voice cracked as I explained her situation. "Jora, you have a transverse myelopathy. I suspect it is from schistosomiasis mansoni, but it could be Guillain-Barré syndrome or another virus." There was nonverbal

---

[1] *The Lancet* 381 (May 18, 2013): 1,788, www.thelancet.com.

communication between us. I felt as if she were telling me, "Please don't say, 'I told you so.'" I didn't. "I am going to treat you with praziquantel and Decadron. That will give you the best chance of recovery. Dr. Narina is very familiar with this problem. It is not new to her. We will do a rectal biopsy to confirm. It won't hurt you." Unfortunately, I knew she would not even feel it.

We gave orders, and the Malagasy nurses jumped to action, starting the IV and giving the medicines. I stepped out. I did not want to watch the rectal biopsy. I wanted to run away.

I was looking out across the driveway, trying not to think, when I felt a tap on my shoulder. "Dr. Barak Shelton?"

I turned, almost not recognizing my name with such a strong Norwegian brogue. "Yes, sir."

"I am Rolf Bjorn, secretary of the Norwegian Mission." He was dressed in a plaid suit with a starched shirt. He moved his bifocals up his nose. "I am sorry not to speak English very smooth. I understand that Jora has severe illness. Is that correct?"

"Yes."

"Thank you, Dr. Barak Shelton. I am quick to make arrangements to transport her back to Norway. The helicopter should be here soon." He looked at his wristwatch. "One hour." He turned and left.

I returned to Jora's side. Thorey was holding her hand. The biopsy was done. "She never felt a thing," Thorey said.

I smoothed her silky white hair. "I'm so sorry, Jora. Arrangements are being made for you to be airlifted to Tana and then back to Norway. That is your best chance for recovery. We treated you for schisto. If I am wrong and you have Guillain-Barré or some other viral transverse myelitis, you need special treatment that is not available here—plasmapheresis maybe." I gasped for breath and grabbed her hand. "I really enjoyed working with you. I'm sorry." I couldn't stop the tears.

"You're a good physician, Barak. It has been an honor to work with you. Take good care of Thorey. Don't let her get sick." She pulled my head down to whisper in my ear, "Don't let her go skinny-dipping in that lake."

After the helicopter left, I felt sick about her prognosis and what had happened to such a fine woman. Would I ever hear from her? It was over. But I still had to make rounds on the TB patients. It took intense concentration to focus on the lab reports and x-rays. I just wanted to go home and cry.

# 40

# MEDICAL CONFERENCE

A MONTH LATER, DR. JACQUES asked me to come to his house for lunch. After the first hour of formality, he told me why he wanted to talk to me. "We would like to have a SALFA conference. We want to invite the physicians from the other SALFA hospitals and have you teach a conference. You would not have to teach the whole thing. The pathologist from Tana would teach, and the doctor from the Alcohol Treatment Center would also teach. One seminar would be cases that each hospital would present and discuss." He took a drink of Coke. "Do you like the idea?"

"I would love to do that. We could go on teaching rounds using the patients here at Antsirabe. That would be great. We could get everyone's input on treatment and diagnosis. It would mean some great discussion. Besides, I would like to meet the doctors from the other hospitals."

"Good. I was hoping you would be willing. The doctors will be arriving in two weeks. What lectures would you give?"

With no time for future planning, my head was spinning. "I suppose I could talk about diabetes and hypertension, and I could give a refresher course on interpreting EKGs."

"Perfect. I will have the SALFA director make the arrangements. There should be about fifty doctors coming."

Two weeks later, seventy-five physicians showed up. It was chaos to find places to house them, and we had to arrange cooks to feed them. The room in which we had planned to give the seminar was too small for such a crowd, so sometime between going on rounds with all the physicians and our first session, Anderson rented a facility down the path from the hospital. I was glad to be out of the loop. All I had to do was discuss the cases we chose to present for morning rounds and give a few lectures—actually, seven lectures.

Every free minute of the previous two weeks, when I was not making clinical decisions, my mind was creating lectures. I had several tablets of notes. As I got ideas in the shower (there was hot water most of the time), in bed (I had to spray for bedbugs again—how had they come back?), and at lunch break (I loved two-hour lunches), I would write down ideas and put them into a folder.

The first session consisted of introductions and speeches. Anderson welcomed everyone and introduced Dr. Jacques as the host. Each physician had a name card, which also designated which hospital he or she worked at. My eye caught on the word *Manambaro*. "Dr. Joel," his card said. I made a point to talk to him.

My one-hour lectures lasted two hours. With translation to French or Malagasy, depending on the subject, and the voluminous questions afterward, I was exhausted after each session. During the lunch break, I got to meet the doctors. The ones who spoke English sat near me at the table and translated questions for the physicians who did not speak English. Sometimes I could answer in French, but they laughed at either my pronunciation or my murdering of verb tenses—I was never sure which.

It was Wednesday before I cornered Dr. Joel. "Tell me what Manambaro is like."

"We are in the jungle. It rains every day. We see lots of infections, malaria, and skin rashes. It's so humid."

I was hardly listening because I was so excited that he spoke English. "I would like to visit Manambaro Hospital. Is there a place for me to stay?" Now I was listening.

"Yes, we have a guesthouse. Would you like to stay there?"

My visa allowed me three more months in Madagascar. I really wanted to work there at least short-term. It sounded so different from the hospital there in the highlands. "How would I get there?"

"You could come with me when the seminar is over."

I knew I would have to talk to Anderson and Dr. Jacques, but it sure sounded safer to go with someone who knew where he was going. In my mind, I pictured the spot that the porter at the hotel had shown me on the map.

# ON THE ROAD TO MANAMBARO

THE RIDE WAS TERRIBLE. I held my stomach and closed my eyes, hoping the nausea would pass as I leaned toward the door and then back toward the center. The last bump sent my head into the ceiling and the contents of my stomach up. I hoped it would end soon. I had just vomited the last breakfast Jacqueline had made for me. After that, I had no appetite.

Dr. Joel seemed lost in reflection in the seat next to me. We were in what the Malagasy call a *taxi-brousse*, an eight-passenger van, crowded together with fifteen to twenty people. I couldn't move my arms. Each shaky mile increased my appreciation for the tenacity Dr. Joel had needed to come to my seminar. As my head reverberated with each skull-jostling bump, I felt like a little kid wanting to ask, "Are we there yet?" but I refrained. After I vomited the third time, Dr. Joel negotiated for me to sit in the front seat.

My nausea settled. I focused on the road ahead. The new problem was that the driver's girlfriend, Simonette, had to sit on my lap for the rest of the trip because the seat was so narrow.

She was a bony, petite young woman who wore a short skirt and a miniscule sweater that revealed most of her anatomy as we bounced along. She talked incessantly in Malagasy. I surmised that maybe that was her purpose—to keep the driver awake. He responded to her with periodic affirmative grunts that kept her talking. I was thankful I couldn't understand her, because her conversation became a constant drone like the sound of the engine.

The road south of Antsirabe was paved for a while but then degenerated to dirt or gravel, depending on one's interpretation, as it coursed through southern Madagascar. When we reached the rocky plateau, the road became the imagination of the driver. I was amazed at how he drove cross-country with no landmarks I could discern yet ended up exactly where the bridge crossed the river.

In the central highlands, the bridges were like bridges anywhere: steel structures that spanned the river. The roadbed was a steel grid. I thought in the United States, they used that grid to attach a concrete driving surface, but these were all singing bridges that caused a high-pitched hum as we drove across the steel lattice.

Farther south, the bridges, if they could be called that, were different. They were under the water. A cement slab just under the surface was meant as the roadway, but there was always some water flowing over the top like a Disneyland waterfall. We stopped and got out of the vehicle each time to assess the depth of water going over the so-called bridge. I appreciated the opportunity to snort the scent of Simonette's perfume out of my nostrils. Meanwhile, the driver sent a local boy to walk over the concrete. If he could walk across without the water being over his knees, we proceeded—that was, if everyone could be found to get back in the taxi-brousse. If someone couldn't be found, then the driver took a nap in the grass, as did several other passengers, until everyone showed up.

During the second night on the road, when I had somehow adjusted myself in the seat and Simonette's bony frame was planted in a comfortable spot on my lap, I managed to fall asleep. Thunder and lightning woke me. I jerked upright and saw no road in the headlights. We hit a bump, and Simonette cried out as her head hit the ceiling. She landed forcefully on a critical portion of my groin. I squelched a scream with my fist and put my arm around her waist to readjust her position. She didn't seem to mind. Holding her close to me like a blanket, I was able to get back to sleep.

Later, I awoke when the driver stopped. It must have rained a lot during the night, because the river in front of us was a torrent. The driver stood at the edge, his sandaled feet submerged to his knees. Everyone else seemed to know what was happening and piled out of the taxi-brousse.

"What do we do now, Joel?" I asked.

"Wait," he said with a smile. "You might want to eat something now, Barak. Judging by the depth of the river, we will be here for quite a while. You won't have anything in your stomach to throw up by the time we leave." I appreciated his medical assessment.

Walking along the raging river, I realized that after two days of sips of water to stay hydrated and minimal food, I was hungry. After about a half hour, a short, petite Malagasy woman appeared with her young daughter. She carried a tray of baguettes, and her daughter carried fruit in a basket. It amazed me how things just seemed to happen in Madagascar. *How did this lady know we were here, in the middle of nowhere, miles from any town and ready to buy breakfast?*

There was no village in sight, but the bread was warm from the oven. *Where did she bake it?* It tasted sweet despite no jam or butter. "It's called *moofo mamy*," Joel explained. "Malagasy for 'sweet bread.'"

Hunger abated, I sweetened my palate with a banana and an orange. Joel and I sat in the shade of a large tree. It felt great not to be jostled about, but as I dozed off, my brain told me I was still moving.

It was early afternoon when Joel woke me. The river was still high, and the driver said, according to Joel's translation, "We will wait till tomorrow morning." Joel suggested we hike to the nearest village to find a place to sleep. We climbed the cut-in-clay steps up from the riverbank. I followed him single file for a couple of miles till we turned onto a footpath leading to a village.

"Are there hotels here?" I asked, sure the answer would be negative.

"Not exactly," said Joel. He kept walking, and I followed, too breathless to ask any more questions.

We went to the marketplace and talked to several people. I shook hands with everyone we greeted but understood nothing of the conversation. After several such meetings, Joel turned to me. "I found a place for us to stay." With that, he headed up the hillside outside of town, climbing more steps cut into the steep embankment. At the top was a large building. As a bell rang, children ran out the door, singing a song. "They put the schools at the top of the highest hill so all the children know where it is," Joel explained.

Children ran in all directions around us, dressed in deep blue uniforms with white collars. They scattered home as a dignified man with hair starting to gray at the temples came out of the building. Joel shook his hand and spoke rapid Malagasy. To my surprise, the man turned to me and spoke in English. "I am honored to have you visit in my village. I am called Albert."

"Albert was a classmate of mine at the university," Joel said.

Albert's wife made a fine meal. She did not speak English, but we still had an understandable conversation as he translated for me. She made us a comfortable bed complete with a mosquito net, as we were out of the highlands, and the risk of malaria was much higher. It did not take any time for me to fall asleep in a comfortable prone position without a bony companion bouncing on my groin.

Joel woke me up before sunrise. I felt ambivalent. I dreaded continuing the bumpy ride with Simonette bouncing on me, but I was also anxious to get to Manambaro. We had a steaming bowl of rice with sliced bananas, courtesy of Albert's wife. I never did understand her name. After breakfast, we headed down the road to find the taxi-brousse.

The level of the river had gone down, so we piled into our places and headed across the river. The water came up to the doorframe. I moved my feet as river water leaked in through the door, but we made it across and sped up the riverbank to the roadway on the top of the cliff above to everyone's cheers.

The road climbed through the mountains and then descended down into a rainforest jungle. Vines and thick undergrowth made it impenetrable. I couldn't see more than a few feet on either side. Roads in the rainforest were muddy, something we had not dealt with since leaving Antsirabe. Twice, we got stuck, and our whole group of passengers became involved in pushing the vehicle out of the mud. Even little Simonette pushed with all her might. The driver didn't seem to mind that she got sprayed with mud when the rear tire caught traction. Besides, she rinsed off in a puddle beside the road to everyone's delight.

The third time we got stuck, even our passenger manpower couldn't budge the vehicle. The tires just spun. I felt doomed, but I underestimated Malagasy ingenuity. Within an hour, there was a plow team of cows—*omby*, the Malagasy called them—attached to the car. With the passengers lined along the road cheering on the omby, the taxi-brousse oozed out of the mud. We piled back in after each passenger shook the farmer's hand,

and we were back on the road. I didn't see any exchange of money, but we all felt obliged to buy some of his wife's pastries when she appeared.

We stopped for a bathroom break demanded by several older ladies jammed in the back seat. I wanted to give them some privacy as they squatted beside the road, so I ventured a ways into the jungle to urinate. I went too far. When I returned to climb into my seat, Joel stopped me. "You'd better clean up first."

"What do you mean?"

"Your legs are covered with leeches." I wanted to scream and stomp my feet as I saw inch-long black bloodsuckers attached to my legs. I restrained myself as I scanned the congregation of women watching to see how an American physician would respond. Joel stooped and graciously pulled them off while my shaking legs tried to maintain composure. When he finished, I had dozens of bleeding sores on my legs and not a bandage for fifty miles or however far it was to Manambaro Hospital. Simonette didn't seem to mind as she jumped back onto my lap. During the next bathroom break, I resolved to just use the opposite side of the road and turn my head. That was sufficient privacy for the ladies.

Joel leaned forward from the seat behind me and patted my shoulder. "It's not far now."

I had no idea what that meant, but I refused to ask. I didn't want to be disappointed. "Thanks for the encouragement, Joel."

"You're welcome. This is the east coast jungle we are in now."

I wondered if Tarzan had to deal with leeches. I didn't recall a scene with Tarzan pulling leeches off Jane's legs. It might have made the movie more realistic.

As I resumed my position under Simonette's bouncing frame, I decided to do what Lily would expect of me. I closed my eyes and counted the things I was thankful for: I was alive, I didn't have diarrhea, I didn't have malaria, and I had slept well in a house with a roof. A jostling bump interrupted my concentration as Simonette's pelvis ground into me, but my attitude had improved. Then I laughed. *I'm thankful for clothes.*

# 42

# MANAMBARO

I must have fallen asleep, because I jerked to consciousness as the van stopped. "This is where we start walking," said Joel as he climbed out of the back seat and opened the front door for me. We had been traveling with these people for three and a half days—well, except for the time we'd waited for the river to go down. They seemed like my distant relatives as we shook hands all around. Simonette said something with a coquettish smile, but Joel refused to translate. Joel and I used both hands to shake the driver's hand as he climbed down from the roof of the van and gave Joel his suitcase and me my backpack. We thanked him profusely for bringing us safely to our destination. Then the group broke into song, with our driver singing the base descant, as we walked up the muddy road to the hospital. They were still singing as they drove around the corner.

My mind returned to the lawyer's office—his overstuffed leather chairs, two picture windows behind his desk, and his clumsy attempt to pronounce *Manambaro*. Now I even knew how to pronounce it. *If he only knew*, I thought.

Avoiding the deep puddles, we walked by houses made of palm tree bark thatched with banana leaves. An elderly woman sat on a grass mat in one doorway, holding a tiny baby. I presumed the baby's mother was off working in the rice fields. Joel waved, and the woman returned his greeting. "She had a strangulated hernia," he said as we passed. "I thought

I was going to lose her. But she is a tough old bird and came through the surgery much better than I expected."

Two young boys pushed their boats made of banana leaves around in a puddle with a stick. They stopped their play and stood at attention as we approached. They greeted Joel with downcast heads, extending both hands, as if to royalty. Then they picked up their boats and followed in our wake. "The older boy had so many ascarid worms that he developed a bowel obstruction," Joel said. "The younger one passed over a hundred. They look much healthier now. I convinced the parents to deworm them four times a year. The medicine works well for ascarides but not for Trichuris."

I quickly reviewed my helminthic pathology. I had not seen many helminthic soil infections in Antsirabe. Ascarides were big, round worms; Trichuris were small but caused anemia.

We headed up a small hill, where I got my first glimpse of the hospital. There was a grand concrete entrance painted blue, with the walls of the hospital extending in both directions. A water tower in back of the hospital was next to a small second-story addition. We walked through the entrance. It led through a one-room width to a courtyard. Roses and tropical flowers bloomed in the central garden. A man with a machete was on his knees, tending to the grass. In the corner grew a palm tree. "The triangular palm tree of Madagascar," Joel told me as we walked past. "Only grows within ten miles of the hospital and nowhere else in the world."

We crossed the covered walkway to an inner circle. Patient rooms opened into the courtyard. The floral scent of the garden competed with the stenches of body odor, pus, blood, urine, and feces that emanated from the patient doorways. When we reached the opposite end of the circle, we entered the nurses' station, which smelled of the same alcohol antiseptic we used to clean our hands between patients in Antsirabe.

Joel was warmly welcomed back from the seminar. He must have been gone for two weeks, judging by the time it had taken us to return. I was introduced to the nursing staff and shook everyone's hand. Joel translated for the head nurse. "They are very glad to have you here to consult on our difficult patients. And they are thankful that you are here to share your knowledge so they can take better care of Malagasy people."

At a sudden loss for words, I said, "I am very glad to be here." Mostly, I was glad to end the taxi-brousse ride.

The nurse's greeting sounded like a trap for a humbling fall. Joel suggested I drop my backpack at the nurses' station, where he deposited his small suitcase. He asked me to follow as we went down a hall through a blue door. With the clothes we had traveled in, we walked right into surgery. They were doing a cesarean section. The baby was screaming as the nurse wiped off the blood. Even behind their surgical masks, I could see their smiles welcoming Joel back to the hospital. The surgeon was sewing up the woman's belly with tough blue proline suture.

He spoke in English for my benefit. "Check on the lady in fourteen, Joel. I am not sure what's going on. Maybe Dr. Barak can figure it out."

*How does he know my name?* We hadn't been introduced.

"She came in seizing last night with a temp of forty. I did a spinal tap. The lab should have results. I started antibiotics, but she was still almost comatose this morning."

Such was our greeting to Manambaro. The woman's spinal fluid showed acid-fast bacilli, and we started treatment for TB meningitis, with which I was now very familiar. The nurses asked us to see several other sick patients. In less than an hour, I was overwhelmed with the severity of the patients' diseases. Most had problems I had only read about and had no expertise to treat. How could I function in that environment?

It was dark when we returned to our travel gear, and Joel led me down the hill to the guesthouse. Something smelled good as we entered. The table was set for three, and there was a large bowl of rice in the middle of the table. Two attractive Norwegian women in their twenties greeted me in English. One was tall, with long brown hair that she was pulling over her shoulder to inspect the ends. The other was a petite blonde with a page cut. She was doing some stretching exercises in the corner. Both wore shorts and tank tops that didn't quite meet. Neither wore a bra. "We were expecting you," one said as they stopped what they were doing and smiled.

Joel dropped my backpack onto the couch and, with a hand on my shoulder, said, "We'll see you tomorrow at seven o'clock for rounds."

"I'll be there," I said.

He left, and I turned to the Norwegians. The tall woman with the long hair spoke first. "We're medical students here on our tropical medicine rotation. I'm Maeva."

The blonde seemed shy. "I'm Aesa. We're your roommates."

An elderly Malagasy woman appeared from the kitchen, bearing a large bowl of fried chicken and a smaller bowl of vegetables. "And this is Ida. Well, that's what we call her. We can't pronounce her Malagasy name. She's our cook," said Maeva.

Her smile revealed no teeth. "Supper," she said in English.

# WORK IN THE JUNGLE

I WAS INTRODUCED TO EACH physician at the hospital. I looked at the paper slip I had in my pocket. No one was named Rakotojoelinadrana that I heard. Maybe he was out of town. But there was no time to think about it. The hospital was full, and there had been several admissions during the night. I was accompanied by a nurse translator and assigned certain wards. Aesa, dressed in scrubs, followed the surgeon. Maeva accompanied me on ward rounds.

I still felt uncomfortable with children. I didn't know the doses of the medicines and was not as confident in examining them. Maeva was pursuing a pediatric residency, so she compensated. In Antsirabe, I had seen few children, except teens who had TB, because the Malagasy physicians had seen most of the young children. It was going to be different there in Manambaro.

Our first two patients were under five, and both were seriously ill with meningitis. A young boy became agitated as I tried to examine him. "Neck is pretty stiff, but pupils react to light, and the face is symmetric. Cranial nerves seem intact. He moves all extremities." I pulled out my stethoscope, describing out loud what I heard. "Lungs are clear; heart sounds fast. Normal bowel sounds."

I told Maeva what antibiotic I wanted to use, and she looked up the dose in her Norwegian pediatric handbook. I wrote it down and handed it to the nurse. "Stat," I said, which was understood across three languages.

Another nurse appeared with two spinal trays. *How did she know what I wanted?* I wondered. Maeva held the boy as I did the spinal tap. Cloudy fluid and elevated pressure suggested that our diagnosis was correct.

The little girl was less well-nourished and was lethargic to exam. Her limbs were floppy, and her skin was dry and hot. She was sick enough to be cooperative, so I let Maeva do the spinal tap. I expected the fluid to be worse. Instead, as Maeva put the needle in the child's back, crystal-clear fluid came out. "Good job, Maeva." I complimented her technique. I looked up at the nurse. "Check with the lab. See if the malaria smear is back. I don't think this is meningitis."

"She sure acts like she has meningitis," said Maeva.

The laboratory technician returned. "Blood sugar is only forty-three, and the malaria smear was positive for falciparum."

"Cerebral malaria with hypoglycemia," I said to Maeva. The nurse came with IV tubing and a bottle of 5 percent glucose in water. I ordered chloroquine IV after Maeva looked up the dose. With the IV flowing, I ordered another of normal saline because the girl was so dehydrated. "Now we wait to see if she responds."

"She is so delicate," Maeva said with tears in her eyes.

The other new admissions were adults, so I felt more comfortable writing orders. A middle-aged fisherman had been whipped by a jellyfish and had a nasty infected sore on his shin. The nurse translated that he had fallen out of his *lakana*—fishing canoe—and scraped his shin on coral. I checked to make sure the hospital had ciprofloxacin and ordered it.

"Why cipro for a skin infection?" asked Maeva.

"There is a vibrio found in ocean water that infects this kind of lesion. Cipro is the drug of first choice." Finally, I faced something I knew something about. For a brief moment, I felt as if I'd made a significant contribution to educating Maeva and patient care.

Next, we made rounds on the patients already in the hospital. Some were routine, such as an elderly woman with a stroke and a teenage boy with rheumatic heart disease and pneumonia. By noon, we had seen all the patients we were assigned, and Maeva and I headed to the guesthouse for lunch. Aesa wasn't back yet. Ida did not prepare lunch, so we were on our own. We washed up and found cold chicken from the night before, baguettes we had not eaten for breakfast, and cheese that Maeva and Aesa had brought from Norway.

"That was a wild morning. I just followed the other doctor around until you came," said Maeva as she took out some Coca-Cola from the refrigerator and poured us both a glass. I sliced the cheese and pulled some chicken off the bones to make sandwiches.

Aesa stormed in and collapsed onto the couch. "I'm never going to get pregnant. Deliveries and C-sections are so gross." Her scrub top was stained with blood. After a moment's rest, she ripped it off. "At least my best bra isn't stained." She headed down the hall to the bathroom.

When she returned scrubbed and clothed in a clean top, she settled down to eat with us. Maeva and I told about our morning, as Aesa's mouth was too full to talk. I was surprised how much a thin, petite Norwegian woman could eat. Satiated, she told us about the deliveries, one of which had been breech, followed by two C-sections. "The second section, the woman had been in labor for four days. She was in shock. We did the section as fast as we could. IV fluids resuscitated mother, but baby died. It was horrible."

There was still an hour before clinic. "I'm exhausted," I said, standing to stretch. "Are you working with me in clinic this afternoon, Maeva?"

"Yes, for the rest of the week, and then Aesa and I are switching. I'm going to work in surgery, and she is going to do medicine. That way, we don't get totally exhausted. The surgery schedule is pretty brutal."

"All right, I'm ready for a nap."

"Tap on my door when you're ready to go back to the hospital clinic. We'll probably rest for a while too."

The clinic schedule was pretty brutal as well. By the time Maeva and I returned to the guesthouse, it was dark. Ida was putting the last touches on one of her specialties: pork and greens over rice. A colorful carrot salad was already on the table as we walked in. Aesa was snoring on the couch.

"She looks so at peace. I don't think we should disturb her," I said.

"She gets real cranky if she misses supper," said Maeva. "I did that once when we first started. I thought she was too tired. I wouldn't want to experience her wrath again."

Aesa aroused to our voices. "I wasn't that horrible, was I?"

"Yes, princess, you were. Supper is ready." Maeva and I headed to the bathroom to wash off the collection of microbes and smell of disinfectant from the clinic. Being in the bathroom with Maeva felt improper, but we were just washing our hands. We dried on the same towel simultaneously and headed to the table for dinner. The smell was enticing.

I liked Maeva. She was logical and precise. She paid attention to detail and asked excellent questions. I tried to ignore her long brown hair; tall, athletic physique; and sweet smile. She was a medical student, and I was responsible for teaching her. She knew pediatrics well, so we were complementary in the clinic. She was hungry for knowledge and ate up my pathologic descriptions of the patients' diseases.

Stuffed together in an exam room in the clinic, we listened for our nurse to yell a phrase in Malagasy neither of us understood; we assumed it meant "Next." The clinic was so busy that there wasn't time to separate out the adults just because I was a board-certified internist, so I was thankful to work with Maeva.

"With children, you have to consider congenital problems. Don't be presumptuous," Maeva said as we examined a child with a chronic cough.

By the first weekend, we had seen a month of pathology. The physician staff was divided into four groups, so I was responsible to be on call one weekend a month. That weekend, I was free. I was exhausted, so when the girls suggested going to the ocean to relax on the beach, I didn't think twice about joining them. The problem was getting there.

"We'll just take the taxi-brousse," said Aesa. "We've done it before."

That night, I had a nightmare about being on the taxi-brousse and never getting to my destination. In my dream, I was trying to get home, trying to get back to Antananarivo to catch a plane, but the rivers didn't cooperate, and I was packed between two women whose babies vomited on me. Nausea woke me.

We had set up a schedule for showers since the water was only hot for an hour from six to seven o'clock. I had the 6:20 time slot. It was 5:40 by my watch. As I went into the bathroom, I noticed that there was no light from under the girls' bedroom door. I thought I would vomit, but the nightmare nausea passed. Slipping into the shower, I gasped, as the cold water felt like icicles tearing down my back. I wanted to scream, but I turned the water off and soaped up. Then I gasped again to rinse off. It was shocking, but I was awake. Just at the end, the hot water came on. *It must be six o'clock.* I toweled off and put on my shorts. It was 6:05.

Aesa was standing in the doorway with her petite china-doll frame wrapped in a towel. She glared at me. Her voice hit a high pitch. "This isn't your shower time."

"I'm sorry. I woke up sick and—"

She raced past me and slammed the door.

I got dressed and went to the kitchen to make coffee. Ida didn't work on weekends, so we were on our own. Sitting at the table and watching the sunrise through the east window, I thought about Lily and the adventure she had forced on me. I was thankful. She had taught me to be thankful. I sipped my coffee and ate a dry piece of baguette with jelly. "I am thankful," I said out loud, mostly to Lily.

At seven o'clock, Maeva appeared, combing her long hair. "You sure got Aesa riled up. What did you say to her?"

"I tried to explain to her that I was nauseated when I woke up, and I went into the bathroom to vomit. Then I decided to take my shower since it wasn't six o'clock yet. But she didn't let me finish. She's a real spitfire, isn't she?"

Aesa appeared. Unfortunately, *spitfire* didn't translate well into Norwegian. There was an explosive exchange in Norwegian before Maeva said in English, "She understands now that you were sick, but she doesn't like being called a dragon and thinks you should apologize."

I looked from Aesa's fiery expression to Maeva's negotiating posture. They were attractive young women, and I was going to the beach with them if I could resolve this. Explaining the derivation of *spitfire* as a fast, maneuverable airplane seemed inane, so I swallowed my pride and said, "I am very sorry that I called you a dragon. Please forgive me, Aesa."

There was an exchange in Norwegian. "She doesn't want you to even think of her as a dragon, or she is going to refuse to work with you next week."

That didn't sound all bad, but I didn't want the tension. "I promise to think of her as an intelligent, diligent medical student at all times."

There was another conversation I didn't understand. "Okay," they both said.

"I made coffee," I said.

They sat in silence at the table, poured themselves cups, and added hot milk and sugar. Aesa said something in Norwegian.

"I didn't catch that," I said.

"It's too profane to translate," said Maeva. "Let it drop. She is just getting back at you for calling her a dragon."

*I didn't call her a dragon,* I thought, but she would never know, nor would I know what she'd called me. "Can we call a truce? I was hoping to have a pleasant day at the beach and then take you two out for dinner. It's been a stressful week."

"You will pay?" asked Aesa.

"Yes, if we can be friends."

She smiled. "I will be your friend." She took a sip of coffee. "This is very good coffee."

Breakfast was harmonious after that. We each packed a day bag and walked down to the road. It was ten miles to Tolagnaro, a beach town called Fort Dauphin by the French tourists, and another couple of miles to the beach once we got to town. A taxi-brousse stopped for us, and we scrunched between two elderly ladies. I was half standing and half sitting, but in a short forty-five minutes, we were in town.

We started walking the couple of miles to the beach. First, we had to traverse the Saturday market. Kiosks selling meat covered with houseflies and fruit covered with the smaller variety of flies presented a noxious-sweet odor until we got out of the market area. Throughout the streets of the business district were stores selling everything from colorful plastic buckets and tin tubs to books and French newsmagazines. A brightly decorated store on the last road before the beach sold beautiful crafts. We stopped in to browse.

The woman at the counter did not look Malagasy. She was too buxom and dark complexioned to be Polynesian. She spoke English with a British accent. "I'm Kenyan," she explained, "but I married a Malagasy man. I set up this business because I was too bored sitting at home."

Colorful baskets, semiprecious gems, and wood carvings were tastefully presented. Maeva and Aesa bought several things. "We are returning to Norway in a few weeks," said Maeva.

"I need gifts," said Aesa.

While the Kenyan woman's English was impeccable, I was beginning to understand that Aesa did not speak English all that well. Maeva kept translating for her. *Clearly, I need to avoid colloquialisms when we work together next week,* I thought. Aesa and Maeva transacted their purchases, and we headed down the slope to the beach. No one else was there. Maeva took a quick scan up the cliff we had just descended and said something to Aesa.

They changed into their bikinis on the beach. The wind off the ocean whipped off their towels, making their attempts at modesty futile. Aesa had a body perfect for a china doll. *If I were only six inches shorter,* I thought.

Maeva had a pleasant figure, but I averted my eyes and changed into my own suit.

We dashed into the waves.

That evening, we climbed the cliff and found a Japanese-owned French restaurant. The food was outstanding, and when the bill came, both women stared. I assumed they didn't believe I would pick up the tab. Smiles graced their faces when I paid for the entire dinner, even their beverages from the bar. We were friends.

The week with Aesa went better than expected. She was clinical and intelligent. If I spoke slowly and enunciated well, she understood. Besides, if I switched to French, she often knew the French terminology better than the English. She was more adept at medical vocabulary than conversational vocabulary. She was pleased that she got to do several spinal taps. She felt it was a learning experience, and my unintended shower faux pas did not seem to interfere with our clinical relationship.

An elderly man presented with a hard liver and ascites, his belly swollen with fluid. "What is this caused from?" Aesa asked.

I explained schistosomiasis, but she seemed confused. "Bilharzia?" she asked.

"Same thing."

I let her do the paracentesis. "It's amazing how this fluid comes out of the belly so fast," she said. She held the catheter and filled two liter bottles. The patient did not speak French, English, or Norwegian, but as she tried to explain his condition to him in French, he seemed to understand her nonverbal antics.

I was impressed with her French. My French had improved enough that I considered speaking French to her as a way of avoiding misunderstanding. I was excited that I had developed some expertise in tropical medicine and how to care for patients in a developing country.

We were almost done rounding, when Joel rushed into our ward. "I need your help right away. We have a patient with multiple trauma. She is in shock."

*Now what?* I wondered.

We followed. Maeva was already there. The young woman was covered in blood. It was hard to see where the trauma was. Her clothes were shredded and covered almost nothing of her torn body. A well-dressed middle-aged Malagasy woman standing beside the victim talked excitedly to Joel.

I started an IV on one arm while Maeva got an IV started on the other. The patient had long slits in her legs and one in her belly. I could see her intestines through the laceration. Her pubic bone extruded through a large cut in her pelvis. When both IVs were running full bore, I asked Aesa for the blood pressure.

"About sixty systolic. It's thready."

"You watch the airway, and make sure she keeps breathing. Can you intubate her?"

Maeva repeated my instructions in Norwegian. Aesa nodded and asked the Malagasy nurse in French to get what she needed. Maeva and I started inspecting the wounds and covering them with sterile gauze. I knew the woman would need immediate abdominal surgery.

Maeva cleaned the long laceration on the young woman's leg as a nurse brought a tray and suture. "You might as well sew it up while we're getting surgery ready," I said.

She was skillful in cleansing the wound and tying off small arteries to stop the blood loss, and she closed the skin just as we were ready to wheel her into surgery. "What's her name?" I asked Joel as he and I were scrubbing.

"It's a long name, but she goes by Izby."

We finished scrubbing and entered surgery. "Well, Joel, let's save Izby's life."

Aesa was acting anesthesiologist, and Maeva helped the surgical nurse prep the belly. "You might as well scrub," said Joel. "We could use more help."

"Not exactly what pediatricians do," she said, but she started to scrub.

I had to admire Aesa. She was detail-oriented and a control freak, just the kind of physician one wanted for an anesthesiologist. She was giving drugs to control heart rate and blood pressure and constantly checking to see that the patient was well oxygenated and that the abdominal wall was relaxed enough for us to explore her belly.

Inside, we found several bowel perforations. "What happened?" I asked. I couldn't understand the situation, and I wasn't a surgeon. Madagascar was teaching me new skills—that was certain.

"She became a Christian without her husband's permission. That was the pastor's wife who brought her to the hospital. Her husband got so mad he threw his spear at her. It hit her in the leg. He pulled out his spear when she was down and stabbed her several times in the belly and pelvis. It's amazing she is still alive."

"What religion is he?"

"Animist. She refused to sacrifice to the hazomanga. It is a sacred carving usually found out in the jungle. So he told her that she was dead to him and speared her."

I held her small bowel as Joel sewed up the hole. Maeva lavaged the peritoneum to decrease the risk of peritoneal infection. We had several bowel clamps on parts of her colon where the spear had run through, so there would be no more soiling. Maeva stuffed a large pack of gauze into the pelvis to control bleeding. We weren't sure what we would find there.

"Blood pressure is stable around ninety. You guys have relaxation?" asked Aesa.

"We're doing fine," said Joel. He told me above his mask, "As long as she is still alive, we keep working."

I checked the surface of the liver; there were no lacerations. The spleen was normal too. If her husband had struck straighter, he would have hit her aorta, but the hemorrhage in the retroperitoneum showed that he'd missed major blood vessels by a couple of centimeters. When the bowel lacerations were all sealed, we checked the pelvis. Maeva removed the pelvic gauze pack.

"The uterus has a hole in it, and the uterine artery is severed," Joel said. He looked as if he were consternating over a decision. He looked up. "If I remove her uterus, she will become a nonperson. She and her husband will never resolve this, and she won't be able to remarry. But if we try to save it, it is bound to be infected—look at the dirt." He picked up the uterus and picked gravel from the surface as he cradled it in his hand. "The side where the spear blade cut is necrotic. We have to sacrifice it to save her life."

With several clamps and a few slices with a scalpel, the uterus ended up on the Mayo stand. Maeva dissected it. I could see tears in her eyes over her surgical mask. Her voice cracked. "She was pregnant," she said as she teased out the dead fetus.

Vessels were sewed together, one ovary was spared, and then we lavaged the pelvis to wash out the dirt. Joel placed a drain in each quadrant as I started sewing her peritoneum. As I started to suture the muscles and skin together, Joel pulled off his gloves and started writing orders. "Now the part we can't control," he said. "Will she get an abscess? Will she survive?"

After four hours on our feet without a break, we were all exhausted. Aesa still had to bring the young woman out of anesthesia, but at least she had been seated during most of the surgery. Joel paused and prayed out loud that Izby would survive as the nurses wheeled her into the postanesthesia ward.

"I'll stay with her for a while," said Aesa.

Maeva and I went to the guesthouse and collapsed on opposite ends of the couch. Ida had probably left an hour before, because supper was set out for us. "I think we'd better wait for Aesa," Maeva said.

"I'm so tired I don't mind waiting." I sighed. "You know, I did not call her a dragon."

"I know. It was partly my mistake. She thought she understood what you said, and when she asked, I translated it literally into Norwegian. I'm sorry." She sighed and adjusted a pillow under her back. "She is actually more like a volcano, but don't you dare tell her I said that. The good part is, after she erupts, she gets over it. She forgives quickly."

I sighed and nodded. There was a long pause. We both had our heads on cushions and our eyes closed.

"She also noticed that you got an eyeful when she changed on the beach. She didn't like that. I noticed you looked away when my towel blew away. Any comment?"

*I need to be very careful,* I thought. *I still have to live with these women for a few more weeks.* "You are both very attractive. You both look very nice nude, if that is appropriate to say. But I assure you I have no lustful intentions. I had a girlfriend who was somewhat of a nudist. She said she was desensitizing me." I looked up at Maeva. Her eyes were still closed. "You know what that means, right?"

"Yes. Continue." She giggled. "I look good in the nude. Nice."

I didn't respond. I didn't plan to say anything more.

"Come on. Continue."

"All right. Well," I stammered, "she taught me that her body … She was physically the most perfect woman. Oh, I'm messing this all up. She said that her body was just the house she lived in and that if I really loved her, I would love what was inside, not the outside. Inside, she was the most delightful, gracious woman." My mind was drifting. "I really respect the two of you; that's why I turned away when your towels blew away. I shouldn't have looked at Aesa either. She's right. I'm sorry. You both look charming in your bikinis. Oh, I guess that doesn't help, does it?"

Maeva's voice was soft. "Did you marry this perfect woman?"

I choked. "She refused."

"She married someone else?"

"No, she died of cancer." I took a deep breath. "I carried her to her bed because she was too weak to walk, and she died that night in her sleep." I cried as quietly as I could.

"I'm sorry, Barak. I didn't know. Aesa and I just thought you were like every other guy. You just wanted to get a good look at our boobs."

"I assure you that you both have nice breasts, if that helps."

She twisted on the couch. "That must have been very painful for her to die in your arms."

"Yes, Lily—that's her name—had her will set up for me to come to Madagascar. All expenses paid if I worked with SALFA for a year. So here I am, at her command."

"When did she die?"

"Seventeen months ago."

"You're still grieving, aren't you?"

"I'm mostly over it. You want to hear a joke?"

Maeva hesitated. "Okay."

"There's no one buried in her grave. The only gravestone in the cemetery without a body." I snuffed my tears.

"Where's her body? Was she cremated?"

"No, they're dissecting it at the medical school. She donated her body to the anatomy lab." I sobbed. "I guess she didn't care who saw her naked, inside or out."

"You're still hurting, aren't you?" Her voice was soothing. She sat up, reached over, and tousled my hair. "And I can tell that you loved her very much."

Aesa stormed in. "Is supper ready?"

"Yes," we said as we climbed off the couch and sat at our places.

Izby had a rough time. She had a forty-degree centigrade fever the next day when I made hospital rounds. Bacteria raged through her bloodstream. I was scared she would die at any moment. Joel came to my side as I was examining her. He asked me to pick antibiotics, but with no cultures, I was just guessing based on clinical trauma studies. I knew of no scientific studies of husbands spearing their wives. I felt desperate to make a decision.

Her belly was tight on exam. Maeva, Aesa, and I checked her every day, sometimes a few times a day, observing for clues to make appropriate treatment choices. The drains we left in flowed with pus. I felt helpless. There was nothing more I knew how to do.

In the meantime, we had patients to see—more children with diarrhea and a few with meningitis, farmers with skin infections, young people with tropical splenomegaly, and always new cases of malaria. It was the jungle after all, and it rained every day.

The last weekend of the month, I was on call with Joel. I was glad not to have total responsibility for every patient. The girls had the weekend off, and since they were leaving the following week to return to Norway, they wanted to do some shopping for people at home.

Izby was still alive. She had been delirious for days, but I must have made some right antibiotic decisions, because she defervesced, much to the staff's surprise. Maybe it was just God's grace, as the pastor's wife was always at her side, praying for her. When she started passing gas and had her first bowel movement, we started feeding her.

The pastor's wife adjusted her silk scarf around her neck and asked, "Can I give Izby rice yet? She was mumbling during the night that she wants rice."

"Go ahead and give her some rice, but be careful; she may not swallow well." I listened to her lungs. They were clear, and her heart rate, rapid since surgery, was almost normal. "Izby?" I called. She said something in Malagasy, and I turned to the pastor's wife to translate.

"She said that she is praying for you to make right decisions. She thanks God for you."

"*Misoatra tompoko.* Thank you," I said as I slipped to the next patient.

When I'd finished seeing the patients Joel had assigned me, I searched to see if he was done. He was writing on a chart. "You're done?" I asked.

"Almost," he said. "One more thing to do." He gave the chart to the nurse. "Follow me."

I followed him across the hospital grounds and into a small building. Three steps went down to a cement-slab floor. The sound was deafening. "Generator rounds!" Joel yelled. He checked the gauges to see if it was running properly.

I stood in awe. There was the behemoth that spewed forth the electricity that made the whole hospital function. I remembered that I needed a picture of it. "I'll be right back," I said, and I ran and got the Polaroid camera from the guesthouse. I returned breathless. The generator was huge and was as loud as a rock band doing an instrumental. Obviously, the building had been constructed around it because it was too massive to fit through the door.

"I need a picture!" I yelled. Joel took the camera, assuming I wanted to be in the photo. I pulled out my wallet. "I'm supposed to have"—I pointed to the name on the paper—"Dr. Rakotojoelinadrana in the picture."

He smiled. "That's me. That's my Malagasy name."

I was delighted. Finally, I'd found what Lily had sent me to do. "Good, but I have to be in the picture too. Who can take it for us?"

"I will!" yelled a voice behind us. I turned and almost fainted. "What are you doing here, Heidi?" I turned to Joel. "This is Lily's mother."

"I didn't know she was Malagasy."

"She's Anishinabe," I said as I gave Heidi the longest, most heartfelt hug I had ever given anyone in my life. I repeated, "What are you doing here?"

She laughed. "I came to take the picture for you!" she yelled in my ear. "I'll tell you more outside after we take the picture."

Joel and I held each other's shoulders in front of the generator. Heidi took the picture. I made sure the demarcation "Lily" painted on the housing of the monstrous machine was evident in the photo. I pulled out a pen and had Joel sign his full Malagasy name over the picture. Then we climbed out of the building to where we could have a normal conversation.

"You invited me to come. Didn't you get my letters? I told you when I was flying in."

"No." I stared. "You flew here?"

"I flew into Antananarivo last night, stayed at the l'Hotel Louvre, and then flew here this morning."

I turned to Joel. "You didn't tell me that we could fly here."

"Yes, there is a flight from Antananarivo three times a week. But instead, you got to see how Malagasy people travel. It was very important for your education, Barak."

I suddenly realized what Joel had done. I needed the education and the experiences that Malagasy people had every day, but I still resented the nausea and vomiting.

# HEIDI'S VISIT

THAT AFTERNOON, WE WALKED THROUGH the hospital gardens and down through the village of Manambaro, talking incessantly about patients and politics back home, and we even discussed my mother and Autumn. "I think Autumn really likes you," Heidi said.

"How can that be? I always thought she considered me to be a parasite on Lily." I thought back to how she had treated me before I left for Madagascar. I admired her, and I was attracted to her, but I'd always thought a relationship was beyond my reach. My heart beat faster. Was it possible that Autumn loved me? Could I love her?

"I think her attitude has changed. She was quite impressed with how you handled Lily's cancer and the requirements of the will. She was impressed that you followed through even against your family's wishes."

I let the discussion drop. We avoided some mud puddles, as it had rained while we were seeing patients in the hospital. "It gets real muddy on this road come November, when the rainy season starts," I said as we avoided a puddle all across the road.

"What is that building with the green cross sign?"

"That's the local pharmacy."

She was interested in what a pharmacy in rural Madagascar was like. That one was a palm-tree-bark hut with a tin roof. The owner explained that he had trained for three months as an apprentice to a pharmacist. "So I know about the drugs," he said in English. Heidi was surprised what could be bought with and without a prescription.

"I can't believe the prices," she said, converting the cost from Malagasy currency to dollars.

Farther down the road, children paraded out of their homes to see the visitor, yelling, "*Vazaha!*" When they saw me, they quieted down because some of them had been my patients. I introduced them in Malagasy, and when they heard that Heidi was Lily's mother, they suddenly became respectful and bowed their heads to her. I explained the surgeries Joel and I had done on some of them, and they quickly lifted their shirts to show their scars. They assumed she spoke Malagasy. I could translate most of what they said. Translating for her only increased her mystique.

Farther down the road, we went to the church and met the Lutheran minister, who spoke excellent English as well as Norwegian and a local Malagasy dialect. He was delighted to meet Lily's mother and invited her to give a speech the following Sunday morning. "I will be honored to translate for you, Dr. Heidi."

She smiled and agreed.

I explained as much as I could as we walked the muddy roads in and out of the village. I was still chattering away when it was time to go to Joel's home for supper. It was a prominent brick house with a tiled roof just south of the hospital, a landmark in Manambaro. I knocked on the door, and Joel invited us inside. He was quick to show Heidi the facilities of which he was so proud, such as the indoor toilet, the laundry room, and an indoor clothesline for hanging up the clothes in the rainy season.

Joel's wife, Josephine, burst into Malagasy when she met Heidi. Joel explained in his wife's dialect, "Dr. Barton is from a different tribe." She seemed puzzled by his explanation. I didn't understand everything she said in response, but judging by her look and reference to Heidi's complexion, I knew she was convinced that Heidi was Malagasy.

Manambaro was known for its seafood. Since the village was ten miles from the ocean, shrimp, lobster, tuna, and shark, as well as many fish I didn't recognize, were always available fresh from the sea. Josephine had gone all out when she'd heard Lily's mother was to be her guest. We had a cold pasta salad with shrimp for our appetizer, followed by seafood chowder. The main course was something to put on rice—*loaka* in Malagasy—and what a something it was: large chunks of lobster and tuna in a spicy sauce that we spooned over our mound of rice. Well, I had a mound of rice. Heidi had a US portion, but after my living in Madagascar for almost a year, a mound of rice had become my staple.

When we were stuffed, Josephine's kitchen help presented bananas flambé with little pastries. "Josephine has been busy all day," I said.

"We were at the hospital, so I was not here to distract her, Barak," Joel said.

There was a gentle tap on the door. Joel went to answer it. He motioned me to the door. "Izby is in shock again; we'd better go see her."

Joel explained to Josephine in Malagasy while I explained in English to Heidi. "I'm coming with you," said Heidi.

Joel smiled at his wife. "Then we will come back for coffee." I had forgotten about that course.

Izby looked pale and listless. Joel palpated her belly while I checked her IV, and Heidi went through the chart. "Your coverage is pretty good, but you could cover anaerobic bacteria better," said Heidi. "That is the most common cause of abscess formation."

"I agree. I think she has an abscess," said Joel. "Look at this red area on her left flank. Let's take her to surgery."

As the three of us scrubbed, I told Heidi Izby's history. "Her husband must have been either drunk or very angry," she said.

We made an incision extending the left flank drain. The drain had been walled off, and an abscess had formed. The procedure didn't take long, and Izby's blood pressure improved when we drained out the pus. Joel added better anaerobic coverage on the order sheet while Heidi and I took a specimen to the lab. The technician Gram-stained it on the spot, and Heidi looked at it through the microscope. "Gram-positives. Anaerobes, I would suspect."

I confirmed her observation, and we reported back to Joel.

The coffee tasted great when we got back to the house, and the conversation was animated. Joel and Josephine were interested in what Heidi's practice was like in the United States, and she told some great stories of recent patients.

It was midnight when we returned to the guesthouse. No one was in the girls' room, and there was a third bed. "I think they must have stayed at the resort on the beach," I told Heidi. She moved her suitcases to the room and hugged me good night.

"Wait," she said. "I have a letter for you that Anderson gave me." She pulled it out of the front of her suitcase. It had a Norwegian stamp on it.

"I'll use the bathroom quickly, and then it is all yours," I said. "No hot water till morning. Sorry."

"Barak, you forget where I grew up. We didn't have hot water till I graduated from high school." She took over the bathroom as I left. I was curious about my letter.

It was in a regular envelope, not a mail-o-gram, which required a lot less postage. I unfolded the letter, and another slip of paper fell onto the floor. I picked it up and sat down on my bed to read the letter.

Dear Dr. Barak Shelton,

After one month of therapy, I am up walking with a cane. I am using the bicycle at the physical therapy department but have not been able to use my own bicycle yet. The therapist assures me that it is a logical goal.

The physician who is caring for me said that without your rapid diagnosis and intervention with steroids and praziquantel, I would have spent the rest of my life in a wheelchair. Thank you for giving me the gift of being able to walk. I will probably not be able to bicycle as fast as I did on our trip, but I hope to at least be able to go again.

Thank you,

Jora

I looked at the piece of paper that had fallen out. It was another letter, but things were scratched out, and a heading had been added. It looked as if it had been crumpled and then straightened and folded before it was sent.

Dear Barak,

I was not going to send this, but when I got ready to send the other letter, I slipped it in. When I got pregnant and the fuck-head left me, I was very angry. I was mad at all men and went out of my way to show them what jerks they were. That is why I [something was scratched out] treated you the way I did. I'm sorry. I expected you to try to fuck me [the line was scratched out and then rewritten], and you didn't. I could tell you treated me with respect. I hope someday to find a man who will treat me like you did. Sorry I left you in the dirt. That was nasty. I can't do it anymore.

Jora

I was shocked at the anger Jora had and the language she used. I could see how my relationship with Lily had not only been my catalyst to become a physician but also prepared me to meet Jora's needs.

The next morning, I expected Heidi to sleep in, but she was up before I was. We had jam and cheese with our baguettes and headed to the hospital for rounds. Heidi had a few suggestions, especially about the pediatric patients. When we got to Izby, I was worried.

Much to my surprise, she was sitting up, eating rice and sweet milk. Her fever was gone, and through my translator, she said that she felt alive, whatever that meant, since it had nothing to do with what I'd asked. Her heart rate was normal, and her lungs were clear. She even had some normal bowel sounds, which I was thrilled about, because if she hadn't, I knew, she would have ended up vomiting the rice she was eating.

We found Joel, and I gave him the report. He was pleased but not surprised. He invited us to come to church with him and Josephine. We accepted, and we changed clothes and arrived at his house. Standing on the porch were three girls and two boys. They were immaculately dressed but barefoot, each holding a pair of shoes in his or her hand. "The two oldest girls and the youngest boy are ours," said Joel. Josephine introduced each child by name. "The others are my sister's children."

"Your sister's children live with you?"

"She and her husband both died. He died of malaria, and she died when Lydia, the youngest, was born."

"I'm sorry to hear that."

Everyone was ready, so we marched down the road toward the church. We paused at a large, flat rock right in front of the church. The children pulled their stockings out of their pockets, put them on, and then put on their shoes. All had smiles of pride as they walked the next fifty feet to the church in their Sunday shoes.

Heidi got out of her seat and danced to the music. She gyrated to the rhythms. After songs by several choirs and congregational music, the minister stepped forward and spoke in English. Then he translated what he'd said into Malagasy. "We have a very special guest here. Dr. Barton has come in place of her daughter, who died of cancer. Dr. Barton is Lily's mother."

The whole congregation hummed. I heard several people say, "Lily's mother," in Malagasy, which I now recognized.

"Dr. Barton, we would be pleased to have you say a speech for us."

I whispered in her ear, "I told you so."

Heidi spoke about Lily's life; many of her quirks, which made everyone laugh; and her deep interest in Madagascar. There was a hush when she told how Lily had made plans to come to the island herself and then gotten sick and died from cancer before she'd had the chance. "So I came to show you her love." Heidi ended her speech and bowed her head.

I looked around the church and saw many tears. Then I heard a murmur. "What are they saying?" I whispered to Josephine.

"They are saying that Lily must have been Malagasy because her mother looks Malagasy."

"I knew that would be a problem." We covered our faces and giggled.

Maeva and Aesa came home late Sunday night and were delighted to meet Heidi. They were comfortable in letting her join them in their room. When I got up to go to the bathroom about midnight to empty my bladder, there was still lively conversation in their bedroom despite no electricity.

When we made rounds in the morning, Maeva worked with me, and Aesa was back doing what she enjoyed: being the anesthesiologist for the surgeons. We walked into the four-bed ward where Izby was staying. She was on her hands and knees, wiping up vomit off the floor.

I squatted beside her. "Were you vomiting?" I asked in Malagasy.

She smiled and said something. My translator shook her head. "She is cleaning up the vomit of the lady in the other bed. She feels fine."

I asked her to lie down, pulled open her lamba dress, and palpated her belly. It was not at all tender, even under the scar where we'd opened the abscess. "*Tsara?* Are you better?" I asked.

"God is healing me, and I am thanking you for helping him" was the translation.

I was amazed. "How could she heal so fast?"

Heidi put an arm around my shoulders. "Great faith," she said.

Each day after that, we found Izby feeding someone, making beds, or curled up next to a sick patient, talking to him or her. "I think she is ready to go home," I told my nurse after we had removed the last drain.

"That is a problem," she said. "It is not possible."

"Why is that?"

"She has no place to go. Her husband is a big man in their village and has promised to kill her if she returns." The nurse ran her hand down Izby's long black hair and looked up at me. "She has to stay here, or she will die."

The next day, I saw her helping the chaplain counsel people. She would sit on the floor and talk to families of children with meningitis. Some days, she would sweep the floor outside the rooms or clean up an incontinent patient. None of that was required of her. She just wanted to help at the hospital "because we gave Izby her life back," my translator said.

One day we admitted an attractive young woman scorned by her husband because she had not been able to get pregnant. She came to get "fixed," but the problem was that her husband had given her gonorrhea. I treated the gonorrhea, but her uterus was so scarred that it was unlikely she would be able to conceive. After I treated the husband's penile discharge, he abandoned her and told her he was going to marry someone else. She turned her head to the wall and wouldn't respond when I made rounds.

Later that day, I saw that Izby had cooked rice for her and was feeding her. The woman was too depressed to feed herself. Izby gave her hope. Several days later, Izby asked the chaplain if there was an orphanage that needed workers.

As I made rounds, I got used to finding Izby somewhere in the hospital but never in her bed. She was always helping someone somewhere. The day before Heidi's flight was scheduled to return her to Antananarivo, Maeva and Aesa promised to take her shopping, so I made rounds on my own. When I put the last chart away, I realized I hadn't seen Izby. "Where did Izby go?" I asked the nurse.

"Fianarantsoa."

"Where's that? Why did she go? Will she be safe?" I fired out the questions.

"The seminary is at Fianarantsoa."

"What does that mean?"

"Dr. Lily's mother gave money for her to go to seminary. Izby will be a minister. She was discharged to her new life as an ordained worker, called a *mpiandry*. She is smart, you know. She went to the university before the headman of her village insisted on marrying her. Now she will minister to many Malagasy people. God has decided she was too good to be married to that headman."

At the end of the week, I said goodbye to Aesa and Maeva. We were friends still, and they promised to write. Two days later, I said goodbye to Heidi and promised to see her when I returned to the USA.

A month later, I was packing to return to the USA. I didn't call it home, because I felt more at home in Madagascar. It was part of me. Madagascar had changed me. I was in love with the people. The SALFA physicians had taught me so much. I felt as if I belonged there. "If I get the chance to return, I will," I told Anderson. Throughout Madagascar, I had found Lily. Her name was stamped on equipment, written on the side of the TB vehicle, and even printed on the generator. She was there. I still felt sad that I had not been able to show her what her generosity had done for so many people—people who loved her but would never know her. As I headed out to the Air France plane on the tarmac, I felt as if I were leaving Lily behind.

# RETURN

THE FLIGHT BACK FROM MADAGASCAR took eighteen hours. A stopover in Paris split the flight into tolerable halves. Paris was enjoyable. I had dinner with Mireille and Claude at a nice restaurant. They were thrilled with the stories I told them. But that was all I got to see of them. They were occupied with their business, and I had not intended to stay long. The problem was that every time I ate a flaky pastry or had an excellent meal, I was reminded that I would never share that with Lily. I wanted to share it with someone. I cut my stay in Paris short and headed to Minneapolis on a direct flight to Detroit and then a quick transfer to Minneapolis.

As I went down the escalator to the baggage claim, there was no one to meet me. I'd called Beth and Jason from Paris. It had been good to talk to them, but Jason was working, and Beth was occupied with the children. I planned to see them soon. In fact, they'd planned a welcome-home party for me the weekend after I arrived. I knew Mom would be teaching, but she was planning on driving down to Minneapolis for the party. Heidi was back from her vacation and staffing clinic back on the reservation. We had made plans to get together after the weekend with my family. I assumed Autumn was seeing clients.

I told myself it didn't matter. Besides, I wanted to spend a few minutes alone at Lily's grave site. It seemed ridiculous. I knew her body wasn't there, just a headstone. Her body was probably wrapped in plastic, dissected into

288

parts in the anatomy lab. Or maybe her intestines were laid out, and her breastbone was split open, with little identification tags on the anatomic parts, ready for the medical students' final exam. I could picture in my mind the students with clipboards scrutinizing her naked body, trying to remember the scientific name of each numbered item. The smart ones would scribble their answers onto their sheets without even a pause. Maybe her liver cancer was trapped in a jar of formaldehyde on a shelf in the pathology lab. That was where the murderous cells belonged.

I found my car where Jason had promised to park it in the short-term lot and drove out to the cemetery. It seemed odd to be driving again after a year. The roads seemed incredibly smooth. Traffic was wild, and all the cars seemed to be going too fast. It took a while to adjust to the pace. My memory served me well as I turned off at the correct exit and found the road to the cemetery.

The office was open, and I parked in front of the cedar bushes in front of the door. I hoped they had little maps marking the grave sites. "It's the grave without a body," I wanted to tell the clerk, but I knew she wouldn't understand. A young woman dressed in a gray suit was seated at a desk, doing paperwork. She looked up as I asked for the plot of Lily Barton, and then she typed the name into the computer.

Lily had prearranged a plot with a stone, and it was the only place I could think to go to be alone to talk to her.

"There is no Lily Barton here," the clerk said. "We have some other Bartons."

I scratched my head to remember her Anishinabe name. "How about Waabigwan-atewaniin Barton?" I asked, and I spelled it for her.

"Yes, that's in the registry. Strange name," she said as she printed a map and circled the site in red ink.

"Strange girl," I mumbled.

"What's that?"

"Oh, nothing."

"Take the first road to the right, and then drive up the hill. Her site is next to the large pine tree." She handed me the map with a red X where the pine tree was located.

It was overcast and threatening rain—typical Minnesota October weather. The wind was quivering the branches of the maple trees scattered throughout the cemetery. I drove to the section indicated and got out of the car. I hiked up the hill toward a grove of trees. A raven cawed in the distance. After a year in the tropics, I shivered as the wind blew through my travel clothes. I should have told Jason to put a coat in the car. Counting the gravestones according to the matrix, I found her stone behind the large white pine. I glanced around. It was the only pine tree in the cemetery.

The stone was engraved with "Waabigwan-atewaniin" and nothing else—no sentiment, no last name, and no statement of her life. After all that time, I still stumbled in pronouncing her name. I pulled out the picture of the generator and knelt beside the stone. "I did what you asked, Lily. Your generator is working just fine. It keeps the hospital going. A little noisy, so they keep it in a building by itself, away from the hospital. They shut it off when they are not doing surgery, but it works well. It's bright yellow. Your name is printed on it in black letters."

My head felt so heavy on my shoulders that I leaned over and rested on the stone. Tears poured out and dripped onto the brown pine needles nestled at the base. I remembered her emaciated corpse that morning, gaunt and breathless. I had to think of a different image. I felt ashamed as I remembered her on the canoe trip, vibrant, athletic, and naked. I remembered her anger as she grabbed my venison steak and pushed me down. I rubbed my buttocks scar. "I'm thankful, Lily," I said in defense to the specter. "I know that I would not be a physician if it wasn't for you. I would have been a high school dropout if it wasn't for you. I loved you, Lily. I really did. Ask Autumn if you don't believe me." I sobbed, holding the memorial stone for stability. When I could cry no more, I put the picture back in my pocket and held the stone with both hands as my body convulsed. I whispered, "I love you."

"She believed you."

The voice was so soft I thought I was hallucinating. Maybe jet lag was getting to me. A gust of wind buffeted my ears as I stood up.

"I love you too," said a voice behind me.

I turned. Autumn was standing beside the pine, holding an urn. The wind was whipping her long black hair across her face. She looked as if she'd come from work, dressed in a black suit with a floral scarf around her neck and a wide leather belt around her delicate waist.

I was shocked and windblown. I didn't know what to say.

"The medical school cremated her body when they were done dissecting it," she said. "I brought her ashes to spread over her grave. She would raise a real fuss about being imprisoned in an urn. She always wanted to be free and naked outdoors." Autumn opened the urn and poured the ashes around the headstone. Some of the bits landed on my shoes. The wind blew the lighter ashes down the hill into a stand of aspens.

She took my hand and walked me back to our cars. "I meant to meet you at the airport, but I was late. Sorry. I had a late client. But I knew you'd be here." She opened the trunk and threw the urn inside.

"What are you going to do with the urn?"

"Put it in the nearest dumpster. Why?" She searched me with her brown eyes. Her eyes hypnotized me like music, soothing my soul. "You know that she would hate that thing."

"She wouldn't want to be confined," I agreed.

I looked back at the gravestone. A gust of wind picked up more of her ashes and blew them in little wind devils around the site. I played with the car keys in my pocket. My hands throbbed with perspiration. I was paralyzed.

Autumn grabbed my chin to face her. "Barak, I'll have sex with you."

My mind spun. I stared at her brown eyes. She was beautiful, but more than that, she knew what I had experienced with Lily. She knew my secrets; she knew my faults. Did she love me?

She laughed and twirled in front of me. Her long hair flew in the wind and whipped across my face. It smelled like spices. "Lily said that would shock you. She was right. You should see the look on your face." She hugged me and kissed me on each cheek, and then our lips met. Her body cradled me from the cold gusts surrounding us. Her tall, lanky form enveloped me; her firm breasts were warm against my chest. I couldn't breathe. Her scent was sweet.

"I didn't think you liked me," I said.

"I didn't. But you've proven yourself. You want to have sex with me or not?"

I grabbed at my car for support. I felt faint.

"Of course," she said, caressing my face next to hers, "when a wolverine mates, it's for life. Waatebagaa insists."

"Would Waatebagaa like to visit Paris?" I said, resurrecting my voice.

"Sure. But why would we go there?"

"For our honeymoon. Besides, it's on the way to Madagascar."

"Are you proposing?"

"Yes."

"I'm ready."

That was our first kiss.

That October was the best of my life.

# *Acknowledgments*

I NEVER HAD A MUSE like Lily, and I have never met anyone like her. I dreamed of becoming a physician when I was five years old after observing a motor vehicle accident in Chicago. Many obstacles erupt along the path to becoming a physician. I am grateful for the people who encouraged me when I lost my vision, when I almost flunked physics, and when I was rejected from ten medical schools. The University of Minnesota, Duluth, accepted me the following year. But acceptance to medical school is only the beginning of the tortuous process of becoming a board-certified physician. Most of Barak's experiences cited in the novel are fictionalized from my own experience. Despair, fatigue, and lawsuits plague every physician's experience, as well as times of joy and miracles.

I am thankful to Melvin Bakk, who hired me to be a canoe guide. He gave me the opportunity to be awed by the wilderness of the Boundary Waters Canoe Area and Quetico Provincial Park, but as Robert Service says in his poem, "the trail has its own stern code."[2] Major fires have burned thousands of acres in the two adjoining parks. A sheer-wind blowdown on July 4, 1999, caused one death and sixty injuries as 370,000 acres were flattened by winds in excess of ninety miles per hour.

I owe a great debt to my Anishinabe friends for the mysticism and cultural background of this novel and my previous novels, *Saving Skunk* and *Releasing Lisa*. Adoption as described in *The Physician's Muse* is documented as far back as John Tanner's autobiography from the eighteenth century.

---

[2] Robert Service, "The Cremation of Sam McGee," *The Spell of the Yukon* (New York: Dodd, Mead, and Company, 1969).

The Sampan'Asa Loterana momba ny Fahasalamana (SALFA) physicians continue to teach me tropical medicine and instruct my resident physicians when we go to Madagascar for our tropical medicine rotation while studying at Western Michigan University Homer Stryker, MD, School of Medicine, where I am an assistant professor. Madagascar is well known for its unique flora and fauna. Lemurs, thousands of orchids, and many other strange plants enrich the island. Today much of this unique ecology is protected, but it is certainly under threat. The roads are bad.

To write this novel, I am deeply indebted to my Anishinabe friends, the Malagasy physicians, and the many preceptors who encouraged me to become a physician. Without my wife's encouragement, I would have given up my dream.

Printed in the United States
By Bookmasters